UNHALLOWED GROUND

UNHALLOWED GROUND

a novel by

Paul Guernsey

WILLIAM MORROW AND COMPANY, INC. | NEW YORK

To my mother,
who read to me

To my father,
who showed me the swamp

Library of Congress Cataloging-in-Publication Data

Guernsey, Paul.
  Unhallowed ground.

  I. Title.
PS3557.U335U54 1986   813'.54   86-8430
ISBN 0-688-06366-7

Printed in the United States of America

First Edition

1 2 3 4 5 6 7 8 9 10

I enter the swamp as a sacred place. . . . A town is saved, not more by the righteous men in it than by the woods and swamps that surround it.

—Henry David Thoreau

SPRING

Chapter 1

*T*hey found the bodies of six murdered children on Grandpa Tarbox's birthday. That was how everything started.

The fact that the old man was turning eighty-one was cause enough for celebration that day. But there was another reason for the party that was being planned; there had been another, stronger reason behind every party they had thrown on the anniversary of Grandpa Tarbox's birth for the past five years. Manny Moreno and his sister, Ida, and his mother and his grandfather gathered with a handful of friends on the same day at the tentative start of each new spring in order to assure each other that what was left of their family was still intact, that they had survived yet another winter since the year a run of bad luck had come at them without warning, dropping on them like a black hail from the sky, and nearly destroying all of them. Grandpa Tarbox always said that by getting together and being merry, they were shaking their fists at the Devil.

It was one of those strange beginning-of-spring days when winter seems to change its mind and tries to come back. A fine, cold drizzle sifted through the air, making the electric power lines crackle, and a thin fog slithered out of the swamp, seeking low-lying places. Crows huddled among the new buds of the trees, complaining hoarsely about the unfairness of the weather. It was Friday.

There were bad signs almost as soon as Manny tumbled out of bed in the attic room of his mother's small, untidy house. He toed his way carefully down the ladder into the hallway, a half-remembered nightmare clinging stubbornly to the back of his mind like a wolf spider on a brick wall. He had sweated despite the chill fog creeping around the foundation of the house; he remembered that. But the dream was gone except for a vague feeling of helplessness. Earlier in the night, there had been the old feeling that someone was watching the house. He got that feeling at least twice a week, had gotten it since even before the bad times first struck all those years ago. But he was fairly certain this new, disturbing dream was a separate thing from the familiar feeling of someone standing near the house observing, or waiting.

Manny was planning to shoot a deer today, and he thought maybe the idea of hunting had given him bad dreams. He never really liked to kill, but the prospect had never given him nightmares before. Perhaps the creaking of the bedsprings and the gutter sounds, the moans, and the words coming from his mother's room below had disturbed him, but he doubted that. He was used to his mother and her boyfriends and their noises after these five years.

The little house had been built by Manny's father and grandfather nearly twenty years before on land the old man had given to his daughter on her wedding day. There was a large living room with a picture window overlooking the tea-colored brook and the swamp that began just the other side of it, a tiny kitchen, and an even smaller dining room that was almost never used. The old Yankee and the young South American had included two bedrooms, and left space for another room in the attic if one was needed. The two had sweated side by side for nine entire months, had fought mosquitoes and cellar flooding.

Being from South America, a continent of witches and ghosts and tragedy, Manny's father had not laughed when Old Man Tarbox cut a wishbone-shaped branch of green apple and wandered the property looking for a well site. The old man held the forks of the branch in his leathery welder's hands, and when the branch had twisted, the bark peeling itself against the alligator-skin callouses of his palms until the stem pointed downward, they dug. The well was still producing eight gallons a minute. Good, happy years followed, and Alexis and Mary Anne Moreno filled the little house on the edge of the swamp with three half-Yankee, half-Chilean children—a fair son, a dark son, and a redheaded daughter. But then the winds started blowing in the other direction, almost tenderly at first, then with the force of a gale. Manny was nearly blinded in one eye during a childhood quarrel with Toby Carver, his best friend. Charlie Raymond, a neighbor and a good friend of the family, went berserk one night and bludgeoned his wife and children to death with a stone before twisting a wire coat hanger into a noose and hanging himself in the backyard. After that, the bad wind seemed to focus its fury directly on the little house Grandpa Tarbox had built with his son-in-law.

Now Alexis Moreno was gone, wandering distant lands. From time to time he sent vague messages to Manny. Grandpa Tarbox was alive and healthy, but he grumbled that his life maybe had gone on for too long now; that the tragedies of two generations were enough for any man, and that this third generation seemed cursed by more than its share of terrors. The old man was once again the owner of the property he had given as a wedding present, had been forced to buy the house and land back from his daughter for one dollar so that she and her children would be eligible to collect welfare money from the state.

Manny's mother and her boyfriend were arguing as he walked into the kitchen in search of coffee. It was their first argument, but then they hadn't been together very long. Flat Top, his face bruised and sagging from too much drinking, was hurling his arms around in a rage, filling the small room. Manny had to dodge a flying arm to get to the stove where a cold puddle of coffee sat waiting in a dented saucepan. He turned up the gas flame under the coffee, and looked up occasionally as he waited. His mother looked bad too, from worry and lack of sleep. Her head was wound in a red rag she used to hide her hair when she had not had the time or the energy to fix it. Her voice was shrill, a dentist's drill in his ear.

They shouted. Something about something someone said in a bar. They ignored Manny, and he tuned them out, standing in a corner to drink his coffee. He liked it with sugar, but didn't want to cross the room again in search of the sugar bowl, so he just drank his coffee black. His mother had done nothing toward cleaning the house, and if they kept fighting, he knew the place would still look like a dump when his grandpa and the other company arrived later in the afternoon. Manny's girlfriend, Jay Lee, and Toby wouldn't mind the mess, and maybe Grandpa Tarbox himself would overlook it, but Toby's mother was coming, and she hadn't attended a party for the past two years. Manny didn't want her to think that his mother was slipping.

He grew impatient as his head cleared and he thought of the deer, the large doe that wandered the swamp behind the house and was only now fattening up after the long winter's hunger. The deer would keep them in meat for a couple of weeks, and they could use the money his mother had coming from the state for something they really wanted, perhaps a down payment on a new television. His mother's last boyfriend had put his heavy foot through the back of the old color set, and it couldn't be fixed. They had been watching black and white for three months now. Grandpa Tarbox often gave them money, had even bought most of the food for his own birthday party and delivered it to the house the day before, but he refused to replace a television that had been willfully destroyed.

The coffee was bitter, and he tossed the remaining half-cup into the sink, where it trickled toward the drain in sluggish rills. Flat Top and his mother continued arguing. Neither had yet seemed to notice Manny was in the room, and he slipped out through the dining room to avoid having to pass between them again.

He went down the stairs to the cellar to get his single-shot .22-caliber rifle and a box of long-rifle shells. His poor, vacant sister, Ida, was in the cellar sitting in the dark. Pretty, fragile, redheaded Ida, whose eyes were like two cold, blue-green cat's-eye marbles, stayed in the cellar almost all the time when there was a new man in the house. She was younger than Manny by three years, and had not been to school since Alexis Moreno, who came from Chile, a country so far away it had winter when it was summer in Connecticut, had packed a single leather traveling bag and fled through the New England snow. Manny's mother still kept the note: *Something's come up. Don't know when I'll be back. Love, Al.*

"Hi, kid," Manny said. He walked to Ida's broken couch and kissed her on the forehead. "Noisy upstairs, huh?"

"Cold," said Ida, and she smiled as if amused and puzzled by something at the same time. She was wearing a frayed gray sweater, and her hands, usually fluttering nervously about like a pair of mourning doves, were buried in her armpits.

"Well then go up," said Manny, his voice soft as if he were talking to the wary doe he hoped to kill that morning. "Go up. It's warm there. Flat Top won't hurt you. Go in my bed."

Ida said, "A ghost is here, Manny."

He studied her in the weak light that seeped through the tiny ground-level cellar windows above their heads.

"What ghost, Ida? There are no ghosts." The dream he could not remember tickled at the back of his mind.

"This ghost can't talk English," she said. "It's one of Daddy's ghosts that goes *rat-tat-tat.*"

He rumpled her hair gently, with a trembling hand. "God, you're so nutso," he said. "Why is my whole family nutso?"

He turned and walked to the gun rack hanging over the workbench. There were slots for three guns on the rack; his own .22 sat on the lowest rung, and his father's old twelve-gauge double-barreled shotgun rested on the topmost. The middle rung was vacant. Manny took his rifle down and leaned it carefully against the workbench. Then he took a box of shells from a drawer and emptied it into his pants pocket.

Ida watched him with unblinking eyes.

"You're going into the swamp?" she asked. Some emotion made her voice go higher; something that might have been fear, though it was always hard to tell with her.

"I'm going. But don't worry about me. I won't go far. I'll stay near the house, I promise." Manny kicked off his canvas sneakers and slipped on a pair of calf-high rubber boots he kept under the workbench. The boots were nearly as old as Manny, were peeling near the top from hundreds of trips into the swamp, but so far they were still warm and had no leaks.

Upstairs, the argument continued, and something made of glass hit the floor and broke.

"The swamp is bad, Manny," Ida said. "Very bad." Her voice continued to rise.

"It is bad, Ida, sometimes," he agreed as he picked up the gun and undid the bolt to the cellar door. "But I love it. Grandpa Tarbox loves it too. Listen, when I come back, I'll go out to the State Road and buy something for Grandpa's birthday. Did you know it was his birthday today, Ida? He's eighty-one, and that's old. It will be from the two of us, okay?"

Ida tucked her legs up under her on the threadbare couch and started rocking back and forth, slowly. "Don't go, Manny," she said.

"There's blood in the swamp." As she rocked, she stared across the cellar at the opposite wall, where Manny knew a wine-colored stain would be visible if there were more light. No matter how many times Manny whitewashed that wall, the stain always returned.

Manny felt his scalp prickle. "What blood?" he said. "Don't be trying to scare me with your ghost nonsense."

"There's blood," Ida insisted, and shut her eyes, stubbornly putting an end to the discussion.

He went up the stairs to the outside, slamming the cellar door behind him.

*I*t was good to be outside away from the arguing and his sister's spooky craziness. Manny shook his head. One time, after she had been home alone, Ida swore that the house had filled with the ghosts of Indians who wore ponchos and played sad tunes on wooden flutes. Some of them had been beating rawhide drums, she told him, and they boomed like thunder. But she had to be heard out, because sometimes she got strong feelings about things that were going to happen. The trouble was trying to decipher the truth from her ravings and childish fears.

He crossed the brook behind the house and waded through feathery tassels of marsh grass to the abandoned railroad bed that was now just a long path of cinders, a black scar through the swamp and the higher woodlands dividing the swamp. The track had once connected a string of farming towns that included Manny's town to Bridgeport, on the shore to the south, by steam train. But with the completion of the State Road, which ran half a mile to the west of the tracks and roughly parallel to them, the trains passed less and less often, and they pulled fewer cars; soon weeds and wild rye were allowed to sprout between the rotting ties. Finally, the line was abandoned altogether, and the crows and the foxes reclaimed it.

All this took place thirty years before Manny was born. He knew about it though, had a clear picture in his mind of exactly what it looked like back then and what had happened, because of his Grandpa Tarbox. The old man was his window into the past. He wove and rewove stories until Manny found himself inside of them. Manny had been there, and was on intimate terms with people who had died decades before his birth. Old Man Tarbox loved the swamp. He taught

Alexis Moreno to love it as well, and the two of them took Manny there almost from the time he could walk.

Now Manny knew this land almost as well as his grandfather knew it. The railroad bed that used to connect his town with Bridgeport crossed two roads at the north and south ends of the swamp; between the roads sat seven miles of water and woods that held many secrets. Manny knew most of the secrets; his grandfather knew them all.

Stagnant water and wet, sucking earth covered only a portion of the area they called the swamp; it was mostly dry woods crisscrossed with singing brooks and broken by hills of glacial rock. But the real swampland, wet and forbidding, surrounded and dominated the other land, giving the area its character and its name. There were caves in the swamp, and abandoned Indian places as well as the leaf-filled cellar pits of the early farmers. There were hidden pools where native brook trout grew large and fat, and places that teemed with muskrat. There were old grave markers too, and strange voices on still nights. Sometimes he saw moving lights or even fires deep in the swamp at night, but he knew better than to investigate.

Manny was brought up in the swamp, felt it was his. He fished out of season and poached an occasional doe in the springtime, when many does were pregnant, because it was his birthright. On paper, however, all the land and water between the two country lanes was owned by a millionaire who had originally come from New York. William Cahill, who was nearly as old as Old Man Tarbox, did not love the land. He never visited the land, not even along the railroad bed where the going was easy, where his electric wheelchair could easily pass. But he owned the property, and he was determined to change it. At the south end now there were houses going in, condominiums mostly, and bulldozers were gouging their way deep into the swamp. They had already filled in one pool where trout had gathered in trembling pairs to lay their eggs. But the north end was worse. The invisible millionaire, who hated the sun, according to Grandpa Tarbox, and stayed indoors all day brooding in the dark, had placed a dump there, a graveyard for old tires. The dump spread two hundred yards farther into the swamp every year.

But retiring old tires was not the only business of the dump; Manny knew that trucks stole onto the ruined land late at night to bury things in secrecy. The swamp was doomed, Manny knew. In the center of it sat a black, bottomless, stagnant well of swamp water known as the Engine Hole. According to Grandpa Tarbox, the hungry pit once swallowed an entire locomotive, and Manny often had a dream that the dump and the new houses finally met, coming together with an explosion at the center of the swamp, and then everything went swirling down the Engine Hole into the center of the earth like the flushing of a giant toilet.

Manny followed the railroad bed north for a time. When he neared the game trail deer usually followed across the tracks, he opened the bolt of his .22 and slipped in a shell. He would have to get very close to get a clean kill with the small-bore rifle, if he didn't want to go chasing a wounded deer around the swamp. But then, Manny was good at getting close to things out here. He found deer tracks in the powdered cinders of the bed, and he stepped off the track, following the game trail through a tangle of wild blueberry bushes. The ground here was wet, water reaching his ankles, and the bushes were high and overgrown. He held the rifle over his head to keep it from getting snagged in the brush.

Then a flock of crows dived out of a stand of pine trees to his right, scolding hoarsely as they flapped overhead and scattered in many directions. They were angry about the gun, he knew. He only hoped they wouldn't give him away.

Manny continued pushing his way through the brush until the blueberry bushes thinned and he came to dry ground. Beech and swamp maple grew here, and small patches of grass were poking up through their winter blanket of fallen leaves. He started to find blood almost immediately. At first there were only a few drops glittering here and there on the ground like ruby pearls. But the earth was torn up, patches of it scraped bare and clumps of new grass lying root-side up on the leaves. As he moved through the trees up a slight rise, gun barrel forward, he saw more and more blood. It was as if someone had taken a paint brush and spattered blood around on the earth; then it began to look as if someone had painted the ground itself, making long, glistening stripes. Manny was dragging his feet by now, and his thumb flicked at the safety catch of the small rifle like the nervous tongue of a snake.

As soon as he topped the rise he saw her. The doe was lying very still against a thick beech tree on which someone long ago had carved a heart with an arrow through it. Her throat was torn out, her insides lay in a steaming heap on the ground, and her long legs were pointed stiffly and awkwardly in all directions. Manny could see that she had been hamstrung to slow her down before she was killed. The eyes,

wide open and glazed, seemed to be fixed on Manny. He took a hesitant, mesmerized step forward, thinking about touching the still-warm
carcass, then he heard himself give a startled shout as a wolf crashed
through the brush near him and drew back its lips to show teeth. He
swung his puny rifle at it, trembling wildly, and the growl seemed to
come from deep within the animal's bowels; it was pure hatred and
jealousy and hunger.

He was afraid to shoot; the muscles in his arms were hopping
beneath his skin like panicked rodents, and he had only one chance
with the single-shot weapon.

"Yah!" he yelled at it. "Yah!" his voice a wordless yelp, but the
animal came still closer, walking on stiff legs, growling. Then, suddenly, four more of them drifted silently out of the woods and stood
around him in a menacing half-circle. They weren't wolves. The first
one looked like a wolf, had a muscular hump on his back and a
pointed, bladelike snout, but he had the colors of a shepherd. He was
a wild dog transformed into a wolf by the sorcery of the swamp.

The others were less changed. One was a lean shepherd bitch
and the rest were all large mongrels. A collar circled the neck of one
of the dogs. They were hideous animals; all of them were missing
patches of hair and one had a reddish, naked tumor covering half its
snarling head. Another dog gave a startled yelp, and then, as Manny
looked on, horrified, swung its head and began snapping viciously at
its own wagging tail.

Manny took a step backward; the air vibrated with a chorus of
growls at his movement. But he took another step and then another,
and then two of the dogs forgot him and went over to sniff the deer
and bury their muzzles in her. There was a sound of tearing meat.
The big wolf-dog followed him until he reached the edge of the blueberry thicket, then returned to the pack.

Chapter

2

*H*e pushed his way quickly through the thicket, looking backward over his shoulder as he walked. Branches raked his face, and a twig poked into his one good eye, blinding him with tears for a moment. He heard a crow soar over him close, screaming *ha! ha! ha!* Behind him he heard the sounds of fighting and then a high, thin wail of pain.

He waited until he reached the brook behind the yard of his mother's house before he opened the bolt of his rifle and slid out the shell. He stuffed it into his pocket where the other bullets jingled and danced. He knelt briefly by the stream to throw a handful of water onto the back of his neck, caught sight of his reflection, and stopped for a moment, looking. It was always strange to see his own face suddenly and judge it, for a split second, as that of someone else. Unlike Ida, who had inherited all her features from the Tarbox side except for the almond shape of her eyes, Manny had the dark looks that had come with his father from Chile. Although he spoke less Spanish than a pet crow his father had taught to talk shortly before he disappeared, his features would have been entirely Indian if he hadn't gotten the stamp of his grandfather's Yankee subbornness on his face as well. Manny was short and quick like he imagined Indians to be, although he had never met any; he was remarkably stingy with words for a seventeen-year-old, was a good worker with his hands, and was often buried deep in his own thoughts, just like an old-time Yankee.

Although the reflection on the water was not sharp enough for him to see his damaged left eye, the one his best friend, Toby Carver, had nearly knocked out with a stick when they were kids, so that the black pupil bled into the surrounding brown iris like the broken yolk of an egg, he was aware of it. He was always aware of the nearly useless eye; he wondered what people thought when they saw it for the first time. Manny often thought that if it weren't for the ugly eye, he might have turned out to be a fairly good-looking kid.

Finally, tiring of looking at himself and mourning his broken eye, he wet the back of his neck and his face and stood.

Looking through the trees, he spied his mother sitting on the front steps of the house his father and grandfather had built for her, swaddled in a great, filthy old spring coat. She sat rocking, her legs tucked up under her, rocking in the addled way his sister had been rocking in the cellar earlier that morning. He watched her for a minute, not at all sure what he should feel, then pulled his black film container of pot and a packet of rolling papers from his pocket. The pot was some greenish stuff, not very good at all, but it was all he could afford until he found a job. When he had a job, Toby Carver would be able to get him the good material, all buds, that he really liked. Toby could get anything he wanted. Manny carefully tapped out grass into a paper and rolled himself a tight joint that was just barely tapered at the ends. He prided himself on his rolling ability; you got the most out of your pot if you could make a joint that burned evenly all the way down.

He smoked slowly, holding the smoke down in himself for a long time. It was harsh stuff, but it did the job, smoothing down the crazy jagged edges of his nerves. The fight with the dogs had left him jumping all right. The blood on the ground . . . the crazy dog attacking its own tail like an enemy . . . that fat drunken bastard putting his filthy hands on Manny's mother when his father might be getting ready to come back to them any day. . . . He smoked everything back into a corner of his mind, shrunk it down to make room for a few good thoughts. The party today, with his grandpa telling stories. He loved to get high and then let Old Man Tarbox put him back in the past, building the house with his father, talking to the railroad gandy dancers, or telling off Cahill when he started to put his dump in the swamp.

The old man did lie sometimes, though; there was no denying that. Like when he said there used to be strange mutated animals in the swamp, bizarre furry things with one eye or five legs that you couldn't find anywhere else. Claimed he and the railroad men trapped them all out because they caught the trout and killed the chickens. Manny thought he was getting a little old to believe that one, but the old man was a good liar anyway. You always believed everything he said while he was saying it.

His grandfather had once told him that his stories were like the Bible in a way: They could be looked at as mere stories, with no point but amusement, or they could be seen as the history of a place and the people in it; they could be seen as the history of the swamp through an old man's eyes. Or if a listener was ambitious, he could take the tales apart like he would the innards of a fish or the gears of an old watch and search for warnings, messages, and morals about life under today's sun.

Sometimes Old Man Tarbox would even put him back playing with his older brother, Terry, in the snow. . . . Manny took a deep, deep drag off his reefer. *Back, back in your corner,* he thought.

He smoked the joint down until it was a tiny roach and went out by itself. He dropped the roach into the film container with the rest of his pot and stashed it back in his pocket. Then he put a shell in his rifle and clipped a branch off a tree high over his head just to see it fly.

It was a stupid thing to do. His mother heard the shot. She stood and started walking toward the brook; she must have seen him by now, so there was nothing to do but meet her. He had hoped to slip out to the State Road, Route 25, by a roundabout way to avoid her and her problems. He crossed the rotting wooden bridge over the brook and met her on the lawn.

She had been crying, he saw. Her nose was swollen and red, a big pale radish, and the soft skin under her eyes hung loose like onion skin. Crying and drunk. She had started showing her age suddenly this past year.

Manny said, "I just saw these dogs—"

"Ed's gone," she told him. "He left. I don't know when he'll be back." Her thin hands came up as if she wanted to hug Manny, but then they stopped, trembling, before her. She made a noise like a wounded bird in her throat; it was a question, a request.

Manny looked down; he rested the stock of his gun on the ground and marched his feet nervously in place. "He'll be back," Manny said. "Don't worry." His voice sounded flatter than he had intended.

"Do you think so, Manny? Do you really think so?" She snatched at his words like a lifeline.

He felt a wave of hatred and pity for her. "Sure," he said. "If you want him to. Where the hell else has that slob got to go?" He raised his hand to touch her on the shoulder, but his arm stalled before he reached her and flopped back to his side.

"There were these dogs in the woods," he said. "Five of them. I thought they were wolves. They killed a deer." He continued marching unevenly in place.

"Ed's not half the man your father was," she told him. She stalked his eyes, but he kept them on the neutral green of the lawn. "But I need somebody. You know that, don't you?"

"That's fucking-A right," he said, barked, surprising himself. "He's not half the man my father is. He's not even a quarter. He's a fucking clown, that's what he is. A fucking drunken clown."

Mary Anne Moreno bowed her head, a dog exposing its throat to another dog's teeth, and it made him want to punch her. "Do you think so, Manny?" she asked.

"You're damn right I think so. I can't stand it when I'm lying up there in my room at night and he . . ." Manny rubbed a quick hand over his face, bit his thumb to make himself stop.

"Well, but your father was a special guy, Manny," she said, her head still bowed. "Maybe we're unfair to expect anyone else to match him."

"A fucking clown," Manny said, softly.

"Do you know he wasn't in this country three months before he was speaking better English than me? He got so that he could correct me, after a while. And he could build houses, built this one right here, and anything that had an engine in it, he could fix it. In the factory, he wasn't there two years before they made him a foreman. The other men were angry at first, him being a foreigner, especially a foreigner that talked like a Puerto Rican, but he showed them he was a nice guy, and then he had them all eating out of his hand. And he told fortunes, Manny, and they were true. He had some funny cards, and he'd deal you a hand one by one and then say, 'You will come into unexpected money,' or something like that and two days later you'd find a ten-dollar bill just lying on the sidewalk someplace."

"Stop that," Manny said. "Stop all that." His head was snapping back and forth and up and down now; he was trying to push everything back into its corner, fighting himself, but then the hot tears went spilling down his face. It was an embarrassment, like wetting his pants, but his mother seemed not to notice.

"What I can't figure out is why he left us like that," she said. "I know him and me were having a little trouble, but not enough to send him running like that, without even talking to me first. He left things unfinished, and that's not like Al. Maybe you know why, Manny, and you won't tell me. Doesn't he ever say anything in those letters he sends you sometimes?"

"No," Manny said. "Nothing. Listen—"

"Because he really was a good man, and if he knew how much he hurt us, maybe he'd come back. And he did hurt us, Manny. We're not even a family anymore, after what happened to Terry, and the way Ida is now, and me with these men that are just big children that like to drink and hit . . . believe me, Manny, I'm just looking for one good one, but look at me now, how can I get one the way I look and I don't think there are any left, anyhow. Good ones, I mean. And you, Manny, don't think that if Alexis was still here you would have quit school at sixteen and spend all your time in that damn swamp and not work and take drugs—" Manny's hand went hard against her cheek and made a sharp noise that startled them both. The side of her face blushed scarlet.

"You can't do that," he said, his voice a pleading quaver. "You can't say those things about us. You can't, Mom."

His mother touched her cheek, made delicate circling motions with her fingertips. "I know," she said. "I shouldn't. Don't worry. I'm not hurt."

"I'm sorry," he said. "I'm a little crazy right now. These dogs in the swamp almost attacked me. They had humps and growths, like monsters. I think something is the matter with them. One of them bit himself, and they killed a deer I wanted to shoot."

"I'm sorry," she said. "I'm a weak person."

Manny hefted his rifle, worked the bolt two or three times, and peered down the barrel through the field sights with his good eye. "Listen," he said. "We've got a party today; Grandpa Tarbox is eighty-one."

"Oh," she said, startled. "I've got to clean that damn house. And cook. Everyone will be here in two hours. But I need a few things from the store up on the State Road. Will you take the car and go for me?"

"I'll go," he said. "I haven't got my present yet, anyway. I'm getting one from me and Ida."

His mother went into the house and returned a few minutes later with a shopping list: black pepper, coffee, napkins, a plastic tablecloth. She handed him ten dollars in ones.

*I*t took him a while to get the old station wagon started. He had to get under the hood twice and jiggle the wires before it caught and ran, and then it ran ragged. He drove out the driveway onto Dark Entry Road, the street that ran between the State Road and the abandoned railroad bed, then turned down the first narrow lane connecting Dark Entry to Route 25. He traveled south on the busy State Road, went down three stoplights past the funeral home, real estate office, and Carvel's ice cream parlor, and parked at a small shopping center that included an all-night grocery store, a liquor store, a sporting-goods shop, and a K mart.

He went into the grocery store first and bought everything on his mother's list. When he was done, he had $1.38 left over, and he pocketed the change.

Then he wandered up and down the aisles of the K mart for a time, saw nothing he really wanted for his grandfather. He thought about buying a flannel shirt for the old man, but then recalled how much Grandpa Tarbox hated to get clothes for Christmas or his birthday. He was like a little kid that way. Manny visited the sporting-goods shop for a while, saw a fishing reel the old man would really be pleased with. But the price on it made it something he could only dream about. All the while the sports-shop clerk tracked him around the store with suspicious eyes, as if expecting him to sweep something into his pocket as soon as no one was looking. And he would have if the bastard hadn't been watching him; something small like a package of fish hooks or a bottle or phosphorescent salmon eggs.

Finally Manny walked into the liquor store and settled on a quart of the thick, sweet blackberry brandy his grandpa liked. The owner asked him if he was old enough to buy liquor; Manny said yes and produced the phony ID card Toby Carver had gotten for him. He bought his bottle, and for good measure a package of blueberry-flavored pipe tobacco he saw displayed in a glass case. There was no gift wrapping in the liquor store, but Manny knew the old man would be just as happy with the brown paper bag the bottle was sold in.

He was pleased with himself when he had finished shopping. His grandpa always grumbled about presents, made a sort of game at making fun of them. Presents were either too big, too small, too bright, or completely useless. Brandy he never grumbled about; he drank it all the time, even in hot summer. Warms the stomach and thins the blood, he always said. Pipe tobacco was another sure winner. He was never happy unless he was puffing like a steam train. He did his best storytelling in a haze of smoke.

Manny set all his purchases next to him on the front seat. He was so happy now, thinking of the party, that he rolled himself a joint, lighting it with the cigarette lighter on the dashboard of the old station wagon. He started the car; miraculously it kicked over and roared on the first crank of the ignition, then he tuned in a New York rock 'n' roll station on the radio. He heard a song from Pink Floyd's *Dark Side of the Moon,* an old album he especially loved. He turned up the radio nearly as loud as it would go, and wheeled smartly out of the parking lot after checking both ways for cops.

He was happy just to drive around for a while; the music was good, and he was getting comfortably stoned. He steered the station wagon down Route 25 through the town's business district, then he turned east and drove a mile up a winding lane into the town center. It was built on a quiet New England green centered around a stone monument to the two men from the town who had not returned from World War Two. There was a Tarbox's name engraved on that monument; Zachary Tarbox, his mother's only brother, whom she barely remembered, had vanished without a trace somewhere in the Pacific. His Uncle Zack, who had killed the last wildcat ever to roam the swamp, had shot it between the eyes one winter's night with Manny's .22.

An old town hall, a spanking-new brick police station, three small Protestant churches, and seven big houses stood around the green. In the fall, usually toward the middle of October, there were always tourists strolling the center, snapping photos of the flaming leaves on the big sugar maples that spread their branches above the churches and the old private homes on the lanes leading away from the green.

Manny crept through the center to avoid drawing attention from the police station. He took shortcuts through housing developments until he reached the beginning of Dark Entry Road. Then he was back on the edge of the swamp, his own territory, and he punched the accelerator hard; he knew every curve in the road and liked to go slinging around the corners, music shrieking and branches clawing the passenger-side window. That was the way to live.

But Manny went flying over one hill too many, flew right into a nightmare. Flashing lights red and blue and a huge white truck, a van, broadside on the road. He hit the brakes, had the sense to pump them as the distance closed rather than locking them and skidding out of control. The truck was backing into the woods on the right side of the road; he saw men walking, a lot of them, so he jerked the wheel and slid past the wide front end of the van just as it pulled out of his way. There were two cops, bluecoats, on the road on the other side of the van, and they jumped. He went between them, his brakes locked up now, and came to a squealing stop twenty feet farther. His reefer was down to an oil-stained roach, so he pinched it out and flicked it under the seat. He was breathing fast now; it seemed as if there was not enough air in the car for him. He cranked the window down; a cop's square, snarling face poked through immediately.

"You're in big trouble," the cop said. He was a town cop. His nose twitched twice, taking in the marijuana smell, then he said, "You're really in big trouble now." There were police cars parked everywhere, with lights twirling and radios barking. The cop, whose name tag said WHITE, called over his shoulder, "Jamison, come over and take a whiff of this car."

Jamison was a large black cop with skin the color of dusky purple grapes. His face twisted with sarcasm as soon as he saw Manny, and he walked slowly over to the driver's side of the car, placing big hands on the door. "You breaking our balls again, Manny?" he asked. "It stinks like shit in here."

"He was right across the road," Manny said. His voice went high as he thought of the near miss he just had. "I saw . . ." A state cop walked out from behind the white van, which was now completely off the road and parked in the swamp. He had his thumbs hooked into his heavy gunbelt, and he was frowning.

Jamison lifted his head over the top of the station wagon. "It's okay," he told the state cop. "Only a kid." The state officer hesitated, then wandered back to the van.

"What the hell is going on here, anyway?" Manny said. "An accident? Somebody get killed?"

Jamison was about to say something, but then he stopped and

his eyes narrowed thoughtfully at Manny. "Seems like I remember something about your family, Moreno, a long time ago. Your brother, I think."

White came up behind, hands on his hips. He had gone over to watch the men in the woods for a moment. He looked impatient. "Let's drag his ass out of there," he said.

"Hold on," Jamison said. "Okay? I can take care of this, Joe, okay?"

White turned and stomped over to the crowd around the white van. There were men putting on rubber suits and rubber gloves and sliding gas masks on over their faces. They looked like deep-sea divers, or moonmen. A man with a TV camera perched on his shoulder like a large blue parrot was talking with a state cop.

"What's going on?" Manny repeated. "You better tell me what's going on now, officer." His fear was gone suddenly, and his voice was sharp.

Jamison studied him for a long moment. Finally he said, "You got any pot on you, Manny?"

Manny shook his head.

"Don't give me that shit. How much have you got?"

Manny dug into his pocket and came up with the container. Jamison took it from him, scattered the contents into the dead leaves on the side of the road. Then he blew the black film container clean and handed it back to him.

"Next time I'll bust your ass," he said. A car going south stopped in the road, the woman driver and three children staring, fascinated by the scene near the white van. Jamison waved them past, then said, "Why don't you get out of the car, Manny?"

Manny stepped out and followed him across the road into the crowd. Off into the swamp twenty yards behind the white van, a group of moonmen leaned on shovels, resting. There was a hole about ten feet square dug into the wet loam of the swamp; Manny couldn't see how deep it was. A fat man with a camera walked around the edge of the hole, squatting now and then to snap a picture. An area of swamp about fifteen yards square was marked off with wooden stakes and yellow tape printed in black with the words CRIME SCENE. It all looked like some kind of movie set to Manny.

A thin man wearing a three-piece suit and mirror glasses was pacing a line between the van and the newly dug pit, his hands clasped behind his back. His jaw worked rapidly at a piece of gum, and he kept glancing at his watch. Finally, the fat man stood, massaging his knees with stubby fingers.

"That ought to do her," he announced to no one in particular. One of the moonmen stepped forward. "Can we pick them up now, Lieutenant? The guys are thinking about getting home sometime today." Without breaking his stride, the thin man said, "Yeah, we're finished now. Take 'em away."

Four men in rubber suits dragged a long, black, zippered bag from inside the van. They marched over to the excavation, and suddenly there were many gloved hands reaching into the pit. Elbows pistoned. The thin man turned away, his pacing ended finally, and the man with the TV camera stepped forward.

"Lieutenant," he said. "Can I go off to the side, there? I want to get some body bag as they're walking past."

The lieutenant stopped chewing for a moment; round muscles stood out on the sides of his jaw. He pointed into the swamp. "Don't you cross that tape," he said.

The cameraman stepped quickly through the swamp. Four men returned with a body bag; it seemed as light as if it were empty. They handed the bag up into the van, and then drew out a new, empty bag and returned to the excavation.

A man with a note pad stepped forward hesitantly. He was dressed in blue jeans and a flannel shirt, and he didn't seem much older than Manny. "Lieutenant Davis," he said. "I'm with the Bridgeport *Telegram*."

The lieutenant stared at him, waiting.

"How many bodies are in there, Lieutenant?"

"Six. Buried about three feet down."

"And they're all children, is that right?"

"Looks like it, but they've been in there awhile. It's hard to be sure about anything right now." The lieutenant's hands remained clasped behind his back; the reporter's pen scratched against paper.

"How long have they been there?"

"It's hard to say at this point in time. They're badly decomposed. Basically, what we have here are six skeletons.

The reporter scratched away; he was excited now, scribbling. "'Any ID on the bodies?"

"Haven't found any yet."

"How did they die, Lieutenant? Is it possible to tell?"

The cop took a breath. "It's hard to say at this point in time. The case is under investigation, and Forensics will have to look at the remains."

"Were these kids murdered, Lieutenant?" asked the young

reporter. The cop snorted, and someone back near the van laughed out loud.

"The case is still under investigation," the lieutenant said. "But I think it's safe to say nobody here died of old age. I think there's a good chance we're looking at a homicide." The pen scratched. Everyone, moonmen and uniformed cops, were watching the interview now, some with crooked smiles on their faces. Everyone but the men in the pit.

"Any suspects yet?"

"No," said the cop. "Nothing. I kinda remember some unsolved kidnappings in the state a few years back; maybe we'll look into them some more."

Manny shouted, "Lieutenant!" and the mirror glasses flashed in his direction. Everyone looked at him strangely.

"Did you . . . was there a dog buried in there somewhere?"

"No dog."

"Are you sure, Lieutenant?"

The cop stared. Manny felt Jamison's powerful hand on his shoulder. "He's sure, Manny," Jamison said.

The reporter glared at Manny a moment, then asked, "How did the police know the bodies were here?"

"We acted on an anonymous tip."

"Any idea who made the call?" There was another laugh from behind them, near the van.

"We don't know. It was anonymous."

Manny stayed and watched them load all six bodies.

Chapter

3

*T*hey called them Day and Night, Salt and Pepper, Black and White. His brother Terry was twelve, two years older than Manny, and he was strong and smart and could whistle to split your eardrums. He was everything Manny wanted to be when he was twelve. Manny thought Terry was his mother's favorite because he was first and because he had moon-colored hair and blue eyes like a Tarbox, and it made him jealous sometimes. But his father always said Manny had gotten all the Indian blood, and Manny knew that pleased him. Alexis would say, "Those high cheekbones and those slanted eyes, kid, and the straight black hair. You can tell you had ancestors that lived higher than the clouds and killed them a Spaniard or two." But when he joked, he would say that Manny's mind was more Yankee than apple cider and Terry's was always up in the clouds, so that they'd be perfect if only their brains were switched around. Sometimes he would grab a knife and fork and make like he was going to do the operation himself, and the two boys would run from him; they sure would run!

Three years earlier, Terry and Manny had moved up into the attic room so their little sister, Ida, could have the downstairs bedroom all to herself. The boys pretended to be mad about the relocation all the time, but they really liked it up in the attic where they could reach and touch the roof and talk without the chance of anybody standing outside the door to listen.

And they planned midnight escapes like the one they were making tonight. The insects and tree frogs were making such a summer racket outside that their hearts vibrated with it. A whippoorwill slowly circled the house, daring them. A chain ladder sat beneath Terry's bed in case of a fire, and as Manny pushed up the screen on the window at the end of the house, Terry wrestled the ladder out of its cardboard box. Terry hooked the ladder on to the windowsill and then let it down to the ground, making sure it rattled only a little against the shingles, not enough to wake their parents sleeping below. Then they shinnied down, quick as squirrels.

Manny and Terry found their fishing poles and a tomato can full of worms behind the woodpile, right where they had hidden them. Butch, their Brittany spaniel, saw them plain as day from across the yard because of the full moon. He stood there almost on point trying to wag his stump, waiting for them to unchain him and free him from his house. He grew angry when he saw them walking toward the brook footbridge without him, and he barked, calling them traitors. Manny wanted to go back for him then, but Terry said no, he'd get lost, and besides, there were skunks at night.

As they crossed the bridge, Manny whispered, "Sorry, Butch," and he was sure the dog heard him because he had ears like radar. But Butch stayed mad and kept right on barking.

They headed up the railroad bed, walking toward the new dump with Terry ahead moving quickly and Manny following. They kept their poles high, but once in a while Manny forgot and let his drift down and it snubbed in the dirt. Terry gave a mean laugh whenever he did that. Then Manny's brother found the mouth of the path they were looking for; it was right off to the side of the Engine Hole. The two of them walked up through the woods, an easy walk because of the moonlight; then they descended through wet swamp that sucked at their sneakers. Off in the swamp they saw a fire burning; it was perhaps the size of a cooking fire and the warm wind brought them voices without words.

"Grandpa Tarbox says those are ghost fires," Terry whispered, and Manny didn't know whether he was trying to scare him or if he really believed that. Just the same, the hair stood at attention on the back of his neck. An owl swept low over them, casting a rippling moon shadow, and it made them duck.

Then they were on dry land again, and they went around a hill that cut them off from the ghost fire. The ground here was covered with brown field grass, and it sloped down sharply toward a line of boulders ahead of them. They heard water singing through the boulders, and their hearts leaped like a pair of trout. Then Terry shushed him, and they moved down to the stream on whispering feet. The stream was black and deep even in the moonlight, and they didn't have to follow it too far before they reached the spot where it bent almost double and formed a wide pool.

The brothers rigged their poles with a number-six hook and a single piece of lead shot. Terry had his line in the water before Manny even finished tying on his hook. His line snapped tight almost as soon as the bait reached the middle of the pool, and then he was fighting a fish that came splashing to the top and jumped, silver in the moonlight. He reeled it in, breathing fast and happy, and said, "Get your hook in, Manny, nothing like a little night fishing!"

Manny cast his line, but Terry broke the neck of his trout and threw it onto the grass and then got his line back in the water and it snapped tight again right away. He pulled in another fish that was maybe an inch or two smaller than the first, and he was ready to rebait.

But suddenly he stopped and cocked his head, listening to the night.

"What is it?" Manny asked, a little envious because his brother was two ahead of him now. But Terry just said, "Shush!" and hit him on the arm hard enough to make it sting. That frightened Manny because Terry never hit him, so he started listening himself.

At first it sounded like a night bird, but Manny knew night birds, and he had never heard one quite like this before. It was a sad noise, and it didn't seem to have a pattern to it like most bird noises. It was moving toward them at about the pace of a swamp bird jumping from bush to bush and it was following the stream right on down. Terry was shaking, and Manny was plenty scared himself. He didn't know whether to reel in his line to get ready to run home or not.

"It's her," Terry told him. "It's really her, Manny. It's the Crying Woman!" The Crying Woman was one of their grandfather's most frightening stories, but Terry didn't seem to be just trying to scare him. Terry seemed scared himself.

"What?" Manny said, but Terry shushed him desperately, blowing spit into his ear. So he listened hard again, and it did sound like crying and it kept getting closer. Then they both heard a twig snap upstream; they looked at each other, eyes wide, then footsteps were coming through the woods at them. Terry growled in his throat, said, "Get down behind that rock and hide," and Manny obeyed at once. He covered his head with his hands and he was just about ready to cry.

Terry hunkered in behind the rock with him, but he stuck his head up a little, looking over the top. The footsteps got louder until they finally stopped right across the brook from them, and Manny felt someone staring down at them. He didn't dare look up, and if Terry hadn't been there to shame him, he would have been bawling by now.

Terry pressed against him, still as ice, and Manny heard the Crying Woman sniff a little and say *"Terry"* as softly as his mother said it when she wanted to wake the older brother without waking the younger. Terry put his hand on the back of Manny's neck, and his fingers were cold as crayfish. Then she said *"Terry"* again, cried it quietly, and there were footsteps and louder crying, then the sounds faded away slowly and were gone.

Manny picked his head up. "Terry," he said, "why did she call you?"

"Shut up," Terry told him.

Manny didn't speak again until they were halfway back to the house. Then, with the fear easing a little, he said, "Terry, why—"

Terry stopped and gathered the front of Manny's shirt in one hand and pulled him close. His eyes were still wide with fright. "Shut up," he said. "Just *shut up.*"

*D*aylight had Manny doubting the existence of the Crying Woman. While Terry slept, he freed the dog from his chain and took him out into the swamp. Near the place where they had been fishing he found nothing. But in the powdered cinders of the railroad bed near the Engine Hole he found a faint line of footprints. They were small footprints; they had been made by a woman, or a child, or a very small man. He followed them until they veered off into the darkest part of the swamp and disappeared.

Chapter

4

*T*here were already people in the house by the time Manny got home. His mother met him at the doorway. Her nose was still red, and her hands were fluttering with nerves. He heard people talking back in the living room, and he recognized Grandpa Tarbox's low rasp as well as the voices of women. He could tell the old man was warming up to begin a round of stories.

"You sure took your time," his mother said, jerking the paper sack of supplies out of his arms. "I thought you were just going down to the store. It's been damn near two hours."

Manny shook his head. He was still numb from watching them load six dead children into the white van. "Something came up," he told her. "Something just came up."

"Something is always coming up with you," she said, and took the stuff into the kitchen where she was struggling at the task of fixing a New England boiled dinner even though Manny had helped her with many of the preparations the night before. Manny rested against the doorframe, wanted to catch his breath before he greeted his grandfather and had to start talking with people.

But Jay Lee heard his voice and came out of the living room to interrupt his solitude. She hugged him, kissed him on his unmoving mouth; she was so short she had to stand up on her toes. Jay Lee was a year younger than Manny, and she had quit school herself the day after she found out he had dropped out.

She pinched him hard on the arm. "What's wrong with you, Manny?" she asked. "You were supposed to call me yesterday. Is it getting so I can't even trust you anymore?"

He looked into her flat black eyes and suddenly wished he was out in the swamp alone, fishing. He swallowed. Manny always had trouble making up his mind whether Jay Lee was really pretty; today he decided, she wasn't. "I called the day before," he told her. "And I knew you were coming to Grandpa's party. Why call yesterday?"

Jay Lee and Toby both lived close by, on the other side of Route 25, so he saw them often. In fact, he saw Jay Lee more than he wanted, sometimes.

She pinched him again. "Because you promised, Manny. You have to keep promises, even if they're just little ones." Then her body turned liquid, and she rolled her hips against his thighs. "That is, if you want me around, understand?"

She stood up on her toes again, clutched the front of his shirt in her short fingers. She closed her eyes and parted her lips slightly, and he bent forward to kiss her. The kiss was dry and pleasureless.

"Yeah," he said. "Sorry. Things have been going on here, Jay Lee. But I should've called, I know that." He kept glancing nervously over her shoulder to see if his mother was coming out of the kitchen. It would embarrass him if she saw them like that.

"You're really sorry?" Jay Lee asked. She tightened her grip on the front of his shirt.

Before he could answer, Grandpa Tarbox brayed from the living room, "Manny! You son of a bitch, get your ass in here!"

"I left his present in the station wagon," he said, and unhooked her fingers.

A few minutes later, Manny walked into the living room, carrying the bottle of brandy wrapped in brown paper. His little sister, Ida, was seated next to the old man on the couch, cuddled into his shoulder. Mrs. Carver, Toby's mother, was there too; she was sitting in a stuffed chair with her hands folded in her lap. Manny noticed that she had had her hair done for the occasion, and even though it was dyed and not real blond, and you could see a little gray at the roots, she still looked nice. She had always been pretty. He kissed Mrs. Carver, just a peck on the cheek, and she said, "Toby's coming over later, Manny. He went to see about a job today. Something he saw in the paper."

Then Manny turned to Old Man Tarbox, who was laughing at him in that silent way of his. He always knew when something was bothering Manny, and he always seemed to think his problems were funny. Grandpa Tarbox had once been large and powerful, a welder, but now age was shrinking him a little inside his skin, so that his flesh hung slack in some places where the muscle had retreated. But he was still good for eighty-one; his broad, open face that had never produced much of a beard was still tight and amused and nearly unwrinkled. The only deep lines on his face were the straight, long ones in his forehead and the two that plunged down from the corners of his mouth, and nobody ever noticed them unless the old man was being stubborn and was puckering his face to show that he couldn't be budged. In fact, Grandpa Tarbox looked remarkably young considering he had worked with his hands all his life, raised two children single-handedly after his wife abandoned him, and then saw his only son swallowed up by a war. When he was telling a story, his wide, thin-lipped mouth would twist a certain way to tell you whether to be happy or scared or angry, and his blue eyes, which saw like telescopes during the day and only gave him trouble at night, when he was blinded by the glare of automobile headlights, would twinkle or flame, according to the tone of the tale.

"Happy birthday, Grandpa," Manny said, and pushed the package into the old Yankee's hands. The old man smiled, dentures flashing, and without looking into the bag said, "Blackberry brandy. Just what I was waiting for."

He reached in and twisted off the top of the bottle, then took a long gulp that made his big Adam's apple work up and down like a piston. The old man handed the bottle back to Manny afterward, and Manny took a smaller sip. Mrs. Carver looked away while they drank.

"Now," said Grandpa Tarbox, still amused. "Where's my blueberry pipe tobacco? You forget it this time?"

Jay Lee, who was out in the kitchen with Manny's mother, laughed out loud and came in with the paper pouch.

"He left it in the kitchen, Grandpa," she said, handing him the tobacco. The old man immediately tore the packet open and filled his pipe. Jay Lee grabbed Manny by the hand and pulled him into a stuffed chair. She sat on his knee and leaned back against his shoulder; he felt suffocated.

Manny said, "That stuff's all from me and Ida, Grandpa."

The old man was sucking a flame down into the packed tobacco of his pipe, concentrating, and when he had the pipe glowing, he crushed out the wooden match in an ashtray on the coffee table. He blew a boiling cloud of smoke into the room, then said, "I know," and kissed Ida on the forehead.

"Thank you, Ida," he said. Ida cooed. Mrs. Carver gave a brave smile as the blueberry-flavored smoke floated over to caress her face and shoulders and then hang about her hair like a stagnant fog.

More gifts followed. Manny's mother came out of the kitchen with a flat gift-wrapped box, and Old Man Tarbox impatiently shredded the paper with his big hands and opened it.

"Well look at this," he said, his face screwed up in disgust. "A sweater." He didn't even pull it out of the box to show it around the room.

"Now, honey, what in hell am I going to do with a sweater? It's almost summer for chrissakes."

"Ah, shut up, Pa," said Manny's mother. But she was smiling as she walked back into the kitchen. "How many bottles of brandy can you drink anyway?" Everyone laughed except Mrs. Carver, who blushed and pretended to look at her fingernails.

The old man then turned to Jay Lee. "Well," he said. "Let's have it, sweetheart."

Jay Lee got up off Manny with a broad grin on her face. She rummaged in her pocketbook, which rested against the couch near Ida, and came up with a small, square package.

Grandpa Tarbox snatched it away from her, and the torn gift wrapping hit the floor a moment later. It was a bottle of cologne, and his head jerked back comically when he screwed off the top and took a whiff. "What's this for?" he asked. "To keep dogs out of the yard? I've run over skunks that smelled better than this!"

They laughed again, even Manny's mother, who had come to the kitchen door to watch. When the laughter died down, the old man blew two more huge clouds of smoke with his pipe, serious all of a sudden, and he stared off into space.

Then Mrs. Carver said quietly, "I too have a gift, but frankly I'm frightened about what kind of reception it will receive." She tried to laugh, but Manny could tell she was embarrassed. At the birthday celebration three years before, Grandpa Tarbox had kidded Mrs. Carver about an ashtray she had brought for him, just as he kidded everyone else about their offerings. It was the old man's way, and he liked to treat Mrs. Carver like a daughter whenever Toby wasn't around. But Mrs. Carver had been upset by the kidding, and missed the next two parties. Now, Manny held his breath, wondering whether his grandfather would spare her. If the old man had a fault, it was that he sometimes didn't learn from his mistakes in dealing with people.

"Well, give it here, then," said the old man, softly this time.

Mrs. Carver reached behind her chair and brought out the present. It was obvious right away what it was, but the old man took his time with the paper, hardly tearing it at all. Then he held up the flannel shirt folded square in its plastic package.

"Now, that's a present," he said. "Take notes, you kids. Number one, it's early spring, and the season for flannel shirts. Number two, all my flannels are in rags. I don't know how Sally knew that. And three, it's green. Green is my favorite color, kids, remember that." Old Man Tarbox boosted himself up off the couch and walked over to Mrs. Carver, still clutching his pipe in one hand. She was blushing mildly when he kissed her on the cheek.

"Thank you, Sally," he told her. "The gift is very nice." Then he lowered his voice. "You know something? I always thought that idiot Tommy Carver had to have lead in his head to run off and leave you with the baby like that. Why you ever broke down and married him—"

"Shush, now," Mrs. Carver said, and turned her head to the side, embarrassed. Her face was red as a tomato, and Manny thought he saw something in it besides embarrassment, perhaps anger.

It was quiet after that; no one quite knew what to say. Manny was glad Toby wasn't there to take offense at the old man's slap at the father he did not remember. Then Jay Lee chimed in, "How about a story, Grandpa?"

Ida said, "Yes, a story."

"Well," said Grandpa Tarbox, after he settled into his seat again. "A story. Ida, which one? The Last Wildcat?"

Manny and Jay Lee both smiled. They knew that the tale about the lonely wildcat who grew tired of life, goaded Zack Tarbox into going after him, and then fell to the hounds after leading a spirited chase was Ida's favorite.

"The Last Wildcat," Ida agreed, and she almost smiled.

But Manny's mother appeared in the doorway shaking her head. She looked nearly exhausted from her unaccustomed efforts, and her hair was hanging down into her eyes. "We're eating in two minutes," she said. "No stories till afterward." So everyone drifted into the kitchen and sat down to corned beef with potatoes and boiled vegetables, a Yankee dinner. But there was a South American dish there as well, a tiny bowl of haddock marinated in lemon juice and hot sauce that stood before the old man's place at the head of the table. Manny's father used to make the fish dish; he called it *seviche*. Grandpa Tarbox fell in love with the marinated fish the first time he tasted it. He rechristened it with a new nickname and insisted on having it every time he visited.

Grandpa Tarbox entered the kitchen last of all; he had taken time to tap the ash out of his pipe and drink a gulp of brandy first. He smiled when he saw the fish dish waiting for him.

"Ah!" he said. "Seven bitches!" He gobbled down the spicy fish while the others were starting on the meat. No one said grace; the custom had ended in the family during the war.

"Anybody else want raw fish?" the old man asked.

Manny smiled, and Jay Lee, sitting next to him with her hand on his knee, made a disgusted face. Ida studied Jay Lee's face a moment, then mirrored it.

Grandpa Tarbox laughed, delighted. "You're making this almost perfect now, Mary Anne," he said. "It's coming out almost as good as when . . ." He let the sentence go unfinished and speared a large piece of corned beef with his fork.

Manny didn't have any appetite, but everyone else ate and joked. When the joke was on him, he smiled until it was over and someone else became the target, then let the smile die and returned to his thoughts. He also made himself smile whenever Jay Lee pinched his knee and hunted his eyes with her own.

In the middle of the meal, a knock came at the front door, and Toby Carver came in a moment later. His blond hair had been recently trimmed, and he was wearing a new brown leather jacket. A small, purple-wrapped package stuck, ill concealed, from the pocket of the jacket.

"Just in time for dinner," he said, accepting the plate Manny's mother pushed into his hands. He kissed his mother and Mary Anne on the cheek and slapped both Manny and Old Man Tarbox on the back. Manny looked up and smiled at him; his grandfather kept his face buried in the food. Manny often noticed that women's eyes lingered on Toby longer than they did on most young men. Toby wasn't very tall, but there was something about his eyes, which were the blue of a deep lake, or the way his straw-colored hair fell across his forehead, or maybe the strong line of his jaw, that they liked.

Sometimes Manny was a little envious of the unearned attention that Toby's looks drew. Once Manny's mother said that Toby looked a little like the actor Robert Redford. Manny had not known what Robert Redford looked like, but he made it a point to see *Butch Cassidy and the Sundance Kid* the next time it was on television, and he had to admit that his mother was not entirely wrong.

Toby's single flaw was that he was missing the little finger on his left hand. One day when he was eleven years old, Toby had come walking out of the swamp with the finger gone and blood running down his arm, and now he kept the hand with the shiny round stub jammed deeply into his pocket when he was around other people, unless he happened to be around Manny. When he and Manny were together, he always seemed to be waving the hand in the air, as if to remind Manny of how the loss had come about. It was a little unnerving to Manny to see Toby's wounded hand fluttering around at eye level, drawing him back to the calamities and horrors of his childhood.

"Did you get the job?" Toby's mother asked, speaking for the first time in half an hour.

"Sure did," he said. "I start next week. I think I'm going to like it." He sat across from Ida, who set her fork and knife down and studied his face with unblinking eyes. He glanced at her once, then looked away.

"What job?" asked Manny, suddenly interested.

Toby grinned at him, showing teeth that two years of wearing braces had made perfect. "That's what I want to talk to you about," Toby said. "But later."

"Oh, you two," said Manny's mother, sitting for the first time. Her nose wasn't so red anymore. "Always being so mysterious. Well, no wonder Toby got the job, looking so handsome and everything today. Where'd you get the beautiful jacket?"

Toby picked up a knife and began sawing at his corned beef. "Bought it," he said, not looking up. "Listen, can I have that milk over here, please?"

"That idiot, Tommy Carver," Ida blurted suddenly, and looked grinning around the table as if she had said something clever. Toby lifted his eyes to her, studying her. Everyone else became absorbed in their food. Grandpa Tarbox's fork paused briefly in midair when she spoke, then continued on to his mouth.

"Ida . . ." Manny's mother began.

Toby set down his knife and fork and rubbed his lips with a napkin. Then he looked over at Grandpa Tarbox, who kept right on shoveling in the potatoes, his dentures clicking.

"So," Toby said. "Gramps. You've been telling them on my father again, haven't you?"

Old Man Tarbox was unrepentant. "His name came up." He kept eating, and Toby glared at him. Mrs. Carver looked like she was about to say something, then she changed her mind and made herself very small in her chair, a wilted flower.

"Oh, really?" Toby said finally. "Were you telling a story? A story about something idiotic he did, maybe?"

"No. I told the Last Wildcat," the old man lied. He glared around the table, daring anyone to challenge him. No one did. "He held the lantern for my boy, Zack, that's all."

"Ah," said Toby. "He held the lantern. Well, tell me, Gramps, what was so idiotic about that? Why is it my father is always the idiot in your stories? Does that seem fair to you? How come he never gets to be the hero like old Zack?"

Grandpa Tarbox threw down his knife and fork now; they clattered against his plate, and the fork bounced into the air and off the table. "Because he broke the lantern, that's why! And because he was a goddamn idiot! I guess I ought to know better than you. I'll tell you, Toby, that Tommy was an idiot and I will call him an idiot for as long as I live, and there's nothing you can do about it."

Toby gave a slow half-smile now, settled back into his chair. He even put a forkful of food into his mouth and chewed it slowly. Then he said, "Maybe you're right, Gramps. I didn't know him. Could be he was as idiotic as you make him out to be. Do you know what I really think, Gramps?"

"I don't really care what you think, Toby," said the old man. His chin trembled as he furiously polished a knife with his napkin.

"Well," Toby said. "I'm going to tell you anyway. I think my father was just a normal kid, and that he was old Zack's best friend. I think the three of you drank brandy and fished and hunted, and that nobody thought anybody else was an idiot."

"I'm not listening to this," said Manny's grandfather.

But Toby continued. "I think Tommy Carver got to be an idiot when his best friend didn't come back from the war, and he had the nerve to marry his best friend's fiancée a dozen years later. Am I making sense, Gramps?"

"You're an idiot as well," said the old man, but it was only a mutter.

"Yeah," said Toby. "You kept hoping, didn't you? Even showed her phony letters you said were from old Zack so she'd stay on the string. If he had only come home, I wouldn't be here right now giving you a hard time, now would I?"

Grandpa Tarbox wore an expression of pain, as if he had been struck. Everyone else at the table winced; it was a low blow. At the time Toby's mother and Tommy Carver had married, Grandpa Tarbox had had to apologize to both of them for having tried to hold things up by forging letters to himself from Zack, who he said was laid up in New Zealand with grave war wounds. The old man, who had always prided himself on his honesty, had been humiliated by the necessity of the apology, and Manny's mother said he had stayed in his house, telling himself stories and not seeing anyone and going for long walks by himself at night for nearly two years following the wedding. And he did not really recover his spirits completely until Alexis Moreno, a man he approved of wholeheartedly, showed up and married his remaining child. True, Grandpa Tarbox now occasionally said that if Mrs. Carver had followed his advice and not married Tommy, she would have been spared a lot of grief. Manny figured Toby had a right to be angry about that, even if it was true, but this was not the time for him to be making a case of it. He shot Toby a warning look, and Toby seemed to get the message at once. Toby sat down and picked up a fork.

They ate in silence after that. Manny's mother had bought an apple pie, and she put slices before everyone at the table without asking. The pie had come in a box, but it was still good. Only Mrs. Carver waved hers away, making a little noise of refusal in her throat. Ida continued to stare at Toby with a strange smile on her rag-doll face until Mary Anne touched her on the shoulder and said quietly, "Eat, dear."

Finally, to break the tension, Manny pushed away a plate of pie crumbs and said, "This sure was a good meal, Mom," and everyone bobbed his head in agreement.

Grandpa Tarbox, recovered slightly from his losing battle with Toby, said, "Where is that pudgy boyfriend of yours, Mary Anne? He's not one to miss a spread like this," and everyone laughed except for Manny, who was not sure how his mother would take the remark.

But she laughed too, and Toby said, "You mean Flat Top, Gramps, you talking about Flat Top?" and everyone laughed more at that. The laughter was a little nervous, but at least it was laughter. Toby and Grandpa Tarbox exchanged a quick look, and it seemed to Manny they were signaling each other for a temporary truce. After that, though, there was still something going on between them, an unspoken conflict now, a cold war with rules Manny couldn't figure out.

Toby said, "Listen, I'm sorry about that outburst, everybody. I guess I've had a rough day, what with the job interview and all. Here, Gramps, no hard feelings, here's my present. Go ahead and break my chops about it, I won't say a word." He took the small package out of his jacket pocket and handed it to the old man, then smiled his thanks to Manny's mother, who was setting cups of coffee on the table and had just placed one in front of him.

Old Man Tarbox studied the package for a moment, turning it over and over in his hands, and finally he pulled off the red ribbon Toby had pasted to the top. He paused to put cream and sugar in his coffee, then he tore off the purple wrapping paper and looked into the box beneath it. He held the small box up near his face when he lifted the lid off, opening it like a poker hand so that nobody else could see; he peered into it for just a second, clapped the lid back on as if he had seen a snake inside, and said, "Thanks," leaving his face carefully neutral.

He wanted to let it go at that, but both Jay Lee and Manny's mother shouted, "Well, what is it, Grandpa?" and Jay Lee snatched the box out of his hand and tossed the lid off.

She looked puzzled, a little like Ida sometimes did, and Ida herself looked into the box and said, "Oh!" startled, then clapped her hand over her mouth and left it there.

"Well, what is this, Toby?" Jay Lee asked. "This is really crummy if you ask me, giving Grandpa rocks for his birthday. Look, Mrs. Moreno, five little rocks with holes in them all strung together on a string." Jay Lee had been Toby's girlfriend long before she captured Manny, had been rejected by him, and now she said nasty things to him whenever she could.

Everyone craned over to look in the box now, and Toby gave a long, scornful laugh, a fake stage laugh, Manny could tell, and he didn't stop until Jay Lee was glaring at him and everyone else looked to him for an explanation.

"You are brilliant, Jay Lee," he said, looking directly into her smouldering eyes. "When they were handing out brains, you were in the girls' room, right? Those things are Indian jewelry; Indians five hundred years ago who were living in the swamp drilled those holes in those rocks, folks. They're stone beads."

Everyone was suddenly impressed; they all reached fingers into the box to touch the stones turned suddenly magical. Even Manny, lost in a wilderness of worries, stood and looked inside. Only Grandpa Tarbox showed no interest, sipping his coffee and staring out the kitchen window.

Mrs. Carver said, "Well, Toby, where on earth did you get these fascinating things?"

Toby smiled, always happy to lecture. "Right where the new dump is now, at the north end of the swamp, there used to be an Indian camp. The bulldozers have wrecked most of it now, but you can still sneak in there after a rain and find an arrowhead or some of these stone beads that have been washed to the surface. I found these a few weeks ago, and I saved them for Gramps. I know he's just crazy about things like that."

The old man grunted and kept staring out the window.

"Now," continued Toby, "there's a story behind the Indian camp, and it ties in with the one about how Charlie Raymond killed his wife and three kids and then hung himself with a coat hanger, and I was hoping this present would sort of inspire Gramps to tell that one. How about it, Gramps?" He grinned like a predator at Grandpa Tarbox.

"No," said the old man, not dropping his gaze from the window. But the women were curious now, and they protested loudly. Even Jay Lee had gone over to Toby's side out of curiosity.

"I never heard that one before, Grandpa," she said.

Manny was not so sure he wanted to hear the story, if the old man was so reluctant to tell it, so he held his peace.

"No," repeated the old man. "I think I'll tell the one about the Crying Woman." He fumbled with his pipe and tobacco, and Manny's mother set an ashtray in front of him.

Manny was sure he didn't want to hear about the Crying Woman, so he jumped off the fence and said, "Tell the Indian one, Grandpa, I haven't heard it in a while."

With Manny's vote, they had the old Yankee treed. "Dammit," he snapped. "That story has Alexis in it. And it's not fit for women and girls to hear." But Jay Lee catcalled about his claim that the story was too harsh for women, said there was blood and guts on TV every day. Manny's mother was quiet for a moment, then said she might not mind a story about her husband.

So the old man fell to the hounds. He started to prepare himself for the story, but Manny could tell he was far from happy about it. His hands trembled when he tried to light his pipe, and when he had it lit, it went out twice before he could build a head of steam. He got off to two false starts before he launched into the story, straight and true and craftsmanlike.

Chapter 5

"Well, this is a pretty recent story, and by that I mean it may be uncomfortably close to some of us, but if that's what everybody wants to hear, I guess I'll have to spit it out. It started a little over six years ago, a year and a few months before Alexis left us for whatever reason he may have had. We had just gotten some new neighbors then, and one set of neighbors was good, as far as we were concerned, and the other set meant nothing but trouble.

"By the bad set, I mean Mr. William Cahill and his damn octopus of a company that bought the entire swamp and even some of the land around it so they could go about destroying history and nature at leisure. Why, that old Cahill even bought the old Tillman mansion on the top of South Hill so he could look out over his condominiums as they swallowed up our swamp. Of course, he picked that side of the territory to live on because not even he had the stomach to watch what his people were doing at the other end, where that damn dump was going in.

"The good neighbor, Charlie Raymond, lived at the north end right across the road from the terrible dump. And he was a good

45

neighbor and a friend, regardless of what he did later. Charlie was retired navy; he had come out of that crazy Vietnam fiasco just a few years before, and he just wanted a place to raise his kids and maybe a few vegetables in peace and quiet without spending all the little bit he was getting from the government. So when that old house on Wolfpit Road went on the block for back taxes, he bought it for a song. Nobody else wanted it, you see, because it was right across from that Cahill monstrosity, and it had gotten pretty run-down to boot. But it was quiet; even though it was across Wolfpit and technically outside the swamp, there wasn't another house around for half a mile. There were trucks going in and out of the dump all the time, sometimes late at night even, when they could only be up to less good than usual, but Charlie figured that was easier on the nerves than neighbors' kids and dogs chasing baseballs through his garden. The well gave good, sweet country water, loaded with minerals, and the house, which was a real handyman's special, promised to be a good, snug home as soon as the proper work was done on it.

"And that's where Alexis came in. That Charlie Raymond sure had plenty of work to do, and he wasn't lazy about doing it, either. But the trouble was, he didn't know carpentry very well, so that putting on a new roof and doing all those other things was a real challenge to him, and he was making slow progress. So Alexis took to stopping over after work that summer, helping Charlie out for two hours every day, and when fall came, they had the house all shipshape.

"By then, the kids were in school, and it was sure no time to start a vegetable garden, so Charlie was sort of at loose ends for a while, drinking a lot of beer and watching baseball on TV. But Alexis had some of the old maps copied for Charlie, and he started taking him around the swamp, showing him the graves and the old foundations, as well as some of the wildlife and things we look for when we go in there. Well, that Charlie became a real bug on swampology really quick. He started going in by himself; he explored all that winter and even bought himself a year-old beagle bitch so he could chase rabbits and squirrels.

"But it was in the early spring, the rainy, thawing-ground time, that he really went nutty on swamp things; it became like a religion for him. One day he called Alexis at work, he was all excited, and told him to stop down the house on his way home that afternoon. So when Al got out that day, he stopped off for a six-pack and then swung by Charlie's house to see what was up. Well, Charlie Raymond met him at the car before he even had a chance to get out, and he stuck a hand, a dirty hand like he had been clawing in mud, right under my son-in-law's nose. He opened his hand real slow, like he had pearls or gold in it and wanted to tease Al a little, and inside were six Indian arrowheads and two stone beads just like those we saw today.

" 'I found these!' he told Alexis, and he was jumping up and down like a kid at Christmas. 'I found them all in one spot. I really think it *means* something!'

"Alexis nearly balked when he found out Charlie had found those things on dump property, thinking of that dog-mean dump boss, Joe Marconi, but he conceded it might be important from a historical viewpoint, and he agreed to sneak over onto Cahill land with him to see what the story was. So the two of them went over that afternoon, with a couple of trowels to dig around in the earth.

"The place where Charlie found the arrowheads was just twenty yards in from Wolfpit Road, and pretty close to the entrance to the dump; they could hear the dozers chewing away at the swamp when they went in there. Luckily, though, there were trees to screen them from both the road and the dump, so that none of Cahill's armed goons, yes they were armed too, shotguns and pistols, could see them working there.

"Alexis recognized right away the spot was just perfect for an Indian camp; a good, year-round stream with a couple of small pools ran right through it, and the land on either side was gently sloping to make for good drainage without being too steep for dwellings. There were also some big, round boulders standing here and there, dumped by the glacier, and they made for good, natural protection from the wind. Quartz chips were scattered all over the ground, indicating someone had once been busy there, flaking stones to make tools. Well, Alexis and Charlie turned over the soil for an hour or so, and Alexis dug up a broken hide-scraper. Then both of them began finding bits of pottery everywhere, some of them pretty big, too, and they knew they had found an old encampment for sure. Alexis was excited now too; he thought that somebody professional, an archaeologist maybe, should come and have a look. Just before it got dark—it was a deep-purple twilight, and the birds were singing themselves to sleep, you know—he went walking upstream from the Indian camp, thinking about who to call in to see Charlie's discovery, and he found what he was sure was an Indian burial on top of a grassy knoll. A bulldozer had gone by and taken a swipe out of that knoll and had exposed one corner of the grave. Al found it by poking around in the dirt with his trowel and turning up bits of bone. Charlie Raymond was so thrilled about that discovery he nearly wet his pants.

"Well, they went back to the Raymond's house and they drank the six-pack Alexis had brought, and then they went to a bar someplace and drank some more beer to celebrate. The next day, Al called over to Yale University, and he made an appointment with some hotshot professor of archaeology there.

"The next week he went over to see the guy, and to show him all the things they found at the Indian site. He even took a topographical map so the professor would know exactly where the camp stood. The archaeologist was impressed when he saw the pottery and arrowheads and stuff and heard the description of the camp, but he insisted on having Cahill's permission before he'd set foot on the land. So his enthusiasm cooled quickly when he made a few phone calls, including one to the offices of Cahill's company in New York, and everyone told him to stay the hell off that property. Joe Marconi even told him— imagine, telling a college professor—that he'd be shot if he so much as put a foot on dump land. The professor kept on the phone for a week, making useless calls everywhere, but finally he told Al there wasn't anything he could do about the situation. He was sorry, but he had his reputation to think about, and he couldn't trespass.

"After that, Alexis and Charlie weren't sure what to do, whether they should dig by themselves or just leave the place alone. But when they found out the bulldozers were working their way toward the Indian camp and the burial site upstream, and that all that history would become part of the expanding tire dump in a matter of weeks, they decided to go to work and save as much as they could.

"My son-in-law went to the library and got books on archaeology and the Connecticut Indians before they lifted a finger; he wanted to do things properly so their work would be of some scientific value if ever someone wanted to study it. Alexis was like that.

"Well, he and Charlie pored over those books for nearly two weeks, and then they started going into the dump with shovels and trowels just after dawn every morning, when chances of getting caught were lowest. They did about an hour and a half of careful digging and sifting every day; Alexis marked on the maps where every relic was discovered, measured how deep into the earth it was found, and took pictures before numbering it with enamel and putting it in the collecting box. Alexis said it was more important to rescue a few carefully documented artifacts than to save everything and have a collection of junk with no story behind it. And they found some beauts, let me tell you. They found two whole, unbroken clay pots that were really works of art, and a mortar and pestle for pounding grain, and maybe fifty quartz arrowheads. They dug down until they found the old fire-pits, so that they knew where most of the dwellings had been. Alexis marked all those on his map, too. The fact that they might get caught added to the excitement of it, and the two of them were like a couple of big kids about the whole thing. As they dug and developed the village on their map, they got a pretty good idea what life was like in the Indian camp back four-hundred-odd years ago, and they swore that the ghosts of those Indians were there wandering through the site while they worked.

"But the bulldozers were getting closer all the time, and it looked like they were going to tear right into that burial upstream before they scraped the camp away. That's when Charlie and Alexis had their first disagreement about the project, and Alexis backed out finally.

"See, Charlie Raymond kept getting more wide-eyed, and, well, almost fanatical about the whole thing as time went on, and he decided they had to go and excavate the burial mound before the dozers got to it. Alexis said no, that they started with the village and they should stick with the village, and he wasn't too crazy about the idea of opening a grave, anyway. Alexis was part South American Indian—you can see the Indian in Manny, here—and he was real superstitious about things like that. No good ever comes of disturbing the dead. But Charlie was insistent, dying to go in and tear up that grave, in fact he almost hit Alexis one time when they disagreed on it, which wasn't like Charlie at all. So Al said it was Charlie's site, Charlie had discovered it, and he could go ahead and excavate it any way he wanted. Alexis quit on him then, but he still dropped over the house at night sometimes to see how Charlie was coming on it.

"It was right about that time things started going wrong around Charlie's house. Charlie's middle child started having a lot of trouble at school. The teachers said he was disruptive, whereas before, he was quiet. They said he'd get up in the middle of class and just holler, sometimes even swear, and he was hitting the other kids. The boy started seeing a psychologist that came to the school once a week, but it didn't help any, and one day at home he cracked his eight-year-old older brother in the head with a hoe and opened a wound that needed about ten stitches.

"Then one day that beagle Charlie had just went nuts for no clear reason and bit his little girl in the face and left her marked for life, although her life never got to be too long. When that happened, Charlie took a gun, an old thirty-eight he had, and went looking for the dog, planning to shoot it through the heart. Turned out there was no need for shooting, though; he found the dog drowned in the stream that ran through the old Indian camp. She apparently drowned herself; Charlie figured she did it out of remorse for biting the child.

"Charlie's wife got a little funny, too. She started slapping the kids, which she never did before, and she cried at odd times, sometimes right in the middle of supper. She said she was tired of living so damn far away from everything, and complained there were strange noises in the house while Charlie was out digging, and that cold invisible hands touched her sometimes when Charlie was sleeping next to her in bed, touched her breasts and private places. Right about that time the whole family started having problems with their eyes. They saw colored lights dancing in front of them and long black tunnels that swallowed the light.

"Charlie was upset by all of this, and he started to do a bit of drinking; hard stuff, not just beer anymore. But he kept at that burial mound, and he was making excellent progress. Charlie got that grave open, and there was a skeleton in it; the skeleton of a tall man facing east, with his knees drawn up to this chest, like the Indians around here used to bury them. The rib cage was pretty well crushed flat from years of pressure from the earth, and the skull was badly crumbled, but the jawbone with all the teeth was in good shape. Charlie spent a lot of time numbering all the bone pieces before he collected the skeleton, hoping to at least be able to glue the skull together later. There were weapons in the grave as well; a big stone axhead, a couple of spear points, and an even dozen arrowheads. He also found maybe two hundred stone beads, just like Toby so generously brought here today; they were scattered through the smashed rib cage, and he figured the Indian was probably wearing a few necklaces of the things when he was buried.

"Alexis really started worrying about old Charlie after he finally emptied the tomb and packed the skeleton and the grave goods into his cellar with the rest of the artifacts they found in the village. My son-in-law went to visit him one night and found the whole house in an uproar. The kids were all crying and acting scared, and Mrs. Raymond wouldn't even talk to Alexis, just nodded her head toward the back porch when he asked where Charlie was. Well, Alexis found Charlie sitting in a rocking chair out back, staring wide-eyed and vacant toward the swamp, a half-empty pint of bourbon on the floor next to the rocker.

"Al said, 'Hi, Charlie,' and Charlie looked up at him, kind of startled, and then started talking right in about how Stone Beads had come knocking at the back door the night before. Alexis said, 'Who?' and Charlie said, 'Stone Beads, the Indian.' Charlie claimed this Stone Beads had banged on the door at about one in the morning until he finally got up and answered it. This Indian, said Charlie, started complaining about how cold it was since Charlie'd opened his grave, and he wanted some blankets. So Charlie took all the spare blankets they had, which was five or six, and went out to the burial site and put them in the empty hole. But Stone Beads wasn't satisfied; he said he needed more blankets, and he started screaming and crying and threatening about it. This shook Charlie up so much he went back into the house and took the blankets right off his wife's back, then went in and stripped the kids' beds while they slept. Of course, everyone woke up, and they were scared—imagine, a woman and three little kids—but Charlie marched right out into the swamp with those blankets anyway. Afterward, the Indian seemed satisfied, and Charlie went back to the house and tried explaining to his family, but that only seemed to make things worse.

"Well, when Alexis heard this story, he told Charlie he probably should stay out of the swamp for a while, and he most definitely should stay off the bourbon. Then he went back into the house to advise Mrs. Raymond to take the kids on a trip for a few days, and he left.

"Al was pretty upset by now, and he went over the Raymond's house again the next afternoon to see how things were going. Well, Charlie was still there, and he was in a bad state. He was drinking when Alexis showed up, and his hands were shaking so badly he could hardly unscrew the cap on the bottle. Charlie said Stone Beads had returned the night before, just as his wife and kids went out the driveway, and the Indian was in a rage. The blankets were no good, this Stone Beads claimed, said they were all infected with smallpox. The Indian ghost told Charlie his people used the blankets, and now all of them were sick and already three of them had died. The worst part was, Charlie said, Stone Beads blamed him for the sickness, said he knew the blankets had smallpox and gave them to the Indians on purpose so he could get their land. The Indian wouldn't listen to Charlie's protests of innocence; he went away calling him a murderer and saying all whites who trespassed on the swamp were cursed, especially Charlie and Alexis and their children.

"It was then that Al told Charlie he should get out of the house right away, maybe come and stay with me for a few days until he could calm down, and then he should go find his family. Charlie wouldn't hear of it though. He said he had brought everything on himself by defiling the burial mound after Alexis had tried to warn him not to, and he had to stay and try to make peace with Stone Beads, or else the Indian would follow him everywhere he went, and maybe try to harm his kids. He was convinced the ghost had caused the dog to disfigure his little girl as well as forced the younger boy to hurt his brother. Well, Alexis stayed there for hours trying to change Charlie's mind about staying, but it was no use, and finally he went home.

"The next day at the factory, Alexis got a strange, jittery feeling, so he left an hour early and went straight to Charlie Raymond's house. Charlie was there by himself, and he seemed calm, almost happy, but he looked awful. He was filthy, caked with mud, and he was a mess of scratches and welts from insect bites. He told Alexis that Stone Beads had showed up the night before with three other Indians, and that they had grabbed him, stripped off his clothes, and tied him with leather thongs. He showed Al the places where the bindings had cut his skin, and he bragged about how he had put up a hell of a fight; the Indians, except for Stone Beads himself, were all small, and it took them a lot of work to overpower him. After they had Charlie bound, they ran a pole between his wrists and ankles, hoisted him like a deer carcass, and ran him about two miles through the wettest part of the swamp. They finally left him on the edge of a blueberry thicket, and they let the mosquitoes and the gnats have at him all night. Charlie said there were clouds of mosquitoes; the stings were bad but the whining they made by your ears was the worst part, and it almost made him crazy.

"But he said Stone Beads came back at dawn with a knife and cut him loose and told him his punishment was almost at an end. That was why he could finally relax, he told Alex; his punishment was almost at an end. Al spent some more time trying to convince him to leave the house, but then they heard a car in the driveway, and it was Charlie's wife and kids, returned to home. The wife came in the house; she seemed pretty calm, and said she and the little ones had been to a motel, but she had decided it was the wrong thing to do, leaving her man like that, and she was back to help him get over whatever it was that was bothering him. Well, Al tried to talk her into going away again and taking Charlie with her, but she refused. And when Alexis looked out the window and saw the kids playing happily in the yard, he thought maybe things were okay now, and he went home. But of course things weren't okay.

"That night Alexis was trying to sleep and not having an easy time of it when the phone rang; Mary Anne should remember this. Well, he answered the phone, just full up with dread, and it was Charlie. Charlie sounded sad as a ghost, and all he said was, 'Al, I've really gone and done it now. Take good care of your children, friend.' And he hung up. Right after, Alexis called me and told me to be dressed in fifteen minutes. Then he put his clothes on and swung by to pick me up.

"They were all dead when we got there, of course. Charlie had gone into the cellar during the night and taken that heavy axhead he found in Stone Bead's grave; it had the numbers *one two three* written on it in black enamel, and he went back upstairs and bludgeoned his wife to death while she slept and then killed the two youngest kids. The oldest boy apparently woke up and tried to run; they found him dead on the stairs. He tried to fight off his father, I guess, because the cops said he had a broken arm along with his head injuries.

"Don't you women look at me like that; you insisted on this story, and now I insist on finishing it properly.

"Anyway, Charlie'd dropped the stone ax right there next to the oldest boy's body. It was all covered with brains and blood, too, and so were the beds and the floors of all three bedrooms. Well, we went looking for Charlie; Alexis had brought along a pistol and planned to put him out of his misery like a mad dog if we found him alive, but of course we didn't. We found his bloody fingerprints on the telephone by the back door; they showed up real well because the phone was white. Then we found Charlie himself in the backyard, strung from a coat hanger he'd twisted into a noose. He must have wanted to die really badly because he was taller than the tree limb he'd decided to use, so he had to lift his feet clear off the ground and set all his weight on his neck and then stay like that for a long while.

"Al and I went to a diner up on Route Twenty-five and called the cops.

"Of course, you all remember that Charlie's empty house burned down a few months later. The skeleton of Stone Beads and all the other relics were still in the cellar at the time, and I imagine they're still buried beneath the rubble of that house."

Chapter 6

Old Man Tarbox blew a huge cloud of blueberry smoke and lapsed into silence. Everyone was quiet for a few moments, then Jay Lee whispered, "Holy shit!"

Ida looked as if she were on the point of tears. "It all burns down," she said, as if the fire had been the most significant part of the story for her. She gave Grandpa Tarbox a look that seemed to say that the two of them shared a secret, and the old man looked away.

Manny's mother sat with her hand cupped over her mouth, her eyes wide, and finally she said, "I didn't think it would bother me." Then she stood and rushed off to her bedroom.

Manny had the uneasy feeling that there was a part of the story missing, a very important part, but he didn't have a clue about what it might be. It was almost as if the story were a big piece in a larger riddle he was supposed to try to solve but was unable even to begin on, because his grandfather was unfairly withholding information. He looked at Toby, and Toby winked.

"Good one," said Toby. "A masterpiece, Gramps." Toby too seemed full of occulted knowledge, and he turned a beaming face at Grandpa

Tarbox. The old man looked as uncomfortable trapped between the gazes of Toby and Ida as if he were caught in a crossfire.

Mrs. Carver wore a look of pain, as if she had a bad toothache. "That was," she said, "the most awful, bizarre thing I've ever heard. I don't think you should have told that, Mr. Tarbox."

The old man tapped his pipe out in the ashtray then, and cleared his throat. "Well, Sally," he said, "sometimes life gets pretty awful and bizarre. In fact, the older I get, the more bizarre and awful things seem to become. I don't know if it's just me, or if the world is coming to an end, just like it says in the Bible."

Mrs. Carver stood and tried to smile. "Well, but we must think only about the good things, Mr. Tarbox," she said. "It's the only way we can survive, isn't it?"

Manny went to the closet in the hallway to get her jacket. There were clothes wrapped in plastic in the closet, shrouded against the dust, and they reminded him of black body bags. Dread was growing inside him like a jagged pearl. Mrs. Carver's jacket was an old one; it had seen at least ten seasons. He took it to her, and she put it on.

"I really must be going now," she said. "I've had a lovely time." She kissed Grandpa Tarbox on the cheek, whispered, "Happy birthday." She started for the door, but when she was halfway out of the kitchen, she turned back to Grandpa Tarbox. "Oh, and I hope you don't still feel badly about having invented a few letters from Zack," she said in a quiet, sad voice. "I know how upset you were when he didn't come home. And perhaps you were right about Tommy. I suppose he was an idiot. He *did* desert us."

Grandpa Tarbox kept his face carefully expressionless for a long minute. Then, slowly, he began to reach for his pipe and his tobacco. "Good-bye, Sally," he said, his voice almost a whisper.

Mrs. Carver turned an apologetic face at Toby, who was frowning even as he stood to accompany her outside. Then Toby and Manny and Jay Lee followed her out to her car. She drove a Pontiac Firebird that Toby had talked her into buying, making payments from her salary as a registered nurse.

Mrs. Carver tried smiling one more time at the three of them before she pulled out of the long, curving driveway and rolled out onto Dark Entry Road.

They watched her go, then Jay Lee said, "Anyone have any pot? I sure could use a buzz after that weird story."

Without thinking, Manny said, "I had some, but the cops dumped it out on me." After that he could have kicked himself.

Toby looked at him, startled. "What cops? When?"

"Today. This morning. Listen, I don't really want to talk about it."

Toby was studying him now, seeking the best way to pry him open. Manny made fists and shoved them deep into his pockets.

"You get pulled over or something, Manny? A ticket, maybe? They didn't take you in, did they?"

"Listen, Toby. Okay?"

Toby studied him some more, seemed to decide the story would take more work than it was worth. He said, "Okay. For now."

Jay Lee looked from Manny to Toby, uninterested in Manny's police encounter. "So," she said. "No pot? Anybody?"

Toby kept his gaze leveled at Manny. "Yeah, I've got a joint, friends. Shall we go behind the house?"

The three of them stepped to the back corner of the house where no one could see them, and Toby produced his silver cigarette case. It was a beautiful silver box, but it had someone else's initials engraved into it; Toby always told people it had been his inheritance from an uncle. This was untrue, as far as Manny knew. Two joints rested in the box; Toby lit one and put the case back into his jacket.

They smoked in silence for a while, passing the joint between them and watching the damp cigarette paper stain a dark brown with the marijuana oils.

Finally, Jay Lee said, "This sure is good pot. Smells a lot better than blueberry pipe tobacco." She giggled.

Toby said, "I got hired for a job today, Manny. And it's not just a job, either, it's an opportunity to maybe get hold of a lot of money, easy."

"Lucky you," said Jay Lee.

Toby told her to shut up. "Listen, Manny," he said. "I don't mean a little money. I mean a lot, a lot of money. And I think there's another job opening too, you know what I mean? We could go to California like we always wanted, you and me."

"Yeah," said Manny. "Tell me about it."

Toby jerked his head in Jay Lee's direction. "It's complicated," he said. "There are a lot of details. We'll go over it later." Lately, Toby's crippled hand always seemed to be hovering somewhere where Manny had to look at it. It was almost as if Toby expected him to study it. The rounded stub, which could change colors rapidly from red to pink to white, reminded Manny somehow of the moody, treacherous eye of an unblinking amphibian. The finger was ugly; sometimes, especially when Manny was drunk or stoned, it could cause his stomach to crawl. At other times, it could inspire inexplicable anger or fear in him.

"Big man," said Jay Lee. "Always with the important secrets. You just want to get Manny away from me, that's all."

Toby told her to shut up, but she ignored him.

"Manny," she said. "You want me to stay over here tonight, or are you going to send me home again?"

Manny looked away from her, aimed his eyes out over the swamp. "I don't know," he said. "I've got something important on my mind, Jay Lee."

She laughed, a crow call. "I sure have heard that before. You're getting just as bad as Toby when—"

"Shut up, Jay Lee," said Toby, and he gave her a shove.

When they got back into the house, Old Man Tarbox and Manny's mother were playing cards. The old man's bottle of brandy stood on the table, and a full shot glass sat before each of them. Ida had another deck of cards, and she was building houses on the kitchen table. She was quite good at it.

Manny, Jay Lee, and Toby wrestled coins out of their pockets, and they sat down to join the game. They played penny poker at first, then graduated to blackjack, with a dime betting limit. Toby got hold of the deal and hung on to it, raking in the coins. Grandpa Tarbox got angrier and angrier the more Toby won, and finally he threw down his hand and wouldn't play anymore. Everyone else tossed in their cards too then, and Manny, Toby, and Jay Lee each took a drink of the syrupy brandy.

After that, Jay Lee said, "How about another story, Grandpa? Me and Manny and Toby are really in the mood for one now." She grinned broadly, and Manny felt like slapping her mouth.

"Maybe we've had enough of stories," Manny said. "My grandpa has to recharge his batteries sometimes."

But Grandpa Tarbox said, "Well, I guess I've got enough pep to tell one for the road." He reached for the pouch of tobacco and began packing his pipe. "Let me see, how about the Last Wildcat?"

The room grew chilly as Toby fixed the old man with a stare. "It seems, Gramps, that you already ran through that one today, or am I mistaken?"

"So I did," said the old man quickly. "We'll let Ida pick the next one. What'll it be, sweetheart?"

"Oh, Ida," said Jay Lee. "Pick the Crying Woman. I always—"

"No," said Manny. "Ida . . ." His stomach cramped at the prospect of his grandfather telling the Crying Woman.

Ida turned her beaming face to Manny, like a flower turning in the sun. He shook his head slowly, but she said, "Yes, Crying Woman."

And so, the old man began.

Chapter 7

"Well, the ghost we call the Crying Woman had a name once upon a time, and that name was Mindwell Hopkins. Mindwell was originally from down on the shore, in Stratford, which is where the people that first settled this part of the state originally came from. She was born and raised there during the years when disagreements between the American colonies and King George of England were growing. When Mindwell was sixteen years old, young William Hopkins drove down to Stratford in a borrowed sleigh one winter day, married the girl, and brought her here to live on his farm.

"The Hopkins farm was pretty small compared to other places hereabouts; the fields were up on the other side of where Route Twenty-five is now, and you used to be able to see where the house stood until they put the shopping center right on top of the site. We buy brandy right now in the Crying Woman's sitting room; think about that. But they were happy, those two; they were both young, unlike a lot of couples in those days where the man was an old geezer working on his third wife, who was usually no more than a girl. The farm produced all they really needed. They had corn and some cattle and some apple trees and a few chickens, and pretty soon the babies started coming along. They had three in three years; two boys first and then a girl. The children all lived, too, which was unusual in those times, although the girl was always sickly, and even when she got older, she had to spend most of her time in the house.

"But when the baby girl was about a year old, Mindwell had a fourth child, whether a boy or a girl I don't know because that one was born dead, and they buried it on its birthday, right behind the house. The grave lies beneath the K mart somewhere; I think maybe under the boys' clothes section, but it could be in hardware too, I'm not certain. That was the beginning of a lot of heartbreaking luck for Mindwell. War broke out right then, so her man shouldered his musket, kissed her good-bye, and marched off somewhere in the general direction of Boston. Well, he never came back, and no one ever heard from him again. It's most likely he was captured by the British and died of smallpox or mistreatment in one of those camps they had, but it's also possible he was shot and fell down in the woods and was never found by anyone, and eventually became loam for the goldenrod and the milkweed. Some gossips in this town even claimed he'd fought till the end of the war, decided he wanted no more part of plowing rocky soil and fighting chicken hawks, and settled down in New York with a new wife and a new name, but that was just idle, mean-spirited speculation.

"Any way you cut it, though, Mindwell was alone. And she was all of twenty-one years old with three tiny kids to feed and a farm to run. Well, she did her best, but she couldn't, you know, do everything by herself. So finally she hired a middle-aged veteran named McCullock, who'd lost an arm to bad surgeons during the war, to give her a hand. McCullock fixed himself up a place in the barn, and his one arm was as strong as all two arms of most men, so he was a big help.

"Things were all right for Mindwell for a time after that, until people started talking, that is. You know how everyone was into everyone else's business in those days, what with the Church and everything, and they still are today as a matter of fact, but nobody has a reputation to defend anymore. Anyway, tongues were wagging that McCullock had taken to sleeping in the house from time to time; whether it was true or not, I can't say.

"But the talk ruined poor Mindwell's reputation in the community, and with it, her chances to marry again. So, when McCullock finally died of lockjaw, she was more alone than ever.

"Well, she was by herself now, after that, and a tarnished woman in the eyes of the community, so men started dropping by to see if they could tarnish her some more. You see, real, authentic scarlet ladies were terribly hard to come by in the Connecticut woods in those days, so when one was discovered, of course she was in great demand.

"Mindwell turned them all away at first; she maybe held out for two years after McCullock died. But trying to run a farm by herself and raise those kids was just wearing her out, and then she was young, remember, still in her mid-twenties, and it's only normal she would think of men from time to time. She tried to take the kids and go back to her family down in Stratford once, but her parents had died, and the rest of the family, her brothers and sisters, certainly didn't want a tainted woman living in their houses and influencing their children. So she was stuck trying to scratch a living out of the farm and fending off the shabby advances of just about all the men in town.

"Then one day along came a young Yale divinity student named Carver, who was the son of a rich man from up in Newtown, to buy some of Mindwell's apples. Whether he was any relation to Toby here, I have never been able to ascertain, but it seems unlikely.

"Anyway, this young Carver apparently liked what he saw, and he came back in a few days for more apples and some corn, and he talked to Mindwell real soft and sweet, not at all like the rough country hicks who had been pestering her. To make a long story short, he courted Mindwell with great patience, and then after a couple of weeks he got what he was after.

"Well, the success went to his head, and even though he was allegedly studying for the cloth, young Carver went through every tavern in the county, crowing about his pathetic conquest. After that, of course, Mindwell became a confirmed floozy in the eyes of the community; some doubt had been growing before because of the fact that she had refused so many men, and floozies don't generally do that. But now, all doubt had been removed, and the eager fellows just would not take no for an answer. She tried refusing people again, even refused young Carver when she heard what he had been saying, but refusal didn't work anymore. One night four young country bucks came around to her house, and she tried to turn them away, but they let themselves in anyway, and they made her be a good floozy with them.

"Whether the kids had to watch that, or even knew what was going on, I don't know, but after that night, Mindwell just sort of gave it all up. She let the farm go to seed—she'd never been much of a farmer anyway—and when men came around she'd let them in if they had a coin or a chicken or a sack of flour for her.

"That went on for a year or so, and then young Carver's father up in Newtown started feeling lonely; he'd lost his wife some years before, and he sent Mindwell a note asking her to visit him. Well, her oldest boy by now was getting almost big enough to handle a musket, and she'd gotten a watchdog shortly after the midnight visit from her four neighbors, so she felt the kids were safe enough to allow her to get away for a night. And after that first time old Carver must have been pleased with her, because he told her that if she came to see him twice a month he'd make sure she had enough money to feed her children and keep her in clothes.

"And that's what she did, all spring and summer and fall, and old Carver got word around the county she was to be left alone from now on, and for the first time in years she was not bothered by callers at night.

"Then one February night, a blizzard started up while she was at the old man's house, and she began to worry about her young ones; the oldest was only nine, you see. Well, she borrowed a one-horse sleigh from old Carver and drove home through the storm, and when she got there, the two boys and the dog were gone. The sickly little girl told her that about two hours before, when the blizzard first began, the dog had started barking at the door, all the hair standing up like quills on the back of his shoulders, and that when one of the boys had opened the door to get firewood, the dog had taken off into the swamp like an arrow, snarling and barking. According to the little girl, the boys called and called for the dog, but he didn't come back, and finally they looked at each other and put on their warmest clothes and started out into the swamp after him. They didn't come back either, and the little girl had been cold as well as frightened, because the fire had died and she didn't know how to get it started again.

"Mindwell got the fire going for the little girl, then she headed out into the teeth of the blizzard to call for her boys. There were no tracks, of course, because of the snow, so she had to just head blindly into the swamp, calling and calling. She didn't find them, and it was so cold she had to give up after a while. She took the sleigh and went to her nearest neighbor's house for help, but nobody was crazy enough to go out and search for the kids until the blizzard stopped. They searched the next day, though, five or six men; those neighbors were real neighborly all of a sudden, but they didn't find a trace of those kids. They spent about a day and a half looking all through the frozen swamp, and then they gave up because they knew it was useless.

"The spring thaw showed up early that year despite a bitter winter, but by that time Mindwell's little girl was dead from pneumonia. I don't know where they buried her. After that, Mindwell sort of lost her reason; she abandoned the house and took to wandering in the swamp, looking for her children everywhere and crying. People said she was sleeping on beds of moss and leaves and eating berries and crayfish and frogs. The farmers tried halfheartedly to catch her a few times, but she eluded them. Then, finally, by the time summer rolled around, her clothes had become so ragged she was practically naked, and she was scandalizing people every time she crossed a road or a field near a house, mostly scandalizing the women, since almost all the men had already seen her naked at one time or another. So one day about twenty men and boys surrounded the swamp and started tightening the circle, little by little. It was great sport; some of them even brought hounds and turned them loose on her, and bets were made as to where she might tree.

"Well, they found Mindwell in that little cave up on the hilltop you kids call the castle; she had crawled in there backwards to escape the dogs. All the men gathered around the cave to get a look, and everyone cheered when two of the fellows finally dragged her out. Some of them sort of poked and prodded her; there were quite a few there that were pretty well lit on hard cider, and some made jokes about who should get her pelt.

"They carted poor Mindwell off to a place for crazy women after that; I don't know where the place was, and it didn't take long for her to die in there. They buried her somewhere with a wooden marker, and her grave was eventually lost.

"She came back to the swamp, though, to look for those kids. People started seeing her ghost late at night, or hearing her crying out there. Kids saw her most of all; she seemed drawn to kids, but she appeared to older people as well. For a hundred years after, whenever an old farmer was found dead in his fields of a heart attack or a stroke, folks said he had seen Mindwell.

"Now, of course, most of the farms are gone, put out of business by competition from the West and these crazy real estate prices. All you see of them are the cellar holes and stone walls that crisscross the woods and the wetlands. I guess I'm about the only one who really knows who Mindwell was anymore. I've seen her six times in my life now, and I always try to be kind to her; I smile and say a word or two, and once I even told her not to worry, that God cares for her, although I don't know if that's really true or not. I know what she's been through and I guess she deserves a little kindness after these two hundred years."

Chapter 8

*T*he old man set down his pipe to signal that the story was over. He stared out the kitchen window into the darkness.

Manny's mother was the first to speak. "Why that poor woman! I guess she never did have a bit of luck. And those people! I guess people were awful damn mean in those days. I'm sure glad it isn't like that now. But something was different this time, than the last time you told it. If I can just think . . ."

The old man smiled at her faintly, but said nothing.

Jay Lee said, "Jesus! That story's a winner, Grandpa! I must've heard it twenty times, and it just gets better each time. And to think they found her in our cave, the one me and Manny and Toby played in when we were kids. It gives you goose bumps."

"I know! I know what it is!" said Manny's mother, rapping a stiff index finger against the top of the table. There was childish excitement in her voice. "You stuck Toby's name in there. That divinity student, the last time he had a different name. Why did you do that?"

Grandpa Tarbox looked startled. "I did?" he said. "I guess I *did*. Isn't that strange." He picked up his pipe and looked at it with wide eyes, as if it had crawled across the table by itself or done something else totally unexpected of a pipe. "That happens once in a very great while," the old man said in a soft voice. "Something will just fall into a story, and there is almost always a reason behind it, and you spend a devil of a time trying to figure out exactly *what.*" Grandpa Tarbox slid suspicious eyes at Toby.

Toby said nothing; he sat smirking at Manny, who was trying hard to keep his face from twisting into a frown of worry. It wasn't working, and Manny knew Toby could tell something was bothering him very much and was just waiting like a vulture for it to come out.

Finally Manny said, "Grandpa, you say you saw the Crying Woman a bunch of times. Did she ever talk? I mean, did she ever say anyone's name or anything?"

Old Man Tarbox fixed Manny with a puzzled look. "Why, no she never talked. Always just cries and looks at you as if she wants to know have you seen her kids. What's this about, Manny?"

Manny looked down at the table, studied the pattern of the scattered playing cards. "Terry and I maybe saw her once when we were kids, fishing in the woods at night."

"And," said Grandpa Tarbox, "she said something to you?"

"Yeah. Listen, folks, I got something to tell; a little story of my own that occurred today. I kind of wanted to hold it till tomorrow, till after the party, but I guess it won't wait. He looked up; they were all staring at him. Only Toby was smiling. He spoke quickly, wanting to get it all out and over with as soon as possible.

"I went to buy some stuff at the K mart plaza this morning; Ma knows that. Anyway, on the way back, I swung through the center of town to come all the way up Dark Entry. Right at the beginning of Dark Entry it was all full of cops, staties and locals both, and there were newspaper reporters and guys with TV cameras and everything." He looked around the table and continued.

"So I stopped to see what was going on, and this guy with mirror glasses says they found six bodies buried in the woods there. Said they'd been there maybe a long time, and they were all kids." Manny started to say something else, but he choked and looked back down at the table.

Grandpa Tarbox opened his mouth and left it open. Ida studied her grandfather's face for a moment, then opened her own mouth.

"Oh my God!" said Manny's mother. "Oh my God, oh my God. I need a pill, no, I need two pills right now." She stood and stumbled off toward the bathroom.

Manny looked up. Tears poured out of him now; he'd held them back all day, and now he couldn't anymore. He was ashamed; that made it twice in the same day, and he scrubbed furiously at his face with the back of his sleeve. Then he shouted so his mother could hear him in the bathroom.

"It might not mean anything, Ma. I asked this lieutenant guy if there was a dog, you know, in there with those kids, and he told me no dog. Could you bring me a couple of those things, please?"

Jay Lee said, "But when will they know if one of the bodies is Terry, Manny?" Everyone looked at her.

"Shut up, Jay Lee," Toby said. He wasn't smiling anymore. He stood and slapped Manny lightly on the back. "It'll be okay, bud. Listen, I'll give you a call in a day or two to talk to you about that other thing, okay? And if you want to talk, or maybe go for a few brews or something, give me a call, all right?"

Manny said, "Okay."

"Let's get our coats, Jay Lee," said Toby. "I'll walk you home."

"But I'm staying—" Jay Lee started to say.

Toby put his hand on her shoulder and squeezed, hard. "Let's go, Jay Lee."

She stood reluctantly and went with him to the closet, then returned briefly to kiss Manny on the cheek. The two of them let themselves out.

Manny's mother came back and put two small white tablets in front of him. Valiums. Her nose was red and swollen, and she seemed beaten down. She said, "Well, it's been a tiring day. I guess I'll go to bed now. Come on, Ida." Ida had pulled her legs up into the chair and was rocking slowly back and forth, staring at the wall.

"Good night, Daddy, and happy birthday," said Manny's mother, She kissed the old man, then took Ida's hand and pulled her out of the chair.

After they were gone, Manny and his grandfather sat together in silence for a long while. Then Manny remembered the pills, and started to put them into his mouth.

"Shouldn't take those, Manny," Old Man Tarbox said softly. "Pills are only for weak people."

"Yeah, well, Grandpa, I'm a pretty weak guy." He swallowed the pills with no water.

The old man blinked at him for a long moment, then said, "Tell me, Manny, did the police say how they found out all of a sudden those bodies were buried there?"

"They said it was a unanimous call."

"Anonymous, Manny."

"Anonymous, then. I should've never quit school."

"Then somebody knew. All that time they knew."

"Sure looks like somebody knew, doesn't it?" They were silent for a long time after that.

Then Old Man Tarbox said, "I guess I'll be on my way home. Got some painting to do tomorrow, and a gutter to fix." He stood, massaging the small of his back with both hands.

"Okay, Grandpa," said Manny. He was starting to feel a calming glow from the pills. "You want a ride home? I've got the station wagon to where it almost runs these days."

"No thanks. I'll just walk right on down the railroad bed. It makes me feel good to take advantage of my right-of-way through Cahill land."

Manny found the old man a flashlight and got his jacket and red-checked hunting cap from the closet. Manny's grandfather put the jacket and hat on, then walked to the door with Manny following. The old man stopped on the top step and looked back at him.

"Things will work out for us, Manny. The important thing is to be strong. It's the only thing."

"Yeah, well, you wrote the book on that, I guess. I'm sorry your birthday ended so shitty, Grandpa." The unspoken portent of a failed birthday celebration hung heavily between them for a long moment.

"I've had much worse," Grandpa Tarbox said finally. "Listen, I want you to come by during the next few days. We'll chop some Cahill firewood together, and then we'll fire up the wood stove and drink some brandy. Deal?"

"Deal, Grandpa. Watch the chuckholes on the way home, all right?"

Manny watched his grandfather cross the wooden footbridge and head down the tracks. He watched the electric lantern bobbing through the woods for a long time; it was a moonless night, and the old man's light was the only thing he could see.

*M*anny slept poorly that night, despite having swallowed the two white pills his mother had given him. Early on, he got the familiar feeling that someone was outside somewhere, watching the house. The feeling lasted an hour or two; it came and went between gray patches of disturbed sleep, then it abated. Later on, Manny thought he heard someone humming or whistling tunelessly up on the railroad bed, but the sound, if it had existed at all, had lasted only a few seconds. He wasn't sure he didn't dream it. A short time later, he was certain he heard his mother or Ida open and close the front door.

Almost as soon as it was light, Manny kicked his way into his Levi's, tugged on an old sweater to insulate himself against the chill of dawn, and went down the ladder to the first floor of the house.

His mother was already at the stove, making coffee. When she saw him come into the kitchen and slide into a seat at the kitchen table, she nodded wordlessly and took an extra cup down from the cupboard. In a minute, she brought over two steaming cups, set them on the bare wood of the table, and then sat down across from him. There was no electric bulb burning in the kitchen, and her face was as gray as ashes in the pale natural light. There were two half-moon–shaped areas of a darker charcoal color directly beneath her eyes.

"I know," she said in a voice that was almost a whisper. "Damn pills are sometimes almost useless unless you take a fistful."

She wrapped both hands around her coffee mug, and Manny took this as a signal to reach for his own cup. He took a sip of the hot, bitter liquid and surveyed the wreckage of yesterday's party; the dishes piled in and around the sink. The faucet was dripping, making a faint tapping sound.

"I heard you go outside last night," he said.

His mother sighed, then picked up her coffee cup, blew across the steaming surface of the coffee, and returned it to the tabletop. "I was worried about your grandfather. He was out dowsing."

"Dowsing?" Manny wondered if the strain of holding herself together was beginning to cause his mother to hallucinate. "You mean witching for water? At night?"

A sudden childhood memory crowded itself into Manny's mind: his grandfather, holding a chokecherry branch shaped like a wishbone in the powerful grip of his leathery hands, with the base of the fork pointed at the sky. The old man had winked at him and then started marching, had marched right toward a spot on his back lawn where he said a powerful underground current of water ran through a channel of gravel and porous rock. As he neared the place, the base of his dowsing rod began to dip as if an invisible hand were pulling it. Then, as he walked directly over the hidden stream, the branch twisted violently in his hands until it was pointing straight down; Manny heard the faint squeal of wood against hard flesh, and he saw the black bark twist away from the white wood.

His grandfather had winced and tossed away the stick then, had shown him palms stained with the juices of green, living wood. "Use apple if you can," he had said. "Or maybe peach. Chokecherry just is not as reliable."

"No, not water, I don't think." His mother's voice pulled him out of a reverie. "I'm surprised you never saw him or heard him; he's out there every so often, way late at night, and he generally hums or sings. I guess the noise keeps him company."

"What then?" Manny asked. The notion of his grandfather wandering the swamp by himself in the dark was disturbing.

His mother looked down at the table and began to rock back and forth ever so slightly in her seat. She took her time in answering, started humming a little under her breath, and he almost told her not to say anything if thinking about it was going to make her come apart at the seams. But finally she said, "Could be lots of things. A dowsing rod isn't just for water; people use them to look for gold, or oil, or hidden treasure. Or things that are lost. Or missing people. Or—" her whole body had begun trembling now; her teeth chattered between words, "or bones resting in the earth."

Manny instinctively reached and put a hand on her slender arm; she stopped shaking almost immediately and looked up at him. Her watery blue eyes had a hunted look to them. "So you think—" he started to say.

"I don't really know," she said. "He used to do that a lot, back before I married your father. Go out water-witching at night, I mean. It was after the war, and he was awful upset about my brother not coming home. It took him awhile to admit that Zack was dead; had poor Toby's mother strung along all that time, saying he was getting letters. He wanted to hold her for Zack so he'd have something waiting when he got home. Later, when he finally gave in and was willing to let Zack be dead, he was desperate for the body to bury, so we could say good-bye to him properly. But the army couldn't find it. There were thousands they couldn't find, and Zack was just one of them, but Pa took it real personal. That upset him more than anything, the idea that his son was on the other side of the world someplace, forgotten and covered over with unhallowed ground. So he started walking at night with his forked stick. He'd go up and down the railroad bed, and across the swamp whenever he could find a path in the dark. I don't know if he thought he was going to find Zack out there, or if that was just his way of thinking or curing insomnia."

Manny's mother was looking back down at the table now. She

was trembling just a little, and two glistening lines of tears crept around the outside of her face and disappeared beneath her chin. Manny felt like crying himself; he depended on his grandfather to be there like a rock when he needed him, and his mother seemed to be saying the old man might be losing his grip on things. It made him feel helpless.

"So now what's he looking for?" His voice came out as a high croak of despair, shaming him.

His mother shook her head. "Maybe he doesn't think Terry . . . that group yesterday . . ." He squeezed her arm, and she stopped trying to talk.

They sat in silence for a long while. Then, strong sunlight finally slanted through the kitchen windows, and the gloom lifted a little. "Did you ever ask him?" Manny said finally.

She wiped her eyes on the back of a wrist, and snuffed loudly. "Once. When I was still living with him. Before I met your father. He got mad and said don't ever disturb him when he's doing that. Not for anything. I guess he doesn't like for people to see that things bother him as much as they do."

Another long silence fell between them as each of them mulled over what had been said. But after a time his mother spoke. "Manny," she said, and looked directly at him, "you hit me yesterday."

Guilt scrambled through him like a hive of angry wasps. He dropped his eyes to the table.

"I know," Mary Anne said, "I'm not the mother you and Ida should have right now. I used to be a good mother until horrible things began to happen to my family. Now, it's all I can do sometimes to keep from going down into the cellar with Ida and curling up into a ball and staying that way forever. You're the man of the family now. Try to be patient with me, Manny."

Manny's throat was too thick to form words. He could only nod.

Chapter
9

*A*t first Manny didn't believe that his father might not come back. But after almost two weeks had passed he began to think more and more about the fights between his father and mother. The arguments had not seemed very serious, but maybe they were, and he was starting to think he might never see his father again. He cried about that, but always in the bathroom so no one would see him. His sister, Ida, had been strongly affected as well; she wouldn't say two words to anybody now except Terry. Terry often went into the cellar where Ida was hiding to talk to her in whispers. Manny felt left out with the two of them always hissing together like a pair of snakes, and his mother had been drinking a lot lately, crying, so he couldn't talk to her either.

The only one left to talk to was his grandfather; Manny walked down the tracks to his house a lot, but Grandpa Tarbox had long, quiet moods now, and he seemed sad. Manny never could get him to say anything about Alexis, because the old man always changed the subject; he'd start in about what trout do in the winter or how the steam engine had plunged into the Engine Hole. All that was interesting, but what Manny really wanted to discuss was his father.

Toby didn't come anymore. Sometimes Manny saw him standing out on the road looking toward the house, but he never walked up the driveway. Too sad for him here, Manny guessed.

*T*hree days before Christmas, snow was coming down hard all of a sudden. It fell in dry flakes like white duck feathers, and there was no heat in the house. The oil for the furnace had run out, and Manny's mother was shut away in her room, so there was nobody to call the truck to come and bring more. Manny was wearing his coat as he looked out the back window, and he shivered as he watched the snow fall thicker and thicker.

Finally, as he watched out the window, Terry came up out of the cellar through the outside door and walked over to where Butch was jumping like a fish at the end of his tether. He let the dog off the chain, and Butch ran in circles, happy, dragging his behind in the snow, and he batted Terry in the chest with his paws a couple of times, leaving dirt and snow on his coat.

Manny jumped up then and ran into the cellar. Ida was sitting on her couch, rocking and crying. Crying and rocking. She looked at him. "Daddy," she said. "Daddy."

"Where's Terry going?" Manny asked. "You know, don't you?"

"Daddy," she said.

"Come on, Ida." He pretended he was going to slap her, but she only squeezed her eyes shut and kept rocking. Tears crawled from under her lids.

So Manny threw open the cellar door and slammed it shut behind him once he was outside. Terry and Butch were already across the brook bridge and walking north on the railroad bed. He called, and started after them.

Terry stopped and turned when he heard the call, and Butch ran back across the bridge, bumped Manny's legs with his head, and went bouncing back to Terry like a rubber ball.

"Go back to the house," Terry said when Manny had reached him. His eyes were red, and he wouldn't look at Manny.

"Come on," Manny said. "What are you doing? It's snowing bad, Terry."

Terry stared at the ground for a while, not answering, and snow piled up on his shoulders. Then he pointed to the ground. The snow was already streaked everywhere with rabbit and squirrel tracks as well as smaller prints that belonged to mice and little birds. "Butch and me are following that rabbit," he said.

"What rabbit?" There must have been a dozen rabbits that had passed by this spot and marked the ground.

"*That* rabbit," Terry said, still pointing. "Now go back to the house."

"What is it, Terry?" Manny asked. "Something about Dad? Ida tell you something?"

Terry reached with both hands and grabbed his coat, jerking Manny closer to him. He moved his mouth as if he couldn't decide which side of his face he wanted it to sit on. "Stupid," he said, "you don't even have boots. Now go back to the house."

*F*rom the window Manny watched the snow for maybe half an hour. The flakes were larger now and they came dancing. Finally he got so worried that the snow would just pile up and cover Terry out there that he put his boots on and ran back outside.

Quickly he picked up their tracks and started following. Manny could tell that Terry was walking fast and the dog was zigzagging, going crazy in the overlapping spirals of the rabbit tracks that were like a Morse code letter repeated over and over—a dot where a single front paw hit the snow, and two dashes for the long hind feet. Dot-dash-dash.

He tracked them up past the Engine Hole. The wind had blown all the snow off the hole so that it sat like a frozen eye in the earth off to the side of the railroad bed. It had always scared him, that hole, and as he passed he wondered how far the engine had sunk with its two drowning men, engineer and fireman, before it came to rest. Grandpa Tarbox said that if you fell in, you might fall all the way through to the other side of the world.

Not too far past the Engine Hole, Terry met someone, met another set of footprints, and he stopped to talk. They were small footprints, probably the prints of a woman or a child, and they seemed to come from nowhere. Manny's heart started pounding now; nobody went into the swamp during a heavy snow, usually not even Manny himself, and he took a quick look over his shoulder to make sure there was nobody behind him. After he was certain he was all alone in the falling snow, he started tracking again. Whoever was there soon led Terry off the railroad bed and into the half-mile of blueberry swamp between the right-of-way and the State Road.

Manny followed them, and they took a winding course through thick bushes that seemed to lead roughly northwest. They had to zig-zag so much to find an open route, it was almost like trailing a rabbit. Then he lost them. He came to a bare spot that was all frozen swamp water blown free of snow, and when he got to the bushes on the other side, he couldn't pick them up again. He went back and forth, back and forth, across ice the color of tarnished silver looking for them, but the swamp had swallowed them up. His feet were numb as two stones, but he didn't care.

Finally, Manny decided it didn't matter if Terry knew he was fol-lowing, and he called out. "Terry!" He shouted "Terry!" until he was hoarse, but the snow drank up the sound before it traveled far.

"Terry," Manny said, quietly now. "Who is walking with you out there?" He picked up a rabbit trail, hoping maybe it was Terry's rab-bit, although he knew it couldn't be. The rabbit made loops and cir-cles and question marks, and finally led him over more clean, gray swamp ice, and then he lost the rabbit too. He almost lost himself in that blueberry swamp, but finally he stumbled up onto the railroad bed and walked down home.

*L*ater, after the police had come and gone, and his mother had cried and put herself back to sleep with three Valiums, Manny went into the cold cellar to talk to Ida. She was no longer crying. She only looked at him with wide eyes that couldn't decide whether they wanted to be blue or green and said, "Lost. He's lost. Terry's *lost*."

Chapter 10

*T*wo days after Grandpa Tarbox's birthday, the weather cleared. It felt like spring for the first time that day; the sun came out and it was a warm, strengthening sun, not at all like the bright, cold sun of winter. The sun drove the fog out of the bogs and the low-lying places of the swamp, drove it right back into the brooks and the ponds, then warmed the ground where the fog had stood. Life started working unseen beneath the sun-warmed leaves on the floor of the woods; when Manny scuffed dead growth down to the bare ground he found insects laboring and tiny green shoots pushing through the wet soil. It reminded him of the time he had pried the back off a broken watch to discover that the delicate hidden gears and wheels inside had miraculously begun spinning again.

Birds were out and moving and battling. Manny saw a flock of crows chasing a red-tailed hawk through the swamp and screaming insults. Male robins staked out areas of the lawn and chased each other home until everyone understood where the borders were. Only the swamp-loving red-winged blackbirds were peaceful; they seemed confused as they gathered aimlessly in a tree behind the house, talking in voices that were so shrill they seemed electronic.

It was a bad day, though, despite the good weather. Somebody from the state police had called early that morning to ask if Terry had been heard from since he disappeared and then wanted to know who his dentist had been. Manny answered the phone; he tried to speak softly and get rid of the cop before his mother overheard, but she came into the kitchen and grabbed the receiver out of his hand. She started shouting; he tried to calm her down, but she swatted at him with her free hand and he gave up.

"This is Mrs. Moreno speaking, Terry's mother. Have you found out . . . Yes, Doctor Rutherford, right here in town. Can you tell me anything, maybe how old the children were? . . . No he has not been heard from. Surely you must know something by now. State police must know something. How old . . . No I don't know the number. I want to know how . . . They hung up, Manny! Just said thank you and hung up! Do you believe that?" She went to the bathroom to swallow one of her pills, then wandered around the house slamming doors; she stuck her head into closets and cupboards, looking for something that wasn't there and banging the doors in anger when she couldn't find it.

Manny swiped a beer from the refrigerator and escaped outside; he wished he had a joint and something to do. Then a dump truck rolled into the yard; Flat Top was back to visit Manny's mother for the first time since the fight on Grandpa Tarbox's birthday. He said hello to Manny as he slung his fat body out of the cab, but Manny just stared.

"Well then screw you too, kid," said Flat Top, and he walked into the house. The two of them started fighting almost immediately, and Manny paced nervously around the yard, kicking an empty soda can and listening. His mother's medley of old songs went from "Where were you, you bastard" to "You don't love me" to "You're not half the man my husband was." After that, she changed themes and started talking about the bodies; how she couldn't stand it, she needed support, couldn't do it on her own, life is hard, and hold me hold me hold me. Except for the part about the bodies, all his mother's men heard these same verses at one time or another. Finally things grew quiet, and Manny knew his mother and Flat Top would be in the bedroom.

He was grateful for the silence, but somehow it made him lonelier than ever. He went into the cellar knowing he would find Ida cowering there, and he tried to coax her out into the sunlight. Ida refused, though; she was sitting on her dirty, threadbare couch, hugging herself and rocking. Her eyes seemed to focus on the wine-colored stain on the wall across the cellar from her couch. After a while Manny gave up and went back into the yard.

He was thinking about stealing into the house for another beer when Jay Lee wheeled into the yard on her old ten-speed bicycle. Manny was glad to see her, and he trotted over to meet her as she was putting down the kickstand on the bike. He kissed her.

"Hi. You got any pot?"

She tried to pout, but he could tell she was happy with his quick attention. "That's the first thing you got to say to me, Manny? If I got any pot?"

"Well, yeah," he admitted. "You know things have been rough around here lately. I'm real happy you came, and if you've got something to smoke, it will make me even happier."

Jay Lee tried to fight off a smile. "You're really glad to see me?"

He knew he would have to work for his reward like a trained seal, so he decided to take a shortcut and kissed her again, long and hard and wet. He put his hands up under her faded sweat shirt and gave her a quick squeeze before he broke away. That made her smile.

"I guess you really are," she said. "And I guess maybe I have a little bit to smoke. I don't have very much, but what I got is good."

"Good," said Manny. "Let's light up."

"Oh no," she told him. "Not around here. I feel like going for a walk in the woods, it's so nice today." In case he didn't get the picture, she winked at him and licked the soft down on her upper lip.

"Let's smoke first, then walk," he said. He was dying for a marijuana buzz to soften his edges.

But Jay Lee took a transparent plastic box out of her pants pocket and flashed it at him. It contained two inexpertly rolled joints. She pocketed the box.

"You catch us, we're yours," she said, and took off running toward the bridge into the swamp.

*J*ay Lee was chubby and slow, so he gave her a full minute before he started after her. It was part of the game, and he knew she'd be mad if he caught her too soon. When she crossed the railroad bed and he couldn't see her anymore, he started out at a dogtrot. She was easy to track in the wet earth, and he saw right away she was headed for the high part of the swamp, the castle and the cave. He didn't like the destination, but Jay Lee was leading the hunt, so there was nothing he could do about it.

The castle was about half a mile from his house; they called it that because some long-forgotten farmer had piled up a high, square stone wall on the hilltop, probably for an animal pen. The entire hilltop was enclosed by this wall, like a fortress, with only one opening where there had once been a wooden gate. Manny and Terry and Toby Carver had once showered sticks and rocks down on imaginary Nazis and Indians from the walls of the castle. The cave, two huge slabs of rock leaning together, shoved together, according to Grandpa Tarbox, by a glacier, yawned darkly three quarters of the way up the hill.

When he reached the base of the wooded, rocky hill, Manny found her sweat shirt lying abandoned on a lichen-covered rock. He picked it up and found her bra hanging on a tree branch not far away. He smiled now; he was beginning to enjoy the old game, and when he found Jay Lee's shoes, he gathered them up and kept running up the steep hill. Her pants were on the path leading around the hill to the cave, and when he reached the cave itself, she was standing there, shivering naked in the shadows, waving her panties on the end of a stick like a flag of truce.

"You won, Manny," she said. "I give up. Boy am I out of breath!"

He ran up to her, throwing down the clothes to hug her, and made her drop the stick with the panties. It felt good to have her shivering and rubbing herself against him naked like that; it made him almost happy and forgetful of everything else, and he felt hot blood rushing everywhere. He decided that he loved her after all.

"I love you, Jay Lee," he said into the hollow of her shoulder. He doubted himself as soon as he spoke, then decided his love was genuine. Finally, as he started gathering the secret parts of her into his hands, he made up his mind that he was confused.

"Really, Manny? Do you really?" She was rubbing him gently with her fingers in all the sensitive spots now, almost making him decide the joint was not so important after all. He started to bite her shoulder, but remembered that she never liked that, so he just nibbled instead.

"Yeah, I really do," he said finally.

She twisted away from him then, stepped carefully on naked feet over to the opening of the cave. The cave was narrow and not more than twelve feet long, and had probably never served anyone for anything other than temporary refuge. "Look at the historic cave!" she shouted. "Let's see if the Crying Woman is home today. Hello Crying Woman," she yelled into the mouth of the cave.

Manny didn't like that; he walked up behind her and grabbed her by the wrist. "Come on," he said. "That's not real funny, Jay Lee."

"Manny," she said, pulling away from him and laughing. "You're afraid of the ghosties! Some hero you are. You know, I would kind of like to screw around in there, just once for the record books."

Manny made himself laugh. "You don't really," he said. "It's dirty in there, and cold. That's why I don't want to. Let's go, up to the castle, I'll race you."

He knew she couldn't resist a race, and he was right. Jay Lee led him the rest of the way up the hill and through the opening in the castle wall. The ground inside the castle was soft with dried grass that had sprouted in the thin loam that covered the gray rock of the hilltop. Slabs of bare rock, gray-green with lichens, peeked through in places. Jay Lee threw herself down on the grass, rolling and arching herself against it like a cat. "You won, Manny," she said. "I already told you. It's warmer in here. You were right." She opened her hand and let the box with the joints fall out onto the grass.

*L*ater, when they had finished the entire joint, smoking it down to a black crumb, Jay Lee giggled and rubbed her legs together. Manny giggled then too. Then both of them were laughing. Everything was funny, suddenly, and Manny felt tears burning his eyes, blurring his good eye and his bad eye alike, and the hot blood started pounding everywhere again, making the air hot and making him breath suddenly fast, in and out. He could hardly see for the tears, and as he reached and touched her everywhere, running his hands over her in a smoothing motion, she said, "Wait, stupid, your clothes." It was a voice from far away.

He obeyed the voice, sat up and stripped his clothes off as fast as he could, laughing, then he fell against her, like landing in a warm feather bed, so soft, and then he wasn't laughing anymore. He was bucking against her, searching for her desperately and not finding her, but then she murmured something and reached, touched him with her hand, and met him. Then he was floating warm and safe and mindless, not hearing and not seeing, rocking gently. He wanted to stay there forever, but after a time he felt himself stiffening, turning to stone, his body reforming itself rigidly. Then he shattered, and light flooded into his eyes, and he heard crows calling out in the swamp, and Jay Lee whispered something.

"Your eyes," she said. "You never close them. I don't like that weird eye looking at me when I'm doing it."

Manny jerked away then, rolled onto his side, feeling lonely once again. Leave it to Jay Lee to say something stupid.

She was quiet after that for a few minutes, then she said, "Manny?" and sat up.

"What's that?" He didn't want to hear any more about his ruined eye. He found himself suddenly wishing he were by himself.

"When you and me came up here for the first time, was that the first time ever for you?" She giggled as soon as she said that.

"What?" he said. It was as if she had kicked him.

"You know, Manny, did you ever do it with anybody else before? Was I the first one for you?"

He rolled over onto his back and squinted at her, pretending he had to screw his face up against the sun so she couldn't read his thoughts. "Of course I did," he told her. "Stupid question if I ever heard one."

She stood, laughing, and Manny wanted to lash out with his leg and knock her down. "Come on, Manny, you don't have to be ashamed. I just want to know the truth."

Manny sat up sharply, angry at this attack on his manhood. "You're a real bitch, you know that, Jay Lee? What makes you think I didn't?"

But she kept laughing, laughed harder as his voice got louder and more strained, and finally she asked him, "Who was it then? Don't be shy. Tell me, who was it?"

"It was somebody," he said. "What the hell do you care? Ah, the hell with you anyway." He started pulling his clothes on, jamming his legs into his pants while she laughed.

Finally, she was quiet again, just smiling now, studying him, and said, "I just asked because you always knew who I did it with the first time, so I thought it was only fair. If you did it before, that is. But I think probably you don't have anything to tell me."

"Shut up, Jay Lee."

"Don't be mad, Manny."

"I'm not mad, so just shut up." He pulled one of his shoelaces tight, and it snapped in his hand. He threw the broken part away, swearing under his breath.

She knelt beside him then, tried to put her arm across his shoulders, but he shrugged her away. "You're a lot nicer than Toby, Manny. He was really strange sometimes. If you promise not to get jealous, I'll tell you about the first you-know-what with him."

"I don't want to hear about it, Jay Lee," said Manny. "What's the matter with you, you think I don't have enough troubles lately, you have to give me grief?" He glanced at her, then looked away; he had finally gotten through to her, thick as she was, and she wasn't smirking anymore.

She said, "I don't know why, but I always wanted to tell you about it. It really bothers me sometimes, and you're the only person I can talk to." She rested her chin on his shoulder, and this time he let her keep it there.

He said, "Look, just save it, okay? You get me mad, and then you want to tell me all about how you got it on with my best friend. I don't care if it was weird and I could write a book on it, save it. I have troubles now, understand?"

She looked sad after that, so he thought for a minute, then put a reluctant arm around her. But he was still wishing he were alone.

Jay Lee finally said, "You're the only person I have, Manny. Since my mom went down to Florida with that guy from the restaurant, my dad never comes home anymore. He's always at the dog track or at jai alai. And when he is home, he doesn't talk to me or anything."

Just to say something, Manny said, "Yeah."

"When you told me you loved me before, down by the cave, did you really mean it?"

Manny said, "Yeah." Then he turned his head and kissed her, because he knew that was what she expected.

After Manny had gotten home and gently persuaded Jay Lee to get back on her bicycle and leave, he was seized with a compulsion to work. He was bored, and suddenly he needed to be doing something with his hands, something useful.

Years ago, his father had stored all sorts of building materials in the rafters of the garage. There was wood in both panels and boards, there were paints, there was wire of many gauges, and sheets of glass, and bundles of fiber glass insulation. Manny took down some of the wood as well as a sack of eightpenny nails, and he gathered all the woodworking tools he could find: a plane, a hammer, a good trim saw, a tape measure, and a square. He backed the station wagon into the driveway, and then, using the garage as a workshop, he began to build. At first, he was not sure what his project would be. He just slowly began to measure wood, and draw careful pencil lines, and cut, and soon his hands, which he had always considered to be the most intelligent part of him, were taken with an inspiration all their own. Manny was drawn deeply into the work, and hours passed unnoticed.

When darkness fell, the better part of a good, solid rabbit hutch stood on the concrete floor of the garage. The hutch contained a run that still needed to be enclosed with chicken wire as well as a shelter box with two rounded entrances and a slanted roof that opened on tiny hinges. Manny was burning to continue the job, but since there was no light in the garage, he was forced to stop. So he stood back and admired his work as darkness crept out of the swamp and surrounded the house; he thought that maybe he would give the hutch to Ida and try to scrape together the money to buy her a pair of black-and-white Dutch bunnies to live in it.

He had a tense dinner of hamburgers and canned spaghetti with his mother and Flat Top that night. When they were finished eating, in what seemed to be an effort to break the tension, Flat Top asked him if he wanted to play poker for nickels and dimes; Manny refused. Instead, he wiped the dishes while his mother washed them; she broke a plate, an old wedding present, as well as a worthless glass.

The next day, he tacked on the wire, then he mixed different paints until he produced a color that was the same blue-green shade as Ida's eyes. He painted all the parts of the rabbit hutch that a bunny's teeth could not reach. Then he set his project in the backyard to dry and for Ida to see when she went out there.

After the hutch was finished, Manny still wanted to build, so over the next couple of days he made a series of elaborate birdhouses in his garage-workshop. He hung some of them in trees close to the house; others he carried deep into the swamp. He even built a box for flying squirrels to nest in, and he took it to a favorite spot on the high grounds of the swamp: nine straight, rough-barked hickory trees standing in a circle like a clique of old men that he was sure only he and Grandpa Tarbox knew about.

About five days after he began to build things, it started to rain. Manny took the rabbit hutch out of the backyard and put it up in the rafters of the garage so it wouldn't get wet. He had meant to take it down again once the sun came out, but somehow he never got around to it.

Chapter
11

*T*he news finally came ten long days after Grandpa Tarbox's birthday, and it was none too soon for Manny.

After the state police had called to ask about Terry's dentist, Manny's mother became like a baby again with the pills after having stayed away from them for over four years. The bottle of tranquilizers in the bathroom medicine chest had stood by, handy but seldom touched, since Terry disappeared and Grandpa Tarbox moved in for two months to make her stop taking them. In the days just before the old man arrived on his mission, his mother had been like a little girl, seeking Valium like candy. But Old Man Tarbox scolded and shamed her away from them until he convinced her that three ounces of vodka a day was enough to lighten the load of grief she carried. With that accomplished, he went back to his own house and his woodburning stove and his pipe-smoke thoughts, leaving Mary Anne Moreno to her booze and her first boyfriend, a thin, shy man who slipped in and out of the house like a ghost, ashamed, during the three months before he was replaced.

This time it was Manny who had to play the part of his mother's father, because Old Man Tarbox now refused to leave the brooding quiet of his home beside the railroad bed. Manny hid the pills; his mother tore up the house looking for them, and finally she drove the old station wagon down to Bridgeport for another bottle. Manny searched her pocketbook when she returned; she swore and slapped at him, but he found the pills and flushed them all down the toilet. She got even by drinking more than her usual three ounces that day and throwing up all over the hallway so that he had to clean it up. Flat Top was in and out during all this time; Manny told him to stay away, but he wouldn't.

Once, when Manny suspected that Flat Top had smuggled some pills into the house, he broke into his mother's bedroom while the two of them were curled up together under the covers, snatched the plastic medicine bottle off the nightstand, and ground the pills to powder under his foot in the hallway. Then, as Flat Top struggled into his pants, Manny went outside and stabbed a tire of his dump truck with the sharp end of a pickax he had found in the garage. Air escaped with a farting hiss.

Flat Top came out ready to hit him, but Manny hefted the pickax, said, "I'll sink this into you, you fat bastard," then told him that if any more pills arrived at the house, he'd chop all six dump-truck tires, and then maybe set the whole machine on fire too, if he felt like it.

Flat Top called him a little one-eyed bastard, said he'd make him pay for the tire, but that was the end of the argument, and no more Valiums came into the house.

Ida would not come upstairs during all that time; Manny had to carry her dinner down there every night, and he couldn't get her to talk to him. She talked instead to Terry, would cock an ear toward a corner of the cellar and say "Yes, Terry," "No, Terry" and nod her head gravely as if listening to something very important.

So when the state cop knocked on the door that morning, it was a relief. Manny was drinking coffee and flipping through an old magazine, and his mother was in her bedroom, alone and asleep. It was Lieutenant Davis with the mirror glasses. Manny waved him into the kitchen and poured him a coffee from the old dented saucepan. Davis asked for Mrs. Moreno, said he had some questions for her, so Manny went down the hall and woke his mother up.

It was hard waking her, but when she finally opened her eyes, she seemed calm enough to talk. Manny told her the state police were there, to get dressed, and he went back into the kitchen.

His mother took awhile to get ready, combing her hair and

dressing, which Manny thought was a good sign. He had been worried that she would stumble out looking like a corpse.

The cop wouldn't say anything to Manny—Manny was just a kid, after all—and he kept his thin lips pressed against the coffee cup. His face was expressionless; his mirror glasses reflected the disorder of the kitchen. Dishes were scattered everywhere.

When his mother finally came out and sat down, Manny could see by the hunted look in her eyes and the way her fingertips trembled against the tabletop that she was dying to swallow a couple of pills before she heard the news. But it looked like she was going to behave herself. She tried to smile at the cop; it was a signal for him to start talking.

Davis cleared his throat and began. "I'll try to make it quick. I've got a lot of work to do. I suppose you read about the six bodies that were found down near the beginning of Dark Entry Road? The newspapers have been full of it lately." He looked expectantly at Manny's mother, and Manny said "Mom" to let her know she was supposed to answer.

"Yes," she said softly. "We heard. They called . . . to ask about the dentist."

"That's right. We checked your son's dental records against the teeth of the victims we found. We did that with the records of twenty or thirty children who have been missing from this part of the state during the past six or seven years. We actually were able to identify two of the bodies that way. But your son was not among those particular victims."

Manny's mother let her eyes fall closed; her body, tensed like a watch spring until then, settled down into the chair like a collapsing balloon. The cop stared at her, his glasses like twin TV screens, waiting for some kind of response.

Finally, her eyes still closed, she said, "That's nice."

The cop shot Manny a puzzled look, took a sip of coffee, then said that Terry's disappearance was still being investigated along with the unsolved disappearances of several other boys that took place at about the same time.

"You mean you're reopening the case?" Manny asked.

The cop now seemed to accept that Mrs. Moreno was not at one hundred percent, and that he was better off talking to Manny. "No," he said. "The cases actually were never closed, but now that we've found some bodies, we feel we have a strong link between a lot of the disappearances. A car pulling a green trailer was seen in the area just before one of the kids we identified vanished from over in Redding. The green trailer was also seen up in Kent just before a twelve-year-old boy became the victim of a homosexual rape and murder and was left alongside a dirt road."

Manny's mother made a strangling noise deep in her throat, her eyes still closed.

"I'm sorry, Mrs.," said the cop. "We tend to believe nothing so horrible happened to your son. We tend to think maybe he just fell asleep out there in the swamp. The only thing that made us include him with the others was the story that someone had seen footprints in the snow shortly after Terry went hunting." The glasses flashed at Manny. "That was you, wasn't it?"

Manny repeated the story of Terry and the snowstorm, and the cop wrote things down in a little notebook, asking a question once in a while.

Then he said, "Well, Mrs. Moreno, the main reason I came over, aside from to tell you that Terry was not one of the boys we found the other day, was to ask if either of you had seen a car pulling a green trailer or anything unusual like that in the neighborhood before Terry was lost. I know it's been a long time, but it's important that you try to remember." He looked from one to the other of them, pen poised over note pad.

Manny said no right away, he was sure he would have remembered, and his mother said, "I don't know. I don't remember much from back then, my life was in such a shambles." She opened her eyes when she said that, and Lieutenant Davis studied her a moment before snapping his note pad shut. Manny expected him to look disappointed, but his face was a mask.

"Well," Davis said, "thanks for the coffee. I've got to bang on a few more doors in the neighborhood today, so I should be leaving. We'll be in touch if anything comes up."

Manny walked him to the door. "Listen, Officer. I mean Lieutenant," he said. "Who made that phone call?"

The cop's thin lips twitched in a faint smile. "That, son, is the sixty-four-thousand-dollar question." He walked out to his car without looking back.

After the visit from the lieutenant, Manny's mother went back to her steady three-ounce-a-day habit, and no longer sought the numbing white pills. Ida seemed to relax a little too; Manny noticed that she was more in touch with reality now that her mother was calm, and she would often agree to go outside with him and walk in the yard when the weather was good. She would never set foot in the swamp, though, would never step even an inch outside the rectangle of new spring grass around the house, which was now almost ripe for its first cutting, and into the undisciplined tangle of dead honeysuckle vines and sprouting weeds thriving right at the edge of the lawn, ready to move in and shroud and strangle and reclaim the yard whenever Manny gave up fighting it. But she would often lie on the lawn on her stomach for hours, watching the insects work their way through the grass and making towers and buildings with sticks that fell from the swamp trees, whose branches hung out over the yard like claws reaching for the house.

Manny would sometimes walk with her around the edge of the yard, pointing out the various plants and birds; he would often reach out into the swamp to pick her a mixed bouquet of early spring flowers, lady slippers and violets. She would clutch the flowers to her chest and smell them and smile so brightly he was almost glad for the way she was, because no girl with a grown-up mind would ever be so happy with anything that didn't cost money. Certainly not Jay Lee anyway; Manny could hear her scornful laugh every time he picked a wild flower.

Ida seemed to get healthier the warmer the weather became; she began to make good, hard sense with a lot of things she said. Manny began to notice too how pretty she really was, in the newness of her young womanhood. He realized that if she were well and going to school, that with her hair the color of burnished copper, and the slightly Oriental lift to her ocean-colored eyes, which seemed to be the only trace of her father's features she had inherited, and the delicate, almost birdlike yet graceful, slenderness of her limbs, she would be a real knockout. One time he decided that if he could get her to overcome her fear of the swamp, it might help her to get better completely, to forget the ghosts and the voices in her head that separated her from everyone else. So, while she watched, he stepped out of the yard and into the rank swamp weeds to pick a dandelion. He held it out to her, said, "Come and get it."

"Bring it to me, Manny," she told him.

"Nope. You have to come here. It's safe, look, nothing happens to me." He shuffled his feet in the weeds and danced a little dance.

She shook her head and looked sad. "It's full of snakes," she said.

"There's snakes, Manny, and things you can't see. Be careful; I don't want them to get you too." She went into the cellar after that and wouldn't come out for the rest of the day.

Ida almost never went upstairs into the house during those days, though. Work had gotten slow for Flat Top, so he was nearly always up there with Manny's mother. They fought and made up and drank and made love in predictable cycles every day. Manny also stayed out of the house as much as he could when the two of them were in there together.

One warm night Toby Carver showed up in his mother's fire-red Pontiac. Manny took one look at Toby's face and knew he was planning a wild evening. That was all right with Manny; he got into the car and greedily sucked smoke from a burning reefer Toby handed him.

"What's up, partner?" Manny asked after he let the first lungful of smoke out the passenger-side window in a long, white blast.

"Wild party in progress," Toby told him. "Are you ready, partner?"

"Okay by me, partner. I've got my ID right here, but the problem is I'm a little short of cash, to be honest."

Toby clucked his tongue. "Who mentioned money, partner? The Carver is flush tonight, and as the Carver's best friend, you already know what belongs to the Carver also belongs to the Carver's partner. Have you the patch, pirate?"

Manny grinned and fished the black eye patch out of his pocket. He slipped the elastic headband around himself and settled the patch over his bad eye. "All set," he said.

The photo on Manny's phony ID card showed him wearing the patch. It had been Toby's idea when the two of them had pictures taken for the cards; Toby said the eye patch would make Manny look older, and that a bartender would be less inclined to question the age of a kid wearing one. So far he had been right on both counts, and Manny grew to like wearing the patch when they went into bars; he thought it made him look mean and would scare anyone who might pick a fight with him.

Toby was wearing the black, skintight turtleneck shirt that he claimed made him most deadly to women he met in bars. And sometimes Toby would score with women when the two of them were drinking together, Manny had to admit that. Usually it would be someone drunk and far past her prime, but once in a while it would be a young college woman, the kind of bright-faced girl Manny would do nearly anything to spend time with. Manny would always be left to walk home from the bar, and on those long, dark walks, envy would gnaw at his vitals like a hungry rodent. He often resented the unearned blond, American-boy good looks that seemed to allow Toby to glide through things in life.

But tonight, Manny was so bored at home, it didn't bother him a bit that Toby was wearing his lady-killing clothes.

Toby churned up some gravel in the driveway as he slung out onto Dark Entry Road, and Manny stuck a cassette into the Firebird's tape player. They drove aimlessly for a while, finishing the joint and listening to music, laughing. Then they pulled into a bar on Route 25, a place haunted by factory workers. The bartender examined their phony IDs, then served up the two mugs of beer and two shots of whiskey that Toby ordered as he slapped a twenty-dollar bill down on the bar top. Toby insisted that they drop the full shot glasses down into the beer and drink them that way. It was something he had seen once in a movie. They drank two rounds like that, then Toby hunched his shoulders and leaned over toward Manny. He began speaking in a slow, secret-telling voice.

"Listen, partner," he said. "This job I have. I've been wanting to tell you about it."

"Oh, yeah," said Manny. "I wanted to ask you, but I forgot with everything that's been happening. Did you quit school or what?"

"No, I didn't quit. I'm working for Old Man Cahill after school every day."

Manny had been chewing a handful of the free popcorn they served at the bar, and he almost choked on it. "Cahill! Holy shit! That's like working for Rockefeller, or maybe the Devil. What is it you're doing for him? Not the dump, Toby?"

Toby smiled; he knew the Cahill name would hit Manny like a bulldozer. "I'm a gardener now, partner. Every day I go up to his house and do yard work and weed the flower gardens and paint stuff, little things like that. Trim a hedge once in a while. The place is big, it really could use a full-time gardener, but the old bastard is so cheap he only wants to pay a high-school kid. Me, he can just get away with giving me a little better than beer money."

"Wow," said Manny. "Old Man Cahill. My grandpa would have a heart attack."

"The thing is, Manny, he wants another guy to work there until the fall when all the leaves have been raked up. I already talked to him about you; he knows who you are, partner, and he likes it that you could work during the morning because you don't go to school. He wants you to go up and talk to him."

Manny sat blinking. Cahill knew him. It was a frightening thought. He thought he would like a little money and something to do during the day; he was sick of being broke and tired of being around his mother and Flat Top. But he wondered if his grandfather would consider him a traitor, working for the man who was ruining the swamp. He guessed he would have to ask the old man what he thought before he made up his mind. Finally he said, "Sounds good. I mean, maybe. Sure would like to have a little cash in my pocket." The idea of money made him hungry. He stuffed some popcorn in his mouth and took a sip from a beer Toby had ordered him, thinking.

"But Manny," Toby said, "you miss the point." He waited until Manny had set his beer down and looked at him.

"It's not just going to be a little pocket money, partner. You're right, that son of a bitch is like Rockefeller and the Devil rolled into one, and he's rich. Listen, you and me, we're going to work for him all summer, get him to trust us, and get to know where all the goodies are in the house, all the money and coin collections and everything. Then, come fall, you know what we're going to do?" Toby was right-handed, but he lifted his beer in his left hand, the hand missing a finger, and held it up at eye level before Manny's face. Manny's eyes were drawn to the stub, which was white with cold from the beer. Toby smiled when he saw that he had caught Manny's eye with it.

"Oh, shit," said Manny. He took a long gulp of his own beer, then slammed the glass against the bar top.

"That's right. We back a pickup truck in there, take everything that's not tied down, sell all noncash items down in Bridgeport real quick, and we're off to sunny Southern Cal, you and me."

Manny took another swallow of his beer, drained the glass. "No," he said.

"Why the fuck not, Manny? It's not like Cahill can't afford it. He's got insurance up the ying-yang. What we'd really be doing is ripping off the insurance company. And he's been making money at our expense long enough, don't you think, ruining the fishing and hunting and privacy for us? When do we get our restitution, partner?" Toby set his beer down and laid his maimed hand on Manny's shoulder. Manny flinched out from under it.

"No," he said. "I wasn't brought up that way. And if we get caught, we go to jail. I'm afraid of jail, Toby. I go to Somers, the only good my eye patch will do me is if I use it to cover my asshole."

"But, partner, we're not going to get caught. Toby baby has everything planned, Sam."

"No." Manny turned his head away to study the candy-store array of bottles behind the bar; he would not look at Toby.

Toby snuggled up next to him then, whispered in his ear so close that Manny felt his damp, hot breath. "Old Man Cahill has a granddaughter, man, sixteen years old, who lives with him. She's a knockout, and she's got class. You see her, you'll get real tired of Jay Lee real quick."

"No," Manny said.

Toby relaxed then, sipped his beer and stared across the bar at the rows of bottles lined up like chocolate soldiers in colored foil. "Those Galliano bottles are nice," he said. "I'd like one for my room."

"Yep," said Manny.

"Listen, partner, you'll change your mind. You're going to think about it awhile, realize it's a good idea, and you'll come over to my side of the table."

"Nope," said Manny.

"Okay," Toby said. "For now."

*I*t turned out to be a long night. They moved from bar to bar all the way down the State Road to Bridgeport until Manny was swallowed in a swirling alcoholic haze. There was a lot of talk, and Toby's finger stub always seemed to be hovering in front of his eyes; he was amazed at how rapidly it could change color, from white to yellow to red. At some point, Toby reached and gathered the front of Manny's shirt in both hands; normally Manny would have taken a swing at him for that, but something in his friend's manner stopped him from reacting this time. Toby, his blue eyes now seething pools, pulled him close.

"When we were kids," Toby said through clenched teeth, spraying him with spit and beer, "I told you I was your best friend. I said I was your blood brother. I said I would die for you, Manny. And I would. Better fucking believe it. I would die for you. I would *die* for you."

Days later, Manny was still bothered by a nightmarish memory of Toby holding a burning cigarette against his own skin, smiling as a wisp of smoke curled up off the flesh of his arm. "Time me, Manny, time me," he had said, and he had been smiling a flickering, jack-o'-lantern smile.

Afterward, Toby dropped him off in front of his mother's house. Manny was stoned and drunk and miserable, so he sat on the front steps for a while, listening to the night birds and the spring peepers and the insects. After a time, he was startled by low singing, or perhaps chanting, coming from up on the railroad bed. He crossed the wooden footbridge as quietly as he could, and when he got out onto the old cinders, he saw the dim silhouette of his grandfather moving slowly north, away from him, in the darkness. By the way the old man's elbows stuck out from his sides, Manny guessed he was holding a forked stick in front of him, divining.

A deep sadness engulfed Manny then; he realized for perhaps the first time that Grandpa Tarbox was as helpless as anybody else. That realization made him feel very small and very alone. The old man disappeared into the night; Manny wanted to run and catch him and talk to him, but he remembered his mother's warning about disturbing his grandfather when he was working his pathetic magic.

Manny let himself into the cellar and fell asleep next to Ida on the couch.

Chapter 12

*T*he dogs attacked on a warm day in May when the swamp was filling with leaves.

Manny was up in the attic room when it happened; he was spying on Ida, watching her as she wandered the backyard, carefully avoiding the edges of the lawn where the feral flowers and weeds grew. She was pacing a jelly roll that started out by the dark wetness of the swamp and closed in tightening loops toward the center of the lawn. She carried a switch with her, a thin whip she had broken off an apple tree. Manny thought that she waved the stick in the air like a magic wand as she paced, and he remembered that spring apple was a magic wood, that the old men like his grandfather who dowsed for water preferred apple over that of any other fruit wood for seeking out underground pools and currents. She sang as she paced, though he couldn't make out the words, and she swung the branch from left to right and then over her head.

When she finally had looped her way to the center of the lawn so that she could loop no more but only spin in place, she stopped singing and moving and froze with the branch held high over her head with both hands. She looked up at the sun—it seemed to Manny she was talking to the sun because he saw her lips moving slightly—so that she did not see the dogs when they came.

There were four of them; he recognized them as the dogs that had butchered the deer, and they melted out of the swamp like wraiths and the weeds barely rustled behind them as they came onto the lawn. Ida was oblivious to them as they surrounded her, blinded by the sun, and they took up the points of the compass around her. The dogs watched her silently for a moment, then they began growling. Manny heard the growls through the open window; they were not loud, but the growl of the dog that looked like a wolf was deep and powerful. The dogs were starving; he could see their ribs, and they were covered with sores, and one was nearly naked of hair, his skin a diseased gray. They growled, unmoving, their heads tilted back to look at Ida, and when Manny shouted through the open window, they did not even glance his way.

He shouted at them again, then shouted "Ida!" which pulled her out of her trance and made her look down at the growling dogs. The branch dropped from her hand. Her eyes widened as she studied the dogs, then she screamed, and the dogs came out of their trance then too, and the biggest dog, the wolf dog, leaped into the air and pulled her down and she disappeared under the churning bodies of the dogs.

Manny yelled one more time; it was just a noise, a shrill yelp. Then he jumped down the ladder that led to the first floor and pushed his mother out of the way as he flung open the cellar door and went down the stairs. He was one fluid movement without thought as he tore his rifle off the wall and poured shells into his pocket and burst through the outside doors of the cellar while pushing a bullet into the breech and snapping the bolt closed. His sister squirmed feebly beneath the dogs, who were tearing at her clothing and her flesh with angry snaps of their jaws.

He ran toward them yelling; they ignored him, and he sighted down on the big shepherd and fired. The dog fell over, then he yelped, then he was up and running through the woods. The other dogs looked up when that happened. Manny shot another animal, the ugly hairless one, and that dog took off quickly and without a sound to disappear into the weeds. The remaining two dogs followed, and Manny sent a bullet buzzing after them, but he missed that time.

Ida was bleeding. Manny tossed aside the .22 and knelt by her, saw that they had bitten her in the backs of the legs and the shoulders and the scalp. She moaned, and when he rolled her over her face was a mask of blood that made him want to cry and beat his head against the ground. But when he tore off his shirt and wiped her face with it, he saw that the blood was coming from her scalp and not her face, and he was relieved. Part of her scalp was loose, a flap of hair and skin, and he pressed his shirt against it to stop the bleeding. When the blood was out of her eyes, she opened them, and said, "Daddy."

Then Manny's mother appeared; she covered her face with her hands, her body trembling like a blade of wild rye in a breeze, and she was saying "Omygod, Omygod." Manny shot his foot out and grazed her leg, told her to go start the damn car, and do it quick. He tied his blood-soaked shirt around Ida's head to hold the flap of skin tight to her scalp, then he hefted her in his arms; she was not heavy. His mother had the car out when he got there, had hit the doorframe of the garage backing it out. He told her to move over, laid Ida gently across her lap, then he roared out of the driveway and onto Dark Entry Road.

A police car picked him up before he got out onto the State Road and followed with flashing lights and a blast of the siren. Then it swerved angrily alongside him; it was Jamison and Joe White. But when they peered into the station wagon and saw Ida and Manny's mother both in shock and the look on Manny's face, they roared ahead and led them down to the hospital.

In the emergency room, they put Ida in a wheelchair and took her away immediately. Manny's mother tried to take her health cards out of her purse and fumbled them all over the floor so that Manny had to stoop to collect them. When she tried to answer questions from a nurse, nothing came out of her throat but a dry squeak, like that of a rusty hinge. So Manny answered the questions, uncomfortable with two cops standing behind him like a pair of blue shadows, then a nurse came out and asked his mother if she wouldn't like to sit down. She sat; they gave her water, and one nurse held a hasty doorway consultation with a doctor, then rushed over carrying a plastic cup with a pill in it.

"Don't give her that shit," Manny barked.

The nurse shot him an offended look and took the cup away.

After Manny had gotten his mother to sign all the papers, the cops stepped in front of him; they were uncomfortable too, he realized, and they asked him to repeat some parts of the story he had told the nurses, and add to them. He said, "Give me a cigarette first," and they did, White lighting it for him, and he said, "Funny, I never smoke." He laughed nervously. "Not cigarettes anyway, officers," and they laughed too, politely.

Afterward, White went to the car to use the radio. Then Jamison, with his friendly face the color of purple grapes, said to Manny, "Brother, your family seems to have way more than its share of problems, if you don't mind me saying so."

Manny was staring back at a nurse who was glaring at him because of the cigarette and because he wore no shirt, and he said, "We'll be all right. I think we're going to be okay."

White returned looking unhappy. "We're supposed to go hunt down those animals," he said. "They're sending a unit from the dog pound to meet us there."

Jamison said, "Really? What was your last marksmanship score? Mine wasn't that great." He laughed, and White frowned at him, saying nothing.

"Manny, you don't mind if we take a look on your mom's property, do you, before we go out into that swamp?" asked Jamison.

"No," said Manny. "I'll even go with you. I'm a pretty good tracker in those woods."

"Oh, you can come, but we can't let you tag along in the swamp. We could get into trouble."

"That's okay then. I'll just wait in the yard; I want to see those things dead. I can't take it standing around here doing nothing, you know what I mean?" He gave his mother the keys to the station wagon, saw that she was okay now, since they had let her know Ida lost some blood and needed a lot of stitches but was going to be all right, and told her he would call her later. Then he went out and stepped into the police car with Jamison and White.

They waited at Manny's house for fifteen minutes before the dog warden's van rolled up. The warden was a fat, gasping man with a pair of long rubber gloves tucked into his belt and he carried a long pole with an adjustable loop at the end for snaring a dog's head. He asked for the story. Manny let White tell it this time, he was sick of telling it, and the dog warden whistled when it was over.

"Haven't had one like that in this town for ages," he said. "Listen, officers, if you have to shoot, don't hit any of them in the head. We'll need to send that to Hartford to have the brain tested for rabies."

Manny offered once again to track for them, said he was sure he could find the dogs, but Jamison said no, sorry, it was a police matter.

So Manny watched them until they were out of sight in the swamp, then he went up into the attic and rolled himself a thin joint with a tiny bit of pot Carver had given him recently. Blowing smoke out the attic window, he looked down at the spot where his sister had been standing. The apple switch was still lying there abandoned. So was his rifle.

They emerged from the swamp after an hour and a half. Manny met them as they crossed the footbridge; the dog warden carried a long bundle wrapped in plastic. The head of the wolf dog stuck out from the end of the bundle.

"Found this one not too far from here," said the warden. "He was already dead. You did a good job, kid."

The two cops were scratched from branches and briars, and the legs of their uniform pants were wet up to the calves.

"We saw one, but we couldn't get anywheres near him," Jamison said. "Guess we could have used you as a tracker in that shit after all. I never knew it was so wild and woolly."

White looked upset. "There's graves out there," he said. "Graves out in the middle of nowhere. I saw them. That ain't Christian."

The warden tossed the dead dog into the back of his truck and left. White got into the squad car and started the engine; Jamison looked at Manny. He tried to say something, then stopped. Finally he said, "You're not really a bad kid, Manny." He slapped him on the shoulder, then got into the car and the two cops drove away.

Manny was trying to watch TV when his mother came in. She looked done in, asked him to get her a drink. So he poured some vodka into a glass and mixed in some orange juice for her. She drank it down in five long, shivering gulps. Then she said, "Ida's going to stay a couple of days. Her face is okay, thank God. I was so worried about her face, Manny."

"You're okay, then, Mom?" Manny asked.

She nodded her head thoughtfully. "Maybe," she said. She tried to smile.

Old Man Tarbox's house had started out huge in the 1920s, but had gotten smaller and smaller as he closed off rooms, finally leaving just enough space for himself to live in. Ten years after he built the house, he boarded off the first room, the upstairs bedroom that was Manny's grandmother's room, which she abandoned when she disappeared with a salesman. Grandpa Tarbox sealed that room so completely that you couldn't know it was ever there unless he told you; he had boarded the two windows over and then shingled the wood and painted the shingles the color of the house. Then, with all her things, her clothes and old letters and presents from him still inside the room, he took the door off the hinges, removed the hinges themselves, knocked out the doorframe, boarded over the doorway, and wallpapered the spot where it had been.

When World War Two ended and it became clear that Zack Tarbox was not coming back, not even starved and sick and half alive from some far-flung Japanese prisoner-of-war camp, the old man closed off his room in exactly the same way. The only thing he saved out of Zack's room was the old single-shot .22 he later gave to Manny. The old man told Manny one time that he had taken a last look into Zack's room before he put the final board in place over the doorway. He hadn't touched the room since his son went away to army camp, and there was a football resting on the unmade bed and the pelt of the last wildcat clung snarling to the wall as if objecting to being cut off forever from the light.

Next, Manny's mother married Alexis Moreno, a smart foreigner who boarded nearby and worked in a factory down in Bridgeport. He shut off her room too after she cleared her things out. Then, inspired, liking the idea that he could keep making his world smaller and more efficient and controllable, he closed off his own second-floor room and the bathroom, and finally sealed off the entire second floor altogether so that the stairs that used to reach there ran smack into a wall, puzzling anyone who did not know the story behind the house. He used the stairs to pile his boxes of books now; they were handy for that.

And now he lived entirely in his claustrophobic downstairs area. The first floor had a living room, a kitchen, and a bathroom. It used to contain a screened-in porch, but recently the old man tore it off, claiming that it had blocked the sun from entering the living-room windows. There had also been a pantry, but he closed that off as well, saying that it sucked heat out of the house and made it cold in winter, and just last year he had boarded away part of the living room. The open space was wasted on him, he said. He heated entirely with a small wood stove that sat in a box of sand in the kitchen now. The tiny space Manny's grandfather had left himself heated quickly when he threw a few chunks of wood on the fire.

One time Toby Carver had gone over with Manny to visit the old man, and he whistled and laughed when he saw all the space that had been done away with. "You're closing yourself up in a real snug little coffin here, Gramps," he had said.

Manny went to visit his grandfather the day Ida got back from the hospital. He walked straight up the railroad bed and found the old man sitting in an old wooden lawn chair in the backyard, contemplating the swamp with his pipe clamped between his teeth. He came out of his reverie as Manny approached.

"How's Ida?" he asked.

Manny said, "Plastic surgeon did a good job. The only thing is she has to have rabies shots, because they can't find all those dogs. I can't even get her to go out of the house now, and she won't hardly talk. Says the swamp is bad, bad, bad."

The old man looked at him with something that could have been mirth or could have been pain, or maybe was a mixture of the two. "I sure wish you'd told me about those dogs long before they got her, when you saw them kill that deer. It was a warning then, I think."

"What warning? That was the day they found those little kids buried, remember? That was your birthday, too. There were just so many other things then, Grandpa."

The old man blew a large puff of smoke, watched it thin and scatter against the blue of the sky that was the same color as his eyes. "But it was a warning," he said. "I would have known if you'd told me. The swamp is starting to move again, Manny; it's not just a couple of dogs attacking a defenseless girl. This is a swamp. There's dry land and wet land and currents moving underneath both. I think Ida is right; I think the swamp has turned against us now, and maybe it's a bad and poisoned place."

Manny said, "You know, I don't think I believe that, Grandpa. I love the swamp, and I think you still do, too. There's no bad places, only bad people."

The old man didn't respond.

"Bad things have happened to us, Grandpa, and bad things are happening now; you say it's the swamp, but I don't think you even believe that. Myself, I get the feeling that someone is watching us and causing trouble for us all around, you know what I mean? Do you ever get that feeling, Grandpa?"

The old man said, "Come in the house, Manny. We'll have a little brandy now, I think."

"You didn't answer me," Manny said. "I asked you don't you think maybe somebody is doing all this to us? Are you hiding your feelings from me now just like when my father disappeared? I was alone then, and I'm starting to feel pretty alone now."

Finally the old man muttered, "Yeah, son. It's the Devil. The Devil is keeping a sharp eye on us. Now come in the house."

They sat at the kitchen table and drank brandy out of coffee cups. Grandpa Tarbox scrounged up two old decks of cards and they played double solitaire, enveloped in a soft, bitter cloud of the old man's pipe smoke. They played until it got dark, then they watched the news on the old black-and-white television in the living room. When the news was over, Manny got up and switched the set off. He turned to his grandfather and said, "Toby has a job working as a gardener for Cahill up at Cahill's house."

The old man was sitting in the old, broken-down armchair that took up half the living room. His frown darkened the house. "Just like that fool to do something like that," he muttered.

"He keeps saying he can get me a job there, Grandpa. Says Cahill is real anxious to have me. Every couple of days he comes over and tries to talk me into it."

"Don't you damn do it."

"No, I—"

"Don't you goddamn work for that bastard."

"No, Grandpa."

"You need something to keep you busy, you go back to school, or you start learning a trade. Anything but that, Manny. Anything."

"Right," said Manny. "Right."

*M*anny was just back from fishing and was cleaning his three brook trout on the front lawn when Toby pulled up in his mother's car. Manny hardly looked up; he was busy operating with his buck knife, using the smooth side of a shingle for a cutting board. Toby got out and stood over him, watching for a time without speaking. Finally he said, "Those are nice ones. That biggest one must run thirteen inches."

Manny opened his largest trout like a wallet; he had already cleaned it, and he pointed to the fiery-orange meat inside. "See that color? That comes from eating little fresh-water shrimp and snails and other shellfish. Nobody stocked these babies; they were hatched right out there in the swamp and grew up there, secret, shooting away if a shadow hit the water above them the wrong way. They were waiting for me."

"Yeah," Toby conceded. "You sure are a good fisherman, Manny. And you know all the spots out in that swamp. At least three times as many as I do."

"Damn right."

"But listen, Manny. I have a surprise for you today, something you're going to like even better than catching trout."

"I don't really like surprises, partner. Why don't you tell me what it is?"

"No, partner. It's something I have to show you. Come with me or you'll never know."

So Manny said okay. He dumped the fish offal down by the brook for the raccoons to fight over that night, then he cleaned his hands and wrapped the trout carefully in aluminum foil and put them in the refrigerator.

Toby handed him a burning joint as soon as he slid into the front seat of the Pontiac. Manny drew deeply on it and held the smoke in until Toby rolled the car out of the curving driveway and onto Dark Entry Road. Then he let the smoke out in a solid white blast and passed the joint over to Toby and said, "That sure tastes good. I don't figure I'd ever get stoned anymore if it wasn't for you, I'm so broke all the time."

Toby laughed but said nothing. Then he turned off Dark Entry and started driving through the maze of Cahill condominiums built on reclaimed swampland and Manny knew suddenly where they were going.

"Toby," he said, "I don't want to go up there. If you're going up there, you let me out of this car." When Toby made no move to turn the car around, Manny reached for the door handle. "I'm not going up to Cahill's, Toby, I told you."

But Toby grabbed his arm. "Manny. Easy. I just want to show you something. Relax. Nothing about working for Cahill, I promise. Nobody's even up there now. Cahill's in New York."

Manny reluctantly took his hand off the door handle. "Nothing about working for Cahill?"

"Promise."

"Okay." He was curious, suddenly.

Toby drove up the steep private road through the open iron gates with ancient, snarling lions' heads welded into their centers, and past the three-story house William Cahill had restored. Manny half-expected it to look like a mansion in a horror movie, but it was a beauty. He had to admit it. It was a birthday cake of gingerbread and bay windows and scrollwork and freshly painted iron railings and brass knockers on the sturdy doors that shone like the sun. The house was surrounded by hedges and fruit trees and screens of blue spruce. There were flower beds screaming with color, and brick goldfish pools surrounded by flowers, and yellow-brick walkways leading everywhere. Behind the house was a restored carriage house and a greenhouse that reflected the sun like a polished mirror. Toby had stopped the car and Manny did not even notice, he was so busy drinking it all in. He finally turned in his friend's direction and caught Toby grinning at him.

"They don't make them like this anymore, eh, partner?" Toby said.

"Jesus," said Manny. "Makes me feel like I live in a shack."

Toby glanced at his watch and the smile died on his face. "Come on," he said. "It's almost time."

They stepped out of the car; Manny was still looking around, wondering what it would be like to own a house and property now, wondering if he himself would ever have five percent of what Cahill had. Toby had to tug on his sleeve to get him moving.

They walked past flower beds toward the carriage house, and Toby stopped him once, briefly, to show him half a dozen tiny marijuana plants growing in a spot between the marigolds. "We'll have our own supply soon, partner," he said. "Come on."

They walked through the front doors of the carriage house, and Manny was amazed all over again. The first floor had been done over like an overgrown dollhouse; there was miniature, antique furniture there, and a little girl's tea set that must have been a hundred years old, and china dolls with blank, cracked sweet faces. Pink curtains covered the windows so that soft pink light filled the entire room. The carriage house made Manny think of Ida when she was five or six years old. *Ida should have had rich, pretty, wonderful things like this, should have them still,* he thought, and he was suddenly bitter. The only adult things in the carriage house were a small phonograph and a small pile of records on one of the miniature tables, along with a pile of girl's clothing, a white sweat shirt and jeans and a bra on one of the chairs.

Toby caught him eyeing the clothes and said, "This place Cahill fixed up for his granddaughter, Stacy, so she can hang out away from the house when she wants to. Personally, I think she's a little too old for this baby shit, but she likes it."

Suddenly, a car door slammed outside somewhere, and Toby said, "Quick, up in the loft." So the two of them climbed a ladder to the second floor of the carriage house; there was nothing here but a plain pine floor you could see right through in places, boxes of old Christmas decorations, and a single bare light bulb hanging down by a cord. Two steel poles supported the roof. Toby led him to the tiny windows overlooking the big house; a girl carrying schoolbooks was walking up a brick path toward the carriage house. A yellow Volkswagen was parked next to Toby's mother's car. "Sixteen and already has a new car," Toby said, but Manny hardly heard him. The girl was tall and had a sweet face and long brown hair, and she walked like a goldfish swam. She was like something Manny has seen in a movie one time, or maybe in a dream. Toby said, "Quick, down here." Manny looked over and he was stretched out on the pine floor, peering down through a crack. Toby looked up just long enough to say "Grab that other crack, and don't make a sound, else they'll find out and castrate us both." So Manny lay down on the floor and aimed his good eye through a wide crack; he could see almost the entire carriage house below him.

The door opened; she came in, humming, and tossed her books down in a chair. Then she turned on the record player; it was something classical, with violins that reminded Manny of brook water pouring over rocks and triumphant horns that made him think of trout leaping into the air and flashing as they hung magically suspended, then falling, falling back into invisibility. She started dancing then, or pretending to dance, as she moved her feet and swung her shoulders and tossed her head back, eyes shut and a look of delight on her face. Manny's heart banged against the floor; he was sure that if the music weren't playing, she would be able to hear it smacking against the old pine boards like a basketball. He was so enchanted with the way she danced, coltlike and graceful and happy, that he didn't for a minute see what she was really doing, that she was slowly unbuttoning her blouse. The flash of white bra and pink skin beneath her shirt awakened him. He lifted his head away from the crack in the floor for a moment, almost frightened by what he was seeing, suddenly feeling the movement of his blood. Then he clapped his eye back down to the floor; nothing could have torn him away now.

With a coltish sidestep she moved over beside a chair and dropped her blouse; her bra came off next, and Manny felt splinters of wood burrowing into his cheeks as her breasts, smooth and small but upward-looking, jumped into his view. Her nipples reminded him of fresh apple blossoms, and for a crazy instant he thought he could almost smell them right through the floorboards. He had a sudden memory of Jay Lee's nipples, brown and tasteless as two buttons on a pair of familiar old seat cushions, but he shoved it out of his mind as soon as it came.

She stepped out of her slacks, kicking them away with the boom of a drum on the record, then she kicked off her shoes and danced, naked except for panty hose, in the glowing pink light of the carriage house. It was uncomfortable now for Manny to lie face down on the floor, but he ignored the discomfort that bordered on pain and said to himself, *Her name is Stacy, Stacy, pink and lacy.* Then another voice in his head, a cruel voice, said, *Jay Lee, Jay Lee, what a Pig-ee.* He almost giggled out loud when he thought of that, but he caught himself just in time.

The dance was over quickly, too quickly for Manny. After she was naked she tugged the white sweat shirt on over her head, then she pulled on the blue jeans that had been waiting for her. Her other clothes, her school clothes, she tossed into a corner of the carriage house, then she picked up her shoes, turned the record machine off, and stepped out the carriage-house door. The door banged loudly behind her, then she was out on the grounds of the mansion calling "Toby! Toby!"

Manny rolled over onto his back, staring at the cobwebs on the ceiling and absentmindedly soothing himself between the legs with his hand. Suddenly Carver's blue-eyed face was hovering over him. He was grinning.

"All yours," Toby whispered. He made a lazy beckoning motion with the hand that was missing the little finger. Then he disappeared down the ladder.

After a minute, Manny stood, the hot loft spinning dizzily around him, and he followed.

*T*he dog Manny had killed turned out not to have rabies. But the authorities were never able to find the other three animals, so Ida had to go through a month of rabies shots just in case one of them had been carrying the disease. The first time, Ida screamed and fought the doctor who came at her with the needle, snapped at the doctor and his nurse like a wild dog herself, so that Manny and his mother and two other nurses had to hold her down. After that, Manny's mother refused to go to the doctor's office, said her nerves were not up to it, and it was Manny who had to take her. They would always fool her into thinking she was there for her stitches and not for the dreaded shot. When the syringe was filled and the doctor was ready, Manny and three nurses would pounce on Ida and hold her down while still another nurse swabbed her with alcohol and the doctor drove the needle home. She would scream once the needle was in her, a shriek that lasted until it was withdrawn, then she would pant and tuck herself into a ball like a frightened animal until Manny could calm her down and get her out of the office. She would not talk to him for a day after that, but Manny didn't blame her. It was only the shot that really bothered her; she was good about her stitches, always careful in her movements to avoid tearing them unless the rabies needle was coming at her. There were stitches in her head, which had been shaved and turbaned with bandages, and in the backs of her legs as well, so that she was forced to walk stiff as a wooden marionette.

*T*he police hadn't made more than a halfhearted stab at finding the feral dogs that attacked Ida; no one else living around the edge of the swamp had been bothered by them. So Manny took to hunting them himself; he prowled the swamp with his rifle for two days, and finally he found two of the dogs. He didn't need the gun; they were already dead, lying side by side near where they had felled the deer. There wasn't a mark on either of them; neither was the dog he had wounded the day of the attack, and after puzzling over this for a while, Manny buried them where they lay. He brought a shovel from his house and dug a pit as deep as he could go without hitting water, then he shoved in the carcasses and covered them up.

It seemed that it was right at that time, when he was digging and burying and covering, with his shirt off, sweating in the late spring heat, that he first heard the worms. They were gypsy-moth caterpillars, larvae, and in their legions they made a distant crackling sound high in the treetops. The crackling came either from their chewing or their shitting, Manny was not sure which, and when he put down his shovel to listen, he could have sworn the sound grew louder and louder until it became a steady rain of noise. It seemed to Manny as if they had been triggered, awakened by his digging and burying and covering up, the same way a bad memory is triggered or awakened by an action, and he grew frightened as he listened to them ravaging the swamp, turning the sweet green leaves of his world into a rain of shit that came crackling through the dying trees.

Over the next days, clear spaces opened in the swamp and the woods as the leaves vanished; except for the heat, it was like winter returning. Manny stayed out of the swamp now; the trout would bite only on flies this late in the season, and the noise of the worms had become a roar, a poisoned cascade of sound. He thought he was the only one who noticed it or was bothered by it, but he was wrong. One day, after Ida had been to the doctor to have some of her stitches taken out, he was helping her out of the car and toward the house when she stopped, froze suddenly, and would not let him lead her. She lifted her head toward the swamp, wearing the same expression a dog wears when it hears something very faint or very strange. She shook Manny's hand off her arm and swept her head through the air, her eyes frightened.

He said, "You hear them too, don't you?" but that was unnecessary because he could tell she did, and they seemed to grow suddenly louder for her just as they had for him. Then she was panting in her rabies-shot terror, and she slapped her hands over her ears. Her scream was a siren wail, louder than any sound she had made when sharp needles slid beneath her skin.

Manny grabbed her by the shoulders now and led her, forced her, toward the house.

SUMMER

Chapter
13

On the day he was supposed to be interviewed by William Cahill for the gardener's job, Manny got a letter that was postmarked Bogotá, Colombia. The letter had been sandwiched into a stack of bills and advertisements and stuffed into the letter box next to the front door. His mother found it as she was sorting through the mail; she froze when she came to it, eyes opening wide at the neatly typed address, which included no return, and the candy-striping around the edges of the thin envelope that set it apart as coming from somewhere exotic.

Manny was on his way out the door to the interview, dressed in the best clothes he could find, a pair of fairly new corduroy pants and a yellow shirt with a tie that nearly matched the blue pants. He caught the look on his mother's face out of the corner of his eye and stopped. She was fingering a loose corner of the envelope, fondling it, and he said quietly, "That's for me, isn't it?" When she didn't answer, he gently pulled the letter from between her fingers, sending the gas bill and the electric bill tumbling to the floor. He picked up the fallen envelopes for her, pushed them back into her hand. Then he bolted up the ladder leading to his attic room. His heart fluttered like a bird as he threw himself onto his bed and tore open the corner of the envelope with a bent nail he always kept on his dresser.

In five years, this was the eighth letter he had received from his father. Each had come from a different place: Mexico City, Santiago de Chile, Buenos Aires, Rio de Janeiro, Caracas, London, Santiago again, and now Bogotá. Each previous letter had been disappointing in the same way. While Manny always awaited word on whether his father would be coming home, or whether at least Manny could visit him or write him, all he got was the same letter over and over: *I am fine, it is warm here in Rio,* or *It is cold here in Buenos Aires,* with an *I hope you are doing okay, and Ida and your mother too. I will let you know when I settle long enough in one place for you to write me.* There was never any explanation or apology, and not one word about Terry. Manny was sure his father knew Terry was gone, because he never mentioned him. Manny always wondered and worried about how his father knew Terry had disappeared.

This letter was a little different, but not by much. Manny tore it from the envelope, wondering at how, as usual, it looked so painstakingly written, as if his father had gripped the pen very tightly to keep his hand from trembling. Sometimes Manny attributed this to the fact that English was not his father's native language, that he was in South America now and probably not speaking much English in any case. Or perhaps the visible labor of the handwriting was to keep more emotion than he intended from spilling out onto the single onionskin pages he sent.

The usual tone of his father's letters had changed slightly in this latest one, however. It read: *Dear Manny, I will not be in Bogotá for long, otherwise you could write me here. The company I work for might send me to Australia soon, but I don't know if I will be there for long either. I am doing fine. I know that you are having troubles now, but you are the Man in the family and you have to be strong, especially now. Love, your father. P.S., as usual, don't show this letter to your mother, because I know it will upset her.*

Manny read the letter over twice, holding it up close to his good eye as if he could absorb more meaning from it that way. Then he set it down, thinking for a minute that he had every reason to be angry and insulted at his father's long-distance order for him to be strong, but then making up his mind he was just sad, as usual, at getting a handshake instead of a hug. He thought hard about the *I know you are having troubles* part. That bothered him, along with his father's unspoken knowledge that Terry had vanished. Manny's grandfather denied communicating with Alexis, but Manny knew someone had to be telling him what was going on in the swamp. The thought made him uneasy.

Manny used the bent nail to pry up a loose floorboard in the attic room, exposing a hiding place he had inherited from Terry. Beneath the floorboard, foil-wrapped fiber glass insulation glinted, and atop the insulation rested a small wooden cigar box that had belonged to Terry and still held some of his older brother's childhood treasures. Manny kept his father's letters and other secret things in his brother's box now; they were mixed in with Terry's poems and snapshots and yellowing pictures clipped from outdoor magazines.

He was about to drop the latest letter on top of the old ones and seal the box away into the darkness under the floorboard when something made him stop just as he was closing the lid. His father's letter had brought Cahill's dump to mind, because the disappearance of Alexis Moreno had so closely followed the tragedy of the Raymond family near the dump. The dump reminded him of Cahill; a remote, faintly sinister figure in a wheelchair, Manny was not even sure what he looked like, and Cahill made him think of Toby. He had a quick vision of Toby's face, only this Toby was a child, eleven years old, and he was laughing and crying all at once, a composite of Toby at that time. He lifted the pile of his father's letters, a thin pile for five years, and found Toby's letter, also thin, resting underneath. Manny's name was written on the envelope in an eleven-year-old's scribble.

Manny lived the pain all over again—the loss, the anger, the loneliness, the horror at what Toby had done to try to make things up to him, and finally his gradual forgiveness—even before he opened the slip of blue-lined tablet paper inside the envelope. His name was repeated inside: *Dear Manny,* it said, *I am sorry I hurt your eye. My mother made me write this letter, but even if she didn't, I would still be sorry. I don't know why I did it, I just got mad I guess, but that is no excuse, and I told the Police and everybody I'm sorry too. If I could give you one of my eyes, I would. But I can't, so I hope you are not too mad at me, and we can play together again when your father and mother says its okay, if they ever do. Your Pal, Toby.*

Manny started to put the letter back into the wooden cigar box, back underneath the pile of his father's disappointing letters, but he changed his mind. He wasn't sure why, perhaps he needed a charm against Cahill evil, but he folded Toby's letter carefully three times and stuck it in his wallet. Then he picked up his father's latest letter, folded that one and put it in the wallet right next to Toby's letter. He wanted his father's letter to be near him, suddenly, with its advice to be strong, although he knew his father no longer had any right to advise him on anything. There was so much that was unspoken in both letters; perhaps they would rub together in his wallet and in his mind, and out of them would come the answers to all the riddles in Manny's life.

His mother was waiting for him at the foot of the ladder, looking summer-hot and summer-worn but with a tiny spark of hope in her eyes. The spark in her died as soon as she saw the look on his face; it left her looking just hot and worn and old.

"He says again for me not to see it," she said with weary certainty.

Manny could not meet her tired eyes. "Yeah, he says it again."

"What else does he say? Anything?"

"Not much. Says he knows we're in trouble here, and to hang tough."

"He knows? How? And why doesn't he come back?"

Manny looked at her now, angry suddenly; angry at his mother, at himself, at his father. "You always ask that," he said. "As if I knew. I still don't know any goddamn more than you do, so stop asking me. I'm leaving." He stalked out to the old station wagon, which was running well now that the hot, dry weather had arrived. He almost covered his ears against the sound of eating, shitting worms in the trees all around him, but forced himself to listen. He hurled like a rocket out onto Dark Entry road.

William Cahill was a lizard. That was what Manny thought as soon as he met the man: a lizard on wheels who had to roll himself into the sun in the morning to warm the cold sludge in his veins. Manny had left the station wagon halfway down the long driveway and walked the rest of the way up to the mansion, ashamed of his mother's car and afraid it would look even more like a junk pile parked next to the birthday-cake house.

The brass knocker made a noise like thunder against the thick oak door. The sound echoed through the house so loudly that Manny thought maybe there was no furniture inside, or that the house was furnished completely with dollhouse stuff as in the carriage house; tiny furniture that could absorb no noise.

A maid answered, a black woman with wide, grave eyes, and she looked at Manny then vanished without a word, leaving him standing there. Manny looked down a wide, black hallway like a yawning throat. An elevator whined at the end of the hall; the door clattered open, releasing a feeble, gray light, and out of the door the lizard came wheeling, a gray silhouette against the gray light. The black hallway nearly swallowed him as he vanished into the shadows for a moment. But Manny felt him there, rolling slowly down toward him; he heard the rubber wheels whispering softly on the tiles of the hallway and thought, *Why is it so cold in here? Is it him?* But then he remembered the air conditioning, and almost laughed aloud at the ridiculous idea of Cahill himself causing the coldness.

Then Cahill appeared in the sunlight; Manny heard the mechanical hum of the electric engine and was startled as the old man materialized before him. Cahill had cold eyes, enraged and impotent all at the same time; he blinked in the sunlight and Manny thought, *He's a lizard.* He must have been close to Grandpa Tarbox's age, but he looked ten times as old, with white skin on his face sloughing away like the skin of a shedding albino snake Manny had seen once in the swamp. His mouth was wide and thin and cruelly expressionless like that of an old snapping turtle. His upper body was wasted; he may have been muscular and wiry at one time, but now he was just shriveled, with small, slow, long-nailed claws for hands. He was covered with a gray blanket from his lap downward so that he appeared to be half lizard and half machine.

Then the snapping-turtle mouth opened, releasing a dry whisper like leaves on a windy autumn night, and Manny was freshly startled.

"You are the new boy," Cahill said. It was a statement rather than a question.

"Yes," Manny said, really worried now for the first time about how his grandfather would take the news of what he would no doubt see as a defection. And he began to worry also about whether he would start to see traces of lizard in Stacy after a time. "My friend Toby—"

"Pronounce your name for me."

This made Manny shiver; it was as if the old man already knew him intimately, and only wanted to hear him say his own name, as if by making Manny pronounce his name, he was forcing him to unlock a secret.

"Manny Moreno," Manny said. He desperately tried to picture Stacy Cahill's sweet face in his mind, but all that came to him was a soft, pink blur atop the uplooking breasts.

"Manny," Cahill said. "Manny." There was a cold edge to the whisper now. "What on earth does *Manny mean,* boy? You were christened Manny?"

"My full name is Manuel. Manuel Moreno." Manny felt his back straightening, thought, *It's true, there is power in a name.*

"Ah," Cahill said; it was a noise like a feeble gust of wind in an attic. "Then you would be Puerto Rican, wouldn't you?" The cold eyes sought him; Manny knew right away Cahill was taunting him, hoping to nourish himself somehow on his discomfort.

He held his back straight, met the cold gray eyes with his own. "No. My father came from Chile. That's in South America. My mother, she's a Tarbox. They've been here for generations. I'm no Puerto Rican."

The old eyes glinted with amusement or scorn, he couldn't tell which. "And what was your father's name?"

Manny thought, *Why am I putting up with this? Why don't I just tell him to go to hell and take my beat-up station wagon to hell out of here?* But he said, "Is. His name is Alexis Moreno. He's back in South America now, working for some company. He travels a lot."

The glint in the old eyes brightened now, became a cold glitter like frost on the windows when the sun slants through. He glittered his eyes at Manny for a long moment, reading him. Then suddenly Manny felt himself blush; he realized the old man was studying his bad eye, probably wondering how it had gotten that way. Manny thought, *If he asks me that, then I will tell him to go to hell. I will.*

But after a long spell, Cahill the millionaire said, as if speaking to himself, "And your grandfather is Nat Tarbox?"

"That's right. He's been living here for years too." Manny expected more; perhaps he would have to answer questions about Terry and Ida and maybe even his mother and her boyfriends. Cahill gave him the impression of knowing enough about him to be able to ask some embarrassing questions. But Cahill just said, "Move."

Manny said, "What?" and the old man said, "Move, you're blocking my ramp." So he stepped aside, puzzled; the old man pushed a lever on the gleaming wheelchair, and he rolled forward, past Manny and down the concrete wheelchair ramp onto the yellow-brick sidewalk.

"Come," Cahill said, without bothering to turn his head toward Manny. "Let us see what you know about gardening." Manny followed the wheelchair, feeling self-conscious even though Cahill was not looking at him. The reptilian hiss of the old man's vehicle seemed out of place in the bright sunlight among the birdsong and growing things.

"What do you know about pruning?" Cahill asked, still not turning to face him. "Do you know anything about it?"

"Sure," Manny said. "I've pruned trees before. They're a lot healthier if you cut off the branches you don't need."

"Don't touch them."

"What?"

"You were about to touch the handles on my wheelchair. Do not ever touch them unless I specifically ask you to."

Manny was startled; he had not even thought about pushing the old man's wheelchair, and would have thought it degrading if he had been asked to do it.

"But I wasn't—" Manny said.

"So, you know all about pruning, eh? And you have cut grass before?"

"Yes, I—"

"And you can edge sidewalks and weed, I suppose?"

"Sure I can. I—"

"Have you done any painting? Don't say you have if indeed you have not."

"I paint," said Manny.

Cahill hit something on the shiny panel bolted to his arm rest, and the chair spun to the left, still wheezing, the tires hissing, and he rolled down a short brick pathway to a kidney-shaped goldfish pool. He stopped with his wheels right on the edge of the pool; Manny thought he heard the old man make a noise, a dry kissing sound, but he was not sure. He looked over Cahill's shoulder. There were half a dozen long goldfish, both red and black, lined up along the edge of the pool awaiting a handout.

"These are my carp," Cahill said in his papery whisper. "I have five carp pools in my property, and all the fish in them are the offspring of carp that have won awards in shows down in New York. All thirty-two of my carp have names, Manuel. I do not expect you to learn all their names. What I do expect you to remember, if you work for me, is that I like my carp quite a bit better than I like most people. When you come here in the morning, you must never forget to feed them, and you must not overfeed them. If I ever discover my carp dying from either starvation or overfeeding, you will be dismissed. Do you understand?"

"How will I know?" Manny asked, suddenly hating the carp, deciding that perhaps he would find some secret way to torment them. "I mean, how will I know how much to feed?"

The old man turned slowly around to face him, the engine of his electric machine working, whining. When he was facing Manny, fixing him with his lizard eyes, there was a click from within the machine and he stopped turning.

"I will be working with you. I am semiretired now, have been for several years, and I have men to handle my businesses for me. I enjoy gardening, Manuel. It is my life now. My bulbs and my carp and my fruit trees provide uncritical companionship I am unable to find among other men. I am not hiring you for your brains or your conversation, and I will be pleased if you do not speak to me unless it is necessary or unless I speak to you first. You will be my hands, Manuel; you will be doing work under my direction that I would do myself if I were not incapacitated. Do you understand?"

"Yeah," Manny said.

"So you want the job then?"

Manny said, "I guess."

"You guess? Aren't you curious what your salary and hours will be? I am offering you one hundred and ten dollars a week for a six-hour day, six days a week. Is that acceptable to you, or do you need time to think?"

"Yeah," Manny said. "I mean, I guess that's okay."

Cahill studied him for a moment; it seemed to Manny the turtle mouth was trying to twist itself into a smile. "Well," Cahill said finally. "I suppose we both have our reservations about this. Let's just say you come here tomorrow at nine o'clock, and we'll both decide in a week or two if it's going to work out. Agreed, Mr. Moreno?"

There was a hint of sarcasm in the old man's whisper now; Manny would have liked to roll him backward into the goldfish pool. But he thought of the money; it would be the first real money he had ever earned, and he thought of Stacy. So he said, "Yeah, Mr. Cahill. Agreed."

Cahill said, "Move."

Manny stepped aside and the wheelchair whined past him again. He followed it out onto the brick walkway, where it turned and rolled in the direction of the carriage house. The old man stopped about halfway to the carriage house, waved his hand out toward an expanse of green, closely trimmed lawn and newly planted fruit trees.

"Those trees, Manuel, your friend Carver planted them this spring; you will have to water them quite frequently," he said. He put his vehicle into gear again, headed straight for the carriage house, and stopped when he was almost touching the front door. He waited for Manny to catch up to him, again not bothering to turn his head and search for him with his eyes, but feeling for him, creaturelike, it seemed to Manny, with the fine white hairs on the back of his neck.

"This is the carriage house," the old man whispered. "I have had it fixed up for my granddaughter, Stacy, so that she can have a place to be alone to study and play her obnoxious music. No one but Stacy is allowed to enter the carriage house, do you understand, Manuel?" Cahill consistently mispronounced the Spanish name, saying *Manual* as in *manual labor,* instead of *Man-well.*

"Yes," Manny said, thinking of the delicious pink light that flooded the building.

"Even if my granddaughter invites you into the carriage house, you are forbidden to enter. Is that clear?"

"It's clear," he said.

"It had better be," said Old Man Cahill, the hiss of his voice becoming a threatening rasp now. "Because if I ever find either one of you boys in that house, you will be punished. Not only will you be fired, but other unpleasant things will happen to you. I am no longer a strong man, but I have strong men in my employ; they will hurt you if I tell them to."

"Wait, Mr. Cahill," Manny said, feeling himself tighten with fear inside, but also feeling something else—feeling the thrill of a challenge mixing with the fear. "I haven't done anything to make you talk to me like that."

"No," Cahill said, his voice simmering down to a cool whisper once again. "No, you haven't. But I just want to make sure that you never do, either. Stacy is almost your age, but she is of a much different class than you; she should mix with her own kind. You may talk to her if she talks to you first, I suppose I can't prevent that. But you are never to leave work to converse with her, or play games, or anything of the sort, is that clear?"

Manny remembered Stacy's voice as she called for Toby, thought, *The two of them have been breaking the rules for weeks now, and the old man doesn't even know.* "Yeah," he said. "No problem."

Cahill said, "Move," and as Manny stepped out of the way, he wheeled his vehicle around and headed back up the yellow-brick walkway.

Cahill didn't look back as he rolled up to the house and disappeared inside. Manny watched him go, then took a walk around the old man's property, feeling a gardener's interest in it now, studied the two acres of lawn that would have to be mowed and the hedges that needed trimming and the birdbaths that were filling with debris, and he thought, *I'll be busy here. I'm going to like this.* He toured the entire outside border of the property; the land was closed off from the rest of the world by a fence buried in a twelve-foot hedge. Then he walked back down the hill to his car.

*H*is grandfather did not come to meet him when he drove into the driveway. Manny left the station wagon there, in front of the old man's house, and walked out to the back. The gypsy-moth worms had gotten into Grandpa Tarbox's yard, and he could hear their droppings sifting through the trees as he walked.

Manny's grandfather was sitting in an old wooden chair, facing out across the abandoned railroad bed into the swamp. He was smoking his pipe, the smoke heading straight up into the still summer sky, and he did not look up as Manny approached.

"Hi, Grandpa," Manny said, suddenly nervous about the coming confrontation. "It'd be a nice day if these worms—"

"It's a bad sign," said Old Man Tarbox, still aiming his sight out over the tops of the ravished swamp trees. "Something's going on here." Manny spotted a half-empty pint of blackberry brandy sitting on the ground next to his grandfather's chair. He thought, *Stuff's a little thick for this weather,* but he stooped and hefted the bottle anyway without being invited, and took a suck of it. It was thick, and too sweet, but it was warming too, and the warmth spread through his body like a good feeling.

"Do you know," asked Grandpa Tarbox, "how there got to be gypsy moths in this country?" Something about the old man's tone let Manny know that one of his grandfather's half-stories was on the way, a cross between a formal story and a lecture on some aspect of nature or life that he thought Manny should be schooled in. Before Manny could answer, Grandpa Tarbox said, "Well, it happened this way.

"Way back in 1869, north of here in Medford, Massachusetts, a naturalist named Leopold Trouvelot was busy trying to produce a variety of silkworm that would be productive here in America. You see, regular silkworms, which came from Japan and other warm places, were too delicate for this climate. So this Trouvelot fellow figured that if he bred those dainty little beasts with some kind of tough bug that was used to the cold, why he'd have a brand new variety of monster that would laugh at cold and illness, gobble down silos full of greenery, and shit bale after bale of thread to make fine clothes for fine ladies. Kind of like trying to produce a bird that lays golden eggs by mating a canary with a crow.

"Anyway, this Trouvelot couldn't find any suitable insect for his matchmaking purposes here in America, so he had a friend over in Europe send him some little moths that were called gypsy moths because the male insect was about the same yellowish-brown color as a gypsy's face. Believe me, Manny, you'll see plenty of those little brown fliers before this summer is over.

"Well, old Trouvelot was happy as a bug, trying to make his new Frankenstein animal, although I don't know how successful he was at it. Then one day he got a little careless; whether he had too much to drink, or his wife was giving him a hard time, or his kid cracked up the horse-and-buggy I couldn't tell you. But Leo the naturalist left a paper box full of gypsy-moth eggs on the sill of an open window at his house in Medford, Massachusetts. Along came a gust of wind, and *whoosh,* that box sailed off into the air just like a magic carpet. Who knows, maybe there was a little gypsy witchcraft involved there.

"Leo was *frantic,* of course. Since he was a naturalist, he knew how dangerous it could be, letting foreign animals into an American landscape. He rushed around for years afterward, trying to track down and kill those escaped moths. But he never got all of them, and because there are very few American creatures that will eat them, they became a plague throughout New England, destroying mile after mile of forest land, and in general just disgusting the hell out of people."

Grandpa Tarbox sighed. "Do you know where evil comes from in this world, Manny? Well do you? It comes from men taking things, taking trees and mountains and birds and animals away forever from a land that needs them, and taking people away from the people that need them so they can go on fighting their big public wars and their private, secret, greedy battles. And it comes from putting things onto the earth that don't belong here, like bugs from another continent, or radioactive poisons, or any kind of poison that nature doesn't create to protect herself."

Manny knew that Grandpa Tarbox was thinking about his Uncle Zack, who had disappeared in one of the big public wars. But he was certain his uncle was only a part of what the old man was pondering. His grandfather was in a complicated mood; Manny would have to step carefully. A sudden recollection, a vision of the old man carrying a forked stick through the swamp at night, blossomed in his mind's eye. Manny crowded the vision away before it could upset him.

"I think you're right," he said, trying to put things off for a few minutes more. "I really think it's a bad sign, too, Grandpa. Ida thinks so; I haven't been able to get her out of the house yet this summer. Of course, those dogs have something to do with that. Myself, I can't go into the swamp with them there, chewing and shitting all the time. Why would nature make filthy creatures like them, anyhow?"

The old man's gaze never left the tops of the trees in the nearby swamp. But after a long, thoughtful puff at his pipe, he spoke. "I guess you *would* be staying out of the swamp now, seeing as you have decided to betray it. Maybe that's what's going on with those caterpillars; the swamp tells itself that if Manny turns against it, it might as well share in its own destruction."

Manny hadn't expected this, but had expected that he himself would be the first to speak harsh words.

"Now, wait, Grandpa," he said. "I came here to explain things to you. You've got no reason to talk to me like that."

But the old man's mouth remained a bitter, unrepentant line, and his gaze did not shift.

Stubborn old Yankee, Manny thought. *Mule-headed swamp-Yankee.*

"I don't know how you found out about it, Grandpa, he just hired me this afternoon. But what I'm going to be doing up there has nothing to do with the swamp. I'll be trimming hedges and mowing lawns and feeding his goddamn goldfish for him." The vacuum of his grandfather's stubborn silence was tearing the words from him.

"I needed a job, Grandpa. He's paying me one hundred and ten a week for outdoor work. I have to work outdoors; I'm not a person that can work in the dark in a factory or push boxes around some stupid warehouse. I can't be closed in, Grandpa."

His grandfather muttered, "Goldfish," and did not favor Manny with a glance.

"And there's another thing, Grandpa," Manny said, thinking, *Why can't I shut up? Why do I let him pick my insides clean? These damned old men that won't look at you, like you were dog shit on the side-walk.* "He's got a granddaughter, Grandpa. She's beautiful. And I was thinking, if I could get to her, maybe just once even, that would be like revenge for what he's done to the swamp, and all the bad things he's done we don't even know about yet." It was the first time that sort of revenge had occurred to Manny; he was surprised at his own words.

The old Yankee did look at him this time, turned smoldering, scornful eyes in his direction. His mouth remained a hard, tight line like a well-sewn seam for a moment. Then he said, "And what about Jay Lee, while you're screwing with this Cahill girl, this little rich one?"

Manny was caught off guard. "What's Jay Lee to you, Grandpa? What's this all about?"

"Well," said the old man, "I guess you just don't have any loyalty to anything or anybody, do you?"

Manny felt himself trembling now, the little muscles under his skin jumping like tiny springs. He tore his father's letter from his wallet and slapped it down on the wide arm of the old man's chair.

His grandfather's expression changed immediately; his hard face melted and took on the soft lines of worry. "What's this about?" he said.

"It's a letter from my father. Read it," Manny said. He reached again for the pint of brandy sitting on the grass, and noted with sat-isfaction that the old man's fingers shook as he slid the paper from the striped envelope. Manny took a long, sickeningly sweet drink of the brandy as his grandfather read the letter. It took him very little time to read it, and when he was done he slid it carefully back into the envelope and set it on the arm of the chair.

"Why are you showing me this?" he asked in a quiet voice. "It's a letter to you."

Manny set the bottle back down and slapped the arm of the chair with his hand, hard. The old man winced, something Manny had never seen him do before. He felt a brief flash of pity for his grandfather, but then his anger returned. "Because he knows," Manny said, not as loudly as he had intended. "He knows we've been having trouble here. I want to know how the hell he knows."

Grandpa Tarbox tried to regain his lost ground, tried to aim his eyes again at the swamp and be remote and offended. But Manny knew it wasn't working for him. He knew the old Yankee was treed, although he wasn't sure why he had been able to tree him so easily this time.

"How should I know that?" said Old Man Tarbox, finally.

"How? Come on, Grandpa. Who else could tell him? You've been keeping in touch with my father, haven't you?"

Something in the old man seemed to break then; he was almost ready to give up and tumble to the dogs. He settled lower into his chair; his hands worried nervously at the now-empty pipe. Still there was something stubborn left in his eyes; he would try to save himself some way, Manny knew. Manny put himself on alert to handle any tricks his grandfather threw his way.

"Yes," Grandpa Tarbox said. "I've been in touch with him. He writes me sometimes and asks how you all are doing."

"And you answer?"

"Yes. I answer."

"Son of a bitch," Manny said. "And you never gave me his address so I could write him? I have to be satisfied with letters that are practically no more than postcards, while you carry on a correspondence with him? What kind of a grandfather are you?" Then he added, didn't want to say it but had to, "And what kind of a father is he?"

The old man's snap and fire came back to him in a rush now. "That last question, don't bother asking me that," he said. "He's *your* father, Manny. And as for why I didn't give you his address, ask yourself why you never showed Mary Anne one of his letters in all these years. Five years and she never saw one."

Manny was off-balance suddenly. He had had the old man treed and somehow let him slip away. Manny felt he had been tricked, but he wasn't sure how. "Hell, Grandpa," he said. "I always wanted to show those letters, but Dad always said keep them away from Mom. So I did."

The old man wore a look of triumph now; his eyes glittered and the seam of his mouth was upturned. "So now you understand why I never gave you one of Al's addresses?"

"You mean he told you . . ."

"Exactly. I don't know why, maybe he just didn't want letters saying come home Daddy chasing him all over the world. I don't know. All I know is he asked me not to, so I didn't. I guess Alexis was so much smarter than any of us, we're all just used to doing what he says, even though he hasn't been around for five years."

Manny was reaching for the bottle again, but Grandpa Tarbox snapped, "Stay the hell away from that. You're too goddamn young." He withdrew his hand.

Manny said quietly, "So why did he leave us, Grandpa? What's the real reason? My mother keeps asking me, and I don't know. You keep in touch with him, maybe he told you."

Grandpa Tarbox was quiet now too, thoughtful and sad. "Manny, I don't know. I really don't."

"Well," Manny said, not really disappointed, beyond disappointment now, "I guess I'll go. See you." He turned and was walking back toward the driveway when Grandpa Tarbox called him. There was a pleading note in his voice.

"Manny," he said. "There are reasons you shouldn't be working for Cahill. Not just that he's ruining the swamp."

Manny turned. "Well, anytime you think I'm ready to hear your reasons, you let me know, Grandpa," he said.

Chapter 14

*M*anny found out right away that he was meant to work outdoors, his hands stained with loam and his knees bright with grass smears. Cahill hovered over him the first few days like a copperhead snake quietly vigilant from atop a tall, flat rock, but Manny soon got used to that. His hands seemed always to know what to do; old Cahill would say, "When you trim this hedge, round the angle where the top meets the side, and Manny's hands would go to work with the clippers and an hour later the hedge would be flat as a wall on top, with a rounded, feminine curve to it as it turned toward the ground. Cahill would roll himself up to the hedge, ready to criticize the slightest flaw; he would find nothing and would have to motor himself away.

Manny enjoyed weeding, felt he was destroying something bad and leaving something good and useful to flourish. It became a game with him to see if he could clear every weed out of every flower bed and garden on the property and have them all clear at once.

He did not even mind the insect spraying; he didn't like the chemicals and knew they were bad if you breathed them or they got on your skin, but he also knew that without the spray the gypsy-moth worms and the other pests would get on the fruit trees and chew and chew and there would be no fruit in the late summer and fall. Manny was determined that there would be fruit, so much fruit that Cahill would have to concede that he had done an outstanding job tending the trees and would award him a basket of pears and apples and plums and maybe a bonus, a crisp ten- or twenty-dollar bill handed over in grudging reward.

It rained often that summer, so Manny had to spray many times to replace the poison that washed into the earth. Toby would never touch the spray equipment; he said it was dangerous and he was not paid enough to do it, but Manny didn't mind that either. He accepted the responsibility for the trees, and he would take credit for the fruit when it became ripe.

Toby was lazy, there was no question. He made himself responsible for cutting the grass, stretched the two-day mowing job out over four days, then hid the rest of the week. Manny would have been angry about it if he had been doing any other job; any job he really minded doing, did not love doing.

And after a few weeks, Cahill began to see the difference between his two gardeners. He often followed Toby, scolded him in his parched whisper, but he said very little at all to Manny. In fact, Manny usually saw the old man only at the very beginning of the day, when he was feeding the goldfish. Then he would hear the rubber wheels whispering behind him as he spread the dry fish-meal flakes across the tops of the yellow-brick pools where the hungry carp were waiting.

When he wasn't supervising Manny and Toby in the garden, Cahill was busy with his visitors. Hardly a day passed without a long black Cadillac or a Mercedes or a fire-red Jaguar from New York or New Jersey rolling up the long, winding driveway, squeezing past Manny's station wagon and stopping before the front steps of the big house. The sportier cars were always driven by young, curly-headed men in snappy three-piece suits. These young men generally came alone, and they invariably carried an expensive box of candy or a live plant for Cahill's greenhouse under one arm. Their shoes gave off a gleam intense as brass in the summer sunlight, and Manny, who usually managed to be busy with his trowel near the front steps when the visitors came, always felt a hard-to-control urge to scatter fresh loam all over their feet as they passed.

The other visitors, the older ones who rode in long, slow, stately cars with chauffeurs, instead of the fast, flashy sports cars, were much more formidable. There were fat middle-aged men with broad, beefy faces and eyes that were either slate-cold or quick and hunted-looking. There were handsome men Manny recognized from TV as state politicians. The politicians carried briefcases and their handsome faces twitched with worry as they stepped from their cars. And there were old men, as old as Cahill and nearly as old as his grandfather, who wore loose-fitting trashy clothes twenty years out of style and whose eyes were never visible because they wore thick prescription sunglasses with black plastic frames. These old men scared Manny more than the others because they were driven by armed chauffeurs who would sit in the long cars, studying Manny with dreamy, feline expressions on their faces and because Cahill himself would come out of the house and roll down the ramp in his wheelchair to greet them.

These visitors bore no gifts.

One time an old man whose skin was speckled all over as if he had been spattered with brown gravy grasped Cahill's hand at the bottom of the ramp and began talking in a hoarse, breathless whisper that made him sound as if someone had just been choking him.

"We have a new customer," he told Cahill. "This is out of Maryland and they want to send up two trucks a week. Bad stuff . . ." Some slight movement of Cahill's must have drawn the old man's attention to Manny, who was crouched in a flower bed, eyes carefully held down to where his hands ruffled the flowers in search of weeds, and he stopped.

"Oh," said the choked voice. "He's not in?"

Manny sensed another gesture from Cahill, then he heard the wheelchair go whining up the ramp and the sound of the visitor's shoes scraping on the stairs. Only when the front door shut behind the two men did Manny look up; he looked at the house, then turned his gaze into the studious face of the visitor's chauffeur, who was giving him an interested half-smile from behind the windshield of his car.

The most frightening visitor of all, though, was Joe Marconi, the dump foreman. Marconi showed up at least three times a week; he always came in either a white pickup truck or a small, dirty Japanese car Manny recognized as Marconi's own. If Manny saw Marconi coming, he didn't rush to the bottom of the stairs as he did with the others, but found a place where he could watch unseen.

Marconi was crazy. His looks were crazy, that was one thing. He was a short, wiry man, like Manny himself, like Cahill must have been when he was younger. He was bowlegged, and his hands and feet were tiny. But his face was all wild and screwy; his chin was like the rounded end of a ball peen hammer, his nose was an ax blade covered with thin white skin, and his eyes were small and black, almost without pupils, set too close together on either side of the nose. They were like bird's eyes, crazy crow's eyes, and they were hot and they jumped in their sockets as if he were constantly enraged or in pain. Because his face was so narrow at the bottom, there was almost no room for his mouth; his lips were rounded and covered an opening the size of an overcoat button. His mouth was always the same; it was too small and misshapen to make expressions with, so Marconi used his eyes and his body to show what he was feeling. And he was a bundle of fierce feelings; he jerked and slammed his body around like a crazed marionette, talking to himself and gesturing even when there was no one near him. He never walked anywhere; he was always hopping, kicking at stones in his way and imaginary stones that were not in his way, throwing his hands in the air, letting his hands express for the expressionless mouth. Sometimes Manny would catch him actually answering himself; he would shrug, or slam his fist into the door of his car, or he would laugh.

Marconi was the only visitor who did not show either fear or respect for Cahill; it seemed to Manny he was too crazy to show fear or respect for anything, and that was what made Manny afraid of him. He always arrived alone at Cahill's house, parking his truck or car crookedly in front of the house, and he would charge up the old man's wheelchair ramp, never using the stairs, his eyes darting to the left and right, searching, burning at Manny if he saw him anywhere and continuing to search if there was no one in sight. He slapped at his pockets and made the change jingle, charging up the ramp as if he were about to kill someone in the house. He would punch at the doorbell once, twice, three times, then march in place, lifting his feet and slapping them back down impatiently, until the black maid opened the door for him. When the heavy door swung open, cautiously, he bulled his way past the maid, saying nothing, perhaps snarling. The door would close then, a dark woman closing the door of a dark house, and Marconi would emerge ten or fifteen minutes later. Sometimes he came out somewhat calmed, absentmindedly rubbing the bald spot on the top of his head or slowly churning the change in his pockets, and sometimes he would be even more enraged than when he first pulled into the driveway, throwing his hands into the air, moving his lips, stretching his tiny mouth, and snapping his head back and forth.

One time when the foreman arrived, Manny was hosing out a trash can by the side of the house. Marconi had come roaring into the driveway too fast for Manny to escape and hide himself somewhere where he could watch while avoiding the burning bird's eyes, so he stayed where he was, carefully absorbed in his cleaning. He heard the car door slam, felt the hot eyes on his back. An unreasonable fear began churning in him, an animal fear that something was very wrong, something out of reach of his senses. Then Marconi called him, startling him and almost making him spray himself with the hose.

"Hey you," Marconi said. Manny looked out of the corner of his good eye, saw the foreman standing at the foot of the stairs. There was no way Manny could get away with pretending not to hear him; he couldn't feign deafness he decided, so after a moment, a long moment of careful trash-can cleaning, he stood and faced Marconi.

"What's your name?" Marconi asked him. He briefly considered remaining mute, then decided it wouldn't work. As he was opening his mouth, something warned him not to say his complete name. He remembered Cahill's *Pronounce your name for me,* and he shivered.

"My name's Manny," he said finally. He felt a hot rill of sweat streak down his side under his T-shirt.

"Manny?" said Marconi. He sounded angry. "Manny what?"

"Manny," said Manny, his last name catching in his throat like a cold sliver of broken glass. He was shaking now; the burning crow's eyes sent fear and hatred washing through him. "Moreno," he croaked, finally.

Marconi changed suddenly then; the craziness fled from his eyes for an instant. Manny thought he saw sadness replace the usual anger, sadness and more than a touch of fear.

"Moreno," Marconi whispered. He dropped his eyes. "Moreno," he said in a voice a man might use to read a name from a tombstone. He remained motionless, staring at the ground, and Manny felt gooseflesh crawling on his arms although it was a humid, sweat-wrenching day.

Then Marconi's eyes snapped up at him, burning once more, but burning coldly, burning falsely and without fury. "Well, get back to work, Moreno," he said, his voice shaking. Then he turned and charged up the wheelchair ramp into the house.

One day the gypsy-moth caterpillars stopped gnawing. It happened on the day he first touched Stacy Cahill, and he took it as a sign of peace from the swamp or from nature itself. Manny thought maybe the swamp was holding an olive branch out to him after many months and years of war. Some tiny voice of Yankee skepticism inside him told him it was a trick, but he had been listening to wintry voices, his grandfather's voice and those in his own head, for so long now he was tired of it and refused to heed them.

The first thing he did when he got to work that day was to strip off his shirt. Manny was self-consciously skinny, but the sun felt too good on his skin to keep his shirt on. He selected a pair of grass clippers from the rack of tools, chose a place in the sun, a circular flower bed behind the carriage house, and started cutting the long grass that grew between the painted white rocks surrounding the garden. With a good marijuana buzz on, it was interesting work; he did it slowly, almost religiously, and two hours passed like a dream.

His heart jumped when he heard Stacy's Volkswagen coming up the hill; he was pleased and afraid, as he always was, and also puzzled, because she was home early. He stood stiffly as she wheeled into the driveway, driving too fast.

She ran up on the lawn and headed for the carriage house, driving with two wheels on the brick walkway and leaving deep wheel ruts in the grass on one side, and when she saw Manny standing there she jerked the wheel and headed for him. He jumped back, ran around the flower bed, knowing she wouldn't drive into the rocks, thinking to himself *There will be hell to pay for this,* but happy with her attention. She circled the flower bed, chasing him, tearing up the lawn and turning up black soil and thin, netlike roots everywhere. He skipped along ahead of her, not really running. Then suddenly something told him to get out of sight of the house. He broke from the flower bed and headed toward the back of the carriage house, and he heard the tinny roar of the Volkswagen close behind him. When he got to the back wall of the carriage house, he stopped and threw his arms back against it, facing her, surrendering. She slowed then, smiling at him through the windshield, and shut the engine off when the bumper was almost touching his shins. His heart was slapping against his rib cage as she stepped down from her little car.

"Where's Toby?" she asked, slamming the door.

Manny let his arms drop; he was suddenly self-conscious, and wished he had his shirt on. "He won't be here for another hour," he said. His heart was so loud in his ears, he was afraid she could hear it. He worried that he would turn red beneath her gaze.

She walked to him, smiling, and took his hand. "Don't stand against the wall like that," she said. She pulled him out from between the car and the building. He let her lead him as if in a trance. Then they were facing each other, very close together.

"Listen, Manny," she said. "You don't have any pot, do you?"

He felt his mouth stretch into a smile of shy happiness. "Well," he said, "yeah. I've got a bone on me. I didn't know you—" He thought of the baby furniture in the carriage house, the soft pink light and the music, then he had a swift vision of her naked upturned breasts, and he choked with embarrassment.

She finished the sentence for him. "You didn't know I smoked? Who the hell doesn't these days?"

"Yeah, I guess," he said. He didn't know what to say, and he wished she would tear her eyes away from his; she was making him sweat, and he had no shirt on.

"Well, light it up, Manny," she said, still holding him with her eyes.

He was shocked.

"You mean right here? All I need is for your grandfather to catch us, and I end up in cell thirty-six down in Bridgeport."

She made a dainty, disgusted sound in her throat. "No," she said. "Listen. There is a Corvette parked in the driveway with out-of-state plates on it. That means Grandfather is tied up in the house with some goon from New Jersey. He won't come out at least until the muscleboy leaves; that will be our signal."

"You sure?" Manny was afraid someone would follow the ruts she had made on the lawn and catch them there, but he did not want to displease Stacy.

"Sure I'm sure. Look." She took a disposable lighter from a tiny handbag on her arm, sparked the flame, and held it up to him, all the time holding him fixed in her gaze.

When Manny saw the flame, he snapped out of his trance and

dug the plastic box out of his pants with trembling fingers. He pushed his last joint between his lips and sucked desperately at it as she passed the flame over the end. When he was filled with smoke, he gave the burning cigarette to Stacy. He was trying to fit the fact that she smoked pot into his innocent image of her, and was not sure that he liked it.

Stacy pinched the reefer daintily between two sculpted, pink-painted fingernails and drew in smoke with a sweet hissing noise. A moment later, when she had released the smoke from her lungs, she said, "You were already stoned when we lit up, weren't you?"

Manny grinned stupidly, felt the grin twist across his face, and he was powerless to stop it. "Yeah. How did you know?"

"Your eyes gave you away."

He was suddenly conscious of his bad eye, tried to imagine what it would look like all glassy and bloodshot with pot smoke, and he had to stop himself from rubbing his hand over it. For something to say he said, "So how come you're home so early? Usually you don't come in till around three." He could have kicked himself then; he didn't want her to know he was keeping track of her. Until now, they had only spoken three times, and very briefly. Once or twice Manny had hung in the background while she bantered with Toby, teased Toby about this or that while Carver made vague, harmlessly obscene remarks the two of them giggled at.

"Why, don't you know, Manny? It's the last day of school. You don't see me coming in here and tearing up the lawn every day, do you?"

His heart leaped whenever she said his name. "Oh," he said. "I guess I forgot it was that time of the year."

"Yes, sir," Stacy said. "Two more years and I'm a free woman."

"Two more? You just became a junior? What will you do then? I mean, when you get out?"

Stacy took a deep breath, then sighed. "Oh, I don't know. Go to Europe, I suppose. Live with a painter in Paris; smoke hash in Morocco. I certainly won't let them pack me off to some dull college, I can tell you that."

Manny remembered suddenly that he was a high school dropout; he didn't often think about it these days, and he was ashamed.

As if reading his thoughts, she stood on tiptoes and brought her face very close to his, almost touching him. Manny felt all the blood go to his face.

"Why did you quit school?" she asked.

"Why?" He sought the lawn with his eyes. "Shit. I mean hell, I don't know. I was having family troubles at the time. School seemed really stupid to me just then. I guess it's just me that's stupid." He felt broken; he hadn't considered that she probably wouldn't lower herself to love a dropout.

"You know what?" Stacy asked.

"What?" said Manny, forlorn.

"I think that's romantic."

"What is?" He was confused.

"Dropping out. Having the courage to do it. To defy society. I wish I could do it."

"Shit," Manny muttered, still confused but suddenly happy.

"Manny. Tell me something." She was standing close to him, her voice a warm whisper.

"What?"

"Have you ever read *Lady Chatterley's Lover?*"

He felt stupid again. "No."

Stacy giggled girlishly. She said, "I think you're cute, Manny." Her face moved toward him, then it moved back; he realized, wonderingly, that she had kissed him. It was all he needed.

She was backing away now, had taken two small steps backward, smiling and sparkling her eyes at him, so he reached out and pulled her forward, grabbing roughly at her hair, and he pressed his mouth down on hers. She clutched at him too, pushing her hands under his arms and around his bare back, and her tongue leaped out and met his for a moment. Then she pushed away, pulling her hands back through his arms and pushing gently off his chest.

"Gotta go," she said. She let her eyes drop to the ground, then slowly raised them to the level of his face, stroking him with her gaze. "I'll be seeing you around." Then she left him, walked around to the front of the carriage house. He heard the door bang shut.

He stood behind the carriage house for a time, catching his breath, and it was then that he thought he heard the steady poisoned worm-rain come to a stop. His breath and his heart were thundering in his ears; they slowed gradually, and then suddenly he noticed that the sound of chewing and shitting had come to an end.

He walked out under a giant pair of twin elms that had been infested with the worms; he strained his ears but could hear nothing in the high branches. He walked along the high outside hedge, listening, and all he heard was birdsong. Manny walked out to the front gate, listening and hearing nothing. Then he started to run. He ran all the way down the winding road leading from the mansion, ran past the condominiums and across the two hundred naked yards of earth that used to be swampland. When he got to the real, untouched swamp, he drove himself into it, tore through briars and blueberry bushes that raked at him. He pushed himself into the swamp, mud sucking at his sneakers, until he was out of breath. Then he stopped and listened, tilting his head back to look up into the trees that were nearly stripped of leaves, and he heard nothing. It was over. He laughed and clapped his hands and did a little dance out there in the swamp, with water up to his knees.

When he got back up to the house, he saw Cahill's wheelchair rolling toward the carriage house. Manny looked at the wreckage of the lawn and caught his breath. He followed cautiously, at a distance behind the wheelchair, hoping Cahill would not turn suddenly and spot him. The old man rolled up to the carriage-house door, rolled halfway through it. As Manny went down the brick walkway, he heard the old man speaking sharply, speaking in as loud a voice as he could muster. He also heard Stacy's high, sweet voice; the two voices mingled, and he couldn't make out the words.

Then Cahill's voice grew less and less sharp, and he heard Stacy laugh. Her laughter sounded like brook water pouring over stones.

As Manny passed the corner of the carriage house, moving slowly, pretending to be on his way to the tool shed, he heard the old man's dry, whispering voice say, "Well, now, don't do that again, Stacy. You won't will you?"

"No, Grandfather," she said, and laughed again.

Manny heard the wheezing and whispering of Cahill's wheelchair; he was almost to the shed when the old man called him.

"Manuel," Cahill croaked, as always, pronouncing his name *Manual,* as in *manual labor.*

Manny turned, expectant, and the old man spread his frail claws to indicate the destruction of the lawn.

"Do what you can about this, will you?" Cahill sounded tired and defeated. He turned his sparkling wheelchair and went wheezing toward the house.

Chapter 15

As the summer wore on, Flat Top and Manny's mother fought more and more and made the bed creak less and less. It was cool through most of June, but when the gypsy-moth worms retreated into their cocoons at the end of the month, the days turned hot suddenly. They were long, still, hot, alcoholic days for Mary Anne Moreno and her man; Manny's mother's three-ounce-a-day limit quickly rose to five and then eight. One morning the front page of the Bridgeport *Telegram* said that the bodies of two children had been found buried in a neighboring town, and she quit counting altogether; she did not let up even when the remains were identified as those of a pair of brothers who had disappeared from Milford three years before. "If one of these isn't Terry, then he'll be one of the next ones they find," she told Manny. "Pa's right; it must be the end of the world. There's bones coming out of the earth everywhere."

Flat Top drank right along with her; he was unemployed now, collecting unemployment insurance, and the two of them started their day with vodka and orange juice at eleven o'clock. Manny's mother stuck with this drink all day long, sipping as she scrambled eggs for

Flat Top and Ida first thing after she got up, and later, when she loaded clothes into the washing machine. By the time Manny got home in the late afternoon, she was totally sloshed, usually arguing with Flat Top over why he didn't wash dishes after he used them or why he didn't change his underwear more often. Flat Top always neglected the orange juice after the first three or four drinks, started drinking his vodka plain over ice and, still later in the day, directly from the bottle itself. The booze made him look like a bloated vulture. Everything about him was big and soft and fat except for his face, which was narrow and wasted-looking. The flesh around his eyes was bruised, and the gray skin hung off his cheeks like dead meat. His broken, uneven teeth and his eyes were the same shade of yellow. Whether drunk or sober, Flat Top complained bitterly and constantly that life had been unfair to him, and often, as he looked Manny's mother up and down with unhidden disgust twisting his face, he would proclaim that he would have been a millionaire years ago if his first wife had not gone off with the vacuum-cleaner salesman and left him with nothing but the bottle for comfort.

Flat Top didn't care for either Manny or Ida. Ida stayed in the cellar whenever her mother's boyfriend was in the house, or she walked in the yard, slowly, still a little sore from the attack by the feral dogs, so that Flat Top never saw her at all unless he looked out the back window when she was walking. He saw Manny often, but the two of them never spoke.

That summer, Manny stayed out of the house as much as he could. He was up at seven-thirty every morning, drank his coffee in the clear coolness of early day, and sometimes coaxed Ida out of the cellar to talk to her about the swamp and tell her about how one day he would buy a big house for himself and Stacy Cahill, a real home where Ida would be welcome and would have dolls and a room with pink curtains all to herself. Then, still dreaming of a home and a new car all his own, he would start the old station wagon and disappear before his mother and Flat Top crawled out of bed.

He worked at Cahill's all day until three. He worked hard, but kept an eye out for Stacy. She was always going someplace: to play tennis, to swim at a girlfriend's house in Greenwich, to the library, to visit people. Sometimes two or three days would pass without his seeing her, and he began to look forward to fall, when she would be in school and on a predictable schedule again. He worried that she had another boyfriend, someone with money and a prep-school education, maybe, and it bothered him that there was no way for him to find out whether she did or not. But something warned him not to mention his fears to her; she was a swamp butterfly, and if he tried to catch her, she would fly away. So whenever she cornered him out by the carriage house to tell him about a Broadway play, or the food she had eaten at someone's house, or how she beat her girlfriend's brother in tennis, he smiled appreciatively and kept his jealousy to himself. He always brought pot for her, and whenever she was about to go out someplace, she would come looking for Manny and his good, seedless marijuana rolled tightly in white rice paper. Stacy usually did most of the talking as they stood behind the carriage house and smoked. She talked about interesting things, things that were fascinating and as distant as the moon to Manny. He was always afraid his mouth would fall open in amazement, and that she would catch him looking at her that way. He spoke very little when he smoked with Stacy. He sometimes tried to talk about the yard work he did, the plants and the goldfish, or about the swamp, but a glazed and far away look would usually come into her eyes. He found the safest things to discuss with her were cars, drugs, and her own life. She never got tired of those subjects.

When they finished the joint, smoking it down to a tiny charred crumb held in the jaws of an alligator clip he always carried in his pocket, she would let him kiss her. He would put his hands lightly on her hips or around her back and he would kiss her with his eyes open, savoring the way her closed eyelids trembled. Then, after a few moments, she would push herself gently away, explaining that she had to go here or there and do this or that, and she would climb into her Volkswagen and disappear. While kissing her, Manny always longed to let his hands creep up to her breasts and down past the small of her back, but something always warned him not to. She was a swamp butterfly, and she might fly away. He was sure that there would come a moment when everything felt right, and then he would tumble her someplace, in the forbidden carriage house or maybe on the lawn at night, and he would touch her all over and kiss her eyelids. He tried to imagine the quality of her moans as he made love to her, and it excited him. Manny figured he had plenty of time.

*E*very day after he got off from work, Manny explored the swamp or listened to Bruce Springsteen tapes on the cheap cassette player in his room to kill time until Toby could leave Cahill's to join him. Toby usually came by with two six-packs of beer and they would sit in lawn chairs behind the house and drink and smoke pot. Ida often sat with them, not drinking and not smoking but with an ear cocked toward the brook and the abandoned railroad bed, as if the swamp were whispering its secrets to her.

Toby would sometimes try to get Ida to drink a beer, harassing her and poking at her with the long-necked bottles until Manny got angry and told him to leave her alone. And when the beer was finished, Toby would invariably begin talking about driving a pickup truck up to Cahill's house and ripping the place off. Manny would stare out over the treetops and refuse to say a word until he changed the subject.

One day it began to snow. Manny was working at Cahill's house when he first noticed it. He was up by the mansion, weeding one of the flower beds, when he looked out toward the back of the property, and saw a column of snow falling beneath a thick elm tree. He rubbed his good eye, thought he was seeing things, and set down his grub hook. When the vision didn't disappear, he stood, massaging his knees, which were stiff from kneeling for so long, and walked back there.

It was snowing moths. There were ten or fifteen of them dancing in the sunlight beneath the tree; he snatched one out of the air and examined it. It was small and brownish, and he recognized it as a gypsy moth. Clinging to the rough bark of the tree was a larger, snow-white moth, a female, and the brown males were dancing around her. The case was hopeless for the dancers, however: One male had already found her and had pushed the entire rear of his body into hers; the two moths sat back to back, unmoving. Manny knew the female would only mate this one time before spilling her sticky mass of eggs onto the side of the tree.

An uneasiness that bordered on dread began gnawing at Manny's insides then; it was the same feeling he had had when the worms first emerged and began to attack the swamp. He watched the two unmoving moths for a moment, sexual curiosity mixing with dread, then he took a stick and mashed them both to a gray pudding against the bark of the tree. The dancers scattered.

In an hour or so, Stacy came back from tennis wearing a white skirt. She came looking for Manny immediately, and as they stood smoking pot by the back hedge, she spotted a column of moths dancing under an old apple tree. Manny tried to take her attention from them, but she went over, waving her hand at them and laughing, saying, "It's snowing, Manny," and he followed. Then he spotted the unmated female clinging to the side of the tree, and he recognized a rare chance to explain something to her that she didn't already know. He told her about how only one in every one hundred moths was female, and that the males swarmed from everywhere, each hoping to be lucky enough to mate her. She was fascinated, and when he went to kill the female, she stopped him. Stacy left him waiting, disappeared into the carriage house, and came back with a tiny insect cage of clear hard plastic and green plastic mesh. She scooped the female moth into the cage with a leaf, clapping the lid on, and laughed. She kissed Manny lightly on the forehead, then ran into the carriage house.

She stayed in there a long time, and Manny went back to work. As he weeded the flower bed, he noticed moths beginning to gather at the windows of the carriage house, flying in place before them and clinging to the screens. Music blared, then Stacy came out in a change of clothes, blue jeans and a T-shirt. She came out running, dancing to the music, and Manny could see by the way she bounced that she was braless. The music was loud, and she danced all across the yard, not once looking at him, the plastic cage held high over her head with both hands.

As Manny stopped to watch, the moths began peeling themselves away from the carriage-house windows to follow her; they formed a ragged line as they fought to keep up. Then more moths came up from other parts of the yard and from the other side of the hedge so that in a minute she was leading a thickening ribbon of flying insects. Soon hundreds were gathered, all of them following Stacy and her captive queen. The music slowed and Stacy slowed her dance; she rolled her hips, teasing the moths, passed the cage close to her breasts and through her legs as they followed. Then the music picked up again; she danced fast, running almost, as she turned, holding the cage high over her head, then snapped it downward. The line of moths snapped too, like a whip. She laughed at this, loudly, and began snapping the cage over and over, until finally the line of moths began breaking up and scattering across the yard like smoke, quickly as they had come. She opened the top of the cage then, still laughing, and turned it over; Manny saw a single plump snowflake drop to the ground.

The music stopped after that and Stacy disappeared into the carriage house. And in a while, Manny found another female moth crawling at the base of a tree. He squashed her underfoot as the males fluttered around him.

One evening as Manny was drinking beer and watching the sunset with Toby and Ida, he suddenly decided he was hungry for pizza. There was a small shop on Route 25 that made them just right, with plenty of mushrooms and a chewy crust. So he took the old station wagon and bought a large pie for the three of them, then sped toward home so they could devour it while it was still hot.

But then, on Dark Entry Road, a cop pulled him over and told him the taillights were out on the car. The cop smelled beer on his breath and gave him a hard time about it, but in the end he let Manny go with a warning and a promise to get the lights fixed. It snowed moths in front of his headlights on the way home.

By the time he got back, the pizza was cold and Ida was no longer in the yard. Toby Carver was sitting by himself in the dark; Manny navigated his way across the lawn by the burning glow of the joint Toby was smoking.

It was a moonless night, and Manny could barely see Toby's face. Carver's eyes glinted with reflected red light every time he sucked hard at the reefer and made it grow bright. The glowing joint also illuminated Toby's maimed hand, made the tiny mound that should have been his little finger reflect light like the eye of an opossum caught in a flashlight beam.

"Pizza's cold," Manny said. "Cop stopped me."

Carver said nothing.

Manny settled into his lawn chair, slapped at a mosquito, and opened the pizza box. "Listen," said Manny. "Where's Ida?"

Toby drew hard on the joint, then offered it to Manny. "I think she went into the cellar," he said.

Manny walked to the cellar door, licking pizza gore from his fingers, and called Ida's name down into the blackness. There was no answer, so he walked back over to where Toby was tugging a slice of pizza out of the box. "Funny," he said. "You didn't try to make her drink beer, did you, Toby?"

"No, I didn't," Toby said. There was a pause, then he said, "I think it was the gypsy moths that scared her."

They sat eating for a while; it was quiet in the house, and they listened to the chirping of the crickets and the frogs out in the swamp. When they finished the pizza, Manny licked his fingers once again and said, "Someday we won't be able to hear this anymore. Everything will be gone."

Toby made no reply.

Then, from inside the house, from the darkened window of Manny's mother's bedroom, something made of glass hit the floor and broke, and Mary Anne shouted, "You son of a bitch!"

Toby opened a beer, gas hissing out of the bottle, then he said, "We ought to get rid of that son of a bitch."

Manny shivered, and reached into his pocket for his plastic joint case.

*T*wo days after it started to snow moths, Manny found Jay Lee waiting for him at the bottom of Cahill's driveway as he was leaving in the station wagon. He was forced to stop because she was standing right in the middle of the driveway, not moving, looking at the ground. Her hair was pulled back into a greasy knot on the back of her head. Wearing an old sweat shirt, she seemed shapeless to Manny; disgust and pity and guilt rippled through him like rings over a quiet pool when you throw in a stone. His hands started to sweat against the steering wheel as he braked to a stop; he rubbed them nervously against his pants.

Manny called out the window, "Jay Lee, what are you doing here?"

She didn't answer; she just left him there with his head craning awkwardly out of the car.

He thought for a long moment, then said, "Well, are you going to get in or not?"

At that, she picked up her head and glared at him through the windshield, unsmiling, then slowly walked to the passenger side and stepped in.

They didn't speak for a long time. Manny drove aimlessly, wiping one hand on his pants every so often, and Jay Lee stared out the window. Then, as they went through the center of town past the police station and the World War Two monument, Manny said, "I'm a little hungry. You want to go with me to McDonald's?"

"No," she snapped. Then she jerked her head around to look at him; he watched her out of the corner of his eye, warily.

"You don't want me anymore, do you, Manny?" she asked.

He opened his mouth to speak, to tell her about Stacy and how much he loved her, but his courage drained away and he closed his mouth without speaking. Then the lies started coming and he couldn't stop them. "That's not true," he said. "I still love you, Jay Lee."

"Manny, I want you to make love to me. I want us to fuck, just like we used to do."

"I don't feel so good right now," he said, sweating.

She pinched his arm, hard. "Nothing ever stopped you before. What's the matter, did it rot and fall off on you from not being used?"

"Christ," Manny said. "Okay. Where?"

At once she was sweet and yielding again. "At your house, in your room," she said. "We'll play some David Bowie on your cassette player."

"No," he said. "My mother and Flat Top, remember?"

"Then up at the castle. Like old times."

Not speaking, Manny rolled along Dark Entry Road, pulled into his mother's driveway, and shut the engine off. Jay Lee was out of the car like a shot; she crossed the brook at a run, and he saw her sweat shirt flash behind the trees up by the railroad bed before she disappeared.

Manny followed at a walk. He found the sweat shirt shortly, gathered it up, and picked up her shoes when he found them. Then he felt something inside himself, felt gentle, greasy fingers stroking the lining of his stomach. He bent over and was colorfully sick onto the dead leaves of the swamp. Manny made a detour to a spring he knew that bubbled up between two rocks; he washed his mouth out there and wiped his face on the sweat shirt. After that he continued on, found Jay Lee's pants and belt, and came to her panties near a tree at the foot of the hill where the castle stood.

The sun was strong throughout the swamp because the worms had taken the leaves from the trees, and gypsy moths were dancing everywhere. He picked up the panties, then trudged up past the cave to the castle, where Jay Lee was waiting for him with no clothes on. She was white as the inside of a mushroom, and she was rolling herself against the dry grass inside the castle, lifting her hips toward him and smiling. Manny dropped her clothes against the wall and started undressing, suddenly self-conscious.

"Hurry up, lover man," she said.

He kicked angrily out of his pants, stripped his undershorts off, and lay down beside her. He had wanted to lie apart from her for a few minutes, catching his breath, but she pounced, jumped on top of him and mashed her face against him. He felt teeth.

Jay Lee bucked and rolled against him for a time, then she reached her hand down and discovered he wasn't ready for her yet. She moaned and began mashing him with her hand; he winced and looked up through the nearly bare trees, thinking to himself, *Fucking worms.*

She squeezed harder and harder, and finally he had to tell her, "Not so hard, Jay Lee." So she rolled off and took her face down there; that made him feel ashamed, and he covered his own face with an arm. She was at it that way for a while; he usually liked it, but this time he didn't, and it just felt wet and rough. Finally she lifted her head; he could tell she was looking at him, glaring, maybe, but he didn't want to see, and he kept his arm right where it was. Then she grabbed him with her hand again, hard, and started working him. Her grip got tighter; it felt like the skin was going to peel off.

Suddenly Manny was sitting up; the back of his hand was stinging and Jay Lee was lying with her head buried in the grass, crying, and he realized he had hit her.

"Sorry," he said. "I told you not so hard."

"You bastard," she said.

He reached to touch her, but she shot her foot out, catching him in the stomach, and knocked the wind out of him.

Manny rolled away from her, gasping, clutching his stomach. Finally, when he caught his breath, he curled his knees up into his chest and covered his head with his arms.

"Sorry," he told her again.

"You cocksucker," she snarled. They lay apart for a long while; Manny listened to Jay Lee's muffled sobs, and told himself, *I'm not really here. I'm in Paris with Stacy, and I am not here in the swamp at all and Jay Lee is all gone. She's married to Old Man Cahill, and he beats her.*

Then the grass rustled as she sat up; he heard her snuff, and the crying stopped. "So," she said. "I bet it's that rich bitch Cahill's granddaughter. Isn't it?"

Manny was tired. "Yeah. It's her."

"And she's pretty, isn't she?"

"Yeah."

"A lot prettier than me, isn't she?" Manny said nothing, so she kicked him in the leg. "I asked you, isn't she?"

"Yeah, Jay Lee, she is."

"Does she fuck?"

"Shut up, Jay Lee."

"I bet she hasn't even fucked you yet."

Manny sat up then, his hands cramped into fists. "I'll hit you again," he told her.

She spat and hit him in his good eye so that he was blinded. "And I'll kick you in the balls if you try it," she said. "She's a little virgin and she won't do it for you. Admit it."

He rubbed his eye out and muttered, "Fuck you, Jay Lee."

"You'd like to, but I guess you can't anymore."

"God—"

"That's why you'd trade a girl who takes good care of you for some little rich piece of shit that would faint if you showed it to her. Can't even make it work."

"Jay Lee, Christ."

"You and Toby. Why the hell do I get all the losers?"

"What do you mean, me and Toby?" He was suddenly curious, and the words were out before he could catch himself.

"Yeah," Jay Lee said, almost to herself. "That kid too. I loved him too, Manny. And I bet you're sick just like him."

"Listen, I've had enough—"

"Do you know that bastard Toby fucked me one time, fucked me for the first time in my life, and then after that he couldn't do it anymore?"

"What?" Manny said. He was frightened and embarrassed and curious all at once. "That's not what Toby told me. You're making it up."

"Don't call me a liar," she shouted. "You're the goddamn liar, Manny." She was getting a little hoarse now. "I told you, he did it one time, then after that, nothing. He wanted . . . he always wanted what I just did to you. I always wanted to tell you this because it bothered me, and you could never goddamn listen, because you're such an asshole."

"Listen," he said. "I'm sorry about things. Maybe we should go now."

But Jay Lee wasn't listening. "Know what else?" she asked. "The one time, it was my first time, and you know what he did?"

"I don't think—"

"We did it right here, where you and I are lying now. It was summer, just like now, only there were more leaves on the trees."

Something was warning Manny that he shouldn't listen to her, that he should leave, but he was paralyzed with curiosity. "Don't tell me this," he muttered.

"We rolled in this brown grass that's always here, and don't think for a minute, Manny, that Toby needed any help like you always do. He knew just how to do it, even though I was scared and sort of half-asking him not to. He went right in, *bang,* and it only hurt a little bit."

"Great," Manny said. "Thanks."

"Afterwards was when it got strange. I felt, you know, good, because I was a woman after that. I was just bleeding a little bit, and I was a little worried I would have a baby, because even then I knew you had to use things or it could happen to you. But like I said, I felt good, and I wanted Toby to hold me and say he loved me, and I was so dumb then I thought maybe he would tell me he wanted to marry me."

"That was pretty dumb," said Manny.

"Shut up, I'm telling this," Jay Lee hissed. "Anyway, Toby didn't do any of that lovey-dovey shit. He just sat up, there was a shit-eating smile on his face like he just beat me at Ping-Pong, and he reached and touched me between the legs. I thought maybe he would say 'Does it hurt?' or 'I'm sorry, the next time will be nicer,' or something like that. But instead he picks up his finger, it had blood on it, maybe a couple of drops, and he holds it in the air, looking up at it like he never seen blood before. Well, that seemed a little weird to me, so I said, 'Toby what are you doing?' But he just said nothing and made a stripe like a cat's whisker on his cheek with my blood."

"Jesus," said Manny, suddenly sorry that he had encouraged her. "I don't think I'll stick around for this. I don't believe any of it." He started to get up, but she leaped at him, tigerlike, and pinned him to the ground. She was heavy, and he was too weak from having been sick to push her off.

"Shut up, Manny," Jay Lee said. "That isn't the worst of it. And if you call me a liar again I'll kick you where it hurts. You hear?"

"Well, hurry up then," Manny said as he considered making an effort to throw her off. His stomach was starting to crawl again.

"Well, Manny, lover man, then Toby spat on me. He hawked up a good one and spat it right into my face, and he said, 'You're a pig, Jay Lee, a real fucking pig. Any bitch that would do this is a pig. Bitches are all pigs.' I swear to God that's what he said. And me in love like I was."

Manny started to protest, but Jay Lee said, "Shut up. You deserve to hear this. He spat on me again, Manny, and I was so shocked I couldn't move. Then he hit me across the face just like you just did, then he got up and laughed and walked away."

"Get the hell off me," Manny said. "I think you made all that shit up. Toby wouldn't do that." But he saw a sudden mental picture of the look on Toby's face when he was burning himself with a cigarette, and it frightened him so much he almost shouted.

Jay Lee laughed; her laughter was cold as icicles sliding off a rooftop. "But I didn't break up with him, Manny, even though I knew he was a fucking creep. Do you know why?"

"I don't give a shit."

She laughed again. "I stayed with him all that time because I didn't have anybody. My mother was gone and my father was in love with jai alai, and he didn't have any time for me. And Toby brought me flowers later, and said he was sorry, and said he loved me. And at first, when he couldn't do anything with me, he was nice about it and said it was because he was ashamed of the way he acted the first time. But later he started telling me it was because he thought I was disgusting. Imagine that bastard saying I was disgusting after what he did." Jay Lee sat up suddenly, her face blank as a stone, tears running down as she stared off into the swamp. Manny sat up too, slowly.

"So then he said he didn't want to see me anymore, that I was too gross for him, and then I was alone. I was all alone for two months and it was the worst thing I ever felt. I was going to swallow a bunch of pills, you know that, Manny?"

"Christ," Manny said, without energy.

"But then I started going out with you. It wasn't the same for a while; you're not as good-looking as Toby, and you don't talk pretty like he can when he wants. But you were nicer to me than him, and for a while it seemed like you were normal about screwing."

"Thanks," said Manny. He started gathering his clothes, put on his shirt and his underwear, and began pulling on his pants.

"And now you're tired of me too. I don't know what I'm going to do."

Manny told her, "You'll survive," and sat on a rounded stone to put his socks on.

Jay Lee flashed him a glance as if what he had said surprised her. She studied him for a long moment. "You know what else about Toby?" she said, finally.

"I don't want to hear anymore."

"He told me he'd kill me if I ever told anyone, but he sleeps with his mother."

"What?"

"Oh, I don't know if he screws her or anything. But they sleep in the same bed. Once when he was drunk he told me his mother started putting him in their bed when he was just a baby and his father ran away, or whatever, and they just never stopped sleeping that way."

"God, you make me sick." Manny was empty, otherwise he would have thrown up again. "I know you're making that up. The hell with you, I'm leaving." He stood and headed out the entrance of the castle.

"The hell with *you,* Manny," she called after him. "Your best friend is crazy and so are you. Just go early in the morning and look in his mother's bedroom window anytime. The curtains are white and you can see right through them."

"Only you would do something like that, Jay Lee," he called back over his shoulder. He kept walking. The swamp was full of the dirty snow of gypsy moths, and he kicked at them as he walked.

Chapter 16

When Manny and Toby were eleven years old, they became summer soldiers, fighting daily wars with sticks for guns. One afternoon, killing Japs and Germans as they went, the two of them conquered the castle. The fight was hard work in the buzzing summer heat, and when they finally got to the top of the hill, they didn't speak for a time. They just caught their breaths and felt the scratches and scrapes they had sustained in the fight, wondering how they got them.

Toby had the best gun, a stick with a wide bottom to it that suggested a gunstock, and Manny was a little envious. So after he caught his breath he blurted out, "Well, Toby, I won't be playing army with a stick for long because I'll be getting a real gun when I'm fourteen years old. It was my Uncle Zack's, and my grandpa has it now, and my father says I can have it when I'm older."

Toby snorted and didn't say anything, and that made Manny angry. "Sure," Manny told him. "My Uncle Zack. I bet he killed lots of Japs, real ones, before they got him. And I'm gonna get his gun. He killed a wildcat with it once. A real one."

Toby snorted again and said, "That gun! I seen it, and it's nothing but an old single-shot."

"Better than what you're getting, 'cause you're not getting anything."

Snort. Toby snorted just like a pig, and Manny felt like swearing at him. Toby said, "That's what you think, Manny. You know the good gun in the Sears, Roebuck catalog, the twenty-two semi-automatic that fires fifteen shots? That's what I'm getting."

He tried to imitate Toby's snort now, but it didn't come out quite right.

Toby continued, "And I'm getting it a lot sooner than you are. I'm getting it real soon. Next week, maybe."

"Bullshit!" Manny could hold it in no longer.

Toby smiled his secret, know-everything smile. Then he said, "I got the money, Manny. I've been taking ten dollars a week out of my mother's pocketbook. She hasn't even missed it. I got sixty bucks now, almost enough to buy that gun. Maybe I'll let you shoot it."

Manny was scared now; the part about stealing money was frightening. But Manny knew Toby had done it, because he did things like that a lot, and it always caused trouble. Sometimes, big trouble. "Wow!" Manny said. His voice shook a little, shaming him. "I don't know, Toby. A real gun."

"Come on," Toby said. "Next week. We come up here and shoot. Real, not with sticks." He looked down at the stick in his hand, and his face twisted in disgust.

Suddenly Manny was hot all over, sweating, and the heat was like little needles stabbing him everywhere. "I can't."

"You mean you won't. You're afraid."

"Listen," Manny told him. "My father. If you knew what he was like. He'd kill me."

Toby kept smiling, but something went out of his smile now, so that he was just stretching his face, showing his teeth, and his eyes were blazing. "Your father my foot," he said. "You're just chicken shit."

"I'm not."

"You are. You think my mother wouldn't be mad if she found out about the money? I'm not afraid."

"Your mother?" Manny said. "You could almost beat her up now. I could almost beat up mine. But a father, boy, when you do something they don't like, they kill you."

"Chicken," Toby snarled. His knuckles turned white against the stick. Manny noticed him getting mad, but it didn't bother him. If Toby ever hit him, Terry would beat him to a bloody pulp. In fact, he enjoyed Toby's anger; it was something he didn't get to see too often. Toby got Manny angry all the time.

"Yeah," Manny said. "I guess if he found out I was shooting a gun, he'd probably beat my rear end off and not let me leave the yard for a month."

"I'm sick of hearing about your father," Toby said.

But Manny kept after him. Toby didn't have a real father. Toby's father was *that idiot Tommy Carver.* The drooling face of an idiot took shape in Manny's imagination. "Jesus, remember the time we were lighting firecrackers and we set the dry grass in the field behind your house on fire? God, did I get it! What happened to you? Nothing, that's what."

"Shut up, Manny."

"And when we found those old twenty-two shells, and we were pounding them with a hammer to make them go off, my father—" Suddenly the heavy end of the stick Toby was holding came and knocked him on the side of the head. Then Manny was on the ground, looking up at Toby and gently touching the spot where the stick had struck him. There was no pain yet; there had only been a touch and then a noise inside his head like the buzzing of a fly. Then, as Manny stared up at Toby, puzzled, the stick came at him again; it came closer and closer, growing larger and darker until it covered his eye; he felt it hit him again, hard, and there were colors and bright lights in his head. Then the stick went away, leaving him in the dark, suddenly, and he reached and touched his eye and his hand came away wet. At first he thought *tears,* and there *were* tears in his other eye, but when he wiped out the good eye to look at his hand, he saw blood. There was a rabbit inside him then, a running rabbit, run for home rabbit, and he was up and running; he couldn't see but his feet knew the way through the woods, and he heard himself screaming, though he didn't know what he was saying and he didn't care what he was saying, he was just a rabbit running home.

Then Toby was there running at his elbow, trying to tug his hand away from the eye to get a look, and he was saying, *"I told you, I told you, Manny."* Toby was scared, that much got through to Manny, and he was saying, "It's not that bad, Manny, wait, slow down, let me have a look."

But Manny just pushed him away, shoved him hard, wishing he were dead, and he went running, running for home.

Manny's eye was bandaged for about a month after that. His father spent nearly that long driving him from hospital to hospital in New Haven, New York, and even Boston in a frantic attempt to save his sight. Every doctor they saw shook his head and told them the eye was damaged beyond repair. One doctor even said that Manny was lucky he still had an eye left.

"Lucky," snarled Alexis, who was usually calm under all circumstances. "*Lucky*. He's just a kid." He began to swear in Spanish at the doctor, who was tall and blond with a baby face and the nasal intonations of the rich.

An orderly escorted Manny and his father from that Boston hospital. Once they were back in the station wagon, which was only five years old at that time, Alexis turned his anger on Manny. "You kids," he said, slapping at the steering wheel. "You goddamn kids. You don't know how to play. You realize you're gonna be almost blind in one eye? *Blind*."

His father was on the verge of tears. This seemed unfair to Manny; here he was having to endure the pain of his broken eye as well as put up with his father's frustration. By the way Alexis was acting, you would have thought Manny had done something unforgivable to *him,* rather than having received unforgivable treatment for somebody else.

About two weeks after the fight, Manny got a letter of apology from Toby. Although he was lonesome, and missed Toby, he didn't answer it and he didn't call Toby on the phone. Toby stayed away until the end of summer, when it was getting to be time to go back to school. Manny was kicking a rusty can up the railroad bed toward where Cahill's earth-eating machinery was starting to chew away at the swamp when he saw Toby for the first time. Just as he was passing the Engine Hole, he looked up and saw someone walking down the track bed toward him. Quickly he saw that it was Toby, holding his hand in the air as if in greeting, but with the palm turned inward. Closer, and Manny saw the blood running in thin, winding ribbons down Toby's forearm and dripping off his elbow. The little finger on Toby's left hand was missing; a bit of glistening bone or tendon peeked through the place where it had been severed, and the blood was flowing from the surrounding flesh.

Manny froze. Some part of him was afraid and wanted to run away. He pointed to Toby's hand, but could not speak.

Toby was smiling, but his smile kept flickering on and off like a light with a bad connection. His handsome face, which was already starting to look like that of a young actor, maybe a young Robert Redford, was as pale as pure quartz.

"Okay, Manny," Toby said. "I think we're even now, what do you think?" His voice was squeaking, and he had trouble getting the words out. Holding Manny transfixed in his huge blue eyes, he said, "I cut it off. Threw it out in the swamp so they couldn't sew it back on. Even Steven, right, partner?"

Manny couldn't answer. He was frozen with his hand in the air, pointing at Toby's wound. The blood continued to flow, and after a minute, the smile died on Toby's face for good. Toby stepped around him then and continued marching down through the swamp. Manny turned and followed, his fingers reaching and gently touching his damaged eye.

When he was near Manny's house, Toby turned and walked across the wooden bridge and went around to the front door. While Manny was walking across the lawn after him, Toby let himself into the house calling, "Mr. Moreno! Mr. Moreno! Look. Even Steven."

*T*hey sent Toby away for two months after that. Alexis told Manny that Toby was "getting his mind adjusted." Just before he came back, Mrs. Carver came over and spent a long time talking to Alexis in the kitchen. Manny and Terry had been sent outside during their conversation, but Alexis soon called out the back window and asked Manny to come in.

Mrs. Carver was trembling, and she kept pulling her lower lip in between her teeth and biting it. She was getting lipstick all over her teeth. She took one of Manny's hands into both of hers; her hands were cold, and Manny wanted to pull away, but he didn't.

"Toby has been very upset since you and he had that fight," she said. "He's been away trying . . . not to be upset. Now he's coming back. He'll be back Thursday."

She paused and looked at him, so he nodded. Then she continued.

"He needs you as a friend, Manny. You and Terry both. I know that he hurt you, and it was wrong and bad of him to do that, but he is very, very sorry. There is not a time that I visit him that he doesn't talk about you or your family. He has always felt just like another brother over here." She glanced quickly at Alexis, who was still seated at the kitchen table. Manny's father gave her a half-smile. "Do you think that you'd like to be friends with him again?"

Manny looked at Alexis. His father nodded once, then looked away. Manny hesitated, then he said yes in a soft voice.

It was evening and the Moreno family was in the living room watching television when Toby came over for the first time since he had cut off his finger. He had walked into the house without knocking, Toby never knocked, and suddenly he was standing in the living-room doorway, smiling at them. There was no bandage on his hand, and the new skin that had grown over his circular wound seemed to glow almost as brightly in the flickering light of the TV as the burning tip of a thin cigar.

"Guess where I've been," Toby shouted.

Manny's parents exchanged a look, and neither Manny nor Terry could bring themselves to ask where. But Toby was not put off.

"To Africa!" he said cheerfully. "Hunting lions!" Toby pressed the imaginary butt of a rifle to his shoulder. "*Pow!*"

Manny and Toby played together nearly every day after that, but their play sessions were mostly mute. They would walk side by side for miles, saying nothing, or they would toss a football back and forth until darkness fell and made it impossible to catch. Terry didn't play with them much anymore; both he and his father would greet Toby when he came around, but they said little to him.

One day in early December, Toby met Manny at the head of the driveway just as he was stepping off the school bus. "You're still mad at me, aren't you, Manny?" Toby asked him. He was not smiling.

Manny dropped his eyes. "Yeah, maybe a little," he confessed. Toby walked away without a further word.

About a week later, Toby again was waiting for him as he got off the bus. It was snowing. Toby held a paper grocery bag in his arms, and as Manny walked up to him, he shifted the bag and Manny could hear glass knocking against glass inside of it. Toby was wearing gloves, and the little finger on the glove that covered his left hand was hanging limply across his knuckles.

"What's this?" Manny asked.

"Look inside. Go ahead," said Toby. "It took me a bunch of days to swipe them all from stores."

Manny tugged the edge of the bag with his fingers and looked down into it. There must have been twenty bottles of what looked like vitamins inside.

"Baby aspirin," Toby said. He wore a hopeful, but trembling, smile. "I thought maybe you and me might take all these together." He was looking not at Manny's eyes but at a spot that must have been in the middle of his forehead. Toby's eyes were watering. "They're not hard," he said. "You can chew them up; they taste like candy. You go to sleep, Manny. You just lie down together and go to sleep."

Manny had been frightened beyond words. He had turned away quickly and begun walking up the driveway to his house. Then Toby was there in front of him, clutching his paper sack in one arm and trying to hold Manny back with the other. The same fear twisted his face as when he had tried to pry Manny's hand away from his bleeding eye.

"I didn't mean it," he said. "Honest, Manny. I wasn't gonna take them. I just wanted to show you I was your best pal. I just wanted to show you I'd die for you, partner."

Although he had doubts, the gesture of loyalty was hard for the eleven-year-old Manny to resist. Together they carried the bag out to an abandoned sandpit deep in the swamp, and they smashed every bottle against a rock, hurling them like baseballs.

Chapter 17

*M*anny sat up in bed. He was sweating; fear and pain and heat leaked out of him like molten lead and ran down his sides. It was the old dream about the day Toby made his world dark on one side, and he tried to get rid of the dream by breathing it out of him, panting. But he couldn't breath, there was no air in the room, only a suffocating staleness.

So Manny kicked himself out of bed, kicked away the soaked sheet and went to the window. The window was open all the way; just the screen was there to keep the bugs out, but the screen seemed to hold the air out, so he pushed it up, his arms shaking, and shoved his head out.

It was cool outside; there was a breeze, and the moon shined down at him like a sweet calming face. The stars were snowflakes. Gradually the breath came back into him. He thought about his eye, got used to the idea all over again that that window would be closed to him forever, would be stained glass instead of clear, and he accepted it.

He sat there for a time, breathing in the cool night. Then he closed the screen and went rummaging through his things for a little pot to put a joint together. He found nothing, not even a roach, even though he was sure he had stashed some someplace, so he decided on a beer instead. Flat Top kept beer in the refrigerator; maybe he wouldn't mind if Manny had one, and the hell with him even if he did. Manny pulled on his Levi's, sweat drying on his skin like icing. He climbed down the wooden ladder to the first floor, his bare feet making damp sucking sounds against the flat rungs. The house was dark and silent. He walked softly into the kitchen, not wanting to wake anyone. Just as he was about to pull the refrigerator door open, he heard a noise.

His swamp instincts made him freeze, his hand on the refrigerator door, listening. In a few moments he heard it again, a faint sound, either a stirring or a murmur, he wasn't sure which. It came from the cellar. The sound was so low it was as if he had sensed it with the hairs on his bare arms rather than with his ears.

Manny stepped over to the cellar door, silently. He waited there for just a moment, until the sound brushed his skin one more time, then he pulled the door open and started down the stairs. He went down as quietly as he could; the door, as he turned the knob and opened it, made only a soft *tick,* the sound of a pin hitting the floor. And he stepped softly, Indianlike, down the steps, feeling the dry, splintered wood rough against the soles of his feet, softly breathing in the damp cool air of the cellar.

As he stepped he heard the sound again; it was Ida, and she had murmured the word *no.* Manny, on the steps, felt someone else in the cellar with her. His heart began to work now, tapping out a warning against his ribs. Four, five, six steps he went, then he could see the whole cellar. It was black down there, like the inside of a well, but objects, Ida's couch and the other old furniture, were blacker, more solidly dark, than the dark air surrounding them. There were two silhouettes on the couch, upright shadows, and he recognized them both. Anger and hatred spread through his blood like maddening poisons. One of the silhouettes was Ida; she was an unmoving shadow on the couch, and the other was . . .

"Manny, is that you?" said Flat Top's voice in the darkness. Flat Top was drunk, and he pronounced the words, *Manny, zatchu?*

The blood gonged in Manny's ears now, flashed brightly behind his eyelids. He jumped, his feet slapping bare, cold concrete at the bottom of the steps, and he hit the light switch on the wall, igniting a bare bulb on the ceiling of the cellar. The sudden light seared his eyes.

Flat Top and Ida both blinked at him, squinted in pain. He took them in at a glance. Ida was fully dressed; she wore Levi's and a T-shirt that said *Atlantic City* and was way too big for her thin frame. Flat Top was wearing nothing but checkered shorts that reached his knees and a pair of rubber shower thongs. His huge stomach, which looked mountainous in the ash-gray light provided by the light bulb, almost hid the half-open zipper of his pants. White cotton underwear peeked obscenely through the opening. Flat Top held a pint bottle in his hand, and he waved it nervously in Manny's direction. He tried to grin, his mouth lopsided and his teeth yellow as a woodchuck's, and he said, "Jus' talkin' to Ida, here, Manny. You wan' a little snort?"

The blood began to roar like a jet engine in Manny's head now. Then there was a loud *snap* from somewhere and Manny was gone, and someone else, someone murderous, was in his body and his head, pulling all the strings.

"Your fucking fly is open, Flat Top," said Manny's mouth. His body already had begun to move forward, slowly like a cat, tasting the air with all its hairs and all its pores. Manny watched himself from somewhere, fascinated and frightened.

"Manny," said Ida.

Flat Top grunted, his mouth opened in surprise. He set the bottle on the floor, where it tipped over and hit the concrete with a cold, sharp *clink*. Then he was digging at himself with the fat sausages of his fingers, trying to close the zipper, and it was hard work for him because he was sitting and the pants were tight on him.

"When I put 'em on musta forgot . . ." He started to get up off the couch, one hand still busy with the fly, and Manny watched himself step forward and throw his right hand into Flat Top's jaw. A shock traveled up his arm to his shoulder; it was a good, delicious, healing shock, and Flat Top fell back against the couch with a grunt. The hand left Flat Top's fly and sought the side of his jaw where he had been hit, and he said, "What the fuck . . ."

Manny watched his arm fire out again, saw it push Flat Top's nose sideways against his face. Flat Top's eyes first went closed with shock, then opened wide with surprise, and Manny's arm pulled back and fired again; a beefy, satisfying sound reached him and his hand went again and again and again. He must have hit Flat Top eight times before his mother's fat drunken boyfriend reached and captured his fist, swallowed it in his own hand that was like a baseball glove compared to Manny's.

Then Manny was on top of him, screaming. Ida was screaming now too, a siren in Manny's ear. He struggled to pull his fist away, fought against the stinking mountain of flesh that held him. He felt Flat Top's free arm go around him and tighten, trying to squeeze the breath out of him, and the person in Manny who was not Manny sent his own free hand to rake nails across the gray, sagging face.

Flat Top bellowed then, shouted, "Manny, stop . . . talk . . ." But he continued to squeeze, causing red flashbulbs to pop in front of Manny's face.

Manny clawed his face again, gasping, "*Bastard, son-of-a-bitch rapist.*"

Flat Top yelled something; he was angry now, and he caught Manny's scratching hand under his chin for a moment.

With both hands trapped, Manny screamed a choked scream and swore and bucked against Flat Top. Then he brought his forehead down hard on the bridge of Flat Top's nose; the chin lifted then and one hand was free.

"Goddamn . . ." said Flat Top.

Manny felt his hand reach down past the arm of the couch and grasp the cool glass of the vodka bottle.

Then suddenly his mother was screaming, "What is it, what's going on down there?" and he slammed the bottle as hard as he could into Flat Top's temple. There was a soft grunt then, almost a sigh, and he had both hands free. He passed the bottle over into his punching hand, which was his strongest, and he pulled it back to bring it down hard on Flat Top's face. But then he felt the big hands on his chest, felt the large, fat body tense, and then he was flying through the air backward.

He landed on his back on the concrete floor. His lights went out for a moment; he might have hit his head, and dimly he heard screaming and the sound of the vodka bottle as it skittered across the floor and shattered against a wall. His mother was screaming, "Stop it, stop it," then he felt Flat Top's baseball mitts close on his arms. His body went crazy then; he swung his arms and kicked and found some loose flesh with his mouth and sank his teeth into it.

Flat Top, howling, lifted him off the floor, pushed and carried him over to the wall, and slammed him into it. The breath went out of Manny like water from a sponge, and Flat Top knocked him twice more against the wall and threw him onto the couch next to Ida. The person inside him that was not him pushed levers and pulled strings, screaming, *get up, get up,* but his body did not respond.

He felt Ida's hand on his forehead, and she said, "Manny," and he heard Flat Top's rubber thongs on the stairs.

"Don't go down," Flat Top was saying in a pleading voice. "He's okay."

"Let me go," Mary Anne Moreno screamed. "I want to see them." The words came to Manny as if from far away.

"No," Flat Top said. "I have to talk to you first. Come in the kitchen." Manny heard their feet scuffling against the floor upstairs. There were more words; his mother was saying, "Let me go to them," and Flat Top kept saying, "Hear me out, hear me out, Mary Anne. They're both okay. Just listen to me for a minute."

Manny's head came up off the couch, then he found he could move his arms and his legs and his back. It felt like there were loose nuts and bolts rattling around inside him. He looked over at Ida; it was painful to turn his head, and he saw that she was crying. She sat unmoving, her face expressionless, but there were rivers of tears streaming from the corners of her eyes. The sight of the tears evicted the intruder who had been moving his body; he came into himself with a *snap.* He reached and wiped at her tears with the back of his hand.

"Did he hurt you?" Manny asked.

She shook her head, slowly, sadly.

"Did he touch you anyplace, Ida?"

She hung her head then, let it drop slowly until it reached her chest. Her hair shrouded her face.

"I asked, did he touch you?" Manny tried lifting her chin, but she jerked her head away from him, violently.

"Son of a bitch," said Manny. He said it again, whispered it. There was no anger in him now, only the cool, clear, inescapable necessity that took the place of the anger. He bent down and kissed Ida on the top of her head, right on the dog-bite scar that ran like a thread through the roots of her red hair.

"I love you, Ida," he whispered.

Upstairs, his mother and Flat Top were talking loudly, both of them at the same time, and he knew they would be down in the cellar in a moment to look Ida and him over. He had to move fast.

Manny stood, his back suddenly full of painful springs that were much too short and much too tight.

From upstairs, his mother's voice called, "Manny, are you all right?"

He hesitated a moment, then called up through the ceiling, "Yeah, I'm okay. Ida's okay too, Mom." Then he walked over to the gun rack, took down the old .22 that used to belong to his Uncle Zack. He opened the drawer beneath the rack, reached in without looking, and took out a box of shells. He opened the box on top of the workbench, slid one brass shell into the gun, closed the bolt, and poured the rest of the bullets into his pants pockets. Then he started for the stairs.

Ida was looking up at him now, tears streaking her cheeks like snail tracks. "Manny, no," she said.

He shook his head and blew her a kiss as he reached the first step; he was crying now himself, and he started up. When he reached the top, he cleared his eyes with the back of his hand, then stepped around the corner into the kitchen. Flat Top was standing with his back to Manny, barring Mary Anne's way to the cellar, and he was explaining himself.

He was scared, talking fast, and he was saying he had just been drunk and had gone into the cellar and had seen Ida and started talking to her. He had a daughter just about her age somewhere, he said. And then Manny had gone down there and gotten crazy and started a fight.

His mother was saying, "All right, all right, just let me see them." She sounded scared too. Then she looked past Flat Top's fat shoulder and saw Manny standing there with the gun. She closed her mouth with a snap and her eyes went wide.

Flat Top caught the look on her face. He looked over his shoulder at Manny and said, "Oh, Jesus!"

"Step away from him, Ma," Manny said. He held the gun casually at port arms; he knew he could drop the barrel and fire in half a second, and his target was so big and so close he couldn't miss. Flat Top knew it too, and the corners of his ugly mouth jerked down in naked fear. Slowly he revolved to face Manny, and Manny's mother took three steps backward away from him.

"Wait, kid," Flat Top said. His voice was shaking. "I was just telling your mother here—"

"She's fourteen fucking years old," said Manny. "And she ain't right in the head."

"I didn't—"

At the same time, his mother said, "Manny, don't—"

Manny said, "Everybody shut up." They both did. Manny studied Flat Top for a long moment, noted with satisfaction the three deep scratches down the right side of his face, one of them starting at the corner of his eye, as well as the fact that he was shaking all over like an old, fat dog that knows its in for a whipping.

"Turn around, Flat Top, and look the other way," he said.

Flat Top just stood there trembling, and Manny's mother said softly, "Wait, Manny. If you're really sure, then there's the police."

Manny laughed, looked at her then, really for the first time. She looked like hell. Her hair looked like a squirrel's nest and the skin of her face was turning gray and coming away loose from her skull, just the way Flat Top's did. There were liver-colored veins spreading south from the corner of each nostril. She had aged ten years since summer started.

"The police," Manny said. "Listen, Mom, how am I going to prove anything to the police? You think Ida is going to talk to cops, when she hardly even talks to us?"

Mary Anne Moreno hung her head, saying nothing.

Manny snapped his eyes back to Flat Top. "You turn around."

Flat Top didn't move, so Manny lowered the barrel of the .22 a fraction of an inch. He started turning then, his shower thongs whispering against the floor. When he was broadside to Manny, Manny lifted the stock of the gun to his shoulder, sighted down the barrel at the big fat ass that was swinging toward him.

Flat Top groaned, "No."

Manny tickled the trigger, and the crack of the rifle, held in and amplified by the walls of the house, slapped his ears.

Flat Top screamed.

Manny, still looking down the barrel of the .22, saw a spot of red blossom against the fabric of the fat man's shorts. Then a big hand was there, covering the spot, and Manny lowered the gun quickly, ejected the empty shell, and slid another in. He slammed the bolt shut just as Flat Top turned to face him again and said, "You little bastard."

"Now," Manny said. "Get out of here. If you come back again I'll shoot you through your fat heart."

Flat Top's expression changed from anger to disbelief. He stared at Manny, trembling, for a long moment. Then, massaging his ass, he turned and lumbered past Manny's mother and out the front door.

Manny lowered the gun and looked at his mother. She stood with a hand cupped over her mouth. Her eyes were glazed.

In a moment they heard the big diesel engine of the dump truck roar to life. Manny listened as the dump truck rumbled out of the driveway, then he opened the bolt of his gun and took the shell out.

He dropped it into his pocket, where it jingled as it rubbed against the other shells.

*T*here was a whole six-pack of Budweiser beer in the refrigerator. It was sitting right on the top shelf; the cans gleamed seductively at Manny as he pulled the refrigerator door open, rifle still in hand, the old, scarred walnut stock resting against the floor. He jerked a can from its plastic membrane with one hand; it required about the same effort as taking a slightly green apple from a tree. Then he popped open the can, still using one hand, took a long gulp—he was drier inside than he thought, and leaned his rifle between the wall and the side of the refrigerator without looking. His mother watched him, unmoving, a hand cupped over her mouth as if she were in deep thought. Manny finished his first beer, wadded the aluminum can with one hand, then took another from the refrigerator.

"Want a beer?" he asked his mother. She shook her head. So he opened the can, took a sip, and looked out the window. The stars were gone, suddenly, like white dust swept off a black table, and purple light was filtering through the trees. Birds were singing from their roosts deep in the swamp.

"I'm sorry about Flat Top," he said, not looking at her. He sensed her trembling then, and a sob escaped through her fingers.

"Shh," Manny said, smiling at her as he would smile at a baby, then turned his gaze back out the window, wondering whether they would come for him silently or with sirens blaring.

His mother stood crying softly for a while, and he let her be. After a time she said, "Is Ida really okay? Did he hurt her?"

"I think she's okay," he answered. "But it's hard to tell with her, you know?" He kept his voice gentle.

"Do you think I should go down there?" There was a pleading note in her voice.

"Yeah," he said, still not looking at her. "I think you should."

She sighed, then shuffled softly to the cellar door, looking old and worn-out in her ratty terry-cloth bathrobe and her gray fuzzy slippers that reminded Manny of drowned muskrats. She paused when she got to the cellar door and looked back at him. She had the look of a beaten puppy in her tired eyes; the look set flames of pity and hatred burning in Manny.

"Do you blame me for this?" she asked. "Is it all my fault?"

He opened his mouth to answer her but no words would come out. So he just shook his head and turned back to the window, took a long sip of beer, and wiped a tear out of his good eye. The cellar door clicked behind his mother. After a time, he dressed, putting on sneakers and a clean T-shirt.

Manny kept his eyes on the clock. Just over an hour after Flat Top had left, three local police cars rolled silently around the curve in the driveway, their headlights flicking off as they turned off Dark Entry Road, and they parked broadside to the house.

Jesus, he thought. *They sent the whole force to get me.* He was proud and fearful at the same time. The idea of jail scared him more than anything else in the world. Squad-car doors opened and closed quietly. He counted six cops standing behind the cars, silhouetted against the pink sunrise like in an old cowboy movie. Apparently they could not see him in the window, and the shadow-bodies twisted and turned nervously, expecting a muzzle flash and the deadly hiss of a bullet at any time. A thrill went all through his guts, made his bladder and his bowels burn and threaten to empty. He heard whispered voices through the open screen, then one silhouette, blacker than the rest, came out from behind a car and walked nervously toward the house, hand resting on pistol butt.

Jamison, thought Manny, feeling relief and an unexpectedly strong wave of affection wash through him. He stepped quickly to the front hallway and squatted below the outside light switch. Then he reached up and flicked the switch for the light over the front door, heard a gasp from Jamison, who was approaching the front steps, and half expected a bullet to shatter the glass window in the door above his head. No bullet came.

In a moment Jamison called from atop the steps. He was standing off to the side of the door, taking no chances.

"Manny," he said. "Manny Moreno. That you in there?"

"Yeah," Manny said. His voice quivered, but not badly.

"You got a gun, don't you?"

"Not on me."

"Sure?" Jamison was nervous.

"You think I'm crazy, Officer?"

Jamison sighed then. "Walk out the door, then, Manny. But come out slow; you don't want to upset anybody out here."

So Manny pulled the front door open, winced as he stepped through the screen door in front of the main door because he knew what to expect. Jamison grabbed him from behind and pushed him up against the wall of the house. Manny was ready, and he stuck his hands out to keep his face from smacking the shingles.

"Good," Jamison said. "Stay like that."

Manny felt the big, warm hands feel up and down his ribs and down his legs.

"Okay," said Jamison. "We got to take you for a ride now." Jamison pulled one of his hands away from the wall; he felt cold metal snap around his wrist and heard a metallic winding noise. Then Jamison grabbed his other wrist and he was handcuffed, his wrists joined behind his back. He stood up straight then, feeling nothing but a strong need to use the bathroom. He was afraid he would wet himself. The handcuffs pinched.

"Those too tight?'" Jamison asked.

Out of the corner of his eye Manny saw the other five cops leaving their positions behind their cars and walking across the lawn toward the house.

"Fuck no," Manny said. He was pleased at the force he was able to put into his voice. But his mouth was dry as ashes.

"Tough punk," Jamison said. His voice was sad and gentle, and Manny felt another unreasonable pang of affection.

Then the black cop leaned forward, urgency in his voice, and he hissed, "You don't say a fucking thing, no matter what happened. You know that already, right?"

"Yeah, I know," Manny said. "Thanks."

The other cops stood around impatiently while Jamison recited his Miranda rights. When that was done, one of them asked, "Where's the gun, kid?"

Manny said, "What gun?" They ignored his answer.

"Anybody else in the house?"

"My mother and sister. They're in the cellar."

Two cops entered the house, another went back to talk into the radio of his police car, and the remaining two stood around outside with Manny and Jamison. After a time, one of the cops who had gone into the house came out carrying his Uncle Zack's .22 by the barrel and said, "Your mother's boyfriend molested your little sister. That right?"

Manny said, "I don't know, is it?" His voice was a little shaky now; he was worried about what his mother was telling them.

The questioning cop frowned, then said to Jamison, "Well, we might as well run him down then." So Jamison put his huge hand on Manny's arm and led him toward a blue-and-white Plymouth police cruiser.

*T*hey didn't let him use the toilet for two hours. He was big news down at the police station; there hadn't been a shooting in town for nearly a year. They booked him for attempted murder, took finger-prints and pictures, then left him alone in a tiny, too-bright room for a while. Then a detective came in and talked to him, using the "nice guy" approach.

"He molested your sister, eh, Manny? Must be a real bastard. Why not tell us about it?"

Manny squirmed in his wooden chair, which, apart from the detective's padded seat and a round wooden table, was the only piece of furniture in the room, and said he wanted to go to the bathroom.

The detective, whose red pants clashed badly with his green plaid jacket, said, "Yeah sure, just a few more minutes, okay?" and went on with his questions. The few minutes stretched into forty-five minutes, and the burning ache between Manny's legs became a dull throb. Then, miraculously, it disappeared altogether except for an uncom-fortable fullness in his bladder. After a while, another detective came in and started all over again. But Manny stuck to Jamison's advice and said nothing.

Finally, both detectives gave up on him. A uniformed cop came and took him down a linoleum hallway to a tiny bathroom, took off his handcuffs, and let him inside. It was funny, but now that they were letting Manny take a piss, he couldn't go. He stood over the toilet for what seemed like ages before a tiny trickle jumped out of him.

After he got started, though, he went on forever; it seemed like he had a fifty-gallon drum buried in him someplace. It took so long that the cop outside opened the door, told him, *"Make it snappy,"* and slammed the door.

When he finished, finally, he walked out of the bathroom and the cop clapped the handcuffs back on him. He led him down a flight of stairs into a dimly lit hallway with jail cells on either side. Each cell had a cot with a bare, blue, pin-striped mattress sitting in the corner. Manny stopped when he saw the cells, realizing for the first time they were going to put him in there, maybe for days, or even weeks. Suddenly he was claustrophobic; his knees shook and he was hot, and he had to drag breath into himself. But something was pushing him forward, something hard at his back, and it took him a moment to realize it was the cop's fingers against his spine. He moved then, stepped forward on rubber legs, and allowed the cop to guide him into one of the cells after removing the handcuffs again. There were no other prisoners in the lockup, and when the door banged shut, it made an echoing noise that sounded like a growl.

The cop said something about food, but Manny wasn't really paying attention, he was listening to the growling, metallic echo of his cell door. The cop started up the stairs. Manny realized he was going to be left alone then, and he wanted to call out to the cop, suddenly wanted him to stay and thought about asking him questions to make him come back. He opened his mouth to call out as the cop scuffed his way heavily up the stairs, his uniform black in the shadows, but he didn't call; something inside him told him the question would find its way out as a high yelp of fear and would diminish all the victories of his already too long day. So he didn't call, and the cop disappeared and he was by himself with the persistent echo of his cell door closing.

A cop came down in a while with a tiny hamburger on a paper plate, a greasy sack of french fries, and a Styrofoam cup of black coffee. "Bon appetite," he said as he passed the stuff to Manny through the bars. Manny was suddenly grateful for the darkness of the lockup; he had been unable to hold back tears once he had been alone, and now, he was sure his face was streaked and swollen.

"Listen," Manny said. "What about my telephone call? And what about my public defender? I told them I wanted a public defender."

"Sit tight, junior," said the cop. Keys jingled on his belt as he walked back up the stairs. Manny took one bite out of his hamburger and ate one French fry. He swallowed all the coffee, which was lukewarm, and then threw the garbage in a corner of his cell. Then he curled up on the cot again and faced the wall. In a moment he found himself crying again.

*T*he roar of his cell door opening woke him up. *I was asleep,* he thought, amazed at himself. His face felt stiff and puffy.

"Okay, sweetheart," called the booming, echoing voice of a cop. "You got an appointment upstairs. Let's go."

Manny stood, blinking at the silhouette of a cop in his doorway. He was aching all over from the pounding Flat Top had given him that morning. He stood shaking with cold as the cop handcuffed him, then allowed himself to be herded upstairs. To his surprise, the handcuffs were taken off in front of the door to the same room where he had spoken with the two detectives, and the escorting cop allowed him to walk inside by himself, without a helping shove.

A thin, balding man wearing a blond moustache and a three-piece suit sat at the round table. He stood, smiling faintly, and stuck his hand out.

"You must be Manuel," he said, pronouncing the Spanish name correctly.

"Manny," said Manny. They clasped hands, briefly and feebly, as the door closed behind him.

"Uh, the state sent you, right?" Manny asked. "You're my public defender?"

The young man's smile changed slightly, took on a fleeting look of amusement. "No," he said. "Mr. William Cahill has asked me to look after you. My name is T. Joseph Lawrence. My firm does a great deal of work for Mr. Cahill in this state."

"What?" said Manny, annoyed and frightened suddenly. "I asked for a public defender. Can't afford any hotshot."

The lawyer laughed. "We aren't going to charge you, Manny. We're doing this more or less as a favor to Mr. Cahill, who is doing it as a favor to you. Accept it. And sit down, please. I have some questions to ask you, and I'm very busy."

Manny remained standing. "I don't need any favors from Mr. Cahill," he said. He had a vision of his grandfather's frowning face. "A public defender is good enough for me, Mr. Lawrence."

The lawyer kept smiling, but irritation bunched the skin around his eyes now. "Mr. Moreno," he said. "You may be in a great deal of trouble. Apparently you have shot someone, and that could mean years in jail, even for someone as young as you are. A public defender would tell you to plead guilty to an assault charge, possibly assault with a deadly weapon, and you would almost certainly spend some time behind bars. Mr. Cahill has asked me to try to keep you out of jail, and I am prepared to do just that, but I can't do it without your cooperation. Now, I suggest that you shelve your pride just this one time and that you sit down and talk to me. This is your young life at stake here."

And so, hating himself, shamed more than tears could ever shame him, Manny sat. The lawyer had Manny recount everything that had happened at the house, from the time he got up that morning to the time they stuffed him into the police car. He kept a small tape recorder on the table during the interview, and wrote things in a tiny notebook. Lawrence kept his face carefully blank as Manny talked.

After the story was over, the lawyer got into some pretty embarrassing stuff. He asked about Manny's father, and his mother's relationship with Flat Top, and about why Ida was the way she was. He also asked about Terry. Every time Manny balked at telling him something, Lawrence reminded him that he would be tried as an adult, and that he could go to jail for a long time. That always made Manny talk again, but he held little things back he didn't think made any difference in his case.

When the questions were over, Manny felt emptied out and hollow. He felt resentful too. It was like standing naked in front of somebody, showing them the blemishes on his body that the clothes hid.

The tape recorder made a *click* as Lawrence shut it off. "Well," he said, "that was very helpful. I can't be sure, but I think there is a good chance we can get you out of this mess."

"But I shot the guy," Manny said. A flicker of unreasonable hope warmed his hollowness.

"Look," Lawrence said. "We have certain mitigating circumstances in the unlikely event we do go to trial. Good circumstances; your age, for one thing, and a good suspicion that Mr. Ed Jakes indeed molested your underage and, uh, emotionally ill sister. But I don't want you to lose any sleep, Manny. I don't think it will get to trial. You said nothing to the police, correct?"

"Yeah," Manny said. "Right."

"Well, then, all we have working against us is the bullet they dug out of Mr. Jakes, which will be matched to your rifle through ballistics, and the unfortunate remarks your mother made to the police when they arrested you."

"That seems like a lot to me," Manny said. Lawrence smiled at him indulgently, and Manny thought, *He thinks I'm an idiot.*

"Not really, Manny. I think we can prove, if we have to, that your mother is an alcoholic, that she was drunk that morning, and that she really doesn't know what happened."

"Christ," said Manny, and he hung his head. Then he thought of something and he looked up. "What about Flat—Ed Jakes?"

The lawyer smiled at him again, and Manny felt like punching him.

"Mr. Jakes is in trouble and he knows it. I believe that with the proper encouragement, he can be induced to leave the state, to just disappear, before he can say one word against you in court."

"Wow," said Manny, awe and uneasiness building in him. Suddenly he realized that the defense Cahill's people were preparing for him was not strictly one of brilliant legal maneuvers. The octopus was working for him now too.

"Now that bullet," Lawrence said, talking almost to himself. "That is the only fly in the ointment. There are many lesser charges stemming from that bullet alone, if they want to make an issue of it. Illegal use of a firearm, discharging a firearm within city limits, other pica-yune things. Perhaps the slug itself will have to be made to disappear before it gets to the State Police Crime Laboratory, but I don't think it will be necessary." He stood, suddenly, and stuck his hand toward Manny.

Manny looked at him, did not stretch out his hand. "Mr. Cahill is good at that, isn't he? Making people and things disappear?" Greasy fingers tickled at his stomach, making him want to upchuck the single bite of hamburger he had eaten.

The lawyer smiled; he looked for an instant like Toby, all teeth and no humor. "Shh," he said, melodramatically. Then, "Listen, Mr. Moreno. That's okay, you don't have to shake my hand. We'll try to have you out in the custody of your mother as soon as possible. I can promise you they will not send you down to Bridgeport at all."

"Why is Mr. Cahill doing this?" asked Manny, half to himself. "I'm just a gardener."

"Ah," Lawrence said, "but you're a good gardener, Manny." He walked past Manny and out the door, nodding to a cop as he did so, then he was gone. They put the cuffs on Manny and took him back to his cell, where he curled up and looked at the wall.

Chapter

18

*S*ometime the next morning, a cop woke him up. He awoke scared and confused, rolling over to face the cell door with his hands in front of his face, ready to receive a blow.

"Relax, tiger," said the cop. "It's only breakfast." It was the same guy who had taken him to the bathroom the day before, but he was smiling now.

Wide-eyed, Manny studied him, releasing his breath, finally, as he took in the wax-papered egg sandwich and the lidded coffee cup the cop held. He was hungry suddenly, and he walked to the bars for the food.

"Had a bad night, huh?" said the cop as Manny took the sandwich and unwrapped it. "Guys told me you were screaming and moaning to beat the band."

Manny looked up, startled. "Must've been somebody else," he said.

The friendliness melted now. "Pal, there ain't nobody here but you," the cop said.

The officer waited for him to finish eating, then walked him up

171

to the bathroom. Manny felt better after he splashed water on his face. But when they took him back to his cell, he started feeling sick, thought maybe it was from the greasy egg sandwich and too strong coffee.

*H*e was tired and he fell asleep again. And after a while they woke him up again. "Let's go, junior," said the cop. He was a big, potbellied guy Manny had never seen before. He walked out of the cell, stiff and sore all over, wondering where they were taking him now, and afraid it might be down to Bridgeport, despite what the Cahill lawyer said. Reflexively he clasped his wrists behind his back so the cop could put handcuffs on him, but the fat man just said, "Move it out, pal. Right on up those stairs."

So Manny walked up, the backs of his legs sore. When he got to the top step, he saw his mother and his grandpa Tarbox standing by the main desk near the front door. He looked behind himself quickly, saw that the big cop was still at the foot of the stairs, hardly paying attention to him, and he rushed over.

His mother reached, and they hugged awkwardly.

Grandpa Tarbox said, "Hi, Manny," and he looked troubled.

The desk sergeant looked up. "You can go now, kid," he said. "Stay out of trouble, will you? We've got a nice, peaceful town here, and we like it that way."

Startled, Manny looked over at him. "What do you mean? You mean I'm released in her custody?"

The desk sergeant snickered. "No," he said. "You're just re-leased."

"How can that be?" said Manny, annoyed. He thought he knew procedure better than this. "I haven't even had a hearing yet."

"Manny . . ." said Grandpa Tarbox.

The cop snickered again. "There won't be a hearing unless you want one. Charges have been dropped. Now go home with your mother, and never darken our door again."

Manny stared at the cop; this had to be a joke, and it was a stranger thing to him than his nightmare had been.

"Manny," said Grandpa Tarbox. "We'll explain to you in the car. Let's go now."

He allowed his grandfather to steer him toward the door with a hand on his elbow. It was bright outside, and the sun hurt his eyes. And when his mother opened the door, a wave of heat charged into the air-conditioned coolness of the police station and nearly knocked him over. It was then that he realized he was going to be free.

Manny snapped his head back toward the desk sergeant, who was looking down at some paper work now. "Hey," he said, almost shouted, a quaver in his voice. "What about my rifle?"

The sergeant looked up. "Don't push your luck, kid. Just get out of here." His grandfather shoved him gently out the door.

It was afternoon; the day was hot and windless, and the air was filled with gypsy moths. There were twice as many moths as there had been yesterday, when the cops were bringing Manny in for shooting Flat Top. They were a blizzard now.

As if reading his mind, Grandpa Tarbox said, "These damn moths are finally peaking out now, I think. Ought to start dying off pretty soon. Then we'll be rid of them."

Manny looked at the old man then, studied him, as the shock of being let out of jail wore off. His grandfather looked tired. The old man slumped in the passenger seat of his mother's station wagon as if his bones had suddenly begun turning soft, and it seemed that new wrinkles had eroded his face since Manny had last seen him. He held his mouth in the tentative, thoughtful way he always did when his dentures were hurting him.

Mary Anne drove; Manny was glad to see she was in shape to handle the car. The three of them sat crowded together in the front seat as they drove up Dark Entry Road, not talking for a time.

Then Manny said, "You feeling okay, Grandpa?"

"I'm doing all right," said the old man, his dentures clicking. He looked out the window as he spoke.

In a tired voice, Manny's mother said, "Mr. Cahill called this morning, Manny. Very early, like about six o'clock. Told me to tell you to be in to work tomorrow at the regular time, and don't expect to get paid for taking two days off."

"*Goddamn* Cahill," muttered Old Man Tarbox, still looking out the window. It was the same exasperated, ill-humored voice he used when Toby beat him at cards.

"So anyway," Mary Anne said, ignoring her father. "I told him you were sick, and that I was sorry I didn't call in for you. Said you were real sick, Manny, you see, I didn't know he knew. . . . Anyway, he laughs, at least I think it was a laugh, sounded sort of like sandpaper on wood. And then he says, 'He is not sick, at least that I know of, Mrs. Moreno. He's in jail, but he'll be out by this afternoon. They'll call you to pick him up.' Then he repeats the thing about you getting to work tomorrow, says be sure to tell you, and he hangs up the phone."

Her eyes, blue and watery, slid off the road for a moment to look at Manny. Manny, uncomfortable between his mother and grandfather, stared straight out through the windshield.

"Yeah," Manny said. "I guess it was Cahill that got me out. I guess he can do about anything he wants in this town."

"Goddamn Cahill," repeated the old man.

"I don't know why Ma, that's the thing. He knows gangsters and people. What's he going to want from me now?"

Mary Anne's voice cracked. "I'm just happy you're getting another chance," she said. They were pulling into the driveway now. "Don't you think so, Pa?"

Grandpa Tarbox was silent for a moment, and when he spoke, there were tears in his voice. Manny was startled; he had never seen the tough old Yankee even close to crying before.

"Of course, I'm happy to have Manny back," he said. "I *am* happy. But why that Goddamn Cahill . . . I just don't understand."

Mary Anne pulled the car into the driveway and shut the engine off, but none of them got out right away.

"He sent a fancy lawyer over to the jail yesterday," Manny said. "The lawyer asked a lot of questions." His mother and grandfather opened their doors then; neither wanted to hear what questions the Cahill lawyer had asked. Manny slid out the passenger side and ran into the house. He found Ida in the cellar with her feet tucked up under her on the old couch, rocking. The rocking was a bad sign.

He sat down next to her, smoothed the damp hair out of her eyes. *It's growing back good now,* he thought, and hugged her. She hugged him back, and her embrace was surprisingly strong.

"Manny's back," said Ida.

"I'm back," Manny agreed. "Are you okay, Ida?"

"Okay," Ida said. Her eyes were far off and dreamy, though; he could tell only part of her was with him.

"You're sure? You're not sad . . . about anything, Ida?"

She shook her head, gravely.

"Well then, what are you doing in the cellar, kid? It's nice outside." He felt her arm move on his shoulder. He turned his head and saw she was pointing at the wine-colored stain on the cellar wall. He turned then to study the mark. It had always seemed shapeless to him before, but now, for an instant, it took the form of a creature, a praying mantis, with its two long, many-jointed catching arms raised for attack. Just for a second, Manny was sure he was seeing the stain the way Ida saw it; it was alive and it made his scalp prickle with electricity. He blinked, and the vision on the wall became a discoloration again.

"Jesus, Ida," he said. "How can you stand it? I just saw—"

"Manny," Ida said. "Tell Grandpa not to go there."

He grabbed her by the shoulders then, realized after a moment he was squeezing her, and loosened his grip. "Where, Ida? Not to go *where?*"

"He knows," Ida said. "Tell him not to." And she closed her eyes, signaling that she didn't want to talk anymore.

So Manny went upstairs. His mother and Grandpa Tarbox were sitting at the kitchen table, drinking coffee. His grandfather had his pipe burning away, and the room was full of blue smoke despite the fact that all the windows were wide open. The air coming in from outside made the smoke swirl and eddy.

Manny sat down at the table. "Grandpa," he said, "Ida just saw something. She says for you not to go someplace you're planning to go. She won't tell me what it's about, but she says you know, and that it won't come out good." Manny did not succeed in keeping the panic out of his voice, but his grandfather only looked mildly amused at his warning.

"Not a thing has come out good for me in the past few years, Manny. What's the difference?"

"Yeah, but—"

"Doesn't matter what happens to an old man," he said, almost to himself.

So Manny let the subject drop. They sat in uncomfortable silence for a while. By the nervous way his mother kept pursing her lips, he could tell she wanted to say something but wasn't quite ready, so he kept quiet and waited.

Finally she spoke. "I think . . . you did right trying to protect Ida, Manny. You got carried away, because you were mad, but you kicked Ed out, which is what I should have done long before."

Manny was embarrassed, and could think of nothing to say.

"I've been a bad mother, and a bad person. I've been drunk all summer."

"It's not all your fault," Manny managed to mumble. He didn't speak louder because he didn't trust his voice. "We've had some luck, boy, recently that—"

"I've been talking to Pa, here, all day yesterday and part of today,

Manny, and I've decided to shape up. No more drinking, Manny. Not a drop. Ever."

"Well, good," mumbled Manny.

"And no more men in this house, Manny."

Grandpa Tarbox kept his eyes carefully aimed out the window.

"You don't have to do that, Ma—"

"At least until Ida is eighteen. And speaking of Ida, she's going to see somebody, a doctor or somebody, as soon as school opens again. Maybe they can help her. I should have taken her a long time ago, but I guess I always kept hoping she'd come out of it by herself."

"Okay," Manny said. "Sounds good to me." He couldn't meet her eyes. He felt no great hope that his mother would be able to follow through on her promises. But still, he thought it was a good thing that she wanted to straighten herself out. Maybe there was a little hope, if he could keep himself from being disappointed later.

His mother's face was becoming red and puffy now, but no tears came to her eyes. It was as if she were too tired to cry. "I really think I'm going to make it with the drinking, Manny. Yesterday was a strange day, and I had three really strong tests. I made it through all three without a single drink. Of course, your grandfather was here and that helped."

"What tests?" asked Manny, alarmed suddenly. "Me getting arrested and what else? You mean Ida, Flat Top, and me—one, two, three?"

"No," she said. "You and Ed and Ida, that was just the first. The second was that that good-looking state police lieutenant stopped by again."

"Oh God," Manny said.

His mother stood and shuffled into the living room. *She's getting old,* Manny thought. She came back with a long manila envelope, pulled two black-and-white photos from it, and set them in front of Manny.

"They caught the man they were looking for," she said. "The one they said drove the car with the green trailer. This is him. I told the lieutenant you were at work, so he left these pictures for you to look at. He wants to know if you have ever seen this guy."

Manny caught his breath and looked down at the pictures. The man was about thirty-five; he was bearded, with a slight harelip that was nearly concealed by his moustache. His eyes were light-colored, and very cold. Manny shivered, thinking that he was looking at the man that might have killed his brother. He let his breath out. "I've never seen him."

"I don't recognize him either," his mother said. "And Grandpa never saw him before. Did you, Grandpa?"

"Nope," said the old man. He was still looking out the window, producing pipe smoke. "I'll tell you what, though," he said. "That state policeman need not have left those pictures. Those same ones are in all the newspapers this morning."

"So they really think this might be the guy . . . at least the one that killed those six kids they found buried?" Manny said. He took another look at the photos. The man didn't look evil enough to murder children. Manny thought maybe it would take someone who looked like Hitler to do that.

"They think," Grandpa Tarbox said. "But I told that lieutenant with the funny glasses that I didn't think that boy got Terry. Told 'em to start checking other avenues as far as Terry was concerned."

Manny looked at the old man, startled, and his grandfather shifted uneasily and pretended to study the swarms of gypsy moths dancing outside the window.

"Why did you tell him that?"

"Because that's what I think." Grandpa Tarbox released an especially large, obscuring cloud of pipe smoke.

"Why do you think that, Grandpa?" Manny's voice had an edge to it now.

"Goddamn it, Manny, because that's just the way I feel. An old man is entitled to his feelings, isn't he?"

His grandfather was concealing something; Manny knew him well enough to tell that. But he knew it was useless to press him. So he turned to his mother and said, "So what was the third big surprise, Ma? I can hardly wait."

She got up and shuffled back into the living room, returned with an envelope with candy-striping around the edges.

Manny's heart hit the wall of his chest and bounced back. He took the letter from her, mumbled his thanks, and, after remaining seated for a polite moment more, stood and rushed up to his attic room.

On the outside, the letter from his father was the same as all the others. Manny's address was neatly typed, with no return address up in the corner. The cancellation seal over the stamp said Asunción, Paraguay, on it. Inside, on a piece of onionskin, a brief message was written in pen. Unlike the other letters, this one displayed open knowledge of recent events in the swamp as passed on by his Grandpa Tarbox.

Dear Manny, it read, *I am fine, but I am working very hard, and am never in one city more than a week or so. Your grandfather tells me things are still tough for you, but I know you are a man and can handle it. One thing bothers me, though, Manny. I understand you are working for William Cahill now. That is bad. Cahill is a crook and a gangster, and you shouldn't trust him. I think you should go back to school and work hard and make something of yourself.*

Please don't blame your grandfather for not giving you an address where to write me. I asked him not to, and I have my reasons. One day I will write you and tell you why. Love, Your father.

Manny read the letter over three times, then stuffed it back in the airmail envelope. He skimmed it across the room, watched it hit the wall and drop to the floor with a whisper. Then he lay back down on the bed, trying to arrange his face so that they would not see how upset he was downstairs. He realized suddenly that he needed a shower.

His grandfather was sending his own ideas about things down to his father in South America, that was apparent enough. And with only the old man's prejudices to go on, Alexis Moreno was trying to call the shots. It wasn't goddamn fair. If his father wanted to run things, he ought to get his ass back up to Connecticut; they sure needed him right now. Paraguay. He was in fucking Paraguay. A place nobody ever heard of.

Angry, grumbling about the letter to himself, Manny found a tiny bit of pot he had hidden and forgotten about a long time before and smoked a thin joint before he carefully stored the candy-striped envelope under the loose floorboard. He smoked angrily, saying to his father, *See, I'm smoking pot, Dad. I'm a high school dropout. I'm working as a Puerto Rican gardener for William Cahill. I shot somebody. All because you aren't here. It's all your goddamn fault.*

When he thought he had all the bad things jammed back into a corner of his mind, he climbed down the ladder to the first floor and walked to the kitchen.

Toby was there; Manny hadn't heard his car. Carver showed his eyeteeth as Manny came into the kitchen.

"Hey, partner," said Toby. "Something catch on fire upstairs? Smelled something burning."

Manny didn't answer. He pulled the refrigerator door open, and he was happy to find four cans of beer left from the six-pack he had been drinking when he was arrested. He opened one of them without offering one to Toby, and took a long gulp.

His mother and his grandpa were still sitting at the kitchen table. His mother sat between Toby and the old man, looking apprehensive.

"Should keep beer out of the house from now on, Manny," said Grandpa Tarbox. "If you have to drink, drink outside."

"What did Al—your father say, Manny?" his mother asked. Her voice was soft, tentative.

"Fuck him," said Manny. He took another sip of beer.

Both his mother and his grandfather twisted in their chairs to look at him. Toby was smiling ferociously out the window; Manny wanted to kick him right in the ass.

"That's no way to talk," the old man said, but he was unable to put any sternness in his voice. His eyes would not quite meet Manny's. His mother looked more sad than shocked.

"Double-fuck him," said Manny. "He's no goddamn father to me. And he sure isn't one to Ida. Look what the hell is happening to all of us. Look at this family. You know where he is right now? Fucking Paraguay. I don't even know where the place is. And he has the balls to write me a letter saying go back to school, Manny. Don't work for Cahill, Manny. Goddamn him and the horse he rode in on." He hadn't meant to say anything about the letter, but it all just came pouring out of him. The can of beer was still half full, and he wound up and pitched it into the hallway. It left a foaming trail of beer all the way across the kitchen floor and up his arm to the shoulder. Then the anger was gone, suddenly.

"Manny," his mother said. "It's not all his fault. You should never say that about your father, even if he never comes back and you never hear from him again.

"Fine," Manny said. "But he's not telling me what to do anymore. Not unless he wants to do it face to face."

Grandpa Tarbox opened his mouth as if he were going to say something, but then changed his mind and turned to face the window again. Toby Carver was still smiling; he was looking at Manny's grandfather and grinning ear to ear. The old man ignored him, and finally Manny said, "What the hell are you laughing about, Toby?"

"Nothing," said Toby. He tried to change his expression then, but without much luck. "Just happy you're out of jail, partner."

Manny opened another beer and sat down at the table. No one said anything for a while, then Toby said, "Hey, Gramps, how about a story?"

The old man looked at Toby then, for the first time since Manny had come down from his room. He was tired; it seemed to Manny something had gone out of him since he saw him last.

"I'm not much in the mood for stories," Grandpa Tarbox said.

But Manny's mother brightened up with the idea, said, "Yeah, Pa, maybe that's what we all need right now, a good story to liven us up. I'm sure Ida would like to hear one too."

"Rabid foxes, Gramps," Toby said. "That's always been my favorite. When the five foxes get in the house with the old lady, and she doesn't have any weapons, but her poodle is there . . ."

"Don't think it will be that one," the old man said.

"So you will tell a story, Pa?" Manny's mother asked.

Old Man Tarbox didn't answer for a while. Then he said, "Well, I will tell one. But it won't be any nonsense about rabid foxes. I guess I'll tell the Last Wildcat." Grandpa Tarbox knocked ashes out of his pipe into an ashtray and started to load it with fresh blueberry tobacco from a paper pouch on the table.

Mary Anne said, "Quick, Manny, go get Ida."

So Manny walked down the stairs to where Ida was studying the wall. "Come on, Ida," he said. "Grandpa is going to tell a story."

She shook her head; Manny was incredulous. She had never missed a story before. "Why not, kiddo?"

She looked at him, only half seeing him. "Toby," she said.

"That son of a bitch. Because he wanted you to drink beer that time, right?"

She smiled then; it was the first time he had seen her do that in a long while. She didn't smile directly at him; it was as if she were enjoying a personal joke he couldn't understand. "Beer," she said. Then her face went stone blank again, like a TV set when the plug is pulled.

"Okay, then," Manny said. He kissed her on the forehead and thumped back up the stairs. His grandfather had already built up a fine head of smoke, and they were waiting for him. He glared at Toby.

"She doesn't want to come up because of Toby. He tried to make her drink beer one night, and she didn't want to."

Grandpa Tarbox frowned deeply.

Toby said, "Sorry, Manny. I'll go talk to her if you want." He was still smiling, and Manny wanted to throw something at him.

"Forget it," Manny said. "She doesn't want to see you, period. Why don't you start, Grandpa?" Manny sat down to listen and took an absentminded sip of his beer.

It was late afternoon now, and the air was starting to cool. The summer sunlight was amber. The old man's eyes glazed over as he looked out the window, his features softened by the pall of smoke that hung about him. His Adam's apple worked up and down several times; finally, he cleared his throat and began.

Chapter 19

"Well, sir, it was way back at the beginning of World War Two, and even then all the wildcats were pretty cleaned out of here. I must admit, I shot a couple myself in my day when I still had poultry and rabbits and things. The other folks around here, they'd go looking for them even if they weren't causing any trouble; hunt them with coon dogs until they treed, then shoot them and let the dogs fight over the carcass.

"So that one day they were extinct as dinosaurs except for one pair, a female and a big tom, that had learned to tiptoe real careful around the farms and houses. They'd learned, you see, that if they bothered domestic animals, that meant dogs and blinding electric lanterns and guns, so they stayed back in the swamp pretty far and killed cottontails and an occasional lame deer or fawn. I used to see their tracks all the time when I was trapping muskrat. They were like friends to me, and I was hoping maybe there'd be kittens sometime and that the race would get started again. Usually they avoided each other, those two, but every so often they'd get together at night and sing a duet out there deep in the swamp that would have every hair standing

182

stiff on the back of your head and every dog for miles around straining furious at the end of his chain.

"Well, but that poor couple had no more luck in life than my
own family, I guess. The pretty little female, she got killed late one
fall night trying to get across the State Road. I saw her as I was driving
up from Bridgeport; the car or truck or whatever it was must have
just hit her because she was still alive. I think it must have been a
truck, because it mashed her whole hindquarters flat against the pavement so that half of her was like part of the road. But the front half
was still struggling to crawl away like she thought she was just pushing herself out of a hole in the road, and pretty soon she'd be on her
way. She was pushing hard against the road with her forepaws, and
she had a real bewildered look on her muzzle like she was wondering why she wasn't going anywhere.

"I stopped the car, went and rummaged in the truck for a weapon,
but the only thing I could find to put her out of her misery was a tire
iron. So I hefted the iron and walked over to her, but I didn't need
to use it after all. I guess she finally realized she wasn't going back to
the swamp ever again, so she lay down without a sound and went
peacefully off to sleep.

"After that, things were pretty quiet for a couple of months. I
didn't see or hear the tom for all that time, and I started thinking
maybe he went walking north, hoping to meet another of his kind
somewhere else in the world. But then I knew it wasn't so, because
he started singing out there in the swamp. He sang all by himself, real
lonely sounding, and he got louder night after winter night. He never
sang from the same place twice, either, and I knew he was pacing the
swamp, side to side, end to end, looking for his lady friend who wasn't
there anymore. And boy, the dogs sure loved that singing! They did a
little singing of their own, all night long, and you could tell they couldn't
wait to see him dropping helpless from a tree branch so they could
tear some spots out of his hide.

"And then he started doing some strange things. That tough bobcat that was always so careful around people before started coming
into my yard every night. He came real quiet, but I always knew he
was there and sometimes I could find a good hiding place to watch
him. At first he didn't go near the rabbits or anything; he was paying
attention to my cat, Sylvia. Mary Anne wouldn't remember Sylvia, but
that cat was real snooty. She was a real society lady, and she'd starve
rather than catch mice. Well, it didn't take me long to figure out that

bobcat was courting Sylvia, and wasn't seeing her as a possible meal or anything. He was real polite, that animal. He'd sit there sometimes and just look at her, and maybe purr a little. He'd never touch the food in her dish, and he never made a move to scare her or anything. When it started getting light, he'd just pad back out into the swamp, quiet as he came.

"But Sylvia never paid him any attention; I guess he just wasn't good enough for her. Oh, she wasn't afraid, but she ignored him at first, not looking at him once in the whole night. She'd just kind of lay there on the back porch and twitch the tip of her tail. Then she got bored with the game, I guess, started to think the tom was getting tedious, and she took to hiding way down in the drainpipe where he couldn't follow her because he was too big. So for a few nights the bobcat sat patiently at the end of the drain, hoping she'd come out. But of course she never did; she was real stuck up, that Sylvia, and he got tired after a while and stopped coming around.

"But that wasn't the last of him. It was just then that he started doing some really strange things. He kept to himself for a while, not singing or anything, and then it was like he finally made up his mind about something because he started showing up around the house again at night. He'd come every night and sit there singing in my yard, only it wasn't singing anymore, it was just yowling, real loud yowling, and he was trying to get on my nerves. And what noises that cat could make! I believe he was reading out of the Devil's own songbook when he sat under my window. He had different growls and threats and curses, but the worst one was a scream he made like a woman with her hair caught in the wringer of a washing machine.

"Of course, I knew what he wanted, but he wasn't getting that satisfaction from me. I'd just open the window and shout, and he'd go away for a while, but never very far, or I'd get really mad and pitch a rock at him off the back porch. That always kept him away a little longer.

"Finally, I guess, he learned I wasn't going to be provoked with evil noises, so then he really went and lit the fuse. I went out one morning after an extraordinarily quiet night to find all my rabbits were dead. He didn't eat a single one; just tore through the chicken wire like it was paper, murdered those bunnies one by one, and then laid them all, and there were seventeen of them, down on the ground in a line, head to tail to head, like he was saying, 'Look what I did, old man. Now what are you going to do about it?'

"After that, it had to be done, of course, but I just didn't have the stomach for it. So I turned the job over to Zack; he's my boy who went off into the Pacific to fight the Japs and was never seen again, live or dead. But Zack was sixteen at the time, and he'd never killed a bobcat. He was kind of eager for it, too, so I told him, well, go to it, because this is the last one. So Zack borrowed two good coonhounds from up in Brookfield someplace, and he took that old twenty-two that the police just took away from Manny, and he got hold of that idiot Tommy Carver to hold the lantern for him.

"The night they went out, the bobcat was kind of prowling near the house, making little noises, just to make sure we didn't change our minds. Those two dogs went nearly wild; they were off and running as soon as Zack opened the car door to let them out. When those dogs went tear-assing into the brush, that cat took off, boy! That wildcat was a real old Yankee. Even if he did sort of have to beg for it, they weren't getting him without a fight. He didn't tree for the longest time; he was enjoying himself, and the dogs had to chase him in figure eights through the swamp. He'd turn every so often and cuff hell out of both of them before he'd take off again, so that the dogs were covered in blood by the time they were finished, and one of them was no good for anything again. Zack and that idiot Tommy Carver tried to follow for a while, but it was really impossible, so they just sat down on a rock with a half-pint of brandy and waited for the dogs to bark treed. Well, the hounds did more yelping in pain for an hour or two before anything else; the cat took them through some nasty briar patches as well as clawing them up, but finally I guess he was getting pretty tired and thought maybe he wouldn't let himself get so bushed the dogs could put him to an undignified death right there on the ground.

"So after he had his fun, the bobcat climbed into a tree and lay down on a low branch where he could spit into the faces of the dogs as they leaped up and tried to latch on to him. The tree is still there now, way off in the swamp standing by itself. You can see where Zack went back the next day and carved into it *Zack Tarbox killed a bobcat here in 1942*. It wasn't a very original thing to carve, but then Zack was young, and he can be excused.

"Anyhow, Zack and that idiot Tommy Carver got there a while later, and the cat didn't even bother moving to a higher branch when they shined the lantern in his face. He just stared into the lantern real patient, his eyes glowing like gas flames and making a nice bull's-eye,

and Zack aimed—it wasn't really any fancy shooting, to be honest—
and put one right between those eyes. The wildcat tumbled and the
dogs had their revenge a bit then, but Zack didn't want the pelt spoiled
so he kicked them off and hoisted the cat by the loose skin between
its shoulders.

"There was absolutely no moon that night; everyone had to sort
of walk back home through the tunnel of light made by the lantern.
They were happy, talking and patting the dogs on the head; they really
deserved it, those dogs, but then suddenly they heard a wildcat sing
way deep in the swamp. The dogs started whining; they'd had enough
of wildcats for a while, and then another wildcat sang off in the distance, then another closer up. Suddenly it was as if every wildcat that
ever lived in the swamp was out there singing and they were close
and far away and there were so many they were like fireflies on a hot
July night. Well, the dogs took off running; they made their way back
to my house and hid under the car until Zack took them home the
next day. And that idiot Tommy Carver got so scared he tripped and
fell and broke the lantern, so they had to finish the trip back home
in darkness with wildcats screaming all around and glowing eyes
peering out of bushes. That screaming of bobcats kept up all night till
dawn; I heard it out my window, even, and then light came to the sky
and they stopped one by one like candles going out until the last one
sang, long and sad, and it was the voice of the big tom Zack skinned
and put in a stretching frame that night. After that, there was no more
singing of bobcats in the swamp; in over forty years, not one has sung,
and I guess none will ever be heard to sing again."

Chapter 20

*G*randpa Tarbox cleared his throat; his voice had gotten hoarse as he talked, and he knocked the gray ashes out of his pipe to signal that the story was over. He looked at Toby, Manny's mother, and Manny in turn, studying each of them for a moment, and then returned his gaze to the window. It was dark outside now, and there was nothing to see except reflections on the panes of glass. Manny's mother had risen sometime during the story to flick on the electric light, but Manny couldn't remember her doing it.

"That was pretty good, Pa," said Manny's mother, her voice flat and her face without expression.

"Yes," said Grandpa Tarbox, still using his dreamy storytelling voice. "And you should've seen what happened that spring after we killed the wildcat. An infestation of cottontail rabbits like I hope never to see again. A sea of starving bunnies pouring out of that swamp onto all the roads. So many of them that the cars kept smashing them down until the entire State Road became paved in blood and brown fur half an inch thick from here to Newtown. And not as much as a radish top left growing in any garden for ten miles around." The old man was interrupted by a fit of coughing that had Manny ready to reach over and slap him on the back. When the spell was over, he continued talking, not waiting to catch his breath.

"Sure," Grandpa Tarbox said, gasping between words now. "You can expect trouble whenever you take away something that belongs in this world, any person or any thing, or you put something in that doesn't belong here at all."

Toby did not quit smiling once during the whole story; his face had become a grinning, mirthless mask. "That was okay, Gramps," Toby conceded. "Even with your 'idiot Tommy Carver' shit. Very optimistic. That wildcat reminds me of somebody, I can't think who."

Grandpa Tarbox did not bother to look at Toby; he looked instead at the grinning face reflected in the window. Then suddenly he began shaking; the pipe dropped right out of his fingers and clattered into the ashtray. His color was bad; splotches of purple came out on his temples and under his eyes.

"Easy, Grandpa," said Manny. "Do you need anything?" A cold terror trickled through him, and it wasn't just because the old man looked sick. It was something else, something that Manny was starting to understand, but that had not yet become clear for him. *What, Grandpa? What is really going on in your mind?* he wanted to ask.

"No," said the old man. "Nothing. A little brandy would be good, maybe, but there isn't any."

Manny's mother rose without a word, walked to the sink, and opened the cold-water tap. She let the water run for a minute before bringing a glass to her father.

Grandpa Tarbox drank the water down. It seemed to do him some good; the shaking eased, and the frightening purple stains on his face faded away.

Manny shot a glance at Toby, saw that he had stopped smiling, finally. He reached and placed a hand on the small of his grandfather's back, felt the old flesh quiver beneath his fingers.

The old man said nothing for a minute as two emotions battled for control of his face. Then he said, "That touching's for women, Manny." Manny took his hand away.

None of them spoke for a while; they all studied their nails or their reflections in the window or drummed on the tabletop. Finally, Toby got up, said good-bye, and left. He was smiling again as he went out the door.

Old Man Tarbox stayed for a while longer, then he too stood and went to the door.

Manny asked him if he wanted a ride, and he refused.

"Want to use my right-of-way on that railroad bed," he said.

Manny was still worried, so he followed his grandfather across the wooden footbridge and onto the cinders of the railroad bed. In the swamp, the insects were singing.

"I could drive you, really," Manny said. "You're not looking too good, if you want to know the truth."

"I could outwalk you right now," Grandpa Tarbox snapped. "You worry about your own health."

"Listen," said Manny. "I think you know something I don't. Why don't you let me in on it?"

"I don't share my troubles with anybody." Grandpa Tarbox was angry now, but he was so tired he was having trouble putting force into his voice. "If I make a mess, I can unmake it. It's no concern of anybody else. Good night, Manny."

He started off down the tracks, slowly. His back was bowed, as if he were carrying a burden.

Manny watched him until he disappeared into the blackness.

Manny walked back across the footbridge and went into the house. There were no lights on now, only the blue-gray glow of the black-and-white television flickering on the walls. He found his mother and Ida in the living room watching a fistfight on the TV. Two large men were holding another, smaller man against the hood of a car and punching him. Police sirens wailed in the background, and the two men ran. Their victim slumped to the ground.

The woman and the girl sat close together on the couch, holding hands and watching the televised mayhem. The sound of the television was turned up too loud; it hurt Manny's ears. He turned the volume down, then went over and sat on the couch next to Ida.

"Guess we had a rough couple of days," Manny said. "Huh, guys?"

Manny's mother turned to him and gave him a weak smile. She looked slightly bewildered, as if she didn't know quite where she was. "Your grandfather is not looking too good," she said. "He's showing his age now. Don't you think so, Manny?"

"Yeah," he said. "I agree. But maybe he just needs a little rest. You probably could use some sleep yourself."

"Yeah, I guess," his mother said.

"But I'll tell you, Ma. I think we're going to be okay now. I think we'll pull through all this. Don't you guys think?" He had to force the words out; his tongue did not want to form them.

"Oh, probably," his mother sighed. She gave him another crooked smile.

He turned to Ida then, bent himself a little in front of her so he could look directly into her face. The police were handcuffing someone on TV and the scene was reflected in the blue-green pools of her eyes.

"Don't you think so, Ida? Don't you think we'll come out of this okay?"

She said nothing, but in a moment a tear leaked out of the corner of each eye and made the reflected television scene quiver and dance. Then she lifted her arm and pointed at the screen.

"That's a bad guy," she said. She blinked, and the tears crept out onto her eyelashes.

*M*anny sat with them a while longer. But fear was chewing at his insides now like a plague of gypsy-moth worms, and he found it hard to sit still. He realized then he had been carrying a feeling of dread around inside him like a tumor for months. Sometimes the feeling faded and almost went away, but when it came back, it was always stronger than before.

He went to his room and smoked a joint with the window open, looking out at the stars and listening to the night insects. The pot smoke turned the fear down a little, made the chewing worms sleepy, but they didn't go away altogether. After a time he heard his mother and Ida go to bed. There was a brief argument; Ida had wanted to return to her familiar couch across from the wine-colored stain on the wall, but Mary Anne told her no, she had to sleep in her bed from now on. Ida didn't resist. It was the first time in weeks she was not sleeping by herself in the cellar.

He waited until everything was quiet on the first floor, then he pocketed his car keys and went out, making as little noise as he could. The sound of the old station wagon starting was like an explosion. He put it in gear and drove quickly out of the driveway, onto Dark Entry Road, and headed toward William Cahill's mansion.

When he got to the top of the hill he found that Cahill's front gate was closed. That surprised him; he had never seen it closed before. He drove up to the gate, expecting to be able to drive right through, and he had to brake hard to keep from bumping the wrought-iron bars with the car. He shut the engine off and got out, studied the chain and padlock that held the gate closed. He was wondering what to do when he heard a rustling in the bushes and looked off to his left. A man wearing a white T-shirt and a pistol holster that crossed his chest on one side was watching him, his fingers touching the handgrip of a gun that peeked out from under his arm. The other hand rested by his hip and held the butt of a flashlight.

"Who the hell are you?" asked the man in flat tones that betrayed no real curiosity.

"I'm Manny. I work here during the day. I'm a gardener."

The man kept his hand on the pistol. "What are you doing up here this time of the night, Manny? It's near ten o'clock."

"I have to talk to Mr. Cahill." Manny took a step away from the gate and moved two paces toward the questioning guard.

The guard studied him for a long moment, then took his hand away from the revolver and pulled a small two-way radio out of his belt. He held it up to his mouth and turned it on with a flick of his thumb; Manny heard a *beep* come from the instrument.

"Yes?" It was the voice of Cahill's maid.

"There's a kid here named Manny says he wants to talk to Mr. Cahill."

There was a pause, then the maid said, "Just a minute."

The guard let the hand with the radio drop hard to his side; he and Manny stared at each other. The guard was large, strong-looking with a beer gut, and had a huge nose that was bent to one side.

The maid's voice: "Mr. Cahill says Manny may come up to the house."

The guard dropped his eyes away from Manny immediately. He stuffed the walkie-talkie back into his belt, fumbled one-handedly with a set of keys he produced from somewhere, and opened the padlock. He pulled the chain through the bars of the gate, it made an angry, grinding noise, then he pulled the gate open without a word.

The maid had already opened the front door for him by the time he crossed the yard and went up the wheelchair ramp. She closed the door after he entered and led him down the wide hallway. Manny had a glimpse of a huge, carpeted living room with a stone fireplace off to the right of the passageway before the maid steered him into a small elevator at the end of the hall.

"Mr. Cahill is up on the second floor in the library," she said. "It'll be the only room up there with a light on, so you won't have trouble finding it." She pushed a button inside the elevator. Thin wrought-iron doors scissored closed, then the elevator began to move. It was a short ride; he soon found himself in a wide, black hallway. He walked out and saw light pouring through a pair of open double doors. It was an oak-paneled room with bookshelves and books on every wall. All the books were bound in the same green leather. Light reflecting off all that muted green gave the entire room a sickly hue.

Cahill was sitting in his wheelchair behind a desk. The desk was of oak and was very old; it contrasted strikingly with the gleaming modern metal of the old man's wheelchair. Cahill had a plaid afghan spread across his lap, and an open book rested on top of the afghan. He pretended not to notice Manny standing there until Manny knocked on the doorframe. His knuckles against the solid old wood made a feeble scratching sound.

Cahill looked up at the noise, and he and Manny regarded each other across the room.

Cahill said "Manuel" in his dry whisper that was like straw rustling in an attic. "Come in if you would."

There was nowhere to sit; Manny crossed the bare oak floor and stood before the desk. He was a little surprised at the stark atmosphere; somehow he had expected to find Cahill surrounded with mementos of his business successes—photos, awards, maybe even a few electronic toys to remind him of how rich he was. But there was nothing in the room besides the scarred old desk and the green rows of books.

"What can I do for you, Manuel?"

"Mr. Cahill, I want to know why you sent that lawyer over to the jail and then pulled all those strings to get me out. I'm nothing to you."

The old man's dry tongue snaked out of his mouth and tried to moisten the thin lips that always made Manny think of a turtle's beak.

"My carp were getting hungry," he said. It might have been a joke, but Manny studied Cahill's face and found no sign of humor.

"That isn't why, Mr. Cahill. That was a big favor; I'm not too stupid or too uneducated to know that. You didn't hire lawyers and make political phone calls just because there were weeds in the flower beds. There is something else going on here and I think you ought to tell me." As soon as the words were out of him, it struck him that he had said nearly the same thing to his grandfather two hours ago. Cahill and his grandfather: two old men with a lot of secrets.

Cahill chuckled then, or perhaps it was only a cough. Manny couldn't tell because no expression tugged at the old man's reptilian face. "You would be surprised," Cahill said, "how easy it was. City and town officials can be had like this . . ." He made a motion with his shriveled hand; Manny looked down and realized he was trying to snap his fingers. "State people come a little harder. Feds you never mess with because they are full of tricks and traps."

"But why for me?"

"Because it was so easy, I decided to make that minimum effort on your behalf. Perhaps I have come to like you, Manuel. You care about things that are growing and living, even if they do not belong to you. That is rare these days. Very rare."

Manny was stunned by the compliment. He opened his mouth to speak, and no sound came out for a moment. But still, something about Cahill's explanation seemed shallow and false to him.

When Manny could talk again, he said, "I really don't buy that, Mr. Cahill. What is it you want from me now?"

Cahill didn't hesitate; it seemed like a question he was used to answering. "I want you back to work tomorrow at nine o'clock sharp. I would like you to consider resuming your education. And I want you to stay out of trouble. If you end up in jail again, you will stay there, with no help from me or my associates."

Manny shook his head, confused and angry and fearful. "What's my schooling got to do with you?"

"I hate waste, that's all. It is just a request on my part, not an order."

"And you don't want anything else out of me? You don't figure I owe you?"

"No."

"Well, I do. Tell me how much that lawyer cost, and I'll pay you back. You can take it out of my pay."

Cahill's throat produced the sound that was not quite a laugh but might have been a cough. "You can't pay me back, Manuel. That lawyer didn't cost me anything. His firm did it as a favor to me. Just as the local people I called here got your charges dropped as a favor to me. You cannot repay a favor with cash."

"So that's it!" Manny said. His finger wanted to lift and poke itself at Cahill; he had to fight it down. "You want favors from me now. Well, you can put me back in jail, Mr. Cahill, because you won't get anything from me except the cash to pay back the lawyer. Soon as you ask me a favor, I'll give you the money and quit. I ain't some three-piece-suit guy from New Jersey. I'm saving all my money, and as soon as you want something from me, I'm giving it to you. No. I don't need favors. And I don't give them out."

"Manny." It was the first time Cahill ever used the name he preferred. "You forget it. What I did for you was easier than passing wind. Just show up for work tomorrow. That boy Toby is not doing a satisfactory job by himself."

"I'll be here," Manny said. The words were angry; he still felt challenged. He wanted to say something else, to hash out his independence a little more with Cahill, to clarify it, but no words occurred to him. So he turned and started to walk out of the library.

"Manny." Cahill seemed to force the name out of himself, as if some part of him did not want him to pronounce it. Manny stopped in the doorway but remained facing into the hall.

"I too was poor as a young man," Cahill said. A strange thickness had invaded Cahill's voice, choking his whisper so that it became almost inaudible. "I too used to work very hard. My father abandoned us when we were living in Brooklyn, and before I was seventeen my mother had died from the spinal cancer that has always run in our family." He paused as if expecting a comment from Manny.

Manny said nothing. It was embarrassing to have Cahill tell him personal things; his feelings were the same as if the old man had pulled up his shirt to show him the scar from an operation. Yet he also felt flattered because he knew there were few people Cahill would confide in.

"Maybe that is part of the reason I got you out," said Cahill, after he tired of waiting for Manny to speak.

Manny didn't doubt that it was part of the reason. But he also suspected that the old man was keeping a great part of his reason to himself. "Tomorrow," he said, and walked through the door and over to the elevator.

*M*anny slept badly that night, and was awake long before the sun came up. The watcher had been out there for a while, he was sure of it. He wondered if it was his grandfather watching the house, on his way back from dowsing for bones in the swamp. With the morning light, the heat began to build up in the attic room until he felt as if he were smothering. He kicked off the single damp sheet covering him and staggered to the window. Hot yellow light was already filtering through the backyard, boiling the morning dew into humidity. The air was full of the dirty snow of gypsy moths; there were so many now that they made a living, swirling blanket two feet above the lawn as well as several thinner layers between the ground and the treetops. As Manny watched, a male robin swooped down out of the swamp to land on the lawn, gave a single startled screech at the veil of pulsing wings covering everything, and veered away toward the brook.

"This is it," Manny said aloud to himself. "They're peaking out now." He watched in awe for a while, ignoring the sweat that ran down his sides, then his head began to throb from the intensity of the waxing light, and he turned and dressed and made his way down the ladder.

William Cahill did not roll out of his house that morning to watch Manny feed the carp. Manny was grateful; he felt he needed more time to decide what he really thought of the rich man's dark gift of influence. He made his regular morning rounds, feeding the fish and taking care of things that Toby had neglected while he was in jail.

By the time he was finished, it was noon, and he decided he needed a nap. He found a hiding place behind some bushes, but it was hot there, and too bright. So he went looking for another spot, a cool, dark place where no one would think of looking for him. He tried the tool shed for a while, but there were spiders in there, and their webs kept brushing across his face whenever he dozed and let his head roll.

Then he thought of the carriage house. It was the perfect spot; the second floor was cool and dark, and nobody would suspect that he would dare to be there. An electric chill ran through him; maybe he would get a glimpse of Stacy changing her clothes when she came back from tennis or wherever she had gone that day. He crept out of the tool shed and looked toward the house. Three Cadillacs from New York were lined up on the driveway, so there was no chance Cahill would even get out of the house before dark.

Manny went to the front of the carriage house, took a last look around the corner facing the mansion to make sure no one was watching him, and pushed his way inside. The brightness of daylight did not pursue him into the carriage house; as soon as he closed the door, he was enveloped in the soft, warm light that was the color of

Stacy Cahill's skin. The light touched him like a caress. The antique dolls watched silently from around the room; they seemed to be listening to the heartbeat that throbbed in his ears. His feet whispered across the floor toward a small, untidy pile of Stacy's clothes. He lifted a T-shirt from the pile and held it up to his face; it smelled of her. The intimate scent was enough to send blood surging between his legs. He moaned softly into the shirt and then, self-consciously, feeling unclean, he set it back down and looked guiltily around him. The old dolls observed him silently.

Manny climbed the ladder to the unfinished loft. He found an old blanket up there, and spread it down on the bare planks of the floor. Then he kicked off his sneakers, lay down, and fell asleep to the droning of insects and the summer song of birds out on the lawn.

He awoke much later to the boom of the stereo in the room below him. He was confused at first, swimming up groggily out of the depths of his sleep, and when he realized where he was, his heart slapped against the wooden floor.

It was the same beautiful, indescribable music she had played the time he and Toby had both spied on her from the loft.

Excited, Manny rolled slowly onto his back so as to make no noise and rubbed the sleep from his eyes. He knew what the music meant; already there was an insistent tightness in the front of his pants, and he didn't want to rush things. He wanted to tease himself just a little before he put his face to a crack in the floor and saw her. He built Stacy in his mind: her little girl's face that belied the wise, rich girl's eyes; her sweet, upturned breasts; her tight, flat stomach, smooth as sculpted quartz; her ass that was as soft and white as a snowdrift, with the wide hips that swung and made her look like she was dancing even if she was only walking across the lawn; and her coltish legs and the soft, blond hair between them that reminded Manny of the white, weightless silk inside autumn milkweed pods. Slowly, still teasing himself, he rolled back onto his stomach and drew back the blanket to expose the cracks in the floor. Snakelike, he crept on his belly to the widest crack and pressed his good eye down against it.

For a moment she wasn't there; she was out of his field of vision. Manny could see the shiny vinyl record revolving on the turntable, and a single stuffed chair. He heard the faint scuff of bare feet against wood above the sound of the record, and heard the floorboards of the old carriage house creak with her movement. Then Stacy swept into view. Manny caught his breath; she was already down to her bra and panties, and she was spinning and letting her arms fly into the air and making her hair ripple and fly like a stand of wild rye in a windstorm. She was a strange mixture of girl and woman, but to Manny, without her clothes she was more girl than anything, with her pink, glowing skin and her effortless dancing that wasn't dancing so much as the joy of life shouted with her arms and legs and head and torso. Stacy tilted her head back, would have been looking directly up at Manny except that her eyes were closed, and she was smiling. The smile reminded Manny of the way Ida had smiled in her sleep years ago in the happy times before everything went bad. Her hands went into the air; she pumped them at Manny one, two, three times, fingers pointed right at him. Then her elbows bent and her hands went behind her back. The hands struggled there for a moment, then her bra dropped to the floor, and it was her breasts now, pink as cotton candy, that were pointing up at Manny. He wanted to laugh with excitement and glee; his finger found its way to his mouth and he bit down on it, hard. She was putting on a real show; it was as if she knew she was being watched.

Stacy did an Indian dance around the chair, her palm tapping her lips in a silent war whoop. Then she started spinning. She spun like a top three times around the stuffed chair, then spun out of Manny's field of vision. He waited impatiently, his breathing ragged, and when she was back dancing below him, her panties were gone. She bent backward, her back pumping to the beat of the music, and her hands rubbed the creamy insides of her thighs. Then suddenly the music was over; Manny heard the needle of the record player skipping at the end of the album.

She froze then, her back arched and her eyes closed and her hands resting on her thighs, and Toby appeared. He materialized like a ghost out of the shadows and into Manny's field of vision. He was smiling and naked, and he went up to Stacy and took her by the shoulders and pulled her straight.

Manny felt nothing. It was like being hit in the back of the head with a brick, and as he watched, the hands that had been jabbing the air at him a few moments before came out and around and circled Toby's back. Stacy and Toby twined like snakes, kissing for a long while as Manny watched, waiting for the feelings to hit him.

After a long moment of kissing, Toby gently pushed Stacy away. Her face was tilted back as they separated; she wore an expression of agony at having to let go of him. Toby moved backward and sat down in the stuffed chair, and she followed him dreamily, drawn by magnetism, and sank to her knees in front of him.

The first feeling came to Manny as she reached between Toby's legs and gathered him into her small, pretty hands. She stroked and petted Toby, cooing as if she were handling one of her antique china dolls. Then she bent over him and her head began to rise and fall in a tidal rhythm, and the rage hit Manny.

His whole body stiffened with rage, every muscle tensed as if a high voltage were running through him. He opened his mouth to scream, and instead of screaming he dug his teeth into the wood of the floorboards. The wood was bitter, and the taste filled his mouth as he plowed splinters with his jaws.

He didn't want to watch them anymore; a voice inside him kept saying, *Roll over, Manny,* but he couldn't roll over, and his teeth kept working away despite the voice, which told him, *Stop biting the floor, Manny. It's crazy.*

Then Toby grunted; his head flew back, and his eyes were wide open, and he was smiling as if he knew Manny was looking right down through the floor at him.

Stacy stood, bent over Toby's face, kissing him, then she danced silently out of Manny's view.

Toby unknowingly held Manny's eyes for a while longer, then he let his eyes fall closed, breaking the spell.

Manny rolled onto his back, quivering now, all the muscles in his body twitching and hopping. His mouth worked open and closed; he wanted to make a noise, but didn't know whether to release an angry sound or a bereaved one.

He heard Toby and Stacy talking below him, then the door to the carriage house opened and closed, and he realized they were gone.

He lay on his back staring up at the ceiling for a long time. Then he twisted violently back onto his stomach, bumping his forehead against the floor. The shock startled him out of his pain for a moment, so he lifted his head and dropped it again against the floor. It felt good, pain to fight pain, so he lifted his head again and brought it smashing down, over and over. The floorboards were loose and had plenty of give to them, so that he really couldn't hurt himself, but his skull slapping against the wood made a satisfyingly loud sound that made him think he was doing more damage than he really was. He banged the floor again and again and again, feeling the anger flowing out of him, until he was exhausted and half stunned. Then he rolled over onto his back, telling himself, *My nerves are dead. I don't feel anything. I can't feel anything. Nothing matters.*

After a time he got up, nearly losing his balance as he stood, and almost falling again as he climbed the ladder down to the first floor. The sunlight hit him like a slap in the face as he pushed open the carriage-house door and reeled dizzily toward his car.

When he heard Toby calling him from somewhere, he began to run, his legs churning drunkenly. He ran toward the car as Toby shouted, "Manny! Manny! Stop!" He pulled the door open, poured himself into the front seat, started the old station wagon, and made gravel fly as he shot out of the driveway and down the hill.

*H*e stopped somewhere to put a little gas in the car and went driving upstate. He didn't even know where he was; he took back roads, speeding, the radio in the car screaming loud enough to drown out his thoughts. He had found a punk-rock station powerful enough to reach him even in the hills of northwestern Connecticut, and he listened to songs about hating and burning and killing and raping. After a time he pulled into a country package store, there seemed to be one every two miles along those country roads, and he bought a case of beer. The girl behind the counter was blond and fat and wore too much blue makeup on her eyes. She didn't even ask to see Manny's fake ID card.

After that, he drove and drank and listened to more songs about violence and the worthlessness of life. He went way north, through a spooky, nearly deserted little place full of high-tension wires called Falls Village. He drove through Salisbury and Lakeville, looking at rich houses and rich people out the window of his car. He knew the New York border was close by, was briefly tempted to cross it and head west, but then realized that he had no money for food or gas, and that he would end up stuck halfway across upstate New York and at the mercy of police and punks and rich people. So, with a head full of beer and death, he turned back.

The gas tank of the old station wagon was almost empty when he rolled down Dark Entry Road and into his mother's driveway. It was twilight, and gypsy moths were snowing down heavily in front of the headlights of his car. Twice on the way back they had gotten so thick he was blinded and almost ran the car off the road. But he made it, finally, and was unzipping himself even before he was completely out of the car so that he could take a long, burning piss on the gravel of the driveway. There were still sixteen bottles of beer left out of the case he had bought; he counted them twice so he would know exactly how drunk he could get. He dragged the case out of the car, leaving the eight empties on the floor of the passenger side, and carried it into the backyard.

The lawn chairs were waiting for him in the singing summer dusk, and he settled heavily into one of the chairs and set the box of beer bottles down on another. He twisted the cap off a beer; the serrated edge bit into his hand. It felt good. He sailed the cap off into the night swamp and never heard it land.

His mother came out after a time wearing a white bathrobe and a concerned face. "Manny," she said. "What's the matter?"

Manny burped. "Nothing," he told her. "Not a damn thing."

"Well, don't you want something to eat?" She was a white-clad wraith in the darkness.

"Nope," he said.

She stood watching him for a while, not speaking. After a time she went back into the house.

Then Ida came out. She came up through the cellar and took a winding, indirect path over the lawn to him, the way a bee zigzags between flowers. She sat down in the vacant lawn chair and stared across at him. Her eyes had a luminous quality in the darkness; Manny avoided them. She said, "Manny, I think . . ." Her voice was full of tears; it had that thick, liquid quality to it.

Manny didn't need anyone crying around him. "Listen, Ida," he said. "I don't need that right now. Go back in the goddamn house." He was sorry as soon as the words were out, but he was hurt, and the anger that was shaking him inside would not let him take them back. He slapped viciously at a mosquito that had landed on his arm. The mosquitoes were out in force now, and they enraged him; they did not respect his grief.

Ida stayed a moment longer, then she rose and drifted back to the cellar following the curious, twisted path that only she could see.

He drank a beer, and then another. Stars blossomed across the sky, and the moon, nearly full, rose above the lawn. Gypsy moths fluttered against the moon as if it were a lantern hanging from a tree. Mosquitoes bit, and Manny slapped, snarling.

In time a car growled up the driveway and parked in front of the house. Manny knew from the sound of the engine whose car it was, and he opened a beer and let the cap sail; it flashed gold in the moonlight before landing in the weeds somewhere. He heard shoes hissing through the high grass of the lawn, and then Toby's silhouette was standing before him at the corner of the house, not daring to come closer.

"Manny," said Toby.

"Fuck you," Manny said. But he was suddenly calm, surprising himself. It was as if saying fuck you to Toby was all he had needed to start the poison draining from inside him.

"Manny, listen. I did it for a reason. I knew you were up in the loft watching."

"That's really great. Get the fuck out of here, Toby."

"Listen, Manny, we're friends. Best friends. Remember that."

"No way. No more." Manny tipped his lawn chair up on the back legs and began rocking.

"Will you listen, you stubborn bastard? That girl is a whore, man, a real pig."

"Yeah," Manny said. "I'll go along with that."

"Well, I knew you were getting all hung up on her, partner. I thought the only way to convince you she was no good was to show you firsthand."

Manny snorted, amused. That had to be the most see-through lie he had ever heard Toby tell. He drained the last gulp from his beer bottle and debated whether to hurl it at the figure facing him in the darkness.

"And another thing, Manny. I think it's getting to be time to do the thing I started you out at Cahill's to do. Manny, we've got to rip that place off and go to California together, and there was no way you'd ever agree to it if you were in love with Stacy Cahill."

Manny cocked his arm and launched the beer bottle.

Toby never saw it coming, and when it hit his chest, he said "Ow!" in a startled voice. Manny heard him rubbing his chest. Then Toby said, "I don't take that personally, Manny. I know you're mad right now. I know you'll come around after you think things over for a while."

Toby's silhouette flinched; he was expecting Manny to throw another bottle at him. He turned and hurried out of throwing range, and in a moment Manny heard Mrs. Carver's powerful car start up in the driveway and go growling out onto Dark Entry.

He sat for a long time, drinking beer, listening to the night insects, and savoring his little victory over Toby. Then he dozed.

Chapter 21

*T*he slam of a car door out in the driveway woke him. At first he thought Toby had come back, and he reached down and started gathering beer bottles near the aluminum legs of his chair. The bottles fell together and made a tremendous clanking racket in the still of the evening.

He heard two sets of feet coming toward him through the long, dew-wet grass, and the two men, cops, came around the corner of the house. He could tell they were cops by the silhouettes of their hats and the glint of moonlight on their badges.

"Manny?" It was Jamison's voice.

He struggled up out of his lawn chair, stiff from the dampness and sloppy with drinking.

The two men stopped as soon as they saw him moving, so Manny advanced on them, his hands theatrically high in the air.

"Okay, boys," he said. "You got me. What did I do this time?"

"Manny," Jamison said quietly. "Your grandfather has had an accident."

Manny stopped and let his arms slide down to his sides. He noticed something swinging at Jamison's side. He looked down and saw the black cop had a camera, one of those Polaroid jobs for taking instant pictures, and he was swinging it by the plastic strap. Then he looked up and saw that the other cop was Joe White.

"What?" Manny heard himself ask.

"Down on Wolfpit Road. He ran his truck off the road onto dump property and hit a tree right across from where Charlie Raymond used to live."

Manny felt himself shaking his head now. "That can't be," he said. "Grandpa never drives at night. He has trouble seeing the road."

"He hit his head pretty hard, Manny, looks like," Jamison continued. "Ambulance guys took him away on a spine board, just in case. But he's alive as far as we know, kid. We came to tell you instead of calling, because we figured your mom might answer the phone. We figured it was better to tell you."

Manny's hands bunched into fists; his nails dug hard into his palms. "Spine board?" he said. "Spine board?" He spat the words angrily.

White spoke then. His voice shook, full of horror. "It was the strangest goddamn thing I seen in my career," he said. "You know those gypsy moths that are everywhere? Well, Christ, when we found him, there were thousands of them things all over the inside of the truck cab, just crawling around. There were big, fat white ones, too, laying eggs on the dashboard. And they were all over his face. You couldn't even see his goddamn face. I never seen anything at all like that. It was—" Jamison reached over and put his hand on his partner's arm.

"Joe," he said. "Why don't you go back to the cruiser? I'll take care of this, okay?"

White obeyed, turning and lumbering across the lawn.

Manny watched him go, then swung his head to Jamison. "What the fuck was he talking about?"

"Nothing important," Jamison said evenly. "He's just upset, that's all. Listen, Manny, this camera." He lifted the camera, pushed it gently into Manny's stomach, and held it there patiently.

In a moment, Manny felt it with his hands. There was a bar of flash cubes attached to the top of it. He took it from Jamison.

"We found the camera in the front seat with your grandfather. We took it out so no one would steal it. We also found a gun, an old, rusty thirty-eight revolver, loaded, but we're going to hang on to that, if it's all the same to you."

Manny nodded woodenly. Then he said, "But what was he doing there?"

"We were going to ask you if you had any ideas about that. Guess you don't, right?"

Manny shook his head. Then his whole body started shaking, and dry gasping sounds came out of his throat. A dam broke somewhere inside and tears rushed out of him, spilling down his face. He was ashamed, but there was no way he could stop.

Jamison was there, suddenly, surrounding him with huge, black, warm arms, and Manny automatically dropped the camera and hugged him back, tight. But it was just for a moment.

"Poor kid," Jamison said, almost to himself. There was pity in his voice.

Manny shoved away from him then, violently, and he lifted his T-shirt and rubbed his face with it. "I'm all right," he barked. "I'm okay. Ain't nothing poor about me."

Jamison stood silently and let him get his gasping under control for a minute. Then he said, "Okay, Manny. You're right. You're a tough kid, I know. That's why we came to you first. We need help with your mom. Can we count on you?"

"Sure," Manny said. "Yeah."

"Good. I think it's probably important that you and Mrs. Moreno go to the hospital soon as possible. You got to tell her the news and get her ready to go, understand?"

"Yeah. You going to drive us?"

"We can't, pal. It's against regulations. But we'll give you an escort and set a pace for you so you don't drive too fast and get hurt. Deal?"

"Okay," Manny said. He rubbed the back of his hand across his face and walked toward the house.

When he got into the house, his mother was already awake and waiting by the door. She wore a bathrobe and the ratty slippers that looked like drowned animals. She was frightened.

"I heard voices," she said.

"Yeah, it's cops." Manny tried to meet her eyes, but he couldn't. "Grandpa had an accident. He's still alive. Get ready, we're going to the hospital."

"Oh," she said. Her hands fluttered up to her face, brushed across her tired, frightened eyes to wipe away tears that had not yet come. "Oh."

"Go on now," Manny said, his voice trembling. "Brush your hair and everything. Get dressed. The police are waiting for us."

She stood unmoving, wiping nonexistent tears with her fingertips, until Manny tapped her lightly on the elbow. Then she looked at him, startled.

"Yes," she said. "Right now." She turned and walked down the hall to her room, frail legs sticking out from her bathrobe. Her door closed; Manny heard drawers opening and closing, and things falling off shelves. He waited for her, leaning against the doorframe. The two cops sat in their cruiser with a light on; they were also waiting.

She came out soon wearing shorts and a new blouse. Her hair was brushed. She didn't look too bad, except for the ruby gash of lipstick she had smeared across her mouth with shaking fingers.

"Okay," Manny said. "Good."

"What about Ida?"

"Let her stay. She's too young to get in, anyway."

"But shouldn't we tell her?"

"Ida already knows," Manny said.

When Manny's mother saw Grandpa Tarbox lying beneath white sheets in the intensive care ward, she tried to scream, but all that came out of her mouth was a sort of hoarse grunt. She broke away from Manny and ran out of the room; he ran after her and found her throwing up in the hallway. She was scrambling down the hall on her hands and knees, being sick, and two nurses came and helped Manny pull her to her feet. The sight of the nurses calmed her a little, and she stood against the wall, panting, her eyes glazed and wild. One of the nurses took out a Kleenex and wiped her mouth for her, clucking her tongue as she would cluck soothingly to a frightened child. Then another nurse appeared carrying a glass of water and a plastic cup containing a white pill. Manny's mother took the pill and drank the water, turning her head from one to another of the nurses as they spoke to her in calming tones.

Manny left his mother with the covey of nurses and walked back into his grandfather's room. He was almost sick himself this time. The old man's body was a shapeless lump beneath the sheets. He was turbaned completely in white bandages, and his mouth was violated by a hose from a breathing machine. The hose was taped into place so it couldn't fall out. The respirator itself stood beside the bed, pumping air into Manny's unconscious grandfather with a steady sighing sound. A needle on the front of the machine jumped with every breath of air it forced into the unmoving body. Another machine stood nearby, echoing Grandpa Tarbox's every heartbeat with an electronic beep. The light in the ward was glaring; it seared Manny's eyeballs. There were other beds, but they were empty.

A nurse came in. She picked up a chart at the end of the old man's bed and wrote something.

"Why does he need that thing?" Manny asked. "The scuba thing?" His voice was unsteady.

"He doesn't seem to want to breathe," she whispered, not looking at him. She glanced at her watch and left, her soft-soled shoes squeaking on the floor.

Manny walked slowly closer to the bed until he was standing directly over his grandfather. Manny knew the old man wouldn't like the respirator if he could see it. And he wouldn't like anyone to see him with his false teeth out and his cheeks sunken in.

"It's your own fault, Grandpa," he said, as if addressing a complaint from the old man. "And you better not die on me. You got some explaining to do. I'm getting sick of your deceitfulness." He wiped a single tear from his eye. He felt numb all over.

Then his mother was back in the room. Her face was ash-colored, but her eyes were dead calm now. A young doctor accompanied her; he glanced at the chart at the end of the bed, explained he was not the doctor that had treated the old man, that he was only the doctor on duty. He said there was no skull fracture or evidence of spinal damage, only a bad concussion along with bad cuts on his scalp and forehead. But the real problem was that the old man had stopped breathing at some time, nobody knew for how long, so there was a large chance of brain damage. Grandpa Tarbox was currently being given drugs to prevent brain swelling, and it was possible he might wake up tomorrow, or not at all. It would be a good sign if the old man started breathing on his own again soon.

The young doctor paused a minute, then asked if they had any questions.

Manny looked at him. "Grandpa hates doctors," he said.
The doctor tried to smile and left.

*M*anny and his mother went home at eight o'clock the next morning.
The old man's condition had not changed during the night; the only
change in the immaculate death-watch room was the occasional whispering presence of a nurse who came in, did things around the bed,
and stole away. When he got home, Manny called up Cahill's house
and told the housekeeper he would not be in that day. Then he climbed
up to his attic room and slept as if he were in a coma.

He and his mother returned to the hospital late that afternoon.
Mary Anne was a well-behaved zombie now; she had gotten a prescription for some Valiums and had gone out and bought them while
Manny slept. When he caught her taking one, he took the brown plastic container away from her and poured the white tablets into his
hand. There were enough for perhaps five days. He didn't have the
heart to throw them away.

"When you're done with these, you won't get any more, will you?"
he asked, weighing the pills in his palm.

His mother followed the rising and falling of his hand with her
eyes, hypnotized. "No," she said, "I won't."

He hesitated a moment, then poured the tablets back into the
container and gave them to her. She stashed them carefully in her
worn handbag.

Later, in the hospital, his mother fell asleep on his shoulder as
they watched Grandpa Tarbox for signs of life. There were no signs,
save the mechanical wheezing of the respirator. They didn't stay all
night this time; they stayed until eleven o'clock, then they went home
in the old station wagon. Before his mother left the room, she went
over and touched Old Man Tarbox lightly on an arm that was exposed
and strapped down to receive intravenous fluids.

"Goody-bye, Daddy," she said.

Manny felt like crying then, for the first time since he had broken
from Jamison's pitying embrace. But he decided then that no, goddamn it, he would not cry, he would never cry again as long as he
lived. He was a man now, the man of his family, just as the infuriating
letters his father sent from South America said, and men didn't cry.

Men did things; they fought and lashed out at dangerous and evil things, they tore themselves apart working, but they did not cry.

.

Summer's back was broken. It seemed to Manny that just at the time his grandfather crashed his truck into a tree and retreated into unconsciousness, the season's decline toward fall began. A breeze came from somewhere, from out of Canada probably, and the heat of summer scattered like a dream. The days were suddenly cool enough that Manny kept his T-shirt on all day while working at Cahill's. At night his mother put on a sweater before going down to the hospital to see her father.

The gypsy moths began dropping everywhere like the petals of wasted flowers. The August breeze seemed to knock them right out of the sky; they lay dead and scattered all over the swamp and floated away toward the sea in fast-running brooks. The birds would hardly touch them when they were alive because of the bitter powder on their wings, but in death they made food for legions of insects that took them away to store them for winter provisions. Ida sat for hours on the lawn watching the ants parade dead moths through the grass.

Once, while Manny sat dozing in a lawn chair, Ida looked up at him and asked, "Is Grandpa dead too, Manny?"

Manny, his eyes still closed, said, "No, not yet," before he could catch himself. He was suddenly frightened then and went out to walk down the railroad bed and pace away his fear.

The new wind brought other changes. Stacy and Toby had a fight; Manny heard them arguing behind the carriage house while he was working late one day. He was out in the orchard picking apples, and he left his work and wandered to the back of the property so he wouldn't have to listen to them. But the cool wind brought their sounds to him if not their words; he heard crying, hers, as well as Toby's unmistakable laughter. The next day she took a plane somewhere for the rest of the summer.

It was a relief not to have her around anymore. He and Toby still spoke rarely, but with the girl away, Manny's hot resentment vanished to be replaced by coolness, like the indifferent briskness of the coming autumn.

One day about a week after Grandpa Tarbox first went into the hospital, Toby stopped by in his mother's fire-red car. Manny, Mary Anne, and Ida were sitting at the kitchen table, eating hamburgers and canned soup, when he walked in the door. No one stood to welcome him, and he made no move to sit. Both Manny and Ida stared down at their plates.

"Sorry to interrupt," Toby said. He did seem sorry. "But I stopped by Grandpa's house today." It was the first time Manny had ever heard Toby refer to the old man as anything but Gramps. "I wanted to make sure the place was secure and locked up and everything so nobody could get in. I guess you all forgot, because I found the back door open."

"Yeah," Manny admitted. "I forgot." His eyes never left his plate.

"Well, I went inside first to make sure everything was okay, and it was. So I was just about ready to shut the door when I saw this pipe sitting in an ashtray on the kitchen table." He drew Grandpa Tarbox's old pipe out of his pocket and set it down before them. The three of them stared at it.

"And it occurred to me that when Mr. Tarbox wakes up, he might like to see this pipe sitting on the table next to him, even if the nurses don't let him smoke it. I'd have taken it over myself, but there's no way I can get into the intensive care. I figure you folks might like to take it in."

Manny looked up now. There was no trace of smile on Toby's face. He felt like crying then, so he stuck a fork between his teeth and bit down, hard.

Manny's mother reached and touched the pipe, stroked it. It shifted slightly under the gentle pressure of her fingers.

"Thank you, Toby," she said. "I really should have thought of that." She looked up at Toby, and Manny saw her smile for the first time in ages.

Chapter

22

*T*he finger-worn old pipe seemed almost to have a magic effect on Grandpa Tarbox. It seemed to remind him somehow that he had one more story to tell, and the day after they set it beside him, the doctors took the respirator out of his mouth and he began to breathe by himself. They watched him for several days; he kept right on breathing, and his heartbeat was strong and steady, so they moved him out of intensive care. The pipe followed the old man down to his new semiprivate room, and by the time August slid into an unseasonably chilly September, he was opening his mouth and saying things.

At first, Manny and his mother were relieved. But it might have been easier on them if Grandpa Tarbox had kept quiet. The old man recognized nobody, and it was obvious from the things he shouted out that there was a continual nightmare waging war against him inside his bruised skull.

"Alexis?" he would shout. "Al, don't go. Don't you goddamn do it. Dangerous people, Al. You don't understand, but I know. Danger, Al. Oh my God!"

Usually he shouted at Manny's father, but sometimes he thought he was talking to Terry. "Terry, stop!" he would say. "It's colder than a tomb out there! Stay home, Terry! Don't you dare leave that house!"

Sometimes he would shout so loudly that the nurses would come rushing in and give him a shot to sedate him so the heart patient who shared his room could sleep. The shot would reduce him to agonized moaning, and sometimes he would still be moaning and muttering the next day when Manny and his mother returned. But when he opened his eyes and saw Manny standing there, he would gasp with horror and the shouting would resume. For Grandpa Tarbox, Manny was Alexis, and all the time Manny stayed in his room, he harangued him with warnings about dark, hidden, deadly things.

Manny's mother was terribly upset about the old man's conversations with her missing husband and son. She broke her promise to Manny and renewed her prescription for tranquilizers. Manny did not oppose her. And she took away the old wooden pipe, convinced that it was haunting her father. But even with the pipe gone, the screaming and pleading continued.

One day in mid-September Manny came home from working at Cahill's to find his mother sitting by herself at the kitchen table. She smiled up at him groggily.

"I think I took too many," she said. She held up the brown plastic pill bottle to show him; it slipped out of her hand, bounced once on the floor, and went rolling away. She bent to retrieve it, and it was only then that Manny saw the wooden cigar box sitting on the table. It was Terry's box, the box where he stored all his father's letters.

The letters were out of the box and scattered all over the table; the sight of them sent blood pounding to his ears. He felt dizzy for a moment, and he snatched at the kitchen doorframe to keep from falling over.

Just then his mother slid from her chair and crashed to the floor. She tried to get up, but couldn't, then lay back with a silly, lazy smile on her face. Her eyes closed slowly, the lids fluttering.

"Goddamn you!" He rushed over and hauled her roughly into her chair by the armpits. The fear was chewing at him hard inside now, and he was sweating. "Why did you do this?"

She tried to smile, but her lips slid lopsidedly down one side of her face. "I had to, Manny," she said in a small, faraway voice. "Those things coming out of your grandfather's mouth mean something, whether you want to admit it or not."

"So you searched my room, is that it? My goddamn room!" He was shouting now; he knew what she had to tell him, and he was desperate to put it off for as long as he could. Put it off forever, maybe. "It wasn't right to do that," he said, blinking at the letters on the table and wishing they would disappear. "It's never right to search a person's things, even if you think it's for a good reason. This—"

"Manny," his mother said. She was struggling to stay upright in the chair. "I didn't have to search. I already knew about that loose floorboard and that cigar box. Terry told me."

"Terry?" His voice was quiet again now, but he was panting desperately.

"Yeah. When he was just a little guy, he wrote his last will and testament on a piece of notebook paper and gave it to me to put in the safe-deposit box at the bank. Real cute; he thought it was a grownup thing to do. Willed everything to you that was in that box and left all his Elvis Presley records to his father. Ain't that just something?"

"Oh," said Manny. He wanted to say something else, but he didn't trust his voice. He was never going to cry again; he remembered that promise to himself, and he forced his grief down the deep well it came from. Then something hit the paper below him; it was a spot of crimson that splashed down on the scattered papers. Another drop hit the paper, and Manny touched his nose. His fingers brought away blood. He pulled a handkerchief from the pocket of his work pants and dabbed absently at his nose.

"You see," his mother said. "I always knew where to find those letters. Guess I really didn't want to look at them. Same reason you didn't want me to see them."

"Oh no," said Manny. The blood was trickling from him steadily now and he had to hold the handkerchief right up against his nose.

"Yeah," his mother said. She wasn't looking at him; her gaze was directed down at the letters littering the table. "I know your grandpa. Know him enough to tell when he's having screaming nightmares because of a bad conscience. Figured maybe if I could tell him what we already knew, I could get him to stop screaming every time he looked at you and maybe help him to live for us. We need him."

"So, what is it?" Manny asked. He was using the handkerchief to cover part of his mouth now. He found it convenient to muffle and disguise the tremble in his voice.

She looked at him then, made the unsteady smile that was weighted on one side. Then her eyes fell back to the table.

"Those letters aren't from your father."

Manny shook his head, tried to signal her to stop, he couldn't catch her eye. She kept her gaze on the table.

"Nope," she said. "Your grandfather wrote every one of them. Did a fairly good job at forging Al's writing, too, but not good enough to fool me."

"Oh," Manny said.

"But I guess I really knew all along. Don't you know those typed addresses your grandfather put on those letters was a giveaway? Al was good at a lot of things, but typing was never one of them."

"God." The blood was coming out faster now, and the handkerchief was soaked. Manny tossed it into the sink and tore enough paper towels off the roll on the counter to cover his entire face.

"And you know, after I found out that I already knew that the letters were not from Al, I said to myself, 'Mary Anne, Manny knows too, or at least he suspects. That's why he never showed you one letter in five years. Because he's not a mean boy, and not to show me, even if his father told him not to, would have been pure meanness, if they were really from my Al.'"

The blood was spurting out of Manny now, running through his paper towels and onto the floor. He was starting to get dizzy.

"So," she said. "Al must really be dead, don't you think?"

"Son of a bitch," Manny said.

His mother looked up at him and saw the bleeding for the first time. No alarm registered on her face.

"Try a couple of ice cubes in a washcloth," she said. "I'd get them, but I'm really too tired."

After that, Manny couldn't stay in the house. First he put a clean handkerchief in his pants pocket in case his nose started to bleed again. Then he crossed the footbridge and went out onto the old railroad bed. He turned and walked south toward his grandfather's house. He picked up a long stick someplace and dragged the tip in the cinders beside him, scoring a long line through the small, hardy weeds that had begun growing there. A flock of crows flew over, breaking into harsh, scolding calls when they spied Manny moving through their territory.

"Dead!" the crows called. *"Dead! Dead!"* Then they were gone.

After a time his feet brought him close to the old man's now-vacant house; he saw the red-shingled roof peaking out over the worm-ravaged treetops. Manny stopped then, suddenly realizing that he would not be able to bear walking on his grandfather's property without seeing the old man there, without hearing the sarcastic, amused greeting: *Thought you forgot how to walk since you got your license.* Manny turned back.

When he got home, Manny saw that the old station wagon was missing. His mother must have gone to the hospital, he thought. He found Ida in the cellar, her eyes wide and glazed, staring at the blood-colored stain on the wall. Manny shivered when he saw her, realizing suddenly that the afternoon had turned cool. He tried getting her to talk; he murmured stupid things about the television programs she watched sometimes and he stroked her red hair, but she did not take her eyes from the wall. She began to rock on the old couch next to him. He got a strong feeling then she was waiting for him to say something about the letters.

"You knew, didn't you, Ida?" he asked finally.

"Daddy's ghost is here, Manny," she told him. "But I can't understand him; he can't talk like us anymore. He makes sounds like *rat-tat-tat.*"

Then she turned away from him, finished with him, and went back to her study of the wall.

He was frightened now, suddenly; he realized for the first time that she probably knew almost everything about the disappearances of his father and brother as well as the nearness of the death of Grandpa Tarbox. Maybe she even foresaw other tragedies not yet suspected by Manny or anyone else, and it was that knowledge that had terrified her and driven her back inside herself. She had gone down a rabbit hole no head doctors would be able to pull her out of unless they found a way to take away the gift of foresight and madness her father had brought her from another continent.

He decided then what he was going to do. His mother was right; for five years the two of them had avoided the truth about the disappearances. Ida had known the truth, and it made her crazy. Grandpa Tarbox knew the truth as well, and he tried to cover it up. But when his lies started to backfire, he took his car and went to prowl Cahill's dump property with a camera and a pistol for some reason, and ran his car into a tree on the way.

Manny decided to look for the truth, now. It was the only way. His father was dead. All right. Terry was dead too, he might as well face it. And at least part of the truth about everything was on Cahill property. The truth was whatever Old Man Tarbox had been planning to photograph there. Something Cahill's people were doing there, maybe.

Manny had avoided that end of the swamp for five years; he realized he had not gone up by the dump even once since Terry vanished. But he would not avoid it anymore.

He kissed Ida on the forehead, then went to find a jacket. The day was cool even though the sun was not down yet. The night would be chilly.

He went up the railroad bed, intending to enter the dump property by the back way to lessen his chances of getting caught by Marconi and his armed guards. Manny's feet scuffed softly through the black cinders of the track bed; black dust puffed into the air with each step. Once, a fox with a limp woodchuck in its mouth crossed his path. It was a red fox, but it wore the blue-gray coat worn by most of the red foxes of the swamp. You hardly ever saw a true red fox's coat here; they blended into the land better when they were dark. The fox stopped for a second to eye Manny, unafraid, then cocked its head back and leaped gracefully, clearing the high weeds at the side of the railroad bed. Foxes were elusive; Manny usually took it as an omen of good luck when he saw one. But he did not feel lucky now. Manny watched the fox trot up through the woods and vanish over a hill.

Long before Manny got to the dump, he could tell he was approaching it. The foliage up at that end of the swamp had become sickly; trees were dying, and many had already perished long before the gypsy-moth caterpillars arrived to devour their leaves. Swirling, circular rainbows of oil sat atop pools that had once been the spawning places of trout and dace and had harbored migrating waterfowl in the autumn and spring.

Manny found four dead songbirds, a thrush and three red-winged blackbirds, within a stone's throw of each other along the track bed. He had known that Cahill's people were doing more than shredding old tires on the dump property, that they were doing far more sinister things, and here was proof. A strange chemical odor hung in the air, and by the time Manny got to the high chain-link fence surrounding the dump itself, the smell was bad enough to make his eyes water.

It was still daylight when he got there. A padlocked gate closed off the railroad bed at that point. A large, white steel sheet painted with square red letters was attached to the gate. The sign read, CAHILL, INC., PROPERTY. KEEP OUT. TRESPASSERS WILL BE PROSECUTED.

Manny didn't want to go over the fence until it was dark; through the dying trees on the other side he could see men walking in and out of the large aluminum building resembling an aircraft hangar, which housed the huge machine that shredded the tires. The shredder was rumbling, and from somewhere on the other side of the huge dump near Wolfpit Road came the low growl of earth-moving machines and trucks. So he waited, peering through the diamond-shaped holes in the fence at the ninety acres of gray mud and tires piled into mountains that had once been nothing but briars and marsh grass and tea-colored streams lined with yellow gravel.

The sun melted and slithered below the dead and dying maples and oaks surrounding Cahill's dump, then it was twilight. Manny toed his way quickly up the fence and dropped catlike on the other side. Then, not knowing what he was looking for, he began to wander aimlessly through the dump, hoping to stumble across whatever it was his grandfather had set out to find when he had his accident. His heart knocked at his ribs; he was sure he would know at once what the old man had been seeking the moment he came to it. He thought perhaps he would discover a burial ground for enemies of the New Jersey mob, or maybe a chop shop for expensive construction machinery. Or—he let his imagination run—a warehouse for drugs. Cahill's friends, if not the old lizard himself, had their hands in everything. This place had to be more than just a dump for old tires and chemicals. Manny was sure of that.

But he was disappointed. All he found were stacks and stacks of bald and rotting tires and foul chemical things. There must have been a hundred thousand tires on the dump land, piled twenty or thirty feet high in places. In between the mountains of tires stood pallets loaded high with steel drums. There were new drums, freshly painted and bearing the unpronounceable names of chemicals on them, and there were old, rusting barrels, some of them leaking evil fluid down their crumbling, dented sides. Many of the barrels bore the word FLAMMABLE in large red letters. The barrels were not always stacked; in the darkness, Manny almost fell into two deep trenches into which barrels had been dumped haphazardly. There were nowhere near as many barrels on the ruined land as there were tires, but there were still plenty of them. There were thousands, Manny decided.

After a time, the tire-shredding machine shut down abruptly, surrendering the night to the sounds of a few trucks moving on the land and the occasional startled screech of a disturbed bird out in the swamp. There were men still moving out among the stacks of tires and barrels; Manny saw two carrying shotguns. But one by one they left their machines, climbed into their cars, and drove out onto Wolfpit

Road until only the men carrying weapons were left.

Manny grew bolder then, moved in closer to the two guards, playing a shadowy hide-and-seek with them among the mountains of refuse. He was frustrated at not finding whatever his grandfather had been risking his life to see, and he began to suspect that the bodies or drugs or stolen vehicles had already been moved and that he had lost his chance. Manny was so angry, a couple of drops of fresh blood oozed out of his nose, and he wiped them impatiently on the back of his hand, where they made long, dark smears; he realized that he was bleeding now every time he had to struggle to keep from crying.

He was considering getting the two guards to chase him in order to vent his frustration when he saw the glare of headlights creeping along Wolfpit Road and then spied a truck turning into the entrance of the dump. The two guards, who had been standing beneath a light on the shredder building, both walked down to the front gate to let the truck in. It was a tractor-trailer.

Manny's interest flared; perhaps the bodies and cocaine were coming now, and he ran through the maze of tires and barrels to get as close to the truck and the men as he could. He reached the corner of the shredder building just as the truck came grumbling slowly up a dirt drive with two men sitting high up in the cab. The guards were following on foot, their shotguns nestled in the crooks of their arms. The truck stopped briefly in the glaring flood of light surrounding the aluminum building; the two guards pointed, shouting "Over there!" and it moved slowly off again, gears grinding. Cahill's gunmen stood a mere thirty feet from him then; he drew in his breath and pressed himself into the shadows along the aluminum wall. But the two men shifted their weapons and slowly followed the truck out into the wilderness of old tires and leaky drums.

He waited a few moments and then followed, staying close to the piles of rubbish as he moved. Once he almost slid into a shining, stagnant pond of foul, tarlike chemicals, and stifled a shout of surprise. He had to pull one foot loose from the sucking muck, and the skin around his ankle where the ooze had touched him began to itch and burn almost immediately.

When he got to where the truck was parked, he scaled a pile of tires to get a better look.

Someone, it must have been one of the drivers, had set two electric lanterns on the ground so that the area around the vehicle was bathed in pale light. But Manny didn't see the drivers; only the two guards were there, cuddling shotguns and looking toward a dark gash that yawned in the ground behind the truck. Then the drivers appeared; they walked around the cab from the far side of the truck. They were strange-looking men; they wore rubber coats and rubber pants as well as rubber boots and hoods. Their faces were covered with clear plastic masks that shone white in the light of the electric lanterns. They were adjusting gloves on their hands as they walked.

Manny had a feeling he had seen men dressed like that before; the feeling made the hair on the back of his head prickle. Then he knew. The state cops who had taken away the bodies of the murdered children last spring had worn similar clothes.

"How much of that you guys got?" one of the guards asked.

"One-fifty," came the answer in a Southern accent muffled by the face mask.

The two men in rubber suits pulled open the back doors of the trailer, then one of them walked to the edge of the ditch and peered down into it.

Manny was close enough to the guards to see one of them lick his lips nervously. "Must be some nasty stuff if you boys are wearing those monkey suits, huh?" he said.

Neither driver answered at first. The man at the ditch continued to gaze down into it; he was shaking his head now. But finally the other driver, also a Southerner, said, "They told us you could get cancer just from looking at this shit."

The two guards laughed nervously and shifted the weight of their shotguns.

Then the driver at the edge of the ditch turned to the guards.

"What the fuck is this?" he asked. "Marconi said he was going to prepare a place. There's no fucking preparation at all here; it's just a goddamn hole in the ground. You think there's root beer in them drums?"

The guards looked at each other, the short barrels of their shotguns circling in the air like antennae. Then one of them said, "Hey, look, man, either dump your shit or take it back to Delaware. We don't care. Just make up your mind."

This time the two drivers exchanged looks. Then, without a further word, they pulled a loading ramp out of the back of the truck, set the end of it on the ground, and began wheeling steel barrels out on a hand truck. The barrels made a heavy, wet thud as they hit the mud at the bottom of the deep trench. The two guards watched for a minute, then drifted away.

Manny quickly got bored with watching the drivers work. Moving the barrels into the pit was slow work for the two men; they grunted and swore and the wheels of the hand truck kept getting stuck in the mud. They must have been hot, but neither shed any of the rubber clothing they wore.

Manny slid carefully from atop the pile of tires. Then he moved quietly away from the two workers, disappointment a bitter taste in his mouth now. All he had seen was Cahill's slow destruction of the swamp. That was nothing new to him, and surely couldn't be what his grandfather had wanted to photograph. When he was out of the hearing range of the two men, he pulled a thick sliver of wood out of the mud, propped his foot on an overturned drum, and began scraping off the muck he had picked up by nearly falling into the chemical reservoir. The skin on his leg where the chemicals had touched was itching badly now; it felt like a rash was breaking out, and it was spreading toward his knee.

Suddenly he froze; he thought that he heard a noise coming from a part of the dump that was far from where the men were unloading their truck. He listened for a moment, hearing nothing but the grunting and swearing of the two Southerners and the heavy thudding of barrels dropping into an earthen pit. The faint sound tickled his ears again; it was so low that he was not sure he wasn't imagining it, as keyed-up as he was from being an intruder in Marconi's territory. The noise was like a distant woman's sob, or maybe it was the call of some night bird, or perhaps it was just a buzzing inside his own skull. It made the little hairs along his arms turn to needles.

The next time he thought he heard the cry, he took his foot down from the drum and walked in the direction from which the sound appeared to come. After a minute's walking between barrels and stacks of tires he stopped, unsure of which way to go, and then the thing seemed to flutter once more at the edge of his senses, just loud enough to start him moving and not loud enough to convince him that it was really there.

But then a real noise reached his ears and made him jump; it was a cough that came from behind him, and he dove behind a pile of empty wooden pallets and looked back the way he had come. A shadow moved back by the barrel where he had scraped the chemical mud off his shoe, then a second shadow joined it. A flashlight went on, silhouetting the two guards and their shotguns.

"Shit," said one of the guards. "I saw him right here."

"Yeah?" said the other. "You sure it wasn't one of those dogs that's always wandering around?" They were speaking in loud whispers that carried in the still night air.

"It was a guy, I could have sworn. Look, there's footprints here in the mud."

"Shit," the second guard said. "People been walking all through here for the last week."

"I know what I saw, man. Maybe we better call Marconi."

The second guard sighed. "Okay, listen, if somebody's here, we can find him ourselves. Forget Marconi. He'll be in a bad fucking mood if we call him this late. You start down the front of the dump, and I'll take the back, okay?"

The two men split up and disappeared.

Manny was startled by what he thought was a soft gasp that came from close behind him, but when he turned around, no one was there. He crouched among the pallets for a long minute, staring at the spot where he was almost certain the noise had come from. Blood made a sound like snare drums in his ears.

Finally he decided that the noise was a hallucination. His imagination had been turned loose by the tension. Still, if the phantom sound had not drawn him away, the guards would have grabbed him. They would grab him still if he did not start moving.

He walked quickly through the dump toward the railroad bed. Strangely, he felt no fear. He felt as if he were swimming his way through a dream.

He heard something and stopped just short of the fence between two pallets loaded high with leaking barrels. The guard passed the narrow alleyway that faced the fence and shined his light down briefly through the barrels. But the weak beam passed over Manny's head, and then the man was past him. He could hear the guard's boots sucking in the mud farther along the fence.

Manny stood and ran to the fence. His fingers slid into the links, and he was ready to climb, but then he stopped. Something white gleamed at the bottom of one of the guard's deep footprints; Manny plucked a quartz arrowhead out of the mud. He rubbed the arrowhead against his pants leg and held it up to his good eye. It was a fine specimen.

"Stone Beads," he whispered.

The swamp was full of ghosts tonight. He stuck the arrowhead into his pocket, then he was up and over the fence and running down through the swamp.

Chapter 23

*T*he station wagon was still missing when he crossed the footbridge into his mother's yard. He kicked off his muddy work shoes, left them lying in the grass of the backyard, and stole quietly into the cellar.

Ida was curled up on her beat-up old couch, snoring softly. Weeds moving by the tiny ground-level cellar windows cast huge, dancing shadows on the cold white walls surrounding her. Manny walked softly up to his sister in his stockinged feet, bent over her, and kissed her lightly on the forehead.

Ida tossed then, turned her face toward the back of the couch. Her hand lightly brushed his nose as she moved.

Ida mumbled. "Daddy," she said.

Manny crawled up the stairs, gently slapping all the steps ahead of him with the palms of his hands. He decided that he was thirsty; he snapped on the light in the kitchen and pulled open the refrigerator. He was hoping for a beer or soda, but there was nothing in there except a half-gallon of milk. He gulped the milk straight from the plastic container, feeling a little guilty because he knew his mother would yell if she caught him. Then he wiped his face in his arm; his sleeve came away dark with milk. Suddenly he wished he had a joint; the craving struck him like a bullet. His heart was still beating too fast, so fast he could hear it, and he needed some pot to calm him down.

But he had not bought any grass recently; had not been able to, actually, because Toby was his only supplier. There were other sources if he wanted to drive up to the high school, but he had never gotten around to it, and now he had run out. He tried watching some late night TV to keep his mind off marijuana, but it was no good. His heart kept whacking away at the same rate, like a pinball bouncing between two bells. He found a stale cigarette in one of his mother's drawers and smoked it; it helped, but not much.

So he took a shower finally, carefully soaping the stinging skin of his leg, and he went to bed. He slept poorly. Every time he dozed he had the sensation of sliding down a steep incline, digging in with his fingers and toes and teeth but sliding faster and faster and faster just the same. Stones like marbles and Indian arrowheads rolled under his chest. He would wake up sweating, his heart fluttering like a dove's crazy wings, then he would doze again and have the same nightmare a few minutes later. Once he thought he had finally shaken the repeating nightmare. He was dreaming of the swamp; he was fishing, and trout were dancing on their tails across the surface of a pool. The sun was bright, and their sides flashed red and gold. But then Toby was there, smiling lopsidedly, hopefully, holding a paper shopping sack in his hands. He shifted his hands slightly, and Manny heard the clinking of glass.

Sometime during the middle of the night he heard his mother come in. He could tell by the sound of the footsteps on the floor below that she was neither sober nor alone. He heard muffled voices, his mother's and a man's. There was stifled laughter too, and then he heard the door to his mother's bedroom open and close. Almost immediately the bed began to groan and creak, the sound filtering up to him through the floorboards, and sooner than Manny expected, sooner than usual, his mother began to cry out in pleasure.

Goddamn her, he thought. *She breaks two fucking promises in the same night. If it's that Flat Top again, I'll kill him.* He wondered if there were any dry shells for his father's old shotgun, now that some town cop's twelve-year-old son had his .22 and was most likely slaughtering songbirds and housecats with it.

Then he had a brief vision of his mother's face as she sat at the kitchen table, his grandfather's forgeries spread before her. After his escape from the Cahill goons, it seemed like an age ago; her mouth that was trying to smile but kept falling down at the corner. But it had just been that afternoon. He felt a sudden rush of guilt then; she had found out that day that her husband was never coming back to her. Without knowing how or why, she knew for certain, finally. And maybe she would start to heal now. She would probably have been cured of her sickness by now if she had faced the truth five years ago, and Manny had shielded her from the truth. Manny and his grandfather.

So maybe now, he thought, *she needed a man to help her heal. Okay,* Manny thought. *She needs it.*

The bedsprings below had paused for a moment, then they started again, rhythmically, like an old washing machine chugging to start. Manny ground his teeth. He still didn't like it.

*H*e was awake for good at first light. His sleep had exhausted him, and he was too tired to sleep anymore. It was chilly. He found an old down vest in his closet and pulled it on over a flannel shirt. He examined his leg before he pulled on his Levi's; the rash was fading away, and it was not itching as badly as it had been last night. He put on a pair of wool socks and toed his way down the ladder.

His mother was already up, rustling around the kitchen in her bathrobe and ratty slippers. She was at the stove with her back to him when he walked into the kitchen.

"Morning," he said.

She gasped, startled, and turned, wide-eyed, to face him. Her temples were furrowed with either pain or guilt, Manny couldn't tell which.

"Manny. What are you doing up so early?" The question was almost an accusation.

"I couldn't sleep."

"Oh! Coffee?" She was near hysteria; he could tell by the way her hands were fluttering around her face.

He thought maybe if he joked a little, it would put her at ease. "Yeah, coffee," he said. "Listen, you were a real show last night. Sounded like the Rolling Stones, with you as Mick Jagger." He tried to laugh, but he could only make a sound like a cough, like Cahill's cold laugh, and there was an edge to his voice he hadn't intended.

His mother turned away then, jerked herself away toward the

stove like a marionette. She tried to pour coffee from the dented saucepan into a cup, but she spilled some and burned her hand.

"Shit!" she hissed.

Manny couldn't stop himself. "Listen," he said. "That's not Flat Top in there, is it? He can't come here ever again. If he does—"

"No," she said. "Not that bastard. Come and get your coffee and leave me alone."

Manny walked to the stove, and she turned and put the cup in his hands.

"Watch, it's hot," she said.

He had the feeling she was going to start screaming at any moment and never stop. He took a sip of the coffee, it was bitter, and he started to turn away from the stove.

She reached and grabbed his chin. Her fingers were hard and cold. "Wait," she said. "What's that on your face? Let mother look."

Manny heard a noise behind him then; he jerked his face out of her hands and turned.

A tall, storklike man with a badly curved back and stringy black hair that reached the collar of his wrinkled white dress shirt was on his way to the front door in stockinged feet. He carried his shoes in one hand, and he froze in the hot focus of Manny's gaze.

"Um, good morning," he said in a voice so high it was almost a falsetto. He drew his lips back in an embarrassed attempt at a smile, revealing teeth as huge and crooked as the yellowed keys of a smashed piano. Then he slipped quickly out the front door, and in a moment, Manny heard a car start up in the front yard.

Manny hadn't planned to criticize, but something about having had to confront the man sent waves of anger and disgust washing over him.

"Mom," he growled, "that's two things. You were drinking too. Two fucking promises in one night." He turned back to face his mother, and found her hugging herself with her thin arms and rocking slightly on the balls of her feet. Her eyes were squeezed tightly shut. It looked like she was about ready to break, to scream and begin to beat herself against all the walls of the house. But Manny was too angry to stop. *Well break then,* he thought. *Get it to hell over with.*

"Mom, you—"

"Manny." She spoke his name calmly, startling him more than if she had screamed. Her eyes were still closed, but she had stopped rocking. "I am trying very hard. It isn't easy for me."

Manny could find nothing to say. He stared at her, astounded, until finally she opened her eyes and looked at him. Her eyes were dull with tiredness.

"Sometimes I can help myself, and sometimes I can't. That's all there is to it," she said. "Give me a chance."

Manny backed off and looked her over, from her hideous slippers to the gray kinked wire of her hair. She kept her arms wrapped around her shoulders, seemed to be keeping herself from flying apart. She was quivering like a sapling in a stiff breeze.

"I needed somebody," she said softly. "And now I'm hung over." She closed her eyes again.

"Listen," Manny said, his voice suddenly husky. "Let me fix you some coffee."

*A*fter that, his mother went back to bed. Manny drove to work feeling a strange calmness now. It was as if a huge storm were beginning to close in on the swamp, brooding darkly on all its jagged horizons, and he was standing temporarily in the still heart of it.

Cahill came rolling down the ramp in his wheelchair just as Manny was tossing food into the first goldfish pool. The old man came wheezing and grinding up behind him, and watched for a moment as he spread flakes across the top of the water.

"Manuel," he said in his attic whisper. "It's almost fall; we'll be bringing the carp inside soon. I would like you to begin cleaning the tanks and preparing the filters today."

"Okay," Manny said.

Cahill regarded him wordlessly for a long minute, then he turned his wheelchair and rolled back to the house.

Manny was busy all day. There was fruit to pick, as well as fifteen large fish tanks to clean and set by the steps of the big house. He lost himself in his work until he happened to look up one time and notice that some of the leaves on Cahill's maples were beginning to turn color. A foxtail red was bleeding into the green; Manny knew all the leaves would be red soon, then they would turn yellow and fall off. After that, he lifted his head every few minutes to look at the changing foliage. It made him feel peaceful.

He was just finishing work on the last fish tank when he heard Toby's car coming up the driveway. He left the tank by the front of the big house and walked quickly to the back of the property so he wouldn't have to talk to him. He got busy back there taking his tree-spraying equipment apart and rinsing it out with a hose; he wouldn't be needing it anymore that year.

By the time he looked up again, the sun was going down, and the air had gotten brisk. The sunset made bands of purple, orange, and pink on the horizon. He stood to look at it, and just then a flock of birds passed overhead, deserting the swamp and heading south for the winter. There were perhaps two hundred of them. Another flock passed, the birds clacking to each other, and then he heard the far-off, lonely cry of migrating geese. They passed over in a V-shaped squadron, honking, silhouetted against the sunset. Two more groups went over as he watched. The cries of the wild geese always made Manny feel like crying himself, all the times before. Now, he only stared, wanting to feel, but empty of feeling.

Then his eyes caught a movement; he looked toward the front of the property and saw Toby facing him. Toby was waving to him; his arm was high in the air, moving slowly from side to side. Manny stared at him; he did not lower his hand.

Manny felt himself nod, once. Then he turned and went back to the disassembled pieces of his spraying machine.

FALL

Chapter
24

*L*eaves began to drop. On warm, windless, Indian summer days, they fell one by one, swaying sadly through branches and making a soft *tick* as they hit the grass. But on other days, the wind stripped them from the trees with a cold fury and sent them swirling across the lawn in agitated flocks until they struck a fence or a hedge or a wall and fell, jumping and twitching, to the ground.

Despite the summer plague of gypsy-moth worms, Manny found that plenty of leaves were left to fall on the Cahill lawns, making a crisp carpet on the hilltop. It was his job to rake them and dump them on the gardens, where they would sit until it came time to till them under the soil the following spring. He was grateful for the solitary work.

One mid-October day, Cahill's housekeeper called him as he worked at the back of the property. He answered and walked toward the house; she met him halfway across the lawn and placed the receiver of a cordless telephone in his hand. His mother. Her voice came panting through the receiver even before he could get his ear to the phone.

"Manny? Manny?"

A feeling of dread washed through him. His grandfather's waxy face blossomed in his mind's eye. He swallowed once, then answered. "Yeah," he said. "I'm here. What's going on?"

"Manny. Thank God. I took a taxi. I'm at the hospital."

"Is he . . ."

"No. No. Listen. He's come awake. Really awake; he knows who I am, and he's been talking about the accident. He says he has to see you right away. Right now, as soon as possible."

"He's talking?" Manny laughed. "He's really talking?"

"Come down here, Manny. He wants to tell you something."

"Okay," Manny said. "I'm on my way."

The black housekeeper was waiting gravely for the telephone. He handed it to her, and she turned without a word and walked back to the house. Manny got into the old station wagon and went shooting down the hill.

*H*e heard his grandfather's voice as soon as he stepped off the elevator onto the floor of the old man's hospital room. He was laughing; the sound made Manny want to laugh as well. Manny turned into the room and saw his mother perched on the edge of the bed, one of her thin hands resting on the old man's arm. She smiled when she saw Manny.

"He's telling me a funny story," she said.

Despite the healthy laughter, there was a milky quality to the old man's eyes, and when he turned them toward Manny, the smile faded from his wrinkled face.

Manny's joy evaporated; the dread rebounded in him strongly.

"That's really Manny?" Grandpa Tarbox said. "I can't see too well all of a sudden."

Manny stepped up and touched his arm, laying his hand alongside his mother's. "It's really me, Grandpa," he said.

The old man jerked his arm away. "Quit touching me, will you?" he said.

Manny buried the offending hand in his pocket. "Okay," he said. He glanced over at his mother; her smile flickered with uncertainty.

"Mary Anne," said Old Man Tarbox with a suddenly gentle voice. "Do you think you could leave us alone for about half an hour? I really do have something to say to Manny."

Her smile died out completely now; her eyes dropped away from Manny. "All right, Pa," she said. She hesitated a moment, then got up and left.

When she was gone, the old man snapped his head toward Manny. "I understand I been out like a light," he said. "But I don't want any goddamn false celebrations. It's not going to last."

Manny spotted a chair and dragged it over to the bed; he sat down backward on it so he could rest his arms on the back. "What do you mean, Grandpa? You've been getting better for two months. Looks like you're improving to me," said Manny.

His grandfather snorted derisively. "I wasn't supposed to come back, you know. I hit that damn tree and the next thing I knew I was floating way up high, looking at my dead body in the truck. I wasn't breathing, Manny." He rolled his head at Manny, squinting his eyes, trying to read his reaction.

Manny kept his face neutral.

"In fact," said the old man, "I guess you could say you're talking to a real live ghost. I saw myself dead before that ambulance got there and they started pumping air into me, just like I was a flat tire."

"Yeah?" Manny said. "You don't look much like a ghost to me, Grandpa. I think you're too mean to die."

"It really was something," continued Grandpa Tarbox. "Those damn moths. I was driving along Wolfpit Road, and they came swirling through the window, maybe a thousand of them, and they started lighting right on my face. In my eyes, Manny. The truck went out of control; I was driving faster than I ought, and I felt the impact. I remember thinking to myself, *This is a punishment, Nat Tarbox.* Tell me, Manny, is it really the sixteenth of October?"

"It is," said Manny. "Listen, Grandpa, what were you doing up there in the first place? You never drive at night. And you had a camera and a gun."

The old man sighed an unhappy sigh and rolled his head away. Manny noticed suddenly that his grandfather's skin was drained of blood and life; he had turned the color of gray slush on a city street.

"Get me a drink of water," he said, his voice suddenly weak. Manny found a silver pitcher on a table nearby and he poured water out into a plastic glass and gave it to his grandfather. The old man downed it all in three gulps, then settled back onto his pillow. He was silent for a time, looking up at the ceiling with his milky eyes. Finally, he spoke.

"It was so peaceful, Manny," he said. "Being dead, I mean. I would never have come back down again for those young medics or whatever they were, except that I remembered you. Or something remembered you, and said you don't deserve to die yet, Tarbox, and made me live again."

"Come on, Grandpa," Manny mumbled. He looked at the immaculate tile floor of the hospital room.

"I owed you something; you know I've made such a mess of things. I owed you at least the chance to be smart and turn down what I have to tell you, a chance for you to tell me you don't need to hear it, before I died and buried everything for good. You're a man now; you're entitled. I guess I should have realized that before."

"I want to hear," Manny said. He lifted his head and looked directly at the old man now.

His grandfather sighed again. "This really is a good punishment for me," he said. "I'm half-blind now, and my head hurts all the time like the Devil himself is in my skull, pounding my brain like a Hawaiian drum. I can't move my goddamn legs, Manny, did they tell you that? And I'm wearing diapers, because I keep pissing myself. Pissing my pants, can you believe it? I'm a goddamn helpless baby. I'll be glad when all this is over with."

"Grandpa . . ." Manny said.

"Ah, shit," said his grandfather. "It seems like yesterday I was a young kid your age, not a care in the world. I was happy. Life is short, Manny, and all the bitterness is saved till the end. Remember that. That's why I'd like you to tell me to forget these things I know, that you don't need to hear them. Put the past behind you, Manny, and go away someplace, maybe out of state. Go back to school and learn a good trade, that's my advice to you. If I tell you what I know, it will just poison the rest of your life, and you're too young for that."

"My life has already been poisoned, Grandpa, hasn't it?" Manny said quietly. "I must be an old man myself, already, in some ways, because things are pretty bitter for me right now."

The old man sighed again, then made a dry swallowing sound. "Well, all right," he croaked. "You really are sure, Manny? Even if I tell you you'll be sorry afterwards?"

"I'm sure."

A nurse suddenly appeared in the room; she was heading toward Grandpa Tarbox's bed, but then she caught something in the expressions of Manny and his grandfather, and she hurried back into the hallway.

"Well, all right. It's a story, Manny. I sure wish I had my pipe and tobacco."

"They won't let you smoke here, Grandpa. I think you can do without it anyway, just this once."

Grandpa Tarbox frowned. "Well, I guess that's just part of my punishment," he said. "I guess I'll have to get along.

"Probably by now you have figured out that your father never went to South America. That he's dead?" the old man asked.

"Yeah," Manny said softly. "I know."

"Well, it took you long enough to figure it out. I was beginning to wonder about your intelligence."

"Go on, Grandpa," Manny said. "No stalling."

"All right, Manny. You asked for it." He cleared his throat twice and began.

Chapter 25

"Well, of course, Manny, you remember the story about Charlie Raymond, your father's friend who killed his entire family with a stone axhead and then hung himself with a coat hanger in the backyard. You know that before the murders occurred, Charlie had told Alexis he was being haunted by Stone Beads, the Indian chief, after he dug into the Indian's grave on Cahill property.

"Well, following those murders, Al was quite shaken up by what happened; it was your father who got Charlie into that amateur archaeology in the first place, and he felt somehow responsible. He didn't mention anything to your mother about how upset he was, because she was always easy to upset herself, and he wanted to keep her out of it. He told me, though. After thinking and pondering and keeping quiet and reading books for nearly six months, he came over to my house one fall afternoon and told me he thought it was possible that something other than a vengeful ghost had caused Charlie to do what he did to his wife and children. Al said the more he thought it over, the more clearly he remembered the strange, bitter smells that used to creep up out of Cahill's dump when he and Charlie were digging in the Indian camp; the smells that were like piss and paint thinner mixed together, as well as the little streams of rainbow-colored oils that used to trickle down into the brook after a rain, and the tiny globs of silvery metal, like jelly, almost, that used to come out of the soil when they were digging sometimes.

"Al told me that maybe, just maybe, something among all those poisons Cahill and his men were putting into the swamp had affected Charlie; something powerful, maybe, that drove him right out of his mind, or something not so powerful, that perhaps reacted with Charlie in a way it wouldn't react with anyone else, and sort of nudged him over the edge. Remember that Charlie'd been in a war a few short years before, and maybe something he saw there had sort of set his sanity to balancing precariously. Charlie could've breathed some poison while he was working in the dump, or had it go right into his skin from the soil, or else something horrible, some evil chemical might have gotten into his well and poisoned the whole family.

"Well, Al concluded that it was more or less his duty to go into that dump and find out what they were doing over there, find out if they were storing any chemicals that could ruin people's health or make them crazy. And he knew what Cahill's people would tell him if he actually asked to go in, so that left him with the option of a kind of guerrilla raid on the dump, a one-man expedition to see what was really in there. So one night he dressed all in black and darkened his face and snuck into the dump with one of those instant cameras and a flashlight and a little notebook to write things down.

"I waited up for him all night that night at my house; I was worried about him, you know, and toward dawn he came up to my back door, his black clothes all covered with mud and reeking of something that smelled like cleaning fluid, and his face still blacked over with charcoal. His eyes were shining though; he said he'd found some things, although he wasn't sure exactly what they meant. Alexis told me he'd found crates of drugs whose expiration dates had come and gone; there were bottles of strong medicine broken right there on the ground and pills strewn everywhere, as well as raw powders that had not yet been pressed into pills. A box of two of those medicines were labeled 'experimental.' And all that stuff was gradually washing down toward Wolfpit Road with each rain, washing right toward Charlie's house.

"He'd also taken some pictures of the labels on some of the poison barrels that Cahill's people buried in there as well as some huge pools of chemicals sitting right on top of the ground. Al said he'd never known before that those trucks from as far away as Maryland that were sneaking onto the property late at night were bringing in such a huge volume of bad things; this was supposed to be nothing but a graveyard for old tires, remember.

"Well, the next day Al walked into the Bridgeport library as soon as it was open; he spent eight hours there researching those labels, and when he dropped by my house later that afternoon, he was upset to the point of tears. I'd never seen him that close to crying, Manny, not even when he'd had a few beers and started talking about his brothers in Chile who had been murdered by political gangsters.

"Cahill had no *right,* Al told me. He was putting things in that dump that could kill people, make them die horrible, painful deaths, or ruin their health, and he had no right to do it. Al said there were herbicides, weed killers, stored in that dump that contained something called dioxin, a chemical that is supposed to be able to cause galloping cancers with just small doses. Those dioxin poisons were leaking out into the swamp; *damn* it, Manny, one of the most poisonous substances known to man was leaking right out into our swamp, and maybe it was finding its way into Charlie's well. Maybe the whole damn family had been *drinking* that poison at the time they died without even knowing it. Al said what if the stuff had given Charlie a brain tumor that sucked and sucked at his mind like a big marsh leech until he went crazy and killed his family.

"Al said plenty of other things in that dump could give you cancer as well, or make you a little nutty just from breathing them. There were solvents like benzene and toluene, and other bad things like something called ketone, and different acids, and I don't know what all. And there were other things Al called heavy metals, compounds that contained mercury and selenium and cadmium and lead, and almost everything else you could imagine. Especially mercury. Al said there were hundreds of barrels with mercury compounds in them leaking all over that dump. He said that under the right conditions mercury can collect in your body, in your brain, and that when it reaches a certain concentration, it can make you go blind, or stupid, or crazy. Like tiny knives, Al told me. The damn metal goes and sticks like tiny knives into the cells of your brain.

"Well, there were just hundreds of chemicals mixing together in a deadly witch's brew out there in the dump. Al wasn't sure if he could pin Charlie's insanity on them for certain, but he knew damn well he ought to let somebody know what Cahill was doing there before somebody else got sick, or crazy, or dead, from what he called the illegal toxic dumping. He decided to get the government in on the problem; he figured they'd close the dump down and give Cahill hell the moment they heard what was going on.

"But then, Manny, your father made his first mistake, and it was a fatal mistake. Instead of going right to the feds or the state, he went to the city. If I had known he was going to do that, I would have tried to stop him; Cahill owns this damn town. Of course, Cahill's people found out what Alexis was doing then. He got a few threatening phone calls, then they took to calling on him at work. They even threatened to lose his job for him. The gist was, they wanted him to lay off, or there was going to be a lot of trouble.

"Al realized his mistake right then and there, and he decided he had to go into hiding. You see, he came from a country where men often were made to disappear by their enemies, so he held no illusion about what could happen to him. He put in for his vacation; figured all he would need was two weeks to get the state in on the problem. Then he wrote that note to your mother and went into hiding in Charlie's old house. He figured it was the one place they wouldn't look, that is, if he was careful and didn't turn on any lights or make any noise. Guess the electricity had been cut by then anyway. And, from Charlie's house, he could always sneak over real quick onto dump property to see what new crime Marconi and his men were committing.

"To be honest, Manny, things weren't going well between your mother and father at the time; that's why he left such a short, unsentimental note, and why your mother thought he might have gone for good. *Something's come up. Don't know when I'll be back.* Your mother and father had been fighting because Al was spending a lot of his time worrying about the Charlie Raymond problem, and before that, he had been in the swamp a good deal, playing, or bumming around with Charlie or me. She reckoned he wasn't spending enough time with her, or with you kids. For his part, he was upset that she didn't share his interests, didn't like to fish, or explore, or hunt arrowheads, and she never read anything. All she seemed to want to do, according to Al, was be a housewife and watch TV and go out to dinner twice a week, and he was starting to get a little bored with her. I guess you probably didn't know any of that, Manny, although you might have felt something was not right between them.

"But to tell you the truth, I'm sure they would have ironed it all out in time, for you kids if not for any other reason. Alexis loved you, Manny, you and Terry and Ida. He would never have left the country and abandoned you, even if he decided to leave your mother. In fact, right before he went into hiding, Alexis told me to take care of all of you in case anything happened to him, in case Cahill's people somehow found him. He told me to do anything I thought necessary to protect all of you in case he lost the dangerous game he was playing with the poisoners of the swamp, who he also suspected of being Charlie Raymond's killers.

"You see, back in South America, sometimes people who had a grudge against a man would go after that man's family, sometimes even after they killed the man himself, I guess to punish him more than torture and death itself could punish. So Al made me swear that I would make sure the Cahill people would not get to you and Terry and Ida and your mother. I have come to regret making that promise. My meddling has done much more harm than good, and I have come to regret that pledge more than anything else in my long and unhappy life. But I'm getting a little ahead of myself here.

"Anyway, Al holed up in Charlie's old house, laying low and sneaking out every day to make phone calls and mail letters and check the post-office box he rented down the center of town. He was trying to get in touch with state people now, planning to tell them at first only about the toxic dumping, and then, when he had their attention, when they knew he wasn't a crackpot, he was going to let them know about Charlie Raymond and his suspicions that old Charlie had been poisoned into insanity. What he didn't count on, though, was how slow the state would be in responding to his proof. He mailed those pictures, real hard proof, but when he called to ask them what they were going to do, he always got stalled by some secretary or underling who treated him like he was a little nuts. Finally he did get a letter from somebody or other, saying they might come down and have a look at things in a month or so. It seems that the state did not really want to tackle Cahill's people; maybe they would do it if they were pushed hard enough, but they weren't going to jump just because some nut with a Puerto Rican accent told them to.

"Well, by the time that lukewarm letter from the state got to him, Al's vacation time was running out. But he figured he would like to make one more stab at it; he'd try to contact the feds, maybe they would do something, and then if that didn't work he was going home and going to work, and forgetting the whole thing. So he started working the federal angle. He wrote a letter and told the feds to call me at my house; told them that I would set up a meeting between him and any federal inspector they sent. And that final ploy did work. Some young man from the government called me shortly after Al sent his letter, said he was very interested in talking to Al, and asked for an appointment. I set a date for the following week; that was the earliest time that federal man could come down from Hartford. And I was all set to tell Al the good news when he dropped by my house that night.

"But Alexis never made it over to my place. Somehow, I have never been able to figure out exactly how, Cahill's people found out my son-in-law was staying in Charlie's abandoned house. They went in there, Manny, and they killed Alexis, and then they burned the house down around his body. Burned it right to the foundation to cover their crime. Since the place supposedly didn't have anyone living in it, the fire department and the police never did make a thorough search for human remains. If they had, they'd have found the bones of your father as well as those of Stone Beads the Indian.

"Manny, I was paralyzed, I'll tell you. I did not know what to do. I was afraid that if I told the police that Al's bones were in the cellar hole of that house, all mixed in with those of the Indian, Cahill's people might kill someone else. Oh, I wasn't worried about myself, I promise you that, I was worried they would get to you children in order to shut me up. They had already killed one person, after all, so I figured they'd as soon do in another to protect themselves. Goddamn that William Cahill. And your mother was acting so badly about Al's disappearance that I was afraid if I told her he was murdered, she might go completely out of her mind, get herself locked up. And if that happened, that would have meant foster homes for you and Terry and Ida, since I wasn't equipped to handle the three of you.

"I remember you walking down the tracks every day through the snow, Manny, to ask me, 'Where's my daddy, Grandpa?' and me not able to tell you. It just about broke my heart.

"But you know, I wanted to get some justice done for Alexis; he was a good son-in-law, and my best friend. So I thought and thought, and pondered and pondered, and I just about had my mind made up to take the risk of squealing on that bastard Cahill when Terry disappeared. What a shock that was, Manny; my grandson falling right off the end of the earth and vanishing. When I heard your story about the two sets of footprints in the snow, I thought right away that Cahill's people had taken him as a warning to me, or maybe to all of us, to keep our mouths shut.

"So I shut my mouth, all right. That federal man called me two days after Terry vanished, and I told him to forget everything. I said my son-in-law was a crackpot who hated Cahill and invented lies about him, and had now deserted his family. I felt like Judas, saying those things, but I thought it was the only way I could keep all of you safe. Which is why, Manny, I can't bear the thought that some filthy pervert made Terry disappear and not Cahill's people, because that would mean I betrayed Al's memory and kept Cahill from justice for no good reason.

"That's why I took the camera and the gun and went out to the dump that night. I finally realized that they had fooled me, and I don't like to be fooled. I was going to take pictures and contact that federal man again, and get things started the way they should have been started five years ago. But I guess it wasn't meant to be, and fate blinded me and put that tree in my way. So now there never will be any justice done, I suppose.

"So anyway, you know the rest, Manny. I started writing those fraudulent letters to keep you from looking too close into your father's disappearance, and as a way to give you advice about how to run your life, to give you a father's counsel. I guess it hasn't worked, though, come to think of it; you quit school and now you're working for the man who killed your father. Oh, I taught myself to forge Alexis's handwriting pretty well, and I had a friend of mine, an engineer who travels all through South America, who remailed those damn letters for me every time he reached a new country. Thought I was pretty clever for a while. I told you not to show those letters to your mother because I knew she'd uncover the forgery. What a fool I have been, Manny."

Chapter 26

Old Man Tarbox sighed a long sigh and lapsed into silence. He turned his head away from Manny, spent. Manny absently wiped his fingers across his nose; he came away with a bright drop of blood. He drew a handkerchief from his pocket and held it to his face. "You okay, Grandpa?"

"No." The answer came as a groan.

"You want me to call the nurse or anything?"

"No." Grandpa Tarbox sighed again. "I would give . . . whatever I had to know how they found out Al was in that house. Manny, it seems that in the past few years, bad things have been happening all out of proportion to the laws of chance. It is unnatural." He coughed delicately, as if afraid of tearing something inside himself.

Manny shuffled his feet against the slippery tiles of the floor. He waited for the blood to stop trickling before he spoke again. "So what do we do now, Grandpa?"

The old man rolled his head back across the pillow to look at him. "*We?*" he said. "Me, I'm going to hell, that's what I'm going to do. You, if you have any sense, will leave here, leave Connecticut. You always wanted to go to California; okay, do it. Take your trip across the country, forget about everything here. Get a job, then go back to school. Make something of yourself."

Manny was silent for a long while, staring out the window of the hospital room. After a time, a sound resembling snoring began to come from his grandfather's half-open mouth.

Finally Manny said, "Did you ever think about killing Cahill, Grandpa?" He said it very softly, almost whispered it, and was not sure he would get an answer.

But the old man stirred and spoke. "Yes," he said. "Every night of my life for the past five years. I always thought it wouldn't be too great a crime against God or Nature, or whatever has made us and pretends to look out for us, to take a single life as long as you were willing to replace it with your own. But I'm not a killer, I'm just not." After a pause, he said, "And you're not either, Manny. I don't think you could build up the proper rage to kill anyone; you'd just start out to do it, and end up not doing it, just getting yourself put in jail. Look at that bastard that molested your sister, Manny; you shot him in the ass. You weren't brought up to kill. It's not in you."

Manny looked down at his fingernails. "I don't know if that's true," he said. "You say a single life, if you replace it with your own?"

"It is true," the old man snapped, a wheeze choking him. "You think it's easy, to pull a trigger and kill someone, but when you look into his eyes, Manny, you won't be able to do it. Now forget all that revenge shit and get out of this state and away from the memories. If you do otherwise, you'll wind up destroying your life. Now, that's my advice to you." In his excitement, Grandpa Tarbox had lifted his head from the pillow. Now he let it drop.

Then, in a gentler tone, the old man said, "You're the last of my line, Manny. Poor little Ida will never be well enough to marry. Even though your name isn't Tarbox, you have Tarbox blood and a Tarbox mind and a Tarbox heart. Don't let us die out. Save yourself; get away from here, and have a son. Please."

There was a long silence, then Manny's grandfather began to snore, for real this time. Manny stayed in the room, thinking. After about an hour, the old man opened his milky eyes and looked directly at him.

"Al," he said. "Don't do it, Al. Don't you do it. They're killers. I know, Al . . ." He began to shout, his hands chopping wildly at the air above him.

A nurse rushed into the room and gave him a shot that sent him muttering into a heavy sleep.

Grandpa Tarbox's wake took place on an overcast, windy night in late October. Bare tree branches pawed and knocked at the windows of the funeral home on Route 25 as the old man lay in his coffin in the cheap black suit Manny's mother had bought for him that morning. The funeral home people had tried to prod the old mouth into a smile, but Grandpa Tarbox refused to smile; his lips had tugged themselves back into a frown. Perhaps he was frowning at the indignity of being placed in a suit for the first time since he was born.

Manny didn't care much for the suit either; he knew how much his grandfather would have objected to it. But he bit his tongue and said nothing in order to humor his mother. The only time he put his foot down was when his mother decided the old man would be more comfortable in death without his dentures, and told Manny she was going to demand that the false teeth be removed. He stopped her then.

And now he sat, lost in a sea of empty chairs that had been set before Grandpa Tarbox's casket. Blood dripped steadily from his nose like a leaky faucet, and he held a handkerchief to his face. There were three people in that casket as far as Manny was concerned: his grandfather, his father, and his brother. He had tried to stop the blood, but it just kept coming, so he learned to put up with it.

During the evening, a couple of bartenders came in, followed by a barber. All three were old men; all were from town. They stood before the casket for a moment or two, then whispered a few words to Manny's mother and walked out. Four old welders his grandfather used to work with entered, sat for a time, talking, and left. Manny sat at the back of the room, apart from his mother and Ida, who were sitting in the first row next to the door. His grief was private, special, and he wanted to be alone with it. His mother had taken medicine to calm her and now she stared, dry-eyed and unblinking, at the old man in his box. Ida had pulled her legs up into her chair, and she was rocking, dipping her body toward the coffin and then away from it. Before the medicine had really taken hold, his mother had tried to get the girl to put her feet on the floor and sit still. But now she let Ida rock.

Jay Lee came in, sat with Manny for a time, not speaking, then went up and settled into the row directly behind his mother. Toby and his mother entered together. They went to the coatroom to hang up their jackets, then Mrs. Carver went over and sat next to Ida. Toby wandered over to the small collection of floral wreaths gathered around the casket.

Mrs. Carver tried for a minute to speak with Manny's mother, found that it was useless, then she took Ida's ankles in her hands and forced her to put her feet on the floor.

Manny recalled Jay Lee's claim that Toby slept with his mother, and he almost smiled.

There were seven wreaths altogether, six tiny ones and one huge offering of red and white roses. Toby worked his way down the line of small ones, reading the cards. They were all from people in town or from the old man's old factory buddies; Manny had read all the cards when he first arrived. Then Toby got to the big wreath and opened the card. It was from William Cahill.

Toby turned and smiled wolfishly at Manny.

Manny turned away.

Toby went over and said something to Manny's mother, bending to touch her arm, then he drifted slowly back to where Manny was sitting. He took a seat uninvited.

"Hello, partner," Toby said.

"Go away," said Manny.

"Don't be like that, partner. Hey, what's the matter with your nose?"

"I got a bleed," Manny said.

Toby clucked his tongue. "Use ice," he said. "Ice will stop it."

"Yeah. Ice."

Toby slid his chair closer. "Listen, pal. That sure is a nice wreath old Cahill sent to Gramps."

Manny didn't answer.

"So listen, I think maybe it's time, what do you think?"

Manny turned to look at him then, saw gleaming eyeteeth. "Time?"

"You know what I'm talking about, partner."

Manny shifted in his chair and looked up toward the front of the room. Mrs. Carver had taken Ida up to the casket, and the girl had reached and clutched the old man's lifeless arm. By the way her back was trembling, Manny could tell she was crying. Mrs. Carver was talking to her and trying to make her let go of her grandfather's jacket sleeve.

After a long while, Manny said, "I got a plan, already, Toby, and you're not in it."

Toby bent closer, almost brushing Manny's ear with his lips. "A plan? What plan, partner?" His hot breath tickled Manny's ear as he waited for an answer.

Manny pinched and wiped at his nose, reluctant to speak. Finally, he said, "I'm gonna kill Mr. Cahill."

"Wow!" There was admiration and excitement in Toby's voice.

Manny had a strange feeling Toby had been expecting him to say what he did; the feeling bothered him.

"You mean really kill him?" Toby asked. "End his life?"

"Yeah."

There was silence for a moment, then Toby said, "Partner, I'll help you."

Manny stared at him. "You're crazy," he said.

Toby grinned.

"No," said Manny. "I don't need your help."

Toby's face was twitching with excitement. "But you do, partner. There's a lot of people in that house. And remember the armed guard outside at night? You'll need guns and handcuffs and drugs and a vehicle and all kinds of things."

Manny could tell Toby was already envisioning his own version of the crime. It had to be Manny's act one hundred percent. "No," he said. Doubt was starting to grow in him, however. Maybe his grandfather was right; he wouldn't be able to look into Cahill's eyes and pull the trigger. But Toby would push him into it if he needed pushing. And it would be good to have someone else with him in the big house.

"Oh, come on," Toby said. "Listen, the old man is all yours. I won't touch him. I don't want anything but to help with the original invasion and to steal anything I feel like. And you'll be the boss, Manny. Whatever you say goes."

"Nobody else gets hurt but Cahill?"

"Agreed, partner, agreed," Toby said. "And afterwards, you and I sell our loot and head for sunny California, like we always planned."

As he spoke, Toby brought his hand up and rested his chin on his knuckles so that the stub of his missing finger pointed directly at Manny's face. Manny's eyes were involuntarily drawn to the smooth peg of flesh; it was as violently and coldly pink as the eye of an albino king snake he had trapped once in the hollow end of a rotten log. Manny was at once revolted by the finger and at the same time unable to take his eyes from it. Toby knew he was looking at it, and he seemed to smile.

Manny glared at Toby. "I don't want any loot. After this thing, I'm turning myself in. If you take a life, you have to replace it with your own."

Toby's eyes grew wide with honest surprise. "Wow!" he said. "Well, but you won't mind if I take a few goodies and split by myself?"

"Toby, I don't care what you do."

"Okay," said Toby. "Cool." They both faced the front of the room for a time, neither of them talking. Then Toby said, "But I do have one small request, boss. Feel free to turn it down if you don't like it."

"Yeah," said Manny. "What?"

"Can we have this little party on Halloween night? Seems like the perfect date."

Manny thought for a moment. "Hell, I don't care."

Toby grinned, his face a jack-o'-lantern now. "Cool," he whispered. "Cool.'"

Chapter

27

*H*alloween fell on a Monday that year. It was a perfect day for Toby and Manny and their plans because they had Sunday free from work at the mansion. Manny was sleeping badly those last few days; the few winks he got were filled with dark terrors and the sensation of falling. He dreamed in color for the first time since he could remember; blood redder than life flashing behind his twitching eyelids. So that on Sunday morning at six o'clock when Toby came bouncing up the driveway in the new pickup truck he had rented and was planning to steal, Manny was already up, sitting on the front steps in the autumn chill with a cup of coffee balanced on one knee.

Toby was all wolfish grins as he jumped out of the cab of the truck and walked over. "Hey, partner!" he said. "Only one more shopping day."

Manny said, "My eyes hurt. I wish there was some damn way I could talk myself out of this." He tried to spit, but nothing came out. His mouth and throat had been dry as baked clay ever since his grandfather's funeral. His frequent nosebleeds were weakening him.

Toby gave him a hearty slap on the back. "Cheer up, partner," he said. "It'll go smooth; you'll see. And once it's done, I think you'll change your mind and head out to sunny Cal with me. You got a whole new life ahead of you."

"Nope," Manny said. "No sunny Cal for me. Somers Prison is where I'm going."

Toby laughed. "You'll see, pal. Suddenly you'll realize—but never mind all that. Come over to the truck and take a look at the new toys I bought for us."

Manny stood; his whole body ached from lack of sleep and sweet, healing dreams, and he followed Toby out to the vehicle. There was an open wooden box in the bed of the truck and it contained hard, sharp-edged things wrapped in flannel rags. Toby snatched one small bundle out of the box, tossed aside the rag, and laid naked a gleaming, nickel-plated automatic pistol. The mirror surface of the pistol caught the autumn colors around it and shone red and gold.

"This little beauty is mine," Toby said. "I'll just be using my weapon for show and intimidation, so I thought I ought to have the flashiest one. Spanish-made Basque thirty-two. Smooth as a girl's ass."

Manny took the gun from him and aimed it out over the treetops. A bluejay flew past, screeching, and he tracked it with the barrel. "Nice," he said finally, returning the gun to Toby. "And what did you get me, a fucking musket?"

Toby giggled an excited giggle. "Manny, come on. We're partners now. Can't we set aside this childish hostility?"

"Partners," Manny agreed. "Not friends. No more."

Toby's smile narrowed, but only slightly. He reached into the box, picked up another bundle, and exposed a .38 revolver. It was nickel as well, but the finish was much duller than that of the automatic.

"This is the actual murder weapon," he said. "Nice Ruger police special for you." He held the gun toward Manny.

Manny accepted the weapon, took the cylinder out and looked down the barrel, then snapped the gun closed again and aimed out over the swamp. He cocked the hammer with his thumb and pulled the trigger; the hammer made a hard, dry *click* as it hit an empty chamber.

Toby beamed. "We've got lots of ammunition, Manny. I figure we'll do some heavy practicing today, if that's all right with you. I got some regular thirty-eight ammo for you to practice with, and then I got some hollow-points for you to use tomorrow up at Cahill's so you can make a real splash in the world." His voice was higher than usual and it shook a little with either excitement or fear.

Manny grunted and stuffed the empty gun into the front of his pants so just the handgrip peeked out. Then he covered the gun with his shirt and jacket. He hadn't had breakfast, and his stomach was crawling greasily inside of him.

"Now, I got some other good things in here, too." Toby took out another bundle larger than the first two. He shook the edges of the rag aside, and six sets of handcuffs appeared, gleaming. They whispered and scraped together between Toby's hands. "Nice ones, these," said Toby, his voice thickening with affection for his purchases. "Smith and Wessons, just like the pigs use. The nice thing about them is you can double-lock them, and they stay just the same as when you put them on, or you can leave them single-locked, and if the bastard struggles, they tighten and tighten on him until they eat his damn wrists clear through to the bone. I don't think we'll need this many sets, but you never know. Some of those New York bastards might decide to show up for a party tomorrow night. I figure I'll carry three and you'll carry three, and we'll both have a key. Here, let me demonstrate." He set down his bundle and picked up a single set of handcuffs to show Manny how to put them on and take them off, how to lock and double-lock them. He handcuffed Manny a few times, front and back, and then he let Manny handcuff him. After that, he put the bright handcuffs in with their mates and drew his silver cigarette box from his jacket pocket. He opened the box and shook five red capsules, three joints, and a small foil-wrapped packet out onto his palm. He dumped everything back into the box but the five pills.

"That other stuff's for us," he said. "These downers are for that monkey who watches the front gate at night. Every evening he takes a thermos of coffee from the house outside with him. He's always already standing there by the time I leave. My plan is this, if it's okay with you: As I'm leaving for home tomorrow night, I stop by the gate, send the gorilla off on some pretext, and then open these capsules and pour the powder into his coffee. Then, by the time we both get up there later on, we catch him either asleep or too groggy to move. We cuff him to the gate, Manny, then the house is ours."

Manny frowned. It seemed to him that Toby was taking everything over, all the planning. It was a relief to him, and at the same time he resented it; resented the feeling of being relieved, of depending on Toby. "What if he doesn't drink the coffee, Toby? Or what if the stuff doesn't affect him like you think it will? It sounds a little iffy to me."

"Listen, it will work. But if something happens, we can just pull our guns on him; he knows us both, so he won't be expecting it. I'd just rather do it this way though 'cause he's the biggest danger up there. After that, it's all cake."

Manny pulled the gun out of his pants and turned it over and over in his hands. "You know," he said, "what I should really do is just go up there tomorrow morning, call Mr. Cahill outside, and then kill him."

"Shit, that's no fun, Manny," Toby said. His forehead wrinkled with sudden worry, and he lifted a hand as if to touch Manny on the shoulder and make him see reason.

Manny ignored him. "But the thing is, I want to talk to him first, to let him know why I have to kill him. Maybe ask him why he got me out of jail that time, whether it was a guilty conscience or what. That really bothers me. I've got to find out, too, if he made Terry disappear or whether it was that pervert creep. And if I pull a gun on him outside in broad daylight, somebody in the house will see, or maybe someone will come up the driveway. I guess it's better to do at night with all the phones torn out and everybody in handcuffs."

"Now you're talking," said Toby. Manny could see that he was greatly relieved, and Toby's relief was somehow disquieting. "We attack the house and we capture it and hold the power of life and death over the occupants. Oh, I want to see Stacy's face when we march in there with guns. That bitch; it's all her fault you and I aren't friends anymore."

Manny snorted, irritated and beginning to feel a chill needle of suspicion pricking his insides, but said nothing.

"Sure, partner. Remember how we used to play army out in the swamp? Remember, we never could decide whether we were fighting Germans or Japs? Well, we're fighting the same enemy this time, pal."

Manny felt uneasy suddenly. "Yeah," he said. "I have something I have to do, that's why I'm fighting. But I don't understand you, Toby. Why are you fighting?"

Toby's eyes gleamed with excitement and something else Manny couldn't fathom, something frightening. "Why, to be with you, partner. I want to prove to you that I'm your best friend in the whole world. I'm really your only friend, actually, even if you say we aren't pals right now. I want to be on your side in the last battle."

Manny scuffed his feet in the dying grass of the autumn lawn. "Yeah," he muttered. "Why not?" He kept his gaze on the ground.

Then Toby said, "Come on, partner. Target-practice time, before your mother wakes up and sees us playing with guns in the front yard." He took the automatic out of its flannel wraps again and stuffed it into his belt. After that, he took a box of .32-caliber ammunition from the wooden crate, and another of .38-caliber, which he handed to Manny. Then, whistling a shrill, almost manic tune, he headed for the brook footbridge without looking back.

Manny followed, slowly.

*T*he swamp had two seasons of heartbreaking beauty: early spring, when new life danced everywhere, and mid-autumn, when the foliage flamed briefly, then died a bittersweet death. Even though the gypsy-moth caterpillars had ravaged most of the swamp that summer, there were still enough leaves changing high in the trees to paint the swamp over in fall colors as well as tint the waters of the stagnant ponds and the bubbling springs and the swift-running brooks with their reflected hues. Manny and Toby headed down the railroad bed in the direction of Grandpa Tarbox's abandoned house, then turned and walked through the woods toward a small, abandoned sandpit that had been worked thirty years before. They passed one of Manny's favorite trout pools on the way; as Manny leaped the stream at the point where a pine-log footbridge had once made the crossing easier, he had a sudden recollection of a huge trout he had taken there when he was nine years old. The seventeen-inch trout, bigger than any his father or brother had ever caught in the swamp and almost as big as his grandfather's largest, had fought him for ten minutes before he was able to drag it flopping onto the cattails that ringed the pool. His heart had nearly exploded with excitement and delight; he had abandoned his fishing equipment right there in the swamp and had run home with the still-thrashing trout, falling three times on the way and skinning his knees and elbows. He hadn't even known he was hurt until his mother spotted the blood.

It hit Manny with a sudden jolt then that he was making his last trip into the swamp, that he would probably never see it again; would never pull a trout from its brooks, or strip tart wild blueberries from its bushes, or carry a rifle through its tall, tassel-topped marsh grass. His insides turned to putrid liquid then, and he had a sudden urge to toss away the evil pistol nestled in his belt. He would have done it too, except the next thing that shoved its way into his mind was the memory of his grandfather lying still in his brass-handled coffin. At the same time, he heard his brother's laugh and his father's voice, with its musical accent: *"You're Yankee as apple cider, Manny. But your brother, he's up in the clouds."*

"Okay," Manny said out loud, feeling himself draw together a little inside. "I give up this swamp. Grandpa was wrong, anyway. It doesn't belong to us."

"What?" said Toby, who was about twenty yards ahead. He spoke without turning around.

"Shut up," said Manny.

There was an old abandoned car at the sandpit. It had been there at least fifteen years, and it was now little more than a pile of brittle rust nearly the same color as winter leaves, well on its way to becoming a part of the wet swamp earth. Silently the two of them agreed on the car as a target, and then they wandered separately through the abandoned pit in search of smaller targets to stack along the roof and hood. They returned with old, rusting paint containers, several beer cans the same color as the rusting car, and the gleaming chrome bumper of a vehicle that had been dumped there more recently than their main target.

Toby wasted no time in jamming a loaded clip into his pistol and going to work on the old car. The first shot was like a blow on the back of Manny's head; violent red spots exploded in front of his eyes and he began trembling, like a beaten dog. The following rapid shots, as Toby stitched a line across one crumbling door of the car, were lesser blows that kept him shaking.

When the clip was empty, Toby turned to him suddenly, grinning wickedly, and caught him with his quivering hands fighting their way to his ears. Toby's smile brightened then, and he reached into his pocket and pulled out four pieces of cotton imprisoned in paper links. He pulled two cotton balls from the paper and stuffed them in his ears, then handed the paper chain to Manny.

Manny accepted the cotton hesitantly, then said, "I don't need it, you know. I can take it."

Toby shook his head. "Not for your nerves, old partner," he said. "For your ears. If you don't use them, your head will be ringing so much tomorrow night you won't even be able to hear a police siren coming up Cahill's driveway."

So Manny gratefully stuffed the cotton into his head, and when Toby took a spare clip from his pocket, fed it into his gleaming pistol and went to work again on the rusty car and the beer cans on the roof, the sharp reports were dulled enough so they no longer danced along his nerves and made him jump.

While Toby shot, Manny opened the cylinder of his own pistol and slid bullets into the smooth, round chambers. With cotton in his ears, the small, metallic noises of the bullets clicking in and the cylinder snapping closed again were mere vibrations that he felt through his hands. Working with the gun had calmed him, had given him a much-needed job to take his mind off the bottomless black hole of his future, and when he finally lifted the gun and aimed it, pulling the hammer back with his thumb, he was steady. He tickled the trigger and a beer can jumped off the hood of the car, landing in dead leaves near one rusting wheel.

Toby lowered his own pistol then and faced him, grinning like a Halloween jack-o'-lantern, and he winked. "Bye-bye, Mr. Cahill," he said.

Manny's stomach churned violently; he would have thrown up except he did not want to humiliate himself in front of Toby. Instead, he swallowed hard, blinked back tears of pain, and emptied his revolver into the side of the car as fast as he could pull the trigger. Toby stood and grinned at him as he fired off the remaining five shots, then he reloaded his clips and returned to shooting his own gun.

By the time their ammunition was gone, it was noon, and the air had warmed. They set down their guns and rested, poking at the bullet holes in the old car with their fingers and kicking with satisfaction at the places where whole sections of the rusty body had caved in. Then they took up their weapons again, hiding them beneath their clothes, and walked back to Manny's house.

Once they were back in the yard, Toby didn't stay long. The two of them stood together for a few minutes, watching a flock of angry crows chasing a clumsily fleeing red-tailed hawk through the treetops, then Toby flipped Manny the thumbs-up sign and jumped into his truck.

"Tomorrow noon at work we'll go over the last details while we're raking leaves," Toby said. "Good shooting with you, partner. And don't forget to clean the barrel of that gun." Then he started the rented, about-to-be-stolen pickup truck and rocketed out of the driveway.

Mrs. Carver called Manny on the telephone that night. She sounded upset; her voice was twanging like a rubber band. "Manny," she said, "I know you don't like to squeal or whatever it is you kids call it, but I want you to tell me the truth. I want you to tell me if Toby is involved in drugs."

Cold fingers closed around Manny's heart. Possible trouble on the way. Trouble that could drown his plans; he was sure that if there was any postponement now, he would never get his courage back to try another time. "No," Manny said, trying to control his voice. "Not that I know of, Mrs. Carver." He paused a minute, trying to think of something that a concerned adult would say. "You didn't find any . . . anything, did you?"

Mrs. Carver was upset enough to be fooled. "No, nothing like that," she said. "It's just the way he *acts*. He's always out late at night and sometimes he doesn't come home; I guess that might be normal for a young man these days. But lately he's been behaving, well, sort of *disturbed*. It sort of worries me that he might hurt himself. You remember, Manny, that he hurt himself a few years ago?"

"Yeah," Manny said quickly. "Yeah, I remember." He felt guilty that he and Toby were causing Mrs. Carver grief. He knew they would cause her to suffer even more before they were through. "Toby was just over here today, Mrs. Carver, and he seemed fine to me. If he's doing some kind of drugs, I don't know about it." Manny shivered as he was speaking this lie.

"You're sure, Manny?" she said. "I know you're his best friend. You wouldn't cover for him, would you? I just think drugs might be the reason he has been behaving this way. I just read an article in *Reader's Digest* about that."

Something warned Manny to be careful. "I don't know if I would cover for him," he said. "But as far as I know, he isn't doing anything like that." The lies were leaving a taste like spoiled fish in his mouth.

"Well, I thought I'd ask you," she said. "And I hope you're telling me the truth. Good-bye, Manny."

"Bye," he said. The telephone whined, and Manny put it back on its cradle. *Disturbed,* he thought. *Disturbed.* What the hell was he getting into? He should cut Toby loose. But he knew now that he would never go up the hill without him. Manny felt cold, suddenly. He was shaking with the cold.

*I*t was Halloween. Manny passed through his workday at the Cahill mansion in a daze. His lack of sleep acted on him like a narcotic; he watched himself going through the motions of raking fallen leaves, packing them in plastic bags, and dragging them to the front gate as if he were a ghost riding on his own shoulders. He had expected to be afraid, but he wasn't. Instead, his only feeling was a deep and aching homesickness for the swamp and an unreasonable yearning to speak for one last time with his grandfather Tarbox.

When Marconi drove into the yard in the early afternoon, his crazy arms flying even before he left the car, Manny lifted his rake from the lawn and stared openly at the deranged little dump foreman, something he had never done before. Marconi had little hands and little feet. His feet were as small as those of a large woman, or maybe even a large child. The possibilities infuriated Manny. He felt a bitter trickle of hatred in his gut for the ugly little man, almost wished Marconi would notice him staring and walk over, walk his twisted face right into the swinging claw of Manny's rake. But Marconi was too busy arguing with himself, hating himself, to notice Manny, and he flew into Cahill's house, raging. He burst out still raging fifteen minutes later, and he drove off without looking back.

Shortly after Marconi left, Cahill rolled his gleaming wheelchair out onto the ramp. The black maid followed him out, cradling a huge oval pumpkin in her sturdy arms. She set the pumpkin down on the top step, went back into the house, and brought out another that was nearly as large.

Manny, raking with his face to the ground and one eye cocked toward the front of the house, saw Cahill lift his head to the maid and say something.

The maid looked out across the lawn at him, calling "Manny! Yoo-hoo, Manny! Mr. Cahill wants to talk to you." Then she returned to the house.

So Manny dropped the rake and started toward the steps, walking slowly.

Old Man Cahill was swaddled in a puffy down-filled vest, a plaid blanket folded across his lap. Wrapped in all that loose cloth, he looked shrunken, feeble, and old. A dying lizard, his blood freezing with the autumn cold. As Manny approached he could see the old man was turning something over and over in his hands; when he got closer, to the bottom of the ramp, he saw that it was a knife. Cahill held the blade up to his chest, the handle pointed outward; blood thumped in Manny's ears when he saw that. For a dizzy moment he was dreaming a dream where he would take the handle of the knife and shove it forward and Cahill would die. It would be so easy.

But then the old man spoke and broke the spell. "Manuel," he said in his frozen whisper of a voice.

Manny's gaze lifted from the knife and he saw a flicker of fear in the old man's eyes, as if Cahill had sensed his murderous fantasy. The look lasted only a second, and then the old eyes were cold and expressionless once more.

"Manuel," he repeated. "Are you much of an artist? Do you think you could take these pumpkins out to one of the gardens and carve some kind of face onto them? It is that day, you know."

Manny looked down at the pumpkins, seeing them really for the first time. "Yeah," he said. "I used to do it all the time as a kid. Me and my father and my big brother used to make a party out of it." He reached and grasped the handle of the knife; Cahill winced, and Manny understood then that the old man felt guilty. That was why he was frightened; guilt was eating him alive from the inside. Manny took the knife from him.

"Scary faces?" he asked. "Or happy ones?"

"The traditional frightening ones, if you please," Cahill whispered, looking away over the swamp. Then he hit a switch on the arm of his wheelchair, turned abruptly, and went back inside the house.

Manny labored for an hour over the jack-o'-lanterns, losing himself in the work. He thought he'd put Joe Marconi's twisted face on both of them, but when he was finished, he decided they looked more like Toby; the sarcastic grin they wore was not one of Marconi's expressions. Just as he was setting the newly carved pumpkins back on the steps of the big house, Toby pulled into the driveway in the rented pickup truck.

Toby was looking at the pumpkins and smiling as he stepped down from the truck. "Fine job," he told Manny. "You did a couple of self-portraits, right?"

"Sure," Manny said. "Self-portraits." Strands of pumpkin gore were drying coldly on his hands, and he was trying to scrape them off against the rough material of his blue jeans. *Disturbed.*

Toby put an arm around Manny's shoulder and steered him out toward the carriage house, speaking in a lowered voice as they walked. "You're still up for it, then?" he said.

"Damn right," said Manny. "Why, are you having second thoughts?"

Toby snorted, the grin broadening on his face. "Not me, partner. Okay, listen to this and tell me what you think. How about this: After we make sure the baboon at the front gate is out and safely cuffed to the fence, we round up everyone else in the house, Stacy and the maid and anyone else there, and take them to the carriage house? I'll stay with them out there so that you can be all by yourself with Cahill for a while. Then if you decide to take off with me to California, at least there will be no witnesses to the actual dirty deed. And afterward, when I go sweeping the house for valuables, nobody sees me do that either, and nobody distracts me or gets in the way."

As Toby spoke, his gesturing hand fluttered next to Manny's face. Manny turned to frown at the offending hand, and he saw the pink, gleaming stub of the severed finger peek at him for a moment before hiding behind the other four wiggling digits. Manny shrugged off Toby's arm and leaned against the back wall of the carriage house. He turned the plan over and over in his mind, looking for flaws, but he found none. Even so, he deliberately took his time in answering, stood watching leaves cartwheel across the lawn for a time, because he didn't want Toby to think he was surrendering control of the plan to him.

Finally he said, "Okay. That sounds all right with me. Another thing, man. How about if we do it at about nine o'clock? That way if any little kids from down in the condos come up for trick-or-treat, they'll be long gone by the time we get here?"

Toby didn't hesitate. "Right," he said. "Perfect."

"But we got to get together before that," said Manny. "Six o'clock, right after you get out of work you come over my house. We'll make sure all the equipment, the guns and handcuffs and all the stuff, is ready, then we'll go out and eat or something. So we're in the mood, you know, when the time comes." The inside of Manny's mouth was dry as dirt.

Toby bobbed his head like a puppet. "Yup," he said. "Right. Maybe we'll even take in a movie."

"Yeah, maybe," Manny said. He nodded his head out over the lawn. "Well, I guess I'm about done raking leaves for the rest of my life. You take over." He pushed himself off the carriage house and headed toward the front gate without looking back. He felt Toby's mocking, questioning eyes on him until he was partway down the hill and out of sight.

Chapter
28

*I*t was almost dark by the time Toby pulled up in front of Manny's house. Manny was inside, sitting by himself at the table in the darkening kitchen, when he came. Ida and his mother were asleep in the living room in front of the television.

Manny watched through the window as Toby walked around to the back of his rented truck, reached into the wooden box in the bed, and fondled the deadly things inside for a moment before leaning against the tailgate, his legs crossed, waiting. Manny let Toby wait for a time in the purple dusk. Then he stood, feeling the .38 revolver pinch the skin of his waist beneath his clothes, adjusted the black patch that covered his bad eye, and walked out the front door.

When he got to the truck, Toby gestured and took the gun from him without speaking. He loaded Manny's weapon with the deadly, flesh-spattering hollow-point ammunition from a box in the truck, and returned it to him. Then Toby loaded his own automatic; slipped the black clip into the handgrip and seated it with a slap from the heel of his palm. Toby smiled his smile then, buried the shining weapon beneath his clothes, and reached again into the wooden box. Handcuffs jingled; he drew out three sets and handed them to Manny.

"Keep them in your jacket pocket. Here's the key, make good and sure you don't lose it."

The handcuffs were cold. Manny stashed them where Toby told him, and he slipped the tiny key into his pocket. He watched Toby's white hand flutter once more into the wooden box; cold metal clinked, then the hand returned as a clenched fist to hover before him.

"Take," said Toby.

Manny cupped his hands beneath the outstretched fist and caught a silver cascade of bullets.

"Just in case you have to reload," Toby said. "Keep them loose in your pocket."

Manny put the .38 shells away. He felt suddenly dry from his lips down through his throat and into his stomach. He had begun to tremble all over, and he felt feverish. He looked out over the dark swamp, wondering if he really would be able to kill, or whether he would freeze up and not be able to do it, just as his grandfather had said. He was so busy worrying, he did not notice Toby take a shard of broken mirror from his pocket and grind a tiny white pebble into a powder against it with a razor blade.

"Here," said Toby, and Manny turned. The mirror, with four thin lines of white powder scored out on it, was balanced on the top of the tailgate. Toby pushed a plastic straw into Manny's fingers. "Hurry, before a breeze comes along and blows it away."

Manny fingered the tip of the straw. "What's that? Cocaine?"

"Good cocaine," corrected Toby. "Help you get your courage up like nothing else. Be careful you don't blow out through the straw when you snort it."

"I don't know," said Manny. The idea of some external courage was tempting, and he almost gave in. But then he thought that if he really was going to murder Cahill, the anger and hatred and power should come from within himself. Otherwise it would be the drug that did the killing and not Manny himself.

"Come on," Toby said. "Hurry up. The wind will pick up any minute."

"No," said Manny. He tried to give back the sawed-off straw, but Toby wouldn't take it.

"What? Manny, snort that shit. Do it now."

"No, Toby."

"Damn it, Manny, I'm worried about you. I think you're going to have second thoughts about pulling the trigger when the time comes— look at you, you're shaking already. Do that stuff like I told you. Those nerves will go away, I'm telling you."

"I'm okay. You worry about yourself."

Toby grabbed the straw away from him. "You sure, partner? No chicken shit when it comes time to splash that old man's head all over the wall?"

"Nope," said Manny as his stomach churned. He again wondered why Toby wanted to go with him when he killed Cahill. He was sure Toby was running some kind of a game that was all his own tonight. The thought made him sick with uneasiness. *Disturbed.* He turned and aimed his eyes out over the swamp, ending the conversation. Out of the corner of his good eye he saw Toby bending over the mirror, the straw screwed into his face. There was a loud sucking *sniff,* and then another a moment later.

"Last chance," said Toby.

Manny didn't answer. In a moment, he heard another pair of greedy sniffs.

Then Toby said, "Okay, partner, let's ride." They climbed into the truck and rolled out onto Dark Entry Road.

"Good-bye, swamp," said Manny.

Toby laughed.

*T*hey went to a pizza place up on Route 25. Toby ordered a large pie with everything on it and jammed slice after slice into his mouth. He ate without looking at his food; his blue eyes were trained on Manny's face. Once in a while he would rub a quick finger against the bottom of his nose and snort, drawing cocaine-laden snot back up into his head.

Manny tried to eat, but he couldn't swallow anything. He would chew a lump of pizza, feel it turn to brains and blood in his mouth, and then spit it out into his napkin, choking quietly.

Toby tracked every move with his laughing eyes. "Can't even taste this stuff; my mouth is all numb with snow," he said, and chuckled.

Afterward, they went to a movie. Toby insisted on a Dirty Harry with Clint Eastwood, said it would get them in the mood for what lay ahead. Manny didn't care what they saw; he knew he would never be able to keep his mind on the story anyway.

The movie was punctuated with screams and snarls and gunfire. Manny, hardly watching the screen, flinched with every shot. Toby giggled, not looking at Manny now, but deeply absorbed in the film. But, every so often he would lift his arm, peel back his sleeve, and read the luminescent dial of his watch. Manny felt icy fingers close around his heart whenever Toby did that.

By the time the movie ended, Manny's heart was pounding so hard and so coldly that he was sure it would freeze and shatter into a hundred pieces.

*T*oby parked just far enough up the driveway leading to the mansion so that no one passing on the public street below would see the truck. When he switched off the engine, the silence of the cool fall evening fell heavily and abruptly upon them. Toby glanced at his watch; the radium numerals glowed greenly, poisonously, in the darkness of the cab.

"Okay," Toby whispered, his sharp eyeteeth gleaming like polished ivory in the light of a waning moon. "We're just a little late, but that's okay, too. Listen, how about you stay here while I climb the hill and make sure Bimbo, the night watchman, is out on his ass? I'll give you a whistle when I have him cuffed to the gate."

Manny once again had the strong feeling that Toby was taking the initiative away from him, and was angry and resentful about it. But he was also afraid; he was trembling like a birch sapling in a strong wind. He had to mutter to keep his voice from shaking. "Yeah," he said. "Okay. But listen, don't you hurt that guy. Don't hurt anybody all through this. Mr. Cahill is the only one."

Toby chuckled, hyenalike. He opened the glove box and pulled out a thick roll of cloth adhesive tape. "Partner," Toby said. "I am not a violent man." Then he slid out of the cab and closed the door with a gentle *click.*

Manny watched Toby sprint up the hill toward the house until he could no longer see him. Then he stepped out of the truck, opened his fly with numb fingers, and made a nervous stream on the asphalt of the driveway. From where he stood, he could just about see the lights of the uppermost floor of Cahill's house. Manny knew that in one of those rooms, the old man was huddled over an oak desk, counting his money or staring broodingly at his books and ledgers in their sickly green bindings. A thought began to run through and through his head: Toby wanted him to kill Cahill. Toby had not been at all surprised when he had told him he was going to kill Cahill. Maybe he had *always* wanted Manny to kill Cahill. For some reason he thought of the eleven-year-old Toby holding a bag full of baby aspirin. He shuddered and leaned against the truck.

After a few minutes, Manny grew impatient and worried waiting for Toby's whistle, and he began walking slowly up the hill. He walked with his hands stuffed deeply into his pants pockets, and he fought an urge to whistle or hum in an effort to break the tension. When he reached the hilltop, he saw a body stretched out near the gate, a large body that appeared to be grasping the iron rails of the fence.

Toby stood over the fallen guard like a hunter over a prize trophy and he was dangling something from his hand. Manny heard a faint jingling and when he stepped closer he saw the keys to the gate glinting in the moonlight. Toby wore a look of triumph.

Then Manny heard a soft moan and looked down. The guard's head was swaddled in white tape; he wore a thick mask of tape across his mouth and around the back of his head. The man shifted; Manny heard metal on metal and saw the short links of the handcuffs the guard wore scraping tautly against a bar of the fence. The guard unconsciously tugged at his restraints, and Manny heard a faint *click* as the handcuffs tightened another notch against his thick wrists.

Single-locked, Manny thought, remembering what Toby had said about how the cuffs would close on a struggling person until they bit into the flesh. His stomach churned. *This is it,* he thought, feeling giddy. *Too late to turn back now.*

The man on the ground groaned again; the noise sounded more like a sigh, really, and he turned his head. It was then that Manny saw the blood that was trickling down from his scalp and running diagonally across his forehead to pool just above his eyebrow. Just at that moment he heard a telltale *sniff* and turned to see Toby vacuuming a line of cocaine off his piece of broken mirror.

"What's this?" whispered Manny. "The guy's hurt . . ." Fear and shame were mixing strongly in him now.

Toby smiled and sucked in a second line of white powder before stashing the mirror and wiping at his nose with the back of his sleeve. "I don't know," he said. "He must have fallen from the stuff I put in his coffee. I found him on the ground just like that. Come on, I've got the keys." Before Manny could question him further, Toby opened the padlock on the gate and tossed aside the rattling chain. Then the two of them were in the yard and heading toward the front steps of the big house.

Manny's heart clunked like an engine with a bad bearing as they stood in front of the wooden door at the top of the wheelchair ramp. The pumpkins he had carved sat on the front steps, candles flickering inside them and bathing the steps in muted yellow light.

Toby's whispering voice was filled with excitement and evil joy. "This is the dangerous part," he said. "If she doesn't answer, we'll have to break in, and then maybe it'll give them time to call the pigs. If that happens, we kill the old man real quick and beat it, understand?"

Manny nodded once, and Toby pushed the bell. In a moment, he reached to push it again, but Manny grabbed his hand and stopped him. A second later slippers whispered in the hallway.

The slow, liquid voice of the black maid: "Darn you! Those batteries go dead on you again? You ought to keep a spare pair with you; it isn't proper for you to be ringing all the time like this." The lock clicked open; Manny stood frozen until Toby pushed him gently out of the way and stood squarely in front of the door, his teeth flashing in the moonlight. The door yawned and Toby's pistol rose to shoulder height as if door and gun were connected by an invisible pulley.

The housekeeper's eyes grew wide as she looked down at Toby and the pistol, and a choking sound came from her. Her fleshy lips trembled, and a single whispered word escaped her mouth.

"Lord!" she said.

Toby jumped then, shoved the gun forward until the barrel almost touched her nose, and grabbed her arm with his free hand, jerking her out of the house and onto the steps. His voice when he spoke was surprisingly gentle.

"Don't yell anything and we won't hurt you. Who's in the house right now? Just the old man and Stacy, right?"

The housekeeper nodded and made a gulping noise. She was trembling all over like a mound of ham jelly, trembling even more than Manny, and when she looked at him, her wide, dark eyes reflected the lopsided moon. Manny had an irrational urge to apologize to her; he opened his mouth but no sound came out.

"Manny!" Toby said in whispered urgency. "Wake the hell up, will you? Go down the hall, see if anybody's in the living room, and wait by the elevator 'case somebody comes down."

"Where . . . ?" Manny asked.

"To the damn carriage house. I'll be back in a minute. Move, now, partner." Toby began tugging the housekeeper gently down the steps, his hand on her elbow as if he were a boy scout helping her across the street. He turned once before he and the woman disappeared into the darkness, shook his fist at Manny, who still had not moved, and twisted his mouth into a silent snarl of rebuke. Then he was gone.

Chapter
29

*M*anny started with dreamlike slowness down the wide hallway. He stuck his hand beneath his clothes and felt the smooth gunmetal; the burn of the cold steel beneath his fingertips added a terrifyingly real touch to his nightmare. He stared into darkened rooms as he walked, his heart leaping as he passed each yawning black doorway, but nothing stirred on the quiet first floor. He reached the closed doors of the elevator, turned, and then he was inside the huge carpeted living room. There were two ornate couches and several chairs around the outside walls, but they were lost inside the huge, high-ceilinged room, and Manny knew that if he spoke, he would hear an echo. A fire of birch logs burned hotly in the fireplace.

Manny stole quickly back to the hallway for a moment, glanced at the silent elevator, then went over to stretch his hands toward the fire. The heat caressed him and made him dizzy. Without warning he became sick; he held his face over the flagstones of the hearth so that his splashing vomit would not ruin the rich carpet. He felt a little better afterward, wiped his face on the sleeve of his jacket and blinked tears of pain out of his eyes as he looked into the friendly fire.

Then the elevator whined, startling him. He moaned softly and dashed across the room, awkwardly tugging the .38 from his belt. He positioned himself in front of the elevator door and raised the trembling gun up before his chest with outstretched arms. The door flew open, and Stacy Cahill was standing before him, gasping.

"Manny!" she said.

"I . . ." said Manny. "I . . ." The gun was flying crazily around in front of him. Something made him jerk back the hammer, and the resolute *click* loosened him inside; he wet himself in a hot spurt.

Stacy covered her ears as she stared at the gun that was weaving drunkenly before her face. "What are you doing?" Her voice was a thin, terrified screech. "Get out! Get out of here!" One of her hands left the side of her head and crept toward the buttons that controlled the elevator, as if he wouldn't notice if she moved slowly enough.

"Stop!" Manny ordered. "Don't!" The gun was still out of control, the barrel wavering between the ceiling of the elevator and the two back corners.

Then he felt a breeze, and Toby rushed past him into the elevator. Toby grabbed Stacy by the hair and said, "Shut up!" punctuating his words with two brutal backhanded slaps across her perfect face. He dragged her out of the elevator, anger and glee mixing in his face.

Stacy's cheeks were bright red where he had hit her, already starting to swell, and her eyes were dazed.

"Here," Toby said, "give me that damn thing." He took the gun from Manny, who still had it pointed at the back of the elevator. With one hand Toby released the hammer and uncocked the weapon before pushing it back into Manny's fingers. He grabbed Manny's arm.

"Listen, partner, are you alive?"

"Yeah," Manny said. "All right."

"Well, son of a bitch, man, don't go cocking that gun unless you're going to use it. Any fucking noise before we have the whole house under control and the cops'll be here. Get it?"

"Toby," Stacy groaned.

Toby hit her again, but not as hard this time. "Understand?" he asked her.

She nodded feebly.

"Now listen," Toby said, turning to Manny again. "Take a deep breath."

Manny breathed, air rattling into his throat.

"Okay, now what you have to do, pal, while I take this bitch outside, is to go up and see Mr. Cahill. You know where he'll be. Just point the gun at him, steady, but don't cock it, and keep him the hell away from the telephone until I get back. He makes a call our ass is grass. Understand?"

"Yeah," said Manny. His panic subsided a little with Toby there and in control of things. He willingly gave up the initiative now.

"Good. Now, what do you have to do?"

Manny took another deep breath. "I go up, point the gun at him, and keep him away from the telephone."

Toby turned then, dragged Stacy roughly down the hall by an arm, and disappeared out the open front door.

Manny stepped into the elevator and punched the button that would take him up to the oak study. He wished the ride would go on forever, but in ten seconds the doors opened onto a darkened hallway. He looked down and saw light coming out of the study. Manny hesitated a moment, his finger flicking tentatively at the trigger of the gun, and he walked down toward the room.

He didn't hear Cahill's rasping whisper until he was almost across the threshold. The sound startled him and he raised his trembling gun before he saw that there was no one else in the room besides the old man.

Cahill sat in his silver wheelchair with his back to Manny, facing the closed curtains of the window closest to his oaken desk. The desk was clear except for an expensive tape recorder with large, slowly revolving reels, a neatly folded newspaper, and a red telephone. The books and folders on the walls bled their single, sickening color into the room.

It took Manny a moment to realize that the old man was talking to the tape recorder. The machine made a faint squeaking noise, and Manny suddenly remembered the telephone. He strode across the bare floor and placed his hand upon it. The plastic was cool beneath his palm. Cahill's white head lifted then, and Manny had the familiar feeling that the hairs on the back of the old lizard's wrinkled neck were straining toward him, sensing him.

"Stacy," Cahill said, with only a faint note of alarm in his voice. "I have told you I don't consider that to be humorous." A withered claw hit a switch on the arm of the wheelchair, and Cahill pivoted with a grinding, electric whine until he faced Manny. His milky eyes widened as he took in Manny's hand on the phone and the nervously bouncing pistol that was aimed at his face.

"Manuel," he said. There was fear in his voice.

Manny said nothing. He stood by the side of the desk as a new, welcome sensation washed through him. Now that he was facing down the old lizard, he had gone beyond fear and nervousness, and a numbness was creeping along his nerves, killing the twitching disease that had invaded his muscles. He felt as if he were dead, or in prison already, and it didn't really matter if he killed Cahill or not. He watched unemotionally as the trembling of the gun in his hand slowed and finally stopped. The barrel focused its dark eye on Cathill's shining forehead.

Manny picked up the telephone and carried it across the room, setting it on a bookshelf and lifting the receiver off the hook. Then he went back and sat down on a corner of the desk. He waved his gun at the tape recorder. "What's this?"

"My memoirs," said Cahill. Manny's tremble seemed to have fled into the old man, and now the raspy, whispering voice was shaking.

Manny reached and shut the machine off, and then he locked eyes with the old man. His enemy. Manny felt no anger at all, just the spreading numbness.

"Well, Manuel," said Cahill, his head shaking weakly, eyes seemingly afraid to blink. "Is this a robbery?" The old man's tone betrayed the fact that he knew it was not a robbery.

"No," Manny's voice said. "It isn't."

Cahill nodded then and swallowed, making a faint ripple in the leathery skin of his throat. "Then what?" he asked.

Manny opened his mouth to tell him, but discovered that he had actually forgotten why he had come. The numbness had made its way into his skull so that past, present, and future were all telescoped into this room; he was here to kill, he had always been here to kill, and he always would be, and life beyond that single purpose did not exist. He was ready to panic, to burst into hysterical laughter, when Cahill himself supplied the reason and brought him out of it.

"Your father . . ." he said in his unsteady voice.

Manny leaped at him then, thrusting the gun forward. Cahill winced and looked as if he were going to cry out.

"Yes," Manny said. "And my brother too! Then, too, there's my little sister, and my mother and my grandpa."

When the gun did not explode before Cahill's twisted face, the old man tentatively opened his eyes. Manny thought he saw tears shimmering. "I see," Cahill said. "And you blame it on me, do you?"

"Yes," Manny said, his voice suddenly calm.

"And you want to kill me?"

"I have to."

Cahill let his eyes fall back closed then as if he were nodding off. Then he said in a dreamy voice, "I didn't need two gardeners, you know. But when that lazy boy, Toby, told me about you, I thought perhaps I could help you, give you a purpose in life, and perhaps convince you to take up your studies again. I did feel responsible, Manuel."

Manny said nothing.

After a long wait, Cahill continued. There was a teary thickness to his voice now. "When you got into trouble that time, when you shot that man, I helped you. You wanted to know why, and you saw through my lies when I told you. But I'm telling you the truth now, Manuel, it was guilt. I have felt guilt."

A wave of heat ran through Manny now, made his jaws snap together and shoved him forward so his face was almost touching Cahill's. "What good does that do me, Mr. Cahill?" Spray flew from his lips and peppered the old man's wincing face. "You think I ever would have shot that guy if my father was around? Never would have met him. You think I'd need your fucking dirty job if he was still here? I'd be damn near ready for college, that's where I'd be. My brother's dead now because of you, and my mother's a whore who takes pills, and my little sister is out of her mind. You don't know, Mr. Cahill. You just don't fucking know." He felt something wet and warm hit his wrist; he looked down and saw a glistening spot of blood. He rubbed his arm across his face and the sleeve of his jacket came away with a bright stripe. Then the elevator whined and they both looked toward the door.

"If that's Stacy, you won't hurt her, will you?" Cahill asked.

"It's not her," Manny said.

Cahill closed his eyes again. "The chickens have come home," he said. There was resignation in his voice.

The elevator door opened a moment later, and Toby walked into the room carrying his silver pistol. He took the scene in with a sweeping glance, and then he grinned. "Good work, partner," he said. "Good evening, Mr. Cahill, is it cold enough for you? This place must run up a hell of an oil bill in the winter. Of course, minor expenses of that sort don't trouble you, I imagine." He walked around the desk, knelt behind the wheelchair, and jerked a cable loose.

"We'll just disconnect your ass," he said. "In case you try to roll away on us." Then he stood and winked at Manny.

"Okay," Toby said. "Party time. Boom-boom. I want to watch."

Manny shook his head. "Not just yet, partner," he said. "I want to talk to him a little more. He's telling me some stuff."

"Well, then, hurry up, partner. Time's a-wasting." Toby sat down on the desk, his smile flickering like a jack-o'-lantern.

"No," Manny said. "Why don't you go back out to the carriage house? I'll call you when I'm done."

"I—"

"No," Manny repeated. "Partner, I'm in charge here. You said so yourself. The sooner you leave, the sooner it will be over with."

Toby gave him an unbelieving look, his mouth hanging slack. He looked like he was about to protest, but then he thought the better of it. Instead he said, "Well, I'll just start piling some things in my truck, if it's all the same to you, captain."

"Do what you want, Toby."

Toby shrugged; annoyance tugged at his face now. But he left the room and in a moment Manny heard the receding whine of the elevator. He turned back to Cahill, who still had his eyes closed.

"So anyway," Manny said, "that's why I have to kill you. I don't think the law will touch you, so I have to."

The old man's bouncing Adam's apple made ripples in his throat. He spoke with choked difficulty. "Would you believe me if I told you I had nothing to do with it, really? Do you know the full story?"

"About how they killed him and burned the house down around him to cover up?"

A thin wail escaped Cahill's throat. "Yes," he whispered, "but, Manuel, it was none of my doing. You see, when I heard he was trying to call down the authorities on my operation on Wolfpit Road, an operation vital to the chemical industry of the East Coast, mind you, I sent my men out to look for him and talk to him. That's all we wanted to do was talk. My people had never before killed a man, and they have not done so since."

"But they killed my father," Manny said, hurling himself into Cahill's face.

The old man whimpered again. "Yes," he said. "Joe Marconi learned that your father was staying in that empty house. He went over to talk, and there was a fight. I understand your father fell and struck his head during this fight, and died."

Manny noticed his gun trembling again; he felt his whole body shaking, but it was with rage and not fear this time. "It was Marconi? Marconi hit my father's head?"

"Manuel," Cahill said. He was pleading now. "There were several men. But yes, Marconi was there. I didn't know anything until after it was over and they had burned the house down, I swear to you."

"So," Manny said, his voice shaking. "You didn't order it?"

"No, Manuel, I did not. Please, that gun—"

"And it was really Marconi who put his dirty hands on my father?"

"I assume so, Manuel . . ."

Something clicked inside Manny; a decision was made. Marconi and his child-sized feet. He crossed the room and grabbed the telephone and slammed it down on the oak desk. "Call him," Manny said. "Call Marconi and tell him to get his ass out here."

Cahill gasped. "I can't."

"You can," said Manny, quietly now. "If you order him, he'll be here. And don't give me away. I've just about made up to take him instead of you, if you do it right, Mr. Cahill." He set the red phone in Cahill's lap.

The old man stared at the instrument, then, slowly, his hands trembling, he lifted the receiver and tapped out a number. Manny could hear the ringing at the other end, and then a faint voice answered.

"Joe?" Cahill breathed. The buzzing voice in the telephone rose angrily. Cahill listened for a minute, then interrupted.

"Yes," he said, "but this is something of an emergency. You must come up here at once." The phone clicked and Cahill set the receiver down.

Manny took the phone then and put it back on the shelf with the receiver off the hook. Then he took out a set of handcuffs and locked the old man's hands together so he could not reach the wheels of his wheelchair. He double-locked the handcuffs so they wouldn't bite into the old gray flesh. Then he went down the elevator to look for Toby; he found him in the carriage house.

Chapter 30

*T*he housekeeper was lying on the floor of the carriage house, her hands cuffed behind her back and her mouth sealed with tape. Her ankles were also bound by the cloth adhesive. Two antique dolls lay on the floor next to her, their faces smashed off, heads gaping hollowly. The woman's eyes screamed silently at Manny as he walked past her and climbed the ladder into the loft.

Toby and Stacy were on the second floor; Stacy was handcuffed to a steel column that supported the roof. Her face was wet with tears and twisted with fright. Toby was sitting on the floor next to her, casually waving his pistol in the air. He was smiling, but the smile died on his face when Manny told him Marconi was coming.

"Holy Christ!" Toby said, and Manny thought he heard fear in Toby's voice for the first time since he could remember. "That guy's crazy! You're crazy! He'll ruin everything."

"He's the one that really killed my father," Manny said. "And it's too late to argue since he's already on the way."

Toby snarled, "You fucked this all up, Manny." The cocaine was making Toby slam all his words together; Manny had to listen carefully to understand him.

"Well, leave then," Manny said. "I don't care. I have to do what I have to do." He walked toward Toby until he was almost touching him.

Toby tried to smile. "Okay. All right. Course I'm staying. Shit, listen then, we've got to pull the truck up here behind the carriage house so he doesn't see it on the way in, and we have to stop him at the gate, because he'll notice the guard isn't there. And we have to move the guard, now. Damn, what a mess, partner."

Toby ran down the hill and drove the pickup truck onto the grounds, then the two of them went to see about the guard. The man was awake, the blood drying on his forehead, and they trained their guns on him and made him crawl along the fence into the woods until he was out of sight. Then they handcuffed him again. Toby found the chain and padlock, and as he closed the heavy gate and wrapped the chain around the bars, they saw automobile headlights coming up Cahill's long drive, creeping along the treetops and the power lines.

"Son of a bitch!" Toby hissed. "What a fucking mess!"

They hid behind trees on either side of the gate. In a minute Marconi's car rifled up and nearly touched the gate; the crazy dump foreman sat gunning the engine, waiting for the guard to let him in. After a moment he began slapping at the horn; Manny could see his mouth working angrily in the reflected light of the headlights. He also saw Toby's face, the corners of his mouth twitching with fear, peeking out from behind a tree on the opposite side of the car. Even though he was aware of the danger they were in, Manny felt a glow of satisfaction in seeing him caught off guard and acting scared. Toby's unexpected fear made Manny think that maybe control of things was swinging back to him now. If they survived the confrontation with Marconi, he would be back on top.

Marconi finally shut the engine off. He got out, swearing under his breath, and slapped at the lock on the gate. "Stupid!" he called. "Hey, stupid!" A blue baseball cap sat cocked at a weird angle on top of Marconi's head.

Manny was shaking again, fear and hatred sharing him this time, but he was able to make himself step out onto the pavement, his gun lifted and aimed. Toby took the cue and stepped out as well; Manny saw that Toby was shaking too, and the observation gave him courage. The two of them closed in on Marconi, who had not yet noticed them, then Manny said, "Okay," as loud as he could, and the little foreman wheeled.

"What the fuck," Marconi said.

"On the ground," said Toby, his voice high and shaking. "Get on the ground, Marconi." They took hesitant steps toward him, and his wild eyes went from one to the other of them. Then his face twisted into a scornful smile that made Manny's heart flutter weakly.

"Punks!" he said. "What the fuck is this, kinney-garten? You two punks think you're taking me out?"

"Lie down," said Manny, "or we'll shoot." The gun was shaking on him again, and he was afraid it would go out of control.

Marconi made as if to lift his hands in surrender, then he took a rapid step toward Toby, grabbing the arm that held the gun, and threw him into the steel bars of the gate.

Toby screamed, "Manny!" as he struggled to keep the gun away from the stronger man, his cocaine bravado vanished now, then he screamed again in wordless pain as Marconi twisted his arm, snarling like a beast.

Manny was frozen with fear for a moment, but then a clear voice entered his head and told him, *That's how he wrestled your father before he knocked his head against the wall,* and he stepped forward and brought the revolver down hard just above Marconi's ear. The blue baseball cap went flying.

Marconi yelped then, a doglike wail, and he fell away from Toby; he settled slowly to his knees. Both his murderous hands went up and cupped themselves over his ears. He moaned, then slowly began probing his head with his fingers. "I'm shot," he said. "Am I shot?"

Toby recovered his balance and his gun, and he looked at Manny with wide eyes as surprise and awe mingled in his face. "Jesus!" Toby said.

Manny cocked his .38 and held it so it was almost touching the dump foreman's neck. "You're not shot," he said in a quiet voice. He was no longer shaking.

"No," Toby said. "Not yet, anyway." His voice was gleeful, but Manny caught a glimpse of his face and saw that his mouth was now a tight angry line. Suddenly Toby brought the handgrip of his own gun down savagely toward Marconi's head. Manny grabbed his wrist at the last minute, robbing some force from the blow, but the dump foreman fell forward without a sound, and his hands fluttered to the bleeding gash in his scalp.

"Hey!" Manny snarled, still holding Toby's wrist.

"Hey, what?" Toby said, shaking him off. "He's the one that did it, isn't he?" He waited for Manny to pull a set of handcuffs from his jacket pocket and snap them on to Marconi's unresisting wrists. Then he said, "Okay, Manny. Do him now. Do it, and let's get out of here." Toby was panting; whether from fright or from the cocaine speeding his blood, Manny couldn't tell.

But Manny lowered his pistol. "Not yet," he said. "I want to be sure."

"My fucking head," Marconi muttered, trying to crawl back onto his knees and falling against the gate. Manny and Toby looked at him, then stared at each other.

Toby sighed, an exasperated hiss. "What the hell are you doing, partner, conducting a trial? We haven't got all week." There was a nervous quaver to his voice.

Manny slid his free hand under Marconi's arm and helped him to his feet. He was heavier than he looked, solid with wiry muscle. The foreman leaned moaning against the iron bars, swearing softly as blood matted his hair.

"I guess," said Manny, awed by the calmness that had invaded him since he had conquered Marconi. "Yeah, maybe that's what I'm doing. Holding a trial. I want a confession from this bastard. Now open the gate, will you?"

They followed Marconi as he staggered up the front steps of the big house. When they were in the hallway, Toby disappeared into one of the darkened rooms for a moment and returned with two long-necked bottles of expensive beer. "Since you want to hang around a while longer, we ought to have a drink," he said.

Manny shook his head. He saw the offered beer as an attempt to put them back on equal footing. He was going to hang on to the upper hand now. "Don't want it."

Toby shrugged angrily and hurled the extra bottle into the huge living room, where it crashed against the fireplace. They took Marconi upstairs in the elevator, steering him down the narrow hallway into Cahill's oak study.

"Hello, Joe," Old Man Cahill croaked, looking up. His face was wrinkled either with sadness or tiredness, Manny couldn't tell which. "It would appear they've mistreated you."

Marconi stared at him, his eyes clouded with pain and confusion. "You set me up, boss," he said.

Cahill sighed. "The chickens have come home, Joe. Not in the way we expected, but they have come home."

"Make him lie down, why don't you, Manny?" Toby suggested, and took a long sip of beer. "And put a set of cuffs on his ankles. I don't have any more left."

Marconi looked at Manny and at Manny's gun, which was still cocked, and he lay face down on the floor without being asked.

Manny knelt and snapped on the cuffs, then looked up at Toby. "Why don't you check the carriage house?" he said.

Toby tried to hide his annoyance with a grin. He hesitated, then said, "Sure, partner. Just let me know when you're done. What's out there is prettier than what's in here, anyway."

"God," Cahill said. "Stacy. You won't hurt her, whatever you do. Please."

Toby laughed meanly and left the room.

"Really, Manuel," the old man whispered, desperate now. "I have money, you know. I would never report this if you would just—"

"No," Manny said. "You know I don't want money. But don't worry, Stacy is okay. He won't hurt her." Manny was not entirely sure, though. With Toby you never were sure, especially now that he was upset about the twist things had taken.

Marconi, his lips almost touching the floor, spoke now. "What is this, anyway, kid? You know you ain't getting away with it."

Manny knelt and lifted the foreman's head by the hair and looked into his wincing face. "I'm going to jail," he said. "I'm not trying to get away with anything. You killed my father." He felt nothing as he watched fear crowd the pain out of Marconi's eyes.

"Wait," Marconi said. "I didn't. Boss, tell him."

Manny heard Cahill's voice, which always reminded him of papers in a drafty attic or leaves blowing down a sidewalk: "It's too late, Joe. Out of cowardice, I already told him. This is Alexis Moreno's son."

"Alexis Moreno," Marconi echoed, his voice a whine.

Hearing his father's name spoken by the two men responsible for his death had a strange effect on Manny; he stood, proudly, and a wave of sadness ran through him. A drop of blood fell from his nose and splashed on the oak floor, mingling with a larger crimson spot that had leaked from Marconi's scalp wound. He felt a movement in the air of the room then, a tiny frigid breeze. Cahill must have felt it too, because he pulled the plaid blanket off his lap with his manacled hands and clutched it to his chest.

"My father," Manny said. "I can take one life; I'm willing to replace it with my own." He stood silently, waiting.

Cahill bowed his head, signaling he had nothing to say. After a time, Marconi spoke up with a trembling voice.

"I've had nightmares, you know, kid, ever since it happened.

Somehow I knew I would have to pay for it one day." He paused. Manny saw his tongue come out and snake dryly along his lips. "I never killed anybody, pal, you got to believe me. With your father, well, it was an accident. Me and two other guys, we went into that old house to talk to him. Just talk, that's all. We wanted to give him some money to shut up."

"Money," Manny snorted.

"Yeah. But he. musta been scared 'cause he came out swinging with a baseball bat as soon as we walked in the door. I had to, in self-defense, you know, grab that bat and try to wrestle it away from him. He was strong, pal, almost as strong as me, and we wrestled our way across the house and into the kitchen. Then we hit the cellar door; it was not shut all the way, and it flew open on us and dumped us down the stairs. When we got to the bottom, I was alive, and he was dead, with a broken neck. That's the way it happened, so help me God."

Another drop of blood came from Manny and hit the floor. He said nothing, but his finger flicked in and out of the trigger guard of his pistol.

Marconi continued talking, as if to himself. "We didn't even have guns when we went in the house. It was just to talk. And right next to the cellar steps, in a box at the bottom, there was a skull. An old crumbled skull. It looked like it was laughing at me. I was scared shitless."

Cahill dared to speak now. "We're not murderers, Manny. What you have is two pathetic, accidental killers who tried to cover their tracks."

Blood was spilling rapidly from Manny's face now. He made no move to staunch it. He was shaking again. "Somebody has to die," he said. "Somebody has to die for this."

"Yeah," Marconi said, still talking to himself. "I sure as hell regret the day I found that damn note."

"The note," Cahill whispered. "I had almost forgotten."

Manny lifted the cocked .38 and waved it between his two prisoners, wary, suddenly, and frightened. They were talking him out of it. "It's a trick," he said.

"No," said Marconi. "It looked like a kid's writing. In my mailbox. Told me where your old man was hiding out. There was no name on it."

"It's a lie, Marconi," Manny repeated, his voice shrill. "I'm going to shoot you before you can lie anymore."

"Manny," Cahill said. "Joe is not lying. The bottom left-hand drawer of my desk. The note is there; Joe gave it to me after your father's death, and my conscience has never let me destroy it."

Manny gently released the hammer of his pistol then, and walked around the desk. He warily opened the drawer; it was filled with newspaper clippings and bundles of letters bound by elastic bands.

"On the very bottom, by itself," whispered the old lizard.

So Manny began tossing things out onto the floor until he reached bare wood. A white envelope rested there; Marconi's name was written on it in childish block printing. Manny's heart was ringing like a church bell as he slid out the letter and read the single condemning line: *Dear Mr. Marconi, Mr. Moreno is hiding in Charlie Raymond's house.*

Manny let the letter drop to the desk top. He stared at it a moment, then pulled out his wallet. He took from his wallet a letter he had stored there months ago and smoothed it down next to the note written to Marconi: *Dear Manny, I am sorry I hurt your eye.*

The writing was identical. Manny read both letters over and over, bleeding over them, stunned by what he saw and trying to convince himself it was wrong. But there was no way around it. He had a sudden memory of a stick coming at him and striking his eye, sending bright colors ricocheting through his skull. *Shut up about your father,* Toby had said.

Manny looked up at Cahill. "But my brother," he said. "You took my brother away to keep my grandfather from causing trouble." There was a questioning quaver to his voice he had not meant to put there.

"No," Cahill said, and looked him in the eye. "I don't know what happened to your brother. It had nothing to do with us. We don't know what happened to your younger brother. I really wish we could tell you something."

Something in Cahill's voice made Manny look at him closely. He thought he saw a tear glisten in the old reptile's eye. Manny looked away quickly.

"Older," he said. "He was my older brother."

"Believe me, Manuel, we are sorry about your father. If we—"

"Damn this blood," Manny said as if he were not even listening. He wiped a long streak onto his arm. Then he went to the window and lifted the curtain aside. He could just see the corner of the carriage house.

"Okay," he said to no one in particular. "All right. I think I understand now." Without a glance at either of the two bound men, he left the room and took the elevator to the first floor.

Chapter

31

The housekeeper had worked her way, wormlike, into a corner of the carriage house. She was hiding behind a chair when Manny walked in; she looked like an oversized, frightened child, and Manny felt a stab of pity for her. Feeble light poured down from the loft from the single naked bulb that hung there.

Toby called out, "Partner, is that you?"

"Yeah," said Manny. "Me." He looked at the antique china dolls with the broken faces and gaping heads as if for the first time; there were four of them mutilated like that. *He did that,* Manny thought. *He's always done things like that. He always liked to hurt.*

He heard muted crying upstairs, and then Toby called out, "Well come on up, partner, and tell me how it went."

"Minute," Manny called automatically. A chill went through him; he thought of the crazed dogs that had attacked him in the swamp that past spring. This was far more dangerous. He tucked the gun into his belt and adjusted the black patch over his eye.

"Help me," he whispered. It was the first time he could ever remember praying. Then he started up the ladder, taking one last look at the wide, scared eyes of the housekeeper.

Stacy was handcuffed to a steel pole; her blouse was open and her pants were pulled down to her ankles. Toby was holding his automatic pistol in one hand and the empty beer bottle in the other. The long neck of the beer bottle gleamed wetly in the dim light.

"Manny," Stacy sobbed as soon as she saw him. "Make him stop. Don't you know he's crazy?"

Toby leered at her, and then, setting down the beer bottle, he reached and touched one of her nipples, which was erect from the cold, making it spring from beneath his fingertip. "Pure beef and lots of it," he said. "What happened up at the house? I didn't hear a shot."

"Yeah, well that's because I put the gun right up to his chest."

"He's dead?"

"Dead," Manny echoed. Blood throbbed in his ears and behind his eyes.

Toby had been looking hard into Manny's eyes until Manny pronounced Marconi dead. After that he let his eyes drift over toward Stacy; a fleeting expression resembling the fear Manny had seen in him during the struggle over the pistol crossed his face like a cloud, but vanished quickly.

"What were his last words?" Toby asked, trying to sound sarcastic, but unable to keep a hint of a strain out of his voice.

A phrase sprang like magic into Manny's mind; his tongue seemed to move with a will of its own. "He said, 'Fuck you, punk.' "

Toby made an unconvincing attempt at a laugh; he was trembling a little now, and Manny could see sweat building at his blond temples as he struggled to divine how much they had told Manny and what Manny was going to do about it.

Manny was sweating as well; he felt molten drops gathering beneath his arms and then diving down his sides under his shirt. It was clear to him now that Toby had gone out of his way to put him in a position to find out how they had known his father had been in the abandoned house. He could only guess that Toby, by coming with him here, had been carrying out some insane ritual of his own. Maybe he had planned to kill Manny at the end of everything. Maybe Toby had wanted to die himself and to take Manny with him. *You just lie down together and go to sleep.* But Toby was now acting as if things had gotten out of his control.

"Well, great," Toby said, his voice sounding as if he had gulped a breath of helium. "But the old man is still alive?"

"Yup."

"Ah, you're a softie, pard. I guess we go in now and pick up a few more goodies, right?" Toby's eyes continued to avoid him.

Manny looked down at the floor, not wanting to give away anything with his own eyes. "Yeah. Listen, you still got any of that coke left? I need a pick-me-up."

Toby made his face grin. "I was wondering when you'd come around. Just so happens I got a little left." He set the gun down on the floor and took the broken piece of mirror, a razor blade, and the foil-wrapped pellet from his pocket. He opened the foil and shook a white pebble out onto the mirror, then began grinding it into a powder. "This is good stuff," he said as he bent over his work. "Real blast-off stuff, if you know what I mean. Yessir." He seemed glad to have something to do, and he did not look up as Manny stood and began to walk around the loft. Manny went back and forth, back and forth, the floorboards cracking like gunshots beneath his feet, and at first Toby seemed to be trying to track him with the corners of his eyes, but he soon had to give that up so he could concentrate on not dumping the cocaine onto the floor with his trembling fingers.

He barely lifted his head as Manny slid behind him, and he made no sound as Manny raised the butt of the .38 revolver and clubbed him to the floor. The cocaine spilled and snowed down through the cracks in the pine boards, and the mirror shattered into tiny blades.

*S*tacy Cahill looked both relieved and frightened as Manny undid her handcuffs with the tiny key from his pocket. She said nothing. He waited for her to adjust her clothes, then he guided her down the ladder. Outside, he wrapped her arms around an apple tree and put the cuffs back on, double-locking them. He returned to the carriage house, went back up the ladder, and sat waiting for Toby to come around.

It took a while; Manny must have hit him harder than he had intended. But after a time, Toby moved and groaned and opened his eyes. He looked surprised when he tugged at his wrists and found himself handcuffed to the column. He twisted himself around to face Manny.

"Hey, partner," he said. "What's this?"

"They showed me the note, Toby," Manny said. "You wrote it."

Toby's eyes locked with his for a second, then bolted away like frightened animals. His mouth fell open long enough to release a dry croak, then it snapped shut again. He hung his head.

Manny waited for a long minute, then a humming began somewhere at the back of his skull; a feeling of unreality began to slip over him. He began to feel almost as if he were watching himself on some dim television screen. The same person that had moved into him and made him attack Flat Top was starting to crowd him out of his own head. He felt a numb finger slip over the trigger of the revolver he carried. "What about it, Toby?" he heard himself say. "Spit it out. *Partner.*"

Toby remained silent, his chin resting on his chest. Manny saw himself reach, cover the side of Toby's face with his palm, and shove his head backward so that it clunked against the steel column that held up the roof.

"Ouch!" Toby yelled, more startled than hurt, and he gave Manny a burning, offended look. He began to breathe hard, blowing spit out into the loft from between wet, rubbery lips like an angry child. "I was gonna tell you, Manny, goddamn it. You don't have to be so fucking impatient."

"When?" Manny heard himself say. Then he felt himself pull in a double-lungful of air and release it all in a single hysterical explosion of sound: "*When?*"

There was silence for another long minute as the two of them stared at each other; a silence that was total except for a rhythmic grating sound that took Manny a while to recognize as the grinding of his own molars.

Finally Toby said, "After you killed Cahill." His voice was small. "In fact, I'd be telling you right now, if you hadn't gone and brought Marconi into it and thrown me off-balance. It was supposed to be Cahill."

Manny's hand went forward, pressed the barrel of the .38 into Toby's cheek right next to his nose, and shoved his head back into the column once again. Toby winced, but said nothing. "Don't fuck me around," said Manny's voice.

Toby sighed; his hands seemed to want to rise and soothe the injured side of his head, but they rediscovered the shackles and settled back to a spot on the pole that was just a little above the floor. "You know, for the longest time, I didn't know why I did it. We were just twelve, you and me, remember, when it happened. But I've been thinking a lot, and I think maybe I finally got a bead on it, partner."

He stopped and looked up at Manny, apparently for some sign of encouragement.

"Go ahead," Manny heard himself say in a surprisingly gentle voice.

Toby swallowed and looked back at the floor. "Well, the whole thing is this. I didn't have a father. Gramps never let me forget that, either, with his fucking stories. You did have a father, Manny, and Terry had him to. And he was a good father."

"Bastard," Manny growled. He saw a bright drop of blood fall from himself and splash against the floor. Toby continued as if Manny had never spoken.

"I wished he was my father too. That's what it was. And you all treated me that way; it was like I was another brother. But then at night I'd have to go home, and there was no father there, and after I hurt your eye, they still let me come around, but it was different; your father was always a little mad at me after that. So I couldn't even pretend anymore, you know? I started to feel like, empty inside. You ever get that, Manny? Where you're all empty inside, and you don't really feel like you're a person at all? Like maybe you're some kind of weird animal that they raised as a person just for a joke, and pretty soon one day they're going to tell you that you're not really a person, and then everyone gets a good laugh on you?"

Manny came back into himself a little after that. "Jesus Christ," he said.

"So I was always around at night, Manny. I was always around your house. Kind of like I was always trying to figure out how to get in. When somebody came out, I'd run away, or sometimes I'd just walk off into the swamp, almost wanting somebody to catch me."

"You," said Manny. He remembered all the nights when he sensed someone waiting outside the house.

"I was around when your father put on his black clothes and went into Cahill's dump. And I was around when he left home for the last time, and I saw him go into Charlie Raymond's house and start hiding."

Manny was fully conscious of his body once again. His legs were asleep, and he shifted them. His arm was tired from holding the pistol in the air, and he let it settle against the inside of his thigh.

Toby continued to bore holes in the floor with his eyes. "So I put that note in Marconi's mailbox at the front gate of the dump." He appeared to try to meet Manny's gaze, but his eyes would not leave the floor. He rubbed his face against his shoulder and bit thoughtfully at his bottom lip. Then, with some effort, he dragged enough air into himself for another burst of words.

"Not that I could figure they were going to kill him, Manny. That's not what I wanted. I didn't even imagine that."

"What, then?" said Manny.

"Well, I guess, and half of this is guessing, but I think I thought they would take him away for a while. Maybe put him in jail or something. Then you would know, Manny, what it was like not to have a father, too, and maybe you'd get the empty feeling, the nonhuman feeling, and you'd be able to understand me. You'd be my brother."

Manny shook his head; anger was gone now, replaced by sorrow and confusion.

"And I think I thought, too, that maybe I'd rescue him from Cahill's guys, and then I'd be a hero. You'd be grateful, and your father'd want me around."

Manny was bewildered. Another drop of blood fell from him and splashed on the floor. Everyone was guilty, yet no one was guilty. The wickedness around him was as complex as it was elusive. It seemed to be having fun with him, knocking him around like a steel sphere in a pinball machine. "I don't know what to do," he said aloud to himself.

There was a long silence. Then Toby said, "Manny, the part about your father is not even the worst of it."

Manny was suddenly charged with voltage; his head snapped up away from the floor, and his arm brought the barrel of the gun up to point at Toby. "What are you talking about?" he said.

Toby squeezed his eyes shut hard, as if he were in great pain. "Remember that gun, that twenty-two rifle we were talking about when we had the fight and I hit you in the eye?"

Manny was back floating again someplace in a corner of the room, and someone else was under his skin. "What about it?" he asked from between clenched teeth.

"Well, I bought it. I had a grown friend of mine buy it for me, a guy who would always get me stuff at the package store when I wanted it. After all the hassle with your eye, and me cutting my finger off and seeing shrinks, it made me feel safe. I thought the gun protected me."

"What about it?"

"I had it with me the day Terry left the house and went out in that snowstorm. I was there, see, just hanging around outside because

I had a feeling something was up. When he left the house, I figured he had guessed where your father was, and he was going to look for him. I crossed through the woods and met up with him and walked with him for a while. I got him to go out over the blueberry swamp."

Manny's breath rattled through the empty loft like the winds of a hurricane. He heard the throbbing of blood. It seemed to be everywhere. Toby's voice came to him now as if from a great distance.

"Finally he told me to go home and walked away from me. Him and the dog. Walked off into the snow that was coming down in a blanket, and I watched him, and then the gun went off, it was almost like an accident, and he fell down. He fell face down and didn't get up."

The storm of Manny's breath became a wordless howl. The gun lifted and leveled off six inches from Toby's face. Then he was back in control of himself, and then he wasn't again; he was in and out and then into his own skin so fast that he felt sick as if from spinning. His howl squeezed down to a whimper, and he pulled the trigger.

Flame licked out over the top of Toby's head; Manny saw a wayward lick of blond hair jerk aside as if brushed by the invisible bullet. Manny moved the gun slightly and fired again and again; Toby hunched his shoulders up over his ears and curled up on the floor like a frightened caterpillar. Manny stood, fired the remaining three shots into the wood in front of Toby's face, and hurled the pistol through the window of the loft. The shattering of glass echoed like wind chimes in his head.

Toby's automatic lay nearby. Manny bent and snatched it off the floor, flipped off the safety catch, and stitched Toby's outline into the pine floor with .32-caliber bullets. When the gun was finally empty, he tossed it into a corner and collapsed on the floor.

*I*t seemed as if he had slept; he was certain fifteen minutes or half an hour or even an hour had passed without his having been conscious of it. A moan or a sigh that had escaped from his own mouth finally brought him around. He sat up to find Toby watching him as he sat hugging the cold steel post Manny had handcuffed him to.

Toby's face was a wooden mask. His cheeks were bloody from the splinters the bullets had kicked up. "What are you going to do, Manny?" he asked.

"I don't know," Manny croaked. He felt empty; he wondered if it was the emptiness Toby had wanted him to share. The thought caused a little chill of fright to leap out into the dark vacuum inside him.

"Do you want to see him?" Toby asked.

"Terry?"

"I'll take you."

Manny studied him for a long minute for signs of treachery. Then he rose, picked the automatic pistol up off the floor, and stuck it into his belt. When Manny unlocked the handcuffs, Toby's face brightened.

"Right," he said, trying to recover his lost bravado. "Right, Manny." He grinned. But there was something hollow and dead about his eyes, and Manny could see that the muscles of his face were working hard to keep the corners of his mouth lifted.

Chapter 32

*M*anny sent Toby down the ladder ahead of him. Toby got to the bottom and stood waiting, tightly gripping a middle rung in one white-knuckled hand as if he could get control of his shaking that way. As Manny descended past the hand, he saw that it was the one Toby had mutilated in exchange for having shattered Manny's vision. In the muted light of the carriage house, the shiny-smooth finger stub gleamed like the eye of an amphibian. Manny shivered when he saw it.

"I think it's getting cold, Manny," Toby said when they were once again face-to-face. "Look at me, I'm shaking. It's got to be cold, partner, don't you think?" Toby could not quite meet his eyes; they seemed to focus on Manny's chin or mouth. He was trying to smile, but every time he parted his lips, his teeth would begin to chatter. His face was covered with blood.

"Yeah," Manny said. "Cold." Instead of giving Toby the comforting look that some part of him wanted to give, he directed his sympathy at the housekeeper, who was still cowering in the corner. The shots from above had frightened her badly, and she was breathing hard, blowing like a horse through flared nostrils.

"We weren't trying to hit you," he said, suddenly feeling stupid. "We're going to leave now. You're safe."

The housekeeper did not react to this news, so Manny said, "Did you understand?" She nodded slightly then, and it seemed that her breathing eased a little. "Sorry we scared you," he added lamely. He was ashamed about the large woman more than anything; she had never done anything to harm him, and, as far as he knew, she was not tainted with Cahill's wickedness the way Stacy and the night guard were. He had probably taken ten years off her life. At that moment the shame almost overbalanced the disgust and hatred he felt for Toby.

Then he saw that the housekeeper's bulging eyes were not focused on his face, but on the automatic pistol tucked into his belt. He looked down at the weapon as if seeing it for the first time; the bright finish was smudged from handling, and he realized that the gun was empty and that he had no more ammunition for it. He thought about going outside to search for his .38, for which his pocket still bulged with shells, but something told him that Toby would take him to Terry's body even if he did not use a weapon to force him to. And if Toby tried anything, Manny was prepared to splinter his skull with the empty gun. He knew he would do it.

Toby was standing now in the open doorway of the carriage house, still trembling and trying to smile. "Ready, partner?" he asked, the tremble in his limbs now having spread to his vocal cords. "Time's a-wasting." And then he did succeed in stretching his face into a horrible, mirthless grin.

Manny wanted to unload the few items that Toby had looted from the house and piled into the truck. Toby gave him no trouble about that, and together they took out a stereo system complete with speakers, a heavy set of silverware, leather-bound books of coins, a small, dark safe that was surprisingly light, and a matched pair of engraved shotguns and set them in the grass by the side of the carriage house. Then, leaving Toby behind for a moment, Manny walked back to the tool shed and felt around in the dark until he found the long-handled spade he had used so often in the gardens around the estate. He carried the shovel back to the truck, tossed it into the open truck bed, where it clanged like the stifled toll of a bell, and jumped into the driver's seat. Without being told, Toby slid in next to him and he began to drive, stopping only to open the front gate for himself and to take a flashlight from the belt of the manacled guard. The guard looked up at him as he flipped on the flashlight and sent the beam streaming through the dark woods on the hillside for a moment. "It's okay," Manny told him. "We're all finished here."

*T*hey parked in Grandpa Tarbox's driveway and walked around the side of the dark house and up onto the railroad bed, heading north. The waning moon had tumbled down out of the sky and was now rolling like a lopsided wheel along the edge of the earth. On either side of the railroad bed, the shadows of trees twisted and struggled like snakes on the floor of the swamp; silver moonlight surrounded the shadows like rippling water. Manny let Toby walk ahead; he trailed behind with the shovel and the gun in his hands and the flashlight stuffed into his back pocket. He swung the shovel like a walking stick, letting the steel blade bite into the sterile cinders of the railroad bed with each step he took. The swamp was silent tonight; there was not even a breeze, and it seemed to Manny that an air of calm expectancy had settled down upon the miles of woods and water. He could almost hear the swamp whispering to him from beneath his feet as he scuffed through cinders and powdered stone. They passed Manny's house, lit by a single dim light in his mother's bedroom, and continued north.

"Not too much farther," Toby said in a subdued voice once they had come upon the Engine Hole. The Engine Hole was full of moonlight, and just as they were passing it, a cloud slid briefly across the face of the moon, causing the silent pool to wink.

Then Toby turned onto the path that Manny and Terry had taken long ago when they had stolen from the house at night to go fishing and had returned home thinking they had seen the Crying Woman. Manny shuddered and hoped Toby had not put his brother's body into the ground near that spot, but Toby pressed on, pushing aside bushes in the overgrown path, leading him down through sucking swamp and up onto higher ground again in the direction of the little brook. Dry brush crackled beneath their feet.

When they were close enough to the brook to hear water singing through stones, Toby said, "Manny, I'm going to need that flashlight." He sounded apologetic.

So Manny caught up to him and passed him the light; the transfer made him think of the story about Toby's father breaking the lantern after the hunt for the last wildcat. Toby took the light, and without turning it on he plunged off into the woods on the side of the old footpath. Manny heard him crashing through brush for a minute, then there was silence. He started after him then, thinking that Toby had escaped and was hiding from him, and he began to curse himself for not having brought the weapon that matched the ammunition in his pocket. His shoes, wet from having come through wet ground, made derisive sucking noises as he stumbled in the direction Toby had gone.

But then the flashlight flared in the darkness, and Toby was calling him. "Over here, Manny," he said. "This is it. I put this stone here."

Toby stood waiting for him, the flashlight aimed at Manny's chest and his gaze directed at some point high over Manny's head. When Manny was standing at his side, Toby dropped the flashlight beam and swept the ground with it; there was a dark stone the size of a pumpkin sitting in the middle of a slight depression in the earth.

"Not much of a headstone, Manny," Toby said softly.

Manny pulled the flashlight out of his hand and pushed the shovel at him. "You dig," he said. Toby took the shovel and began to break the ground.

But a few minutes later, after Toby had gotten about a foot beneath the soil and said, "I think there's something here," Manny shoved him roughly out of the way.

"Don't you touch him, Toby," he said, and, dropping to his knees, he set the gun and the flashlight aside and began to scoop cold dirt up out of the hole with his hands. He felt something solid; he thought maybe it was a root. But turning the flashlight on it for a moment, he saw that it was a yellowed thighbone. He began to breathe rapidly, throwing dirt with both hands, and he felt other bones taking shape in the dirt below him, ribs and hips and an entire hand. When his fingers fell into the eye sockets of the skull, a moan escaped him, but he kept clawing away at the earth. Then he felt something strange, and he stopped a moment to turn the light to it. It was the skull of a dog. Manny was panting now.

"A dog," he whispered. "You fucking asshole. You buried a dog with my brother."

He flung a handful of dirt at Toby's unmoving silhouette, then he flung another and another and another. He would have kept throwing dirt until he fell exhausted into the shallow grave except that once, as he was reaching, instead of closing his fist on earth, he touched the skeletal hand of his brother.

"Jesus," he said, and collapsed to the ground. "You fucker. I'd like to kill you. God, I wish . . ." His words turned to a strangled wail in his throat. He wanted to cry, but he couldn't cry; he couldn't even bleed anymore. He lay twitching and shuddering next to his brother's unhallowed grave.

Then Toby was kneeling in front of him, coolly passing the flashlight beam over Manny's prostrate body. He reached and picked up the pistol Manny had discarded, and, holding the flashlight under his armpit for a moment, slipped out the empty magazine and tossed it away. He dug into his pants pocket and drew out his spare clip.

"Did you forget I had this, Manny?" he asked. He fed the clip up into the pistol and seated it. Moonlight danced along the silver barrel.

"I don't care," said Manny. "All you bastards . . ." Manny was aware, suddenly, that he had made a fatal mistake. But at that moment Manny cared little whether Toby shot him or not. He was tired of everything. So tired he felt like crawling into the dirt with his brother's bones and covering himself with loam and sleeping there. There just was no dealing with the evil in the world.

"Partner," said Toby. "Remember that I told you that I didn't mean to shoot Terry? Do you believe that I meant that?" There was a brittle, pleading quaver in his voice.

"I don't know," said Manny. "Leave me alone."

"Look at me, Manny."

"Fuck off and die, Toby."

"*Please,* Manny."

So Manny looked up. Toby was holding the Spanish .32 loosely in his right hand and shining the flashlight on his own face with his left. His face was black as a coal miner's from the earth Manny had pelted him with. He was expressionless, except for two wet lines that cut straight channels through the dirt and disappeared under his chin.

"Do you believe I meant that?" Toby repeated.

Manny pulled himself into a sitting position. "Maybe you meant it," Manny said sharply. "Cahill cried, you know."

Toby looked surprised. Then he said, "Things happen. People aren't always in control, you know, partner? I didn't mean to shoot him in the first place; it was just something that I did because I was scared. I wanted to be able to tell you about your father in my own way, and it looked like he was gonna blow it for me. I figured they'd get Cahill, and Cahill would talk about the note, and they'd pin it to me, and you'd hate me, Manny. The rifle just sort of lifted itself and went off; I wrapped the fucking thing around a tree and then burned it after that. Not because I wanted to hide it, but because . . . it killed your brother."

He met Manny's gaze for a second, then he let his eyes slink away. His face took on a pained expression, as if Manny's eyes had burned him.

"Believe me, Manny, the second I shot Terry, if I could have brought him back . . . I would have." He laughed nervously, pain still plowing furrows in his face. "The damn dog, I had to chase that dog forever, Manny. I was freezing. I will never forget that. I wanted you to go ahead and kill Cahill, Manny, that would've meant that you put most of the blame on him. See, believe me, I always wanted to tell you about everything, but . . . in my own way, so that maybe you could forgive me just a little bit. Maybe you'd tell me that I still deserved to live, and I think I do, don't I, Manny? I'm not bad a hundred percent. And everything I did, I did as a kid. I've changed a lot." He was shaking badly now; the gun in his hand was pointed at Manny's chest, and it was shaking too. Toby was getting out of breath from talking so fast.

"You don't believe me, do you, Manny? I told you I'd die for you, and you still don't believe me. Partner, I wanted you to start finding out, that's why I was always trying to goad Gramps into telling you different things to get you moving toward Cahill. I gave him those stone beads on his birthday for that reason. I was pretty sure he knew about your dad, and I wanted to smoke him out. That's why I got you up at Cahill's to work. I wanted you to know, dammit, I just didn't want you to find out it was partly me until you knew it was mostly Cahill and blamed him for it. So I was always worried Gramps with that damn forked stick would find Terry, even though it was stupid, thinking he could, out here in all this swamp. But I used to follow him at night, sometimes, when he was wandering around, and it'd really make me sweat if he was getting hot, I'll tell you." He laughed nervously again.

A worm of curiosity worked its way through Manny's revulsion and hatred. "What about all those other bodies, Toby? Did you murder those six kids they found last spring?"

Toby was crying steadily, soundlessly and with no expression on his face. Just as Manny began to ask his question, he rubbed at his dirty, tear-streaked face, appeared surprised to feel the wetness, and abruptly snapped off the flashlight, leaving them with only the moonlight to see each other by. The pistol and Toby's teeth shone eerily in the silver light.

"Me? Shit, no. What do you think I am, partner? I did know those bodies were there, though. I found the freshly turned soil a couple of years back, and I thought it might be something Gramps had done. So I dug in there myself a little one night, and found 'em. Sort of forgot about them for a while after that, but then when I wanted to give Gramps a little push and get the ball rolling, I called the cops and said they were there. Had no idea there were as many as six there, I'll tell you that."

"Who killed them?" Manny was feeling sick to his stomach; his insides squeezed with a couple of dry heaves, then they settled down.

"I don't know, Manny, I swear. Maybe that guy they caught. Who knows, partner, the world's full of crazies."

"How did Terry get here? You murdered him in winter when the ground was hard."

The question did not seem to phase Toby. "I had him in different places. During the winter, I had him piled under stones from a stone wall. Then when the ground was soft, I took him and buried him up near the dump. But your grandfather was looking up there with his forked stick, and he even started to do some digging, so I brought him here. I . . ." Manny heard him sigh deeply. He was silent for a minute, then he said, "There's no way, is there, Manny? Even if I went to jail for the rest of my life, you still wouldn't forgive me even a little, would you?"

Manny thought of the gun, but he decided he didn't care. "No," he said.

"Well, not forgive, exactly, but maybe understand a little bit." The pleading quaver came back into Toby's voice, and it irritated Manny. "Like maybe I need help, you know, or something. 'Member we always said we were brothers? I never had a father, and you were the only person I was ever close to." Toby seemed to be whining now, and Manny's annoyance grew, along with his disgust. The bitter hatred he had felt seemed to have been vanquished by his exhaustion. The gun continued to bounce in Toby's hand to the beat of a steady pulse.

"No, Toby. A brother who kills my brother is not my brother anymore." Irrationally, he squinted to protect his eyes from the muzzle flash he expected to come licking out of the gun like a snake's tongue. The pulsing of the gun stopped; the barrel froze and the bore was like a yawning cavern in the darkness.

Then Toby said, "Kill me, then, Manny. I deserve it. I want you to. Take the gun." But he made no move to offer him the weapon.

Manny slowly climbed to his feet, still expecting to be shot. Toby rolled his head backward, following his movement, but he did not shoot.

Then Manny reached, all the time expecting a gun blast, until his hand covered the automatic. He tugged gently; Toby released it from his grasp.

"I can't," Manny said. "You know I wanted to before, but I couldn't. Now I'm not sure I want to. It's like Grandpa Tarbox told me; it's not in me." As he said it, Manny discovered that this was true. The hate he had felt had burned almost entirely to clean, white ash. He wanted to go home. He wanted to sleep. If Toby had decided to shoot him, that would have been another kind of sleep, a deeper rest, and maybe that wasn't so bad either. Maybe now he would wake up in a day or two and tell the police, and maybe he would decide not to tell anyone. It seemed, suddenly, that he had already done the important thing. He had found his brother.

He started to walk back through the woods toward the path, the gun dangling from his hand. In a minute he heard Toby coming through the bushes behind him. He did not turn around. When he was up on the gravel of the track bed and heading down toward his house, he heard the crunching of Toby's feet on the broken ballast. He began to move faster, to escape.

Then, when he was well past the Engine Hole, Toby called to him. "Manny. I said I'd die for you."

Something made Manny loosen his fingers; the gun slipped from his hand and hit the cinders of the railroad bed with a muffled thud. He kept walking.

A moment later he heard Toby's lonely cry: *"Manny!"* Manny could have turned around then, but that was not in him any more than killing was in him. He kept right on walking, and the shot came half a minute later. It was not as loud as he had expected.

Manny walked back slowly. He found Toby quivering, with his eyes squeezed shut, almost as if in orgasm. A trickle of blood ran from the corner of his mouth. The automatic pistol lay in the weeds, three inches from the tip of a finger that kept pointing at it and then curling back toward Toby's palm. Toby quivered like that for a quarter of an hour, then he lay still.

Chapter 33

*M*anny squatted in the cinders of the railroad bed for the rest of the chilly night, keeping a vigil by Toby's body. He remembered his grandfather telling him that everyone was valuable in his own way, and that the loss of any person upset the balance and harmony of things. Looking down at Toby's still shell, Manny supposed that the rule was valid even for his poor murderous friend. He was glad suddenly that he had not killed Cahill, or Marconi, or Toby.

Once Manny reached and stroked Toby's blond hair for a moment. The touch filled him with grief for all of them—for Terry, for his father, for Grandpa Tarbox, and even for Toby himself. Grandpa Tarbox had been right: Manny was no good at hating.

Dawn came and crows gathered, complaining in the high branches of dead trees. A squabbling pair of young raccoons crossed the track bed a little ahead of Manny and entered the weeds on the other side without even looking in his direction. In the new light, he saw how dirty Toby's hands were; they were at least as dirty as his own. He knew there would be questions about that. Manny rose, massaged the stiffness out of his knees, walked back up the tracks, and began pulling branches and loam and leaves over the top of his brother's shallow grave. He knew that a trained eye could easily pick out the disturbance in the ground, but he didn't think anyone would bother with it. He dug a small hole off to the side of the track bed near Toby's body, and stabbed the shovel blade into the damp earth next to it so that the handle pointed skyward. Then he walked down toward his house, stopping only to wash his hands in the brook.

*T*he police arrived about fifteen minutes after he called them. A squad car carrying Jamison and White slowly rounded the curve in the driveway, followed by an ambulance van. Two detectives came along later.

They all asked him questions. Jamison's eyes were wide with horror or fear or maybe just disbelief, and his voice was sharp. They asked him questions even as the ambulance men bent over Toby, touching him delicately, as if he would crumble to dust beneath their fingers, and then zipped him into a black body bag and carried him off.

Manny told them he did not know why Toby had been digging in the swamp. He said he had gone for a walk in the early morning hours because he couldn't sleep, had found Toby lying there just like that.

They took him to the police station for more questioning. He almost expected them to catch him in a lie; he was so tired he didn't care. He said he didn't know why Toby's head was all bruised. Maybe a fight at the high school; he was always getting into them. He said he had no idea how Toby had gotten wooden splinters buried in his cheeks.

He expected them to say something about the mayhem at Cahill's house. But no one mentioned Cahill, and after a time someone spoke with Mrs. Carver. She told them that for a long time she had been worried that Toby was using drugs. Manny told them that yes, Toby sometimes used drugs, marijuana and even cocaine. If they tested his blood, they might even find some, he suggested. They let him go then; Jamison even drove him back to his house and dropped him off at the mouth of the driveway.

*F*or days, he waited for something bad to happen. He felt wrung out, exhausted, and he slept most of the time. His sleep was dreamless, and during the twilight periods between slumber and wakefulness, he half-expected to be jerked out of bed by rough policemen's hands and accused of killing Toby or kidnapping Cahill and Stacy. No heavy footsteps sounded on the ladder to his attic room, however; the only noises in the house were the faint footfalls of Ida and his mother moving about below him. Sometimes he would hear them talking. Twice during those days his mother called up into the attic to tell him that Mrs. Carver wanted to speak with him; he would climb down the ladder and mumble condolences and reassurances into the telephone while Mary Anne hovered nearby, almost glaring at him, standing first to one side and then to the other as he twisted away and wrapped himself in the phone cord to avoid her eyes.

At just about the time Manny had made his mind up that the police were not going to visit him again, the day arrived for Toby's funeral. His mother woke him up that morning; she had already put on the dress she had worn at Grandpa Tarbox's services.

"Ida's ready too, Manny," she said. "Don't you think you ought to be getting up?" Then she stood at the foot of his bed, fixing him with her questioning stare, until he flapped a dismissing hand at her and slowly began to slide out from under his blankets.

He dressed and drove them to the funeral home in the old station wagon. The room where Toby lay was large and nearly empty, and decorated by three lonely flower arrangements. Mrs. Carver was Catholic; Manny had never known that, and a thin, effeminate priest with little round glasses on his face came in to read words in flat, practiced tones before asking the handful of mourners to drive down to the church.

Mrs. Carver had no one there, and she clung to Manny's arm throughout the service and the burial. She didn't cry, but her eyes looked dead. She told him she had been taking Valium to keep her calm.

The priest had never known Toby. But he said that Toby was a sensitive boy who had probably been crying out for help and had not been heard. He told them that Toby, at this moment, was probably sitting with God. He did not mention the suicide directly. The priest prepared bread and wine; he asked if anyone wanted to take communion, and no one, not even Mrs. Carver, stepped forward. So he performed his miracles, ate and drank by himself, careful not to waste a single crumb of the host. He rang bells, and afterward he wiped the cup clean with a piece of white linen and set the folded cloth across the top of the polished vessel.

At the cemetery, the priest said more words, sprinkled water on Toby's coffin, and then poured some sterilized sand from a silver tube onto its rounded lid. The sand rolled like marbles off Toby's smooth box.

The men from the funeral home had brought the three wreaths that had stood near the coffin and had set them up around the gravesite. Two of the flower arrangements were small, the third was as big around as a manhole cover. On his way back to the car, Manny passed by the large wreath and opened the card. It said, *From William Cahill and Stacy.*

Manny and Ida and his mother visited with Mrs. Carver at her house for a while. Mary Anne had made a casserole, and a few friends had brought other dishes. No one ate any of it.

As they were preparing to go home, Mrs. Carver came up to them. "I'm leaving," she said. "I'm selling the house and moving away from here." The skin of her face hung from her skull like uncooked dough. Manny nodded, and his mother patted her on the shoulder. "I'll visit you," she said. "I'll come soon."

*B*ack at the house, Ida turned on the television and curled up on the couch to watch *Wheel of Fortune.* Manny's mother pulled a frayed gray sweater on over her good dress, made herself a drink with vodka and orange-flavored Hawaiian Punch, and sat down by herself at the kitchen table, staring out the window. Manny went up to his room to take a nap. He slept for about an hour, and when he rose and went back downstairs, his mother was still gazing into the front yard, the ice cubes nearly melted in her glass.

"Are you okay?" he asked, feeling his insides tighten in apprehension. She turned to look at him, one thin hand covering her mouth.

Then, letting her fingers drift from her lips up into her hair, where they traced trembling paths, she said, "Manny, something is all wrong here. I think I know you a little better than you think, and you've been strange about things." He held her gaze for as long as he could, then he looked down.

"Did you kill Toby?" she asked.

His breath caught; he stared down at the kitchen floor until the spots on the dirty linoleum began to dance. He let the air back into his lungs slowly and, without looking up, he shook his head.

"Well, what happened to him, then?" she asked in a soft voice.

He looked up then; his mother was shaking slightly, but her eyes were locked on to him, and it seemed that she was pulling herself together from inside to handle anything he might have to tell her. But he still couldn't be certain she would not shatter if he let her have everything all at once.

"It's just like they said," Manny told her. "Toby shot himself."

There was a long silence, then his mother said, "You know, this is just like when your grandfather kept shouting out your father's name, Manny. I know something rotten is behind it all, and if I don't find out what it is, my imagination will go to work on it, and I'll imagine things ten times worse than the truth, and it will make me crazy. Don't let me go crazy, Manny; I'm nearly there already. Why did Toby kill himself? It has something to do with you, doesn't it?"

"You're shaking," Manny said. It embarrassed him that his own voice was trembling now. He was exhausted again, suddenly, wanted nothing more than to crawl up the ladder to his attic room, pull the covers up over his head, and fall down the dark well.

"I'm all right, Manny. Can't you see how hard I'm trying?"

He looked at her, then let his eyes fall away. "You're doing a good job," he conceded. "Okay. Put on some old shoes, Mom. We have to go for a walk."

*I*t was late afternoon when they left the house. His mother caught her breath when she saw Manny take a shovel from the garage, but just the same she followed him across the rotting footbridge and into the swamp. They said nothing until they had reached the site of Terry's shallow burial and Manny had scraped away enough dirt and vegetation to expose the bones.

"It's Terry," he said in an unsteady voice, and squatted down to await her reaction.

She stood mute for a time, both hands touching her lips, then she settled down to the ground next to him. He was afraid she would begin to rock back and forth in the disturbed way that Ida sometimes did, but instead she let a hand fall away from her mouth and flutter toward the open wound in the earth; she briefly touched a yellowed rib and then drew her hand away.

"It is . . . how do you know?"

"I know," he told her, his voice sounding like a hinge that needed oiling. "Butch . . . Butchy is in there with him." He looked away over the tops of the trees so he would not have to see her face. "Toby killed them. He told me." It was a terrible effort to choke out the words, but he continued. "It was that same day they walked away."

There were no words for a long time; the two of them watched the November sunset together, neither looking into the face of the other. When his mother finally spoke, her voice was tired but surprisingly strong.

"Tell me everything, Manny," she said. "I'm not sure, but I think I'm ready to hear it now."

*T*hey left Terry right where he was for about a week. Manny and Ida and his mother all stayed to themselves in the little house, and when they happened to come together in the living room or the tiny kitchen, they never mentioned him. Then one morning, Manny was seized with an urge to build; he backed the car out of the garage, began to pull down all the wood that had been stored there in the rafters, and set to work. He hardly knew what he was doing, he just knew that his hands had to be busy; it was the same feeling that had taken him when he constructed the rabbit hutch for Ida. When he ran out of wood, he went down the railroad bed and took some old pine that his grandfather had stored at his house.

Very quickly, as he sawed and planed and hammered, a long box took shape atop the two sawhorses he used as a workbench. He was half-considering putting tiny windows in it and painting it and making it into a giant dollhouse for Ida when his mother came out to watch him. She stood with her arms folded across her chest for a time as he worked, then, very softly, she said, "I think you're right, Manny. I don't think we want strangers touching him."

So Manny built a lid, and his project became a coffin. When he was finished, Mary Anne lined it with old blankets and pillows and tacked some material she had once used to make curtains around the sides to hide the bare wood. The material was white and printed with pictures of crossed fishing rods and little black fish with yellow eyes and yellow tails.

When the job was done, Ida surprised them by appearing in the garage dressed in the clothes she had worn to the funerals of Toby and Grandpa Tarbox. She carried an old bottle of My Sin perfume that she had taken from the top of Mary Anne's dresser. The inexpensive scent had been a Christmas gift from Terry many years before, and Ida took off the top and sprinkled it liberally around inside the padded box.

After that, Manny took a shovel and went off by himself into the swamp. He selected the grassy top of a knoll where he had always seen Queen Anne's lace growing in the summer, and he began to dig. He was tired when he first broke ground, worn out from his work on the coffin as well as weary from the heaviness he had been carrying inside ever since Toby had killed himself. But the deeper he went into the ground, the lighter he began to feel; it was if he were drawing energy from the damp soil of the swamp itself. Once or twice he stopped to crumble the wet earth in his fingers and to smell its richness. When his work was finally done and he boosted himself up out of the hole, his muscles were crying for more work, and a breeze that crept down from the higher parts of the swamp was so sweet it made him dizzy. He paused for a moment to breathe in that good air and let it fill him up.

Manny and Ida and their mother carried the new coffin out into the swamp and set it down next to the spot where Toby had buried Terry. Manny took the lid off and leaned it against the side of the wooden box, and then, after hesitating a moment, he knelt and lifted the skull up out of the ground. He looked from his mother to Ida and then said, "It's Terry. This is Terry."

They both reached and touched for a moment; Ida said, "Good-bye, Terry," and Mary Anne was about to say something, but tears came to her eyes and she closed her mouth decisively. Manny settled the skull in on a pillow, and when he knelt again, they knelt with him and the three of them began taking the bones and placing them gently in the homemade coffin.

They left the remains of the dog where Toby had put them; Manny quickly covered them up with the shovel, then they lifted the box and carried it up into the woods to the new grave. Manny remembered that the Indians of the swamp had thought heaven lay in the direction of the rising sun, and that they had always buried their dead to face in that direction. He opened the lid of the box one more time before it went into the ground to adjust Terry so he was facing east. After that, Manny and his mother lowered Terry down on ropes while Ida wandered through the swamp in search of dried flowers. When she returned, she handed each of them a small bundle of the dried brown heads of marsh grass and goldenrod, which, along with a single sprig of bittersweet that held only five or six berries, were all that she had been able to find. Ida shoved the bittersweet into the middle of her own bundle and tossed it down onto the lid of Terry's coffin. Then Manny threw his. His mother was the last to drop her flowers.

They covered Terry with earth and walked back to the house.

WINTER

Chapter

34

*I*t was the last day of the old, tired year, the dead day before the New Year was born, and a few weeks over six years since Alexis Moreno walked out of his house and never came back. It was snowing lightly, and the big, soft flakes came down like white duck feathers.

Manny and Ida and their mother were playing poker at the kitchen table, using toothpicks in place of money. The cards were very old and worn and soft; the gaudy queens and the winking jacks were witnesses and veterans of many games with Grandpa Tarbox, and the three of them would not have changed them for a crisper deck even if they had had one. Ida's attention wandered from the game frequently; she would slowly turn an ear toward a corner of the kitchen as if listening for something, her small pretty mouth slightly agape. Usually she would come out of the reverie by herself in a second or two, shaking her head slightly and looking back down at the table. But sometimes Manny would have to tap her on the elbow and call her name.

"Ida," he would say, "pay attention. And hold your cards up; I don't want to see them."

Ida would look from one to the other of them then, smiling

crookedly, as if in apology for her distractedness.

A half-pint bottle of blackberry brandy sat on the table at Manny's elbow. From time to time he would lift it, screw off the top, and take a short sip. Twice during the game Manny pointed the open neck of the little bottle in his mother's direction; she smiled, shook her head, and turned to the contemplation of her cards. The second time, he said, "Sure? I'll even get you a glass."

But his mother just said, "No. No thank you, Manny."

The game went on, nobody raising, nobody bluffing. There was little talking in the warm kitchen, just the comforting whisper of card against card and the ticking of toothpicks tossed into the center of the table.

Then, just after she had shown them three kings and swept a tiny pile of toothpicks to her side of the table, Ida cocked her head again, this time in the direction of the window.

"Ida . . ." Mary Anne said.

"Someone's coming," Ida said. "On the driveway." Then she gathered up the cards in her thin fingers and began to shuffle.

Manny and his mother looked out into the falling snow. In a moment a metallic blue car that Manny recognized as a Lincoln Continental came around the curve in the driveway and stopped a stone's throw from the house. Mary Anne and Manny exchanged glances, and then continued playing. After several minutes, a man stepped out of the driver's side and stood looking toward their window, his gloved hands at his sides.

"Shit," said Manny. He tossed in his cards and went to the closet for his jacket. Then he went out the front door, hands in his pants pockets, and walked up to the visitor. It was T. Joseph Lawrence, Cahill's lawyer, and the skin of his bare and balding head was pink with the cold. He looked miserable in the open air, even though he wore gloves and a heavy overcoat.

"Manuel," he said. He peeled off a leather glove so slick it looked as if it had been shined with oil, and he pushed his hand toward Manny. Manny stood looking at him.

"Oh yes," Lawrence said, vapor boiling from his mouth. "I had forgotten." He replaced the glove, then clenched and unclenched his fist, as if making sure the fingers still worked.

"So," Manny said. He watched the puff of vapor produced by the word *so* thin and vanish against the gray sky. It made him think of his grandfather's pipe smoke.

"Yes," Lawrence said. "Well. Mr. Cahill has asked me to relay his regards." A corner of the lawyer's mouth twitched as if in an attempt to smile.

"How is Mr. Cahill?"

"Not well, Manny," said Lawrence. "He suffered a terrible stroke about six weeks ago. He is bedridden."

"That's too bad," said Manny. He said it with sarcasm, but he was surprised by a pang of true regret that sliced through him.

Lawrence smiled now with his own sarcasm. "Well, he did ask me to visit you, Manny. A drive into the woods is not my idea of a swell New Year's Eve. Not even to see such a close friend."

Manny nodded. "Okay," he said. "What is it, then?"

Lawrence fumbled in the pocket of his overcoat and pulled out a rumpled sheet of paper. He smoothed it between his gloved fingers and cleared his throat.

"Fucking lawyers," said Manny. Lawrence ignored him.

"Mr. Cahill wishes me to tell you that he is concerned about you, that he has always respected you, and that he even admires you in a way." Lawrence's sarcastic smile returned, and he even met Manny's eyes for a moment.

"Go ahead," said Manny. He tilted his head back and stared directly up into the falling snow.

"He wishes me to tell you that he was both surprised and thankful that you did not go to the authorities concerning the whereabouts of your father's remains and the information you have on our Wolfpit Road activities. You could have caused us a great deal of trouble and expense."

"You would've killed me too."

"That is not true, Manuel. And Mr. Cahill said that would not have stopped you if you had made your mind up to do it."

Manny was still facing the sky. He held his breath for a long moment, then exhaled a blast of white vapor. "Read your shit," he said. He heard Lawrence sigh.

"Mr. Cahill wants you to know that he has purchased the property containing the ruins of the house where your father's remains now lie. He of course cannot deed that land over to you, but he promises that he will not develop it or sell it and that you and your family may visit there any time you wish. He only asks that you don't erect any kind of marker there, and that if you want the body retrieved, you allow us to do it, so that we can do it discreetly."

Manny turned his eyes on Lawrence now. The lawyer looked embarrassed, but he continued.

"We would prefer, that is, Mr. Cahill said he would prefer, that you not—"

"We don't need to dig him up," Manny said. "And we don't need any marker."

Lawrence nodded, suddenly grave. "He said he thought you'd—"

"Go ahead and read," said Manny. He was surprised at the sudden gentleness in his voice.

"Well, there isn't really much left, then," said the lawyer. He looked down at the paper in his hand, crumpled it, and put it in his pocket. "Mr. Cahill said he thought you would like to know that the illegal part of our dump operations will probably be discontinued by spring. The company has decided that the area is becoming too populated. Some of the chemicals will be taken out and placed in another site."

"Sure," said Manny. "Bury it in somebody else's backyard. Fuckers like you and Cahill and Marconi are going to wind up killing all of us with your poison and your money and your politics." His stomach churned with a sudden bitterness.

Lawrence was embarrassed again. "Even we . . . sometimes have a conscience, Manuel. Some of us. The things we do, well, we do them because we think they're right. The world has to develop. It's just that once in a while—"

"Once in a while is too much," Manny snapped. "What else?"

The lawyer dug once again in his overcoat pocket. He pulled out another piece of paper; it was a check.

"Piss off," said Manny. "Back in your fucking car."

"Wait, Manuel. Just at least look at it. It won't burn you."

Manny took the check; his hands were numb and he could hardly feel it in his fingers. "Blood money," he said.

"No, Manny. Mr. Cahill says please don't look at it that way. He says please see it as restitution to you and your family. Think of it as a penalty he has to pay to you for what he did to your father. Let's say for the sake of argument that you took us to court over all that's happened. Let's pretend, too, that Mr. Cahill couldn't buy the court's judgment with his superior lawyers, and his ability to distort evidence and testimony, etcetera. The imaginary fair lawsuit. Why then, Manny, the court would award damages to you and your family. Look at this as damages."

"I don't think so," Manny said.

"Manuel. It is actually not that much money. It's not anywhere near what you should really get; Mr. Cahill does not want you drawing attention to yourself and possibly to us with sudden affluence. Think of it as back wages if you want. But you know your family needs it. Your mother and your sister."

Manny held the check for a moment longer; his mouth watered as he looked down at it. Then he tore it in half lengthwise and watched the two strips of paper flutter away in the wind.

"It's not that we couldn't use it," Manny said. "It's just that Mr. Cahill has to get over the idea that everything can be fixed with money."

Lawrence's eyes were wide with surprise. "But what will you do? I mean, Mr. Cahill will want to know."

Manny glanced back at the house for a moment. "I'm gonna start looking for a real job. And if that's not enough, maybe we could sell one of the houses. This one or Grandpa's."

Lawrence coughed into one of his shiny gloves. "Your grandfather's house? Well, there could be an arrangement there, as well. Once it clears probate, we might buy it from you. We'd of course give you much more than the building and property are actually worth—"

"Forget that," Manny said. "If we do sell it, it won't be to you."

Lawrence studied him for a long while as snowflakes fell between them. "Okay," he said finally. Then, softly, with his eyes to the ground, he said, "Joe Marconi is also ill, Manny. Some kind of tumor. It may have been caused by—"

"The dump," said Manny. "Un-fucking real. That doesn't make me happy. Did you think it would?"

Lawrence sighed. "I don't know. Well, good-bye, Manuel." He pulled open the heavy door of his Lincoln, seemed to think about stepping into it, then he looked up at Manny. "Mr. Cahill also asked me to tell you that he is deeply sorry. If he could make things different—"

"You tell Mr. Cahill I hope he starts to feel better," Manny said. His voice was suddenly thick.

"That isn't likely, but it will please him that you said that," Lawrence said. He got into his car and drove away.

Manny took a long walk after that. He waved at his mother and Ida, who had been watching his meeting with Lawrence through the lighted kitchen window, then he walked out over the rotting footbridge and onto the abandoned railroad bed. It was snowing hard now; the snow reminded him of the day he had gone looking for his brother in the blizzard and had not found him. To keep that memory at bay, Manny turned south and traveled in the opposite direction from that other long, sad walk; he walked down toward his grandfather's house. It was growing dark and he walked quickly.

The house looked dismal, standing unlighted in the snowstorm. The sight of it caused a lump to appear suddenly in Manny's throat. Snow was already piled high on the arms of the old wooden lawn chair where his grandfather had always sat, smoking. Snow stood thick on the roof, a sight that was hard to take when there was no smoke curling up out of the chimney.

Manny had wanted to go inside to look around, and perhaps also to call Grandpa Tarbox's name out loud once or twice to assure himself that no bitter ghost was brooding in the house. He now knew that he wouldn't be able to do it, however.

But then suddenly, a flash of motion caught his eye. Around the corner of the house came a fox. The fox carried something in his mouth; Manny was afraid at first that it might be a housecat, but as the animal approached, he saw that he carried a cottontail rabbit. The fox came toward him steadily, the pads on his feet squeaking faintly in the wet snow, and when he reached the railroad bed, he stopped for a moment a mere ten feet from Manny and studied him with shining black eyes that revealed no fear. It was a male fox, a dog-fox in the prime of life, and his thick pelt was a true red; the first red pelt Manny had ever seen in the swamp, where all the red foxes wore gray or black to allow them to hide more easily. Against the snow, in the falling twilight, the red fox seemed to glow as if lit from within.

The fox moved his head; Manny knew that he was probably just adjusting his grip on the limp rabbit, but the motion made him appear to nod. His eyes twinkled with secret intelligence, or perhaps humor.

Then the fox walked to the edge of the railroad bed, where a snow-laced mound of briars separated the sterile cinders from the beginning of the deep woods. He gathered himself for a leap, glanced for a second in Manny's direction, and sprang over the briars. Swallowed by snow and darkness as soon as he left the ground, the fox seemed to leap forever.

ABOUT THE AUTHOR

Paul Guernsey was born in Milford, Connecticut, where he currently resides. He is a graduate of the University of Arizona, in Tucson. Mr. Guernsey has also lived in Phoenix, Arizona; Guadalajara, Mexico; Kenai, Alaska; Caracas, Venezuela; and Rio de Janeiro, Brazil. He has worked as a forklift driver, a machine mechanic, a packer in a salmon cannery, a newspaper reporter, and a wire service correspondent in South America.

Unhallowed Ground, his first novel, was a winner in the PEN American Center's 1985 Nelson Algren Fiction Award.